Somewhat Of An Animal

A Novel

Written By

Jacqueline Vincent

For those who believed in us,
We love you all.

And for Marija

Oh, My skin, like the black gold of heaven,
its exquisite balm sends you to madness,
and hold fast, servant, to the lowest deep of your own mind...
stay there, as you look upon me, your saviour and your jailer
both.
My skin.
Like the black gold of heaven

R.B

Book One

Introduction: Queen Of Worlds

South Western Guinea.

The ascent looked arduous, insurmountable almost. Even the seasoned merchants from the surrounding villages, all slim and sinewy, huffed arrogantly at the pathway as it stretched upward toward heaven. They idly strode on, tapping at the flanks of their mules.

Rose welcomed the challenge with every sure step. Her strong body was free of all fatigue and weakness.

"Please, tell me again of the man who wishes to meet us," she asked her guide.

"Well, Madam, in these lands there are many shamans, but he is not that, nor is he a conjurer," Cheikh announced in French. "He does possess powers, indeed, the man is highly revered, Madam. He is the eldest known living descendant of an ancient royal line... royal in the old African sense. I am referring to the times before these lands were known as the Empire, before they were joined with neighbouring countries like Mali and Senegal, Madam."

Rose smiled as he spoke. His voice was musical and had a nice ring to it that trilled with the birdsong around them. Although the twelve year old boy hadn't said much until this point, she knew he was among the very best and his knowledge had impressed thus far. He had spent many days assisting her, for which he would be paid handsomely.

They both climbed the steep trail as it snaked skyward, and while passing through a dense forest, Rose thought she saw a couple of baboons peering at them from the undergrowth.

At last they saw the lone hut in the clearing, smoke curled from the small chimney. A small girl with dreadlocks was busy stacking fat cassava roots against the side of the hut.

3

Cheikh spoke to the girl in the Kpelle dialect and she nodded and wiped her hands of soil before entering through the small door of the hut. She appeared again, beckoning them both. They approached and she began to speak.

Cheikh translated. "She says it is her great great grandfather. She tells us his fathers come from the times before Mandinka."

Rose looked down at the two children as they squeaked together.

"Before Islam came here, even in the age before the language of Mandé, his people had always been farmers, but she says they had possessed powers of healing."

"Cheikh, ask her if we might meet him."

"On the contrary, Madam, she tells me that the old man has been waiting for you," he laughed. "Isn't this truly great, Madam?"

Rose entered first, taking in the woody scent. The hut resembled less of a liveable dwelling and more like a tiny place of prayer, presumably an area in which the old man could meditate. Many bottles and bowls of varying shapes and sizes were placed all along the inner walls of the round space.

The old man sat cross legged in the centre of the floor. A calabash gourd was positioned before him, steam arose from the murky liquid. His eyes were shut.

Rose could hear the girl whisper something to Cheikh behind her.

The old man opened his eyes with a start and immediately looked agitated. Once more Rose heard the girl speak to her guide, although now with more urgency.

"Cheikh, talk to me. What is she saying?" The boy was silent.

The old man looked serious and concerned about Rose. He began whooping and chattering, the young girl screamed and ran out.

She began to feel alarmed, and asked again, "Can you tell me what's happening, boy?"

4

There was a pause before Cheikh began to stutter, apparently attempting to follow what the distressed old man was saying.

"Err, Madam… when… when he was a young man…"

Rose waited and glared at Cheikh again, who was frowning, listening. The man's distress grew, whipping into a feverish fury as he knocked over the gourd, its entire contents spilling on the earth at his feet. Rose and Cheikh both stepped backwards to avoid the hot liquid.

The old man continued to chatter harshly. Cheikh shook his head. "I want to go home, Madam. Please forgive me."

"You can't just leave here without telling me what he is saying."

"I think we should leave, Madam."

"Cheikh, please!"

Cheikh turned to the old man again as he became more and more distressed.

"The man said he knows you, that you are from this land."

Now, Rose became confused. She frowned sceptically, looking back at Cheikh.

He went on. "He said he's seen you before." The young boy became reluctant but Rose urged him to reveal more. His frown creased his face up intensely. "He has seen you, he has seen you; he keeps repeating it, Madam."

Rose panicked. "Where has he seen me?"

The boy then turned to look at her. "I do not want to say."

Rose now ordered him to give up the information. Cheikh was shaking. "He said he has seen you ten thousand years ago; the time when the moon and the sun kissed."

The boy looked at the man and Rose asked again, but he kept listening, until he finally spoke. "Grande soeur, I cannot be here any longer, please let me go."

Rose went quiet. She appreciated the boy's fear and didn't wish to upset him further. She felt bad about her imperiousness towards him.

But Cheikh spoke again. "He tells me you bring a whirlwind. He said you are a judge on the surface of the earth."

She looked down at the old man in disbelief. He seemed spent as his chattering ceased. He glared back at her with wide eyes.

"Madam, for all of his life he had taken a vow of silence; he has never spoke, Madam. Never in his life... until the moment we came here on this day."

"Oh dear," Rose said, almost silently. She remained tense and stared at the man in disbelief, his large eyes glared at her implicitly, as if pleading, bloodshot and swollen. He then prostrated himself at Rose's feet, as much as his old body would allow, whilst wailing and chanting.

Cheikh finally told her, "Madam, he tells me he is your servant and messenger. He says you still have work to do, that you should exercise your rite – the rite that expresses your rule over the world. He sees a god in you, Madam."

The man chanted, mantra-like, urging her to hear, to listen to his prayer: "*Reine des mondes... Reine des mondes... Reine des mondes... Reine des mondes...*

Sarah Allen

"Why didn't you do something, anything, to save her?"
"I was… scared…"

***

Nineteen years ago.

The rain spilled out of the sky and seemed to hang there forever like some rotten grey curtain.

Its constant downpour added to the sheer darkness of the huge residential tower that had been her home for the past two years, and made Rebecca Sinclair feel like it was raining all over the world.

She gazed from her small bedroom window. A daydream, thoughts of clearer skies and happier memories, momentarily averted her from a responsibility that barked at her from the outskirts.

"Right, baby, have you got everything?" asked Martha as she breezed through the room, shoving on a shiny black Adidas tracksuit top.

Rebecca glanced back at her in disbelief; even in these situations, Martha still managed to be glamorous. "Yes, Mother. I have the forms, all the documents they gave me the last time."

"Good baby." Martha clutched her daughter's face and proceeded into the usual ritual, a well executed but modest MOT. Even now, at the age of sixteen, Rebecca still welcomed her mother as she checked her appearance, eyelashes, the whites of her eyes and her hair. "My baby, you're so beautiful."

Not as beautiful as you, Rebecca thought. As a child, her mother had reminded her of a young Diahann Carroll.

"Are you sure you want to do this? I mean, are you ready, baby?"

I am not, Rebecca thought.

***

"Hello, which emergency please?"

Rebecca sniffed. Her attempts to speak were laid to waste due to her decreasing vocal chords.

"Hello? Could you state which emergency service you require?"

A pause. Then Rebecca's dialogue dotted and trailed as if gripped by mortal panic and the inability to speak. With all her strength, she attempted to gather herself before the operator repeated her inevitable query. Doing so was hard.

"Please help," she whispered.

"Okay, we'd really like to. Listen, stay on the line, and take your time. I'm here, luvvie. You can start when you're ready, okay?"

"My best friend has just been attacked... I think she is dead."

Chief Superintendent Robert Wright reached over and pressed the stop button on the cassette player.

"Is that your voice?" he asked. Rebecca nodded. "For the purposes of the tape, Miss Sinclair has just indicated that it was her voice on the tape."

He spoke methodically, a touch stoical. "Tell me, was that hard to hear? Did it make you feel uncomfortable?"

Martha sat to Rebecca's left and she had disliked Wright's attitude right from the start. She deduced it was obvious her daughter's fear was serving to frustrate him in some way.

"What kind of questions are you asking? Do you think she would be pleased to hear that?"

"Mrs Sinclair…"

"Miss Benoit. My name is Benoit; I have told you this twice already."

"Miss Benoit, apologies, these questions are unfortunate, I'll grant you, but they have to be asked, if only to determine where we're at, you understand?"

Both women didn't, they let his question float by. Martha stared at him icily, while Rebecca, withdrawn, maintained her lowly status, head bowed and silent.

"Now, Rebecca, do you think you'd be able to try again?" he asked.

"That's why we're here, isn't it?" Martha said, calmly. "She said she would. What's the matter with you?"

Her accent was sophisticated, not at all indicative of her life in Kingston, Jamaica and Harringay respectively. Yet there was something in the way she applied her words; cutting but highly authoritative.

Wright silently thought about the discretion he believed he was using which was going by unnoticed.

Martha turned to her daughter and tilted her head up. "Baby, look at me. You can do this, okay?"

Rebecca blinked her huge reddened eyes, the tears spilling down over her cheeks.

Her hand was encased within Martha's, a tightly clenched union of love, which rested on the surface of the horrible grey table before them.

Rebecca cleared her throat. With all the reluctance in the world – she began.

"I had lost her. She was with me all night but I looked at the clock at about 10pm and I realised I hadn't seen her for a while."

"How long is a while, exactly?"

"About ten, twenty minutes. I wasn't worried, not at that point. There was all the sixth form teaching staff everywhere; they were dancing more than the students."

"The fact you had teachers there gave you no cause for alarm, correct?"

"Yes."

"This is still at the prom dance? In the hall?"

"Yes."

"How long after that did you begin to look for Sarah?"

"Pretty much then…"

"You said you weren't worried."

"I wasn't. I wanted to find her. That doesn't mean I was worried."

Wright frowned. "Okay, where did you look first?"

"Well, I walked all around the hall. I couldn't see her so I looked in the toilets next…"

"The ladies' toilets?" Wright asked. Martha looked back at him blankly. "I'm sorry, silly question. Rebecca, could you tell me how long you were looking for Sarah Allen before you found her?"

Rebecca stared at her mother's hand and thought about the answer. "I can't remember for sure, I think it seemed like another twenty minutes." Her sentence meandered into more of a question than an actual statement.

Martha was aware that her daughter was approaching the part of the story that had caused her the most problems in the past. During all their prior police meetings, hours of interview time had always turned fruitless during this point, giving way to hysterics. She squeezed Rebecca's fingers tighter.

Wright also knew. "It's okay. In your own time, Rebecca."

Her eyes began to water again. She paused before breathing in heavily. "It was in the locker rooms, like, the changing rooms. There was a door that led into another room."

"Yes, is that the door you hid behind?"

"Yes." Rebecca swallowed.

"Could you please get her a drink?" Martha asked as she glanced at her daughter.

"Of course."

"A cold drink."

Wright indicated to his colleague. A flimsy plastic cup half-filled with murky warm water was presented to her. Rebecca sipped just enough to moisten her throat.

"To start with, it was his voice that scared me. He had a deep voice."

"Are we talking about Andrew Baker?"

"Yes, Andrew Baker."

"Do you believe you arrived at the scene as it began?"

"Yes I do. They were kissing. It was okay; Sarah was okay at this point."

Superintendent Robert Wright looked up from his notes. "Consensual?"

"Yes, but it didn't last long. I noticed two others, sat in the dark at the other end of the room."

"Did you recognise any of them?"

"Yes. They were Andrew Baker's friends."

"Okay, um, their names…" he broke off purposefully, expecting Rebecca to pick up where he left off.

"Ricky Gomez. Steven Freeman."

She looked at her mother and breathed in. Martha looked back and smiled proudly.

"They got up and came closer, one of them said something, something like 'it's my turn' or 'me first'. Something like that. I could hear the music from a long way off, kind of vibrating. Sarah said to Andrew that she wanted to go back to the dance, he told her to shut up."

Rebecca paused at this point, mirroring exactly what had happened on previous interviews.

"Carry on, baby."

"Ricky Gomez was the first to take a hold of her…"

Martha looked on as Rebecca finally melted, tears ran down her cheeks and her fist slammed down on the table in frustration.

"Rebecca, take your time; I understand it's hard. You have plenty of time." Superintendent Robert Wright's support lacked feeling as he half-heartedly offered a tissue.

"Baby, I want you to do something for me." Rebecca looked into her mother's eyes, never failing to be influenced. "I cannot do this anymore, not this time. If I could, you know I would in a heartbeat. But you need to tell this story. Now, if you don't relate the statement, they can't put these bastards behind bars. We don't want that to happen. Just think about that, that's all it is, talking, telling it like it was – that's all you need to do. After you've said it all, they'll get the justice they deserve. We need them to face justice, don't we, baby?"

Rebecca nodded and lost herself in Martha's eyes, a light brown swirl of beauty and persuasion. Likewise, her tone was both magnanimous and authoritative. She continued nodding gently, conceding to everything Martha told her, and in doing so, she could feel a burst of strength.

"Tell this guy your stuff, baby. Let's put a line under this and go home."

***

An arm grabbed at Sarah from behind, she felt herself being fixed, held in position. "Why are you doing this, you bastard?" she screamed at Andrew.

Standing in front of her now, she recognised him. If Andrew Baker was smoothly handsome, the scruffy Ricky Gomez was his polar opposite. Looking like an indie-band reject, he was the only one of the three attackers who wasn't wearing a suit.

He hoisted her dress up high. She struggled against his hasty actions, tears came down from her eyes as she looked at Andrew in disbelief, himself oblivious, reaching into his jacket and pulling out a small packet. He poured the powdered contents onto the surface of the dirty bench beside him and started to cut into it with a credit card.

The dark stench of the locker room dominated. She looked back in terror at Ricky Gomez. He hurriedly unzipped his pants, instantly releasing his penis, it flopped out before he forced himself inside her roughly. The pain as the thing invaded her was unbearable. Void of lubrication, it almost crunched through her vagina. Bucking back and forth, harder and harder, herself being thrown about on the end of his harsh movements.

Huffing and puffing, his gruff face was grotesque as he gave out a long groan while ejaculating. She slumped into a heap on the cold damp floor.

Steven Freeman appeared in front of her. "No sleep for you yet, you bitch!" he said angrily, "Get on your knees."

She didn't move, and was roughly hoisted up. Steven Freeman placed her head to meet his blood filled crotch and stuffed himself into her mouth. She instantly struggled, doing her utmost to avoid it, and was punched in the face for doing so.

His penis was huge and she gagged on it, choking on its fluid. After he'd climaxed, he turned her around and attempted to place himself between her buttocks. After fixing her in position, he took her waist with his large hands, ferociously pushing and pulling on her, grunting and yanking her head back. The agony she felt in her vagina was now joined by the pain in her rear.

Satisfied, Steven tossed her aside like a rag doll.

While trying to fend of unconsciousness, all Sarah could hear was their laughter and abuse. Their words were like heavy rocks being hurled at her face. The pain of what Steven Freeman had just done was immense. It felt like she was dying from the inside. Her body was limp and aching. A stinging feeling swam through her as her life's blood felt like it was made entirely of nails.

"Right, come here, you fucking bitch," Andrew called enthusiastically.

Within the sound of Ricky and Steven's encouragement, Andrew had tied her arms up above her head with his tie – the purple tie she had so admired earlier in the evening.

Not at any point that evening had Andrew displayed evidence of anything untoward. He had looked after her so well, engaging with her intelligently as they spoke. Sarah's self esteem flew far away as she thought about what was happening to her. Tears burned her eyes as he stared blankly back at her.

She knew what was about to happen again. She tried to stay calm by taking deep breaths but it was no use. Her underwear, torn and strewn around her bruised knees, was whipped away and suddenly her whole body went rigid, his hard penis was now thrusting deep inside her sore and bleeding centre. Sarah tried to scream but nothing came out, only a slight broken wheeze. He tore her apart, himself like relentless machinery pulverising what remained of her, and she collapsed onto her knees.

Seeing the sight of her declining body sent Andrew into a frenzy, fuelled by the cheap drugs he had just snorted up his nose. Taking a nearby baseball bat, Andrew lunged at her; first to her jaw, then as the momentum of her body weight pulled her downwards, he followed through with a crack to the back of her head. Her left leg juddered as she hit the floor. Foam collected at the corners of her mouth. Sarah no longer moved as the room fell eerily quiet.

***

"I walked over to them," Rebecca said, weeping. "It seemed like I wasn't there, like I was seeing it in a dream or something."

Chief Superintendent Robert Wright was silent, himself an unwilling recipient of Rebecca's terrifying truth.

"My body felt like it was still back behind the door. But, my brain…" she swallowed. "It was like everything was in slow motion. I looked down at her, but she wasn't moving. I had an urge to touch her, to pick her up, or something. Then I looked at the three of them. I remember the looks on their faces. Like a cross between fear and rage. They looked like wild animals."

She paused, silence where not even breathing could be heard. The noiseless sounds of the small office buzzed and made everyone's ears rattle. Martha looked at her daughter and reached over with yet another fresh tissue.

"Andrew held me up, and Gomez punched me in the face. The other one, Steven Freeman, then forced me to look in the mirror at my broken nose. I remember scrunching up my eyes, refusing to look at my reflection."

Martha breathed inwards. She kept her tears locked inside.

"They just walked away. Dragged her body from the room. Like it was normal. I had no energy. I felt like I was dying."

***

It had taken Rebecca almost two hours to relate the details. Martha clutched her daughter to her side with both her arms.

Only now did Wright display signs of fully genuine panic and concern. Pale and teary-eyed, he blew out heavily, his hands criss-crossed over the back of his head.

"Thank you, Rebecca. That was… you did really well, you really did," he said finally. "And thank you, Miss Sinclair, you should be so proud of her."

"It's Benoit. Miss Benoit. Write it down."

No one else spoke.

Sapphire

Present Day, NYC

Adele, her secretary, telephoned to let her know that her driver was waiting.

Rose Benoit switched off her laptop and picked up the evening's outgoing mail. She grabbed at her handbag and headed for the door.

Reaching the ground floor, the heavy glass parted and she stepped from the lift out into the lobby. The sound of her *Louboutins* resounded loudly across the marble, echoing up towards the high ceiling.

The journey home to her apartment was never long, especially if her driver kept to the west of Fifth Avenue. Rose noticed his wandering eyes in the rear view mirror.

The familiar ring of her phone sounded in the back seat of the vehicle. Julie's name flashed on the screen. "Sweetie, talk to me."

"Uh, Rose, I can't tell you how pissed I am."

"Excuse me?"

"Dumb-ass guys."

"Oh no, another one?"

"They're all damn near the same."

Rose adored Julie Ross's Bronx accent; its fire and its colours made her smile.

"Okay, so what was this one like? This was the gentleman with the cars, *oui*?"

Julie laughed cynically, "Gentleman? Fucking gentleman made me go all the way up past frickin' Westchester."

"Westchester? I thought he was from New Jersey?"

"Oh, I don't know where the hell he's from. Don't care now. Anyway, Westchester. Stayed there, didn't I? I thought he was one of those car-type dudes, you know. He looked the type. Smooth white boy, window pulled down,

16

driving me places, driving around in his land cruiser or sports convertible."

"And was he?"

"Nah, you see? Who got it wrong again? He *fixes* cars."

"Pardon?"

"You heard me, baby. He mends vehicles in his daddy's place, up in the Hudson Valley or somewhere."

Rose laughed. Then forced herself to stop due to Julie's silence.

"You think this is damn amusing? There I am, black and red evening gown, and I'm like – *bam* – everything's perfecto, dressed to kill, you know? I get there, fool's got me looking all over for him; he's nowhere to be seen. I thought he'd be waiting for me in the lounge or someplace, wearing some nice suit. I'm calling his phone, calling out his name. I'm wandering around in *his* damn house looking for the guy, right? Anyway, no answer. So, his family's got this waiter or butler type dude, he tells me he's in the garages. So, I go out there and he's underneath this car, in his overalls, asking me to hand him a damned wrench!"

"Oh my," said Rose, whose driver had so far glanced back at her a total of seventeen times.

"Oh my? Don't you think that type of shit's weird? This stuff could only happen to me."

"So what did you do?"

"I grabbed my bag and my ass and cut out. Driving back in my heels like I was damn crazy. Got back early this morning 'cause I left so late."

"Where are you now?"

"In Brooklyn, round my sister's place. Listen, are you home yet?"

"Almost."

"Well, I'll leave here in twenty, that okay?"

"Yes, darling, that's fine."

Aside from their engagement with Oleg Gribkov, last year's winner of *The Observer*'s power list, they had planned for dinner. Rose's unyielding attempts to fix Julie

17

Ross up with a date were now becoming customary.

Finally, the Bentley stopped outside her apartment. The chauffeur got out of the car, ran round and opened Rose's door.

"Your name," she asked, refusing his assisting hand.

The man immediately tensed and looked down. "Err, my name is Kubit, Madam."

"Kubit, your services are no longer required," she announced coldly. Kubit's kind face morphed into a tense frown. Rose cut him a glance and his expression softened.

He watched her walk towards her building, despite the dismissal, admiring her physique.

Once inside, Rose immediately selected some Verdi.

Her Manhattan loft, she had been here for some time now. Ever since she'd set foot in the wide expanse of the flowing apartment, she had fallen in love and knew instinctively that she would want to live inside it. She had heard it had once belonged to Marlene Dietrich; an added bonus.

She eased off her restrictive clothing and footwear and walked into the wet room. The cool invigorating water running down her hot skin felt good as it cleansed and rejuvenated her.

Wearing the tiniest red mini-dress, she stepped out into the warm night and climbed in to Julie's passenger seat.

"Wow, you never told me it was *that* kind of night," Julie said, eyeing Rose's dangerously high pair of red heels. They kissed.

"Be not concerned with my attire, baby; tonight's the night you're going to bag yourself a lover."

***

They would always hit *Casa Mia* first, one of their most favourite establishments. Being prime time, it was busy as usual, but there would always be a table awaiting Miss Benoit.

Rose adored the restaurant; situated right at the heart of

bustling West Village, the place never failed in transporti.... er back to Tuscany.

The Maître D greeted them, politely asking if they wanted drinks while handing them a menu each.

"Julia, I sacked my driver tonight."

"So what's new? Do you hate every driver in New York?"

"Possibly."

"None of those guys ever last more than two weeks. What did the fool do this time, sneak a glance at her majesty through the rear view?"

"Correct."

"Oh, for crying out loud, Rose. I can't believe you sometimes. You iced him for looking at you?"

"Darling, I care not for disreputable help. It will not be tolerated."

"Yeah? Well you're crazy."

The sommelier arrived presently with two chilled glasses and a bottle of the Chardonnay they had selected.

"Jules, tell me about your date."

"I told you already. The car guy?"

"Non. The black guy. The date you had on Monday?"

"Oh, that fool," she began. "He was another one of those jerks, babe. Oh, he was pretty, I guess, you know? We went out, I dressed good, I felt good. That was until he started talking about himself, and wouldn't stop. The brother was more interested in his own reflection than what I was trying to say."

"What were you wearing?" asked Rose.

"Shorts. Like, *Saint Laurent*."

"Goodness, did he not care?"

"Nope. The boy wore a baggy sweater as if it was nineteen ninety eight."

Rose looked down and frowned slightly.

"I think I scare men away, Rose. I must do; I'm single *again*. These days it seems nobody sticks around more than a damn week."

Rose listened intently, her eyes fixed upon Julie as their

waiter positioned oil and focaccia on their table.

"But, at the end of the day, I don't really give a damn... they're all a bunch of fucks anyway."

"All of them?"

"Sure, why not? How come every single guy on this planet is obsessed with sex? Why can't I just meet one dude who doesn't want a blowjob on the first date?"

Rose smiled and placed a pinch of bread into her mouth.

"I mean, what is it about blowjobs? Why the hell would any chick suck on a guy's dick after ten seconds?"

Nodding, Rose silently agreed.

"I'm just so whack."

"Oh heavens, Julia, it's true: you really do meet a lot of slime, darling. But I honestly don't know what else to say that I haven't said already. I actually believe the sights you set on men are in the wrong departments."

"What makes you say that?"

"Sheer evidential fact is what makes me say it, dear. Take a look at the proof. Take a look at where we work. There's more to life than power-crazed banker boys, or narcissistic hip-hoppers. Both are truly dreadful. Kindness and good intentions are like kryptonite to them. You need to stop what you're doing and look elsewhere."

"Girl, where? I mean, I been *everywhere* round here. From Yonkers and all the way down past Staten Island."

That is true, Rose thought. Julie Ross had even succumbed to the online dating phenomenon, failing miserably.

"I think it's 'cause they see me, see that I'm biracial, and they think... wow, I like those light-skinned bitches, all that shit, right? Then somehow they switch, they recoil when I open my goddamn mouth."

"Nonsense."

"Why nonsense?"

"They aren't equipped to handle you, that's all, darling," Rose smiled.

"Say what?"

"Listen. You're a feisty lady, everyone knows that. You

like to be in control…"

"Yeah, so do you. And?"

"Yes, but because you're assertive, because you take no nonsense, and the type of men you go for are the same, you will always clash. It's never going to work, honey; it's always going to collide."

Julie shrugged, a symbol that only ever antagonised Rose.

"Let me ask you this, Jules: when was the last time a guy you dated ever paid you a compliment? And I want you to be honest now, baby."

Julie turned her nose up. "Yeah, they pay me compliments, so what?"

"When?"

"I can't remember," Julie replied.

Rose raised her shoulders and widened her eyes, as if illustrating that she had proved her point, but Julie continued: "Listen, I get compliments, okay?"

"Okay. What kind of compliments?"

Julie thought. "Um, I got nice ass."

"That's correct, you do, well, for someone as thin as you are. What else?"

"That I have a good pair of tits, you know? All that shit. For crying out loud, fools say it all the time."

"Julie, they're not compliments. It's just hogwash that men say before they get down to business."

"Hogwash?" Julie asked.

Rose rolled her eyes. "Oh, goodness. Yes. Hogwash. It means nonsense."

"Bougie Rose, with your Duchess of Roseumpia type ways…" Rose could hear Julie smiling.

"Kindly refrain from digressing. It *is* nonsense. Men say it for themselves. Listen, you're a fine woman, right? They have to remind themselves they're going to be getting down with a hot piece of ass like you. They say it because that's what they see, and want. You hear me?"

Julie burst into laughter, "Rose, you're so full of shit."

"Listen, it's true. When was the last time anyone told

you they liked your hair, hmm?" she said, while Julie abruptly stopped laughing. "Tell me the last time a man said you had a nice smile? They liked your clothes? Or that you are just a nice person? No, the majority of these guys, no matter where they're from, they only want one thing. Not all men, please do not misunderstand, but many."

"Yes, Ma. I hear ya', Ma." Julie took a sip of her wine. "Okay, so tell me, what is it you want me to do?"

"Just go wide, darling; don't go down that same old road. And also, look at yourself, you really are a fine-looking woman. Don't sell yourself too short. You are quality, so you deserve quality, not some rat-bag skanky-dick."

"Sister, please." Julie typically waved off Rose's words.

"Hush," said Rose. "Don't *sister please* me. *Sister please*? Who the hell is *sister please*? She a nun?"

Julie chuckled. "Rose, you really are something else, you know?"

"Believe me. This sister does not tell lies. Look, I'll ask this guy," she said brashly as their waiter arrived with their meals.

"Rose," Julie hissed, loudly whispering, "Don't you dare."

"Tell me your name," Rose asked the young man discourteously.

"Um, my name is Rossi, Madam."

"Rossi Madam, okay. Tell me, Rossi Madam, my friend here… you think she's pretty?"

The boy turned to Julie, who stared back at Rose, calm on the outside, volcano on the inside. "Of course, she is very pretty."

"Come now, Rossi. Pretty? Is that all? Do you not think, Rossi, that she is absolutely gorgeous, undeniably beautiful?"

Rossi, awkwardly still holding their heavy plates, looked at Rose then lowered his head for a second in an attempt to compose himself. He eyed Julie again, who was now, indeed, gazing back at him.

"I hope you don't mind," he said, turning back to Rose, nodding, "but I think she is extremely beautiful." Rossi was sincere and began to turn a dramatic shade of crimson.

"There you go, Julia. Rose rests her case."

***

Rossi arrived back at their table a little while later. "Ladies, was everything satisfactory with your meals?"

"Rossi, darling, you are such a sweetheart. Is he not just the sweetest, Jules?" Rose asked as she sat back and sipped her wine.

Julie turned towards the waiter. "Rossi, please ignore her."

"The food was delicious, darling, be sure to send our compliments to your magnificently adept chef."

"Certainly, Madam." Rossi grinned from ear to ear as he proudly stepped away from their table.

"Oh, Rossi," Rose called, as she poured more wine into Julie's glass, "kindly come back here."

The man spun around, with a touch of doubt. "No need to look so worried, darling, I am not going to bite you," she smiled.

"Rose, let the kid alone; he's suffered enough," Julie said.

"Here." Rose placed a napkin before him and supplied him with her pen. After a moment Rossi finally twigged, quickly sketching the digits to his cell phone.

"Thank you, Rossi. I shall keep this for future reference." She took the napkin and folded it in half, "You may go, Rossi. I bid you a pleasant evening."

Rose continued to play with the napkin, smiling, eyeing Julie.

"I hope that ain't for me, babe. I would hate to think you were wasting your time."

Rose ignored. "Don't call this week. Too eager. Next Friday."

"For crying out loud, Rose. Why you gotta do me like that? He was about twelve."

"Early twenties, possibly. He's younger than you, no doubt. I wasn't aware that was a crime."

"Okay, what if he ain't single?"

"Julie, darling, relax. Rossi is single, trust me."

"Oh crap," Julie said suddenly checking her wrist. "Shall we get out of here? I reckon we're late."

"*Oui*, let's go." Rose signalled for the bill, which she paid. Rossi receiving the largest tip he'd ever seen.

***

Oleg Gribkov's gnawed red face, bitten by a lifetime's worth of Vodka consumption, was stamped with bitter impatience at being made to await their arrival. He sat, sullen, unsmiling as he omitted all the bad tidings one would expect from one of the most formidably powerful tycoons in both the western and eastern hemispheres. He was sat between four of his business partners and various members of his management team. They were becoming edgy, fearful of a customary eruption from the eighty one year old.

"They're on their way, rest assured, Comrade," said the bravest.

His fat face immediately lit up on seeing Julie Ross and Rose Benoit as they sashayed through into the lobby.

Air kisses all round before they all finally seated themselves.

Oleg's colleagues would be forgiven if they were to assume their choice of venue had been his idea, but *Private Eye's* was one of Rose's most favourite haunts. They sat within a VIP booth, segregated from the boisterous young bankers and the sullen Ray Ban wearing Arab princes.

Surrounded by three dancers of Rose's choosing, and supplied for obvious reasons, the women writhed against one another, before placing themselves closer to Oleg, two at his front and one holding him from behind. The man was well and truly buttered, lapping it up like an oversized geriatric cat.

More ladies arrived. Rose was seated at the head of their table. She smiled and rolled her shoulders in time to the music. She was almost obsessed by Sapphire. Her milk-white flesh enraptured her, and her plus-sized attributes sent her into a frenzy whenever she looked upon them. Sapphire swayed and moved her hips expertly, which made Rose Benoit quiver with delight. She had no choice but to recall fondly the late night parties they had both attended near Périgueux.

"Rose, baby. Keep your eyes on the prize," Julie reminded her, clicking her fingers in front of Rose's face, rousing her from her fantasies.

***

It was their second engagement with the Russian. So engrossed with the pair was Gribkov that he decided to place his interest in them without even finalising a formal appointment with their finance department. What impressed him most was the almost devastating way the pair had put their mark on Wall Street. Within their first year under their *Nubian Rose* banner, a promotions company, they had shattered through the investment bankers like a sledgehammer, procuring millionaire status during the run of their second year. Once established, they expanded, with facilities in London and Paris. Their ruthless reputation and image in the press, powerful yet glamorous, was countered by their humanitarian exploits. It made for a genius balance. Everybody in New York wanted to be near them. Oleg Gribkov was no exception. He considered himself fortunate to be investing in *Nubian Rose*.

"Well, this is splendid news," said Rose, raising her glass. "Gentlemen, I speak for Miss Ross and myself when I say we are delighted with this development. We look forward to a future with you with eagerness, and with sheer excitement."

They toasted and smiled, and began putting their merger proposals into effect there and then – Julie looked serious with her reading glasses, checking terms and conditions, with Rose signing contractual forms while sat high upon Sapphire's lap.

Mister Jack

Enfield, Middlesex.

Jack Sargent's back problem had returned. He'd had lumber issues in his twenties but this was much worse. Back then, Ibuprofen had worked reasonably well when the pain began; it quelled just the right amount of discomfort to enable him to go about his business. Lately, however, he'd been advised to swallow larger tablets – a stronger dosage with a much more bitter taste.

He approached *New Horizons* in the same way he might have walked up to a firing squad. The last time had gone badly; Daniel had thrown a tantrum, totally out of character for the usually thoughtful nine year old.

Daniel's carer was Madge Markham and she glanced sadly at Jack as he signed himself in. "He feels awful, Jack. He's been so worried about it all this time. He's even drawn you a picture."

Jack smiled at her but avoided eye contact after a couple of seconds. He was aware the woman liked him. He chose not to display signs that might be misconstrued as anything other than mild friendship.

She escorted him through into Daniel's empty room. "He's obviously still at lunch, Jack. You want me to tell him you're here?"

"No, it's okay. Let him finish," he said, looking around.

"Very well. It'll be a nice surprise." Madge smiled and closed the door.

"I hope so."

Jack walked over to the wall above Daniel's bed. All the usual pictures hung in a display that comprised a huge white arc. They all seemed to feature the same house with a chimney and shining sun in the background. He would often be holding hands with Daniel in the foreground. Sometimes they would both be driving a sports car.

The door opened slowly, and Daniel almost failed to notice Jack sat in the chair beside his bed as he entered.

"Mister Jack!" he shouted, and ran towards him with his little arms open wide.

***

Sat together in a modest dining room that often doubled as an area that was reserved for special occasions, they had laughed together as Jack told Daniel his rubbish Christmas jokes.

It didn't take long, however, before he noticed something underlying within Daniel's behaviour. But Daniel was a receptive child, and he soon talked willingly of his problems.

"I am sorry, Mister Jack, about the last time you came to see me."

"You don't have to apologise to me, Daniel, about anything."

"I was…" he paused, as if trying to magic up the correct word, "sick."

"I don't think you are sick, Danny. I just think it's because you're sad sometimes. Do you think?"

"Yes, I think so, probably, Mister Jack."

"I think I know why you're sad, too."

They both looked at each other, both silently acknowledging their friendship. Jack was aware that although the child was young, he nevertheless possessed a sharpness that he himself had never occupied at that age.

"I do not want to be sad, and complain about these homes, Mister Jack, really I don't. But I don't like this one, Mister Jack. Ever since they brought me here, I feel like I'm not comfy."

"Comfy, as in… you don't feel at home here?."

"Yes. I don't feel right."

It broke Jack's heart to hear him say such things. "I think that's just because you're in a new place, Daniel, that's all. At least Madge is still with you."

"Yeah, I really like Madge; she's very nice all the time. And I think she wants to marry you."

"Um." Jack cleared his throat. "She told me that you've drawn me a picture."

"Oh yeah," he said excitedly. "wait there, I will get it. Close your eyes, Mister Jack."

Jack had to scrunch them shut as tightly as he possibly could, anything less would be cheating. He heard the sheet of paper waft through the air as the boy retrieved it from its hiding place.

When told to open his eyes, Jack was greeted with an A4 rendering of himself and Daniel on a small boat. Blue wobbly waves rolled and pushed them towards a stretch of land that resembled something from *The Lord Of The Rings*. The entire canvas was generously utilised with colour and detail; not a single corner had been left neglected, and his pencil shading had improved since the last few pictures. It was quite safe to say that this was his best work so far. The blue sky seemed lovely on face value, but as Jack looked further into it he saw an approaching storm, some birds were trying to avoid its arrival, flying off in the opposite direction. Jack wondered if these details were intentional or just childish blips. All the same, these things were further illustrations of the depth Daniel clearly held in abundance.

"Do you like it, Mister Jack?"

"Are you kidding me? It's wonderful. I love it. I really like the boat."

"Is that your favourite part of it?"

"I think all of it is amazing. What's that over there?" Jack pointed directly towards a castle on the right hand side in the distance. The building looked peaceful and serene. Its golden walls glimmered and radiated the sunshine perfectly.

"Oh yes. That's your house," Daniel said.

"My house? Wow. I'd love to live in a house like that."

"You can't yet."

"Why?"

"Because, silly, you have to rescue the princess who's in prison inside. There's always a princess inside, Mister Jack," he said seriously.

"Oh yeah, of course, how could I forget that?" Jack pretended to shoot himself in the head with his two fingers.

PR

South London. July.

Andrew Baker stepped out of the people carrier and walked quickly through the bunch of oncoming photographers. His stiff, tightly-fitting suit, although fashionable, gave him the air of arrogance that his image and reputation suggested. Flanked at his side by Red, his PR manager, he looked towards the entrance of the giant amphitheatre that was to be his place of employment for the next five seasons.

Although approaching the twilight of his career, soccer genius, Baker still possessed promotional potential. Samantha, his previous girlfriend, had been discarded. Apparently the pretty brunette proved unable to boost the right kind of media-friendly profile. Certainly not the kind of woman who should be seen with the most hotly tipped signing of the year. If his new premiership club, with its powerful manipulation of the press, could dispose of the rumours and scandal of rape and murder in his younger years, then sending Samantha packing back to Devon would be easy.

"She was stupid anyway. Shit in bed. Total disappointment," said Andrew shaking his head. "Sometimes women can be useless."

Red nodded in agreement. The man was skinny, apart from his rounded stomach, which made him look disproportionate, his over-expensive designer suit looked ridiculous. He handed Andrew more glossy A4 sized pictures of Kelly Williamson – the most popular member of *HashTag*, the latest girl group whose new album had just topped the download chart on both sides of the Atlantic. Her image found favour with Andrew. His eyes searched through the images, with the lad's mag photo-shoot his favourite. He liked the way they'd dressed her in skimpy outfits.

"Yeah, she's fit. She's the one," he said, finally.

"Good, good choice, Andy. And she's new, you know? Fresh!"

Andrew smiled whilst letting wind.

"So, you want her, yeah?" Red asked, crudely raising his eyebrows.

"Yep, she looks the dirtiest. And little too; I'll bet she's tight, know what I mean?"

Both men laughed. Red picked up the receiver. "Yeah, get in here."

His assistant could have been his mother – the woman looked at least twenty years older than Red's mid forties.

"Yes, Mister Redding?"

"Kelly Williamson," he said over his shoulder. "Andrew's chosen Williamson, okay?"

The woman nodded and closed the door.

"Andrew," he sighed, as if demonstrating their time for laddish machismo had reached its end. "I've been asked to talk to you about this court thing."

"Oh, don't start that again."

"I know, mate. But it's just something you and I have to cover, I'm afraid." Red stood and quickly strode towards the drinks cabinet behind his desk. "Scotch or scotch?"

"I ain't supposed to drink, you know that."

"Listen, that murder they accused you of, I don't care if you did it or not. I couldn't care less, Andy. But I do care about you. You've been coming on leaps and bounds ever since you left that shit-house you came from. You are our golden ticket, Andrew Baker." He placed a small glass inside Andrew's hand and clinked it with his own. "We are not about to lose you just because of some stupid fabrication that happened fucking years ago. Old news, Andy, very old news." He glared at Andrew, stern, convincing.

"Okay, so why bring it up?" Andrew smelled the liquid in his glass, recoiling slightly at the aroma.

Red dropped back into his seat opposite and inhaled

deeply.

"Andy. They want some kind of answers. They've started to put the heat on us, so we have to be seen to give this thing some consideration."

"What's that mean?"

"It means we have to pretend like we care. Some people out there believe you actually did it. People don't really like you, Andy; they say you're arrogant and cold. You have to work on making them think otherwise."

"So what the fuck do you want me to do about it?"

"Next time you do an interview, warm up. Be nice."

"Oh screw that, Red," Andrew said, turning his nose up. "I can't pretend to be something I'm not. I'm not fake. There must be some other way of doing this."

Red shook his head. "Andy, calm down." The man thought momentarily, appearing as if contemplating some other random option, but Andrew knew from experience Red had this conversation planned from the start.

He spoke finally. "Those two other suspects?"

Andrew frowned. "What about them?"

"I'm going to make this easy for you to understand, Andy. Basically, if one of them gets sent down for this, then this problem will not be our problem anymore." Red's stern gaze persisted, now intense, almost angry. "Do you understand, Andy?"

Habanera

She felt good as she placed the leather mask over her face and viewed herself in the mirror. Her eyes could be seen beneath the slits, arrogantly seductive.

She had earlier feasted on the Champagne and Beluga, and appreciative of the exquisite standard, she had thanked the food and beverage manager personally.

The hotel apartment boasted all the typical spoils of grand Las Vegas. The glossy vanilla-coloured furniture suited the sparse white of the huge interior.

Priceless fineries, legendary bejewelled eggs and giant objects made from gold and diamonds served to entice her senses and mood. The vast space of the master bedroom was breathtaking in warm white with its floor to ceiling windows. Outside, beyond the huge balcony terrace, the heat-drenched hum of the boulevard seemed a thousand miles downward.

She touched herself, her fingers gently tracing a line from her bosom down to her navel.

The studded corset housed her breasts perfectly and the noise her *Choos* made as she trip-trapped slowly from the master suite had just the desired sound upon the marble floor.

On her entry to the adjacent living space, the three men roused themselves from the extensive wait they had endured. Seated and tied to their stools, they pleaded, their whines muffled beneath the gags placed in their mouths as tears ran from their bruised eyes.

During their previous beating, she had referred to them as numbers one, two and three.

Carmen's *Habanera* came rushing loudly from the surround speakers like a wild horse, Maria Callas stabbing their ears.

Slowly, Rose Benoit walked over and approached the middle prisoner, although she placed her hand on top of the head of *number one* sitting to his right. She ran her fingers through his hair then stroked his face, her gaze still fixed upon *number two*. He looked on, gripped with fear.

Number one was then pushed over, bringing the stool crashing down, still attached to his seated behind. He fell awkwardly, the side of his head smashing against the marble. Once floored, he was kicked to one side, enabling her to walk over his upturned body.

Rose grinned and *Number two* wept.

She squatted down over *number one,* leaving his face inches from her groin, and presented a small knife. Using her left hand to prise open his mouth, she pinched out his shy tongue with her index finger and thumb. She cut cleanly, and as the organ was released from the back of his throat, it became limp in her hand.

As she stood and turned, *number one* omitted an array of loud guttural noises from behind her, choking and spitting blood. After casually inspecting it, she gently popped the bloody piece of flesh in the chest pocket of *number two'*s torn shirt, his body contorting and protesting against the foul deed.

Rose made her way towards *number three* and stepped onto his lap. She looked down at him whilst putting her arms around his shoulders. Bruised and battered with the beatings she'd previously bestowed, he looked up, pleading.

Her generous cleavage engulfed his face as she reached past him to take a hold of a lighter and a box of cigarettes from a shelf. Daintily pinching one from the box, she attached it to a long ivory cigarette holder before placing the end between her black shiny lips. The man whimpered as she inhaled, taking a huge draw. She removed his gag and took a firm hold of his face with both hands whilst prising his mouth open. She lowered her head and pulled his upwards enabling their mouths to close together. She then passed all her inhaled smoke down into his throat. When finished, she raised her head and continued to hold his mouth closed, keeping it all inside. He coughed under her strong hand, his body whipped and bucked beneath her. He tried to move his head, intensely frustrated at her strength, which limited his movements. A moment later she sucked in another large amount of tobacco and repeated the same cruel treatment. After the third time his red eyes watered. After the fourth time his bladder released, urine dripping from the seat beneath her large posterior, which was by now crushing his lower body. After the fifth time, Rose noted his face, greenish and shrunken. Still, she relentlessly repeated the exercise until the cigarette had burned down to the filter. She then placed one hand back inside his mouth and prised out his tongue in much the same way she had done with *number one.* The burning filter was pressed on to it, thus finally extinguishing the cigarette butt, which he was prompted to eat.

Ashy spittle and drool ran down his chin. His stomach was bloated and burning and his throat had holes in it. He looked up at her powerlessly, wishing for an ending, urging her to move on to his fellow prisoner.

Rose glanced down at him, a serene easiness upon her face. *Number three* pleaded pathetically and tried to out-shout Maria Callas, but to no avail.

Rose moved her shoulders seductively to the cello stabs of the second verse then slowly arose. Her graceful hips swayed low and rhythmically to the movements of the music as she stood free of his lap.

Closing her eyes, she mouthed the lyrics, elegantly illustrating and conducting the words using her fingers. The sound of the aria had always given her a sense of power. Her eyelids fluttered as she allowed herself to be taken away by the sheer lust the song evoked within her.

Swooping slowly past *number two* and stepping over an almost lifeless *number one* on the floor, she left the main area of the apartment. Quickly, the remaining seated men looked at one another, as if her departure had presented a chance, a gap in which they could do something to stop further abuse. Their muffled inaudible shouts were still no match for the omnipresent ear-splitting soundtrack, thus making it impossible for them to communicate.

Rose re-entered the room holding a golf club she'd found among their belongings. She moved towards *number three* and looked down at him once more. His face said it all – he *knew*.

Taking a grip of the handle more firmly with both hands, she lightly tapped the side of his cheek. He shrieked and averted his head while she gently rubbed the tip of the wedge iron against his face. Rose's lips parted slightly, her tongue nestled between her teeth, as she saw his avoidances. She raised the club aloft, drawing it up high before quickly swinging it back down, landing it on the left side of *number three's* skull. The sound the bone made as it cracked prompted *number two* to cry out. *Number three's* head slumped forward on the impact as his neck broke.

Number two was inconsolable as he began to shake with fear as she moved towards him.

With her fingers, she lifted his head by his chin and pressed her lips against his gagged mouth, mocking him and breathing heavily. Her allure confounded him and made him feel contrite.

She seated herself on his lap and lowered the volume to the music before reaching round to untie his gag. He moaned once his mouth was free.

Rose calmly whispered in his ear. "I am most curious, darling. At no point whatsoever have I merely laid a finger upon you that would warrant such cry-baby behaviour. Yet, of the three of you, you have been by far the most wretched specimen."

He wept and looked down in shame.

"There, there, baby, don't cry."

He looked up at her and a slight impression of hope became evident in his contorted features. His eyes momentarily fell at her perspiring breasts.

She stroked his face tenderly and his sobbing abated, almost. Rose grinned, the man's false sense of security was exactly what she wanted.

"Why have you done this?" he asked. His Russian accent was now less obvious due to the damage to his vocal chords. "What is this all about?"

She hummed whilst still looking him in the eyes. "Why don't you answer me?"

The newly found assurance disappeared as his attempts to reason with his captor brought no results. The rejection and desperation returned to his face.

"I'll do anything. Please tell me... am I able to make you release me?"

"No, darling, unfortunately not." She saw more tears as terror once again gripped him.

"Actually, on saying that, I have an idea," she said suddenly. "I know a little game we can play, you and I. Wouldn't that be fun?"

He looked up at her with his big damaged eyes, listening intently for more slim hope.

"Okay, listen. I'll turn around, and walk slowly to where I left the golf club over there. If you have managed to release yourself from this stool by the time I reach the club, I shall permit you to leave this apartment. However, on the other hand, if you have not managed to free yourself by the time I reach the club, I shall beat you. I shall beat you severely. Darling, what do you think?"

"I think you are a fucking bitch," he spat. "You are a lunatic. I should have slit your throat as soon as I saw you."

She tutted. "Now, now, darling, there's no need for that kind of talk."

She got up and resumed humming, before turning around. "I shall begin now. Please try your best for me, baby."

"Fuck you... You are not human... like an animal. I will kill you!"

Still humming, she walked slowly towards the golf club.

"You are a bitch. Ugh...you are an animal." Rose had to hold back a smile. She found his use of the English language endearing. She continued humming.

"How could you do this to me? I am a wealthy man."

Still humming.

"You need locking up. You think you'll get away with this?" he shouted.

Humming.

"Fucking crazy black bitch, damn you!"

He twisted his shoulders and arms and tried desperately to break himself away from the stool.

By this time, she had reached her destination. She turned and looked back at him.

"Damn you to hell, you bitch. I will get away, and I will make misery for you. You'll regret what you are doing… you'll regret it!"

Rose walked back towards him, holding the end of the golf club with her fingertips.

"Please!" he screamed. "Not me. Please!"

As she approached, slowly gyrating her hips, she raised one leg in the air before neatly placing the sole of her shoe on his chest, pushing him and the chair down backwards. He landed roughly on the floor, breaking his shoulder on the impact.

"I have to say I am disappointed, darling," she cooed as she stood over him. She bent over and stuck the full extent of her posterior in the air for dramatic effect while reaching inside his shirt pocket to retrieve *number one*'s tongue. Holding it high above in line with his mouth below.

"Supper time, baby."

"Fucking stupid, cruel whore. Never trust a whore; you're all the same," he screeched angrily, drool and mucus ran down the sides of his grimacing mouth.

"Eat," she uttered, as her fingers released it. The gland splatted upon the surface of his face and he moved his head from side to side in attempts to shake it off.

She lowered herself on top of him and retrieved *number one*'s tongue with her fingers.

"When I ask you to do something, I expect you to do it," she said, stuffing it inside his mouth. "Bon appetit."

Rose maintained her hold of his orifice, which offered

him no other option but to facilitate her orders. The flesh was finally consumed.

After digesting, he was defiant. "Is that really all you have? You want me to eat his tongue? Easy, I did it, see?"

Number two munched defiantly, even though the thing was no more, "Is that all you have?" He spewed mock laughter, which sounded more like choking. "Is that all you can do, huh?"

Rose smiled. Slowly she straightened and placed her right heel against the top of his head, securing it in place so it was unable to move in spite of his desperate attempts.

"The views on the Shadow Peak Course are so beautiful, darling," she said simply. "I found the cool air this morning most refreshing as I undertook preparations towards my '*A*' *game*."

Raising the wedge club high, she brought its full force crashing down upon the bridge of his nose. Just the one blow was fatal enough. His broken skull pressed against the soft tissue of his brain beneath it.

Rose hummed, walking away from his still jittering body. She gently leaned the club against the wall and turned the volume up once more.

Grabbing her long leather coat she walked casually from the room and out of the apartment.

Real Daddy

After his second burger, Daniel attempted to explain the reason for his sudden fondness for junk food. Jack Sargent disliked this; a nice sandwich would have been more satisfactory.

"But they're feeding us wrong, Mister Jack. Like, there's this long piece of meat type of stuff that looks like plastic poo." He frowned in a way that always amused Jack.

"Have you told Madge?"

"I did, and she said she'd tell the dinner ladies." Jack made a mental note: *talk to Madge about food.*

"So, Mister Jack, what are we going to do today?"

"Well, Daniel, I actually wanted to talk to you today, about a couple of things."

Daniel shuffled in his seat. Football or the zoo would have been a better answer, but the boy nodded and smiled.

"Okay, Mister Jack, what about?" he said, before destroying the remaining piece of his quarter pounder.

"Firstly, I wanted to ask you how you feel about spending time with me. Do you like it when I visit you?"

Daniel immediately lit up. "Oh, Mister Jack, I love when we go places. It's the best thing in the entire world!" The boy didn't hold back. "It's the best thing I do. Because you're my best actual friend, Mister Jack."

Jack's insides glowed, as if lighted by Daniel's innocence and fervour.

He looked him squarely in the eye. He had previously rehearsed the words, constantly repeating them in the mirror every morning for weeks. The whole speech had become like a mantra after a certain point. But this day, at this moment in time, the words left him, flying away like useless pieces of paper. A new plan was hastily thrown together.

"I wanted to know what you'd say if I told you there

might be a chance of seeing more of each other."

The boy looked back at him – it was hard to tell what he was thinking. Jack went on. "That is to say… would you like that?"

Daniel remained still. It was Jack who now shuffled in his seat. He felt bad at his fumbling conduct. It had been wholly unsatisfactory. He knew Daniel had been told this before. He'd been approached by *lovely new families*, telling him they adored him, that they wanted him to be a part of their lives. The nights he had spent crying when his saviours had backed out…

There was a silence. Daniel's indifference made Jack think he was losing him. "Daniel. You are my best friend, too. We're best buds, remember? I wanted to ask you if you would let me be your guardian."

Daniel swallowed, and as usual, gave the question careful consideration before proceeding to speak, finally releasing Jack from his guilt-ridden torment.

"Mister Jack, you wouldn't be my guardian." A tear appeared and fell down from his huge eye.

"Why not?"

"Because… if you did this… you'd be my real daddy."

They held hands. Afterwards, Jack took him to the park, still oblivious that Daniel only liked to play football with him because Jack looked funny when he ran.

Guardians

The landing was narrow and dark and strewn with rubbish. Ricky Gomez tumbled down the staircase in such a fury that the declining timber steps were almost broken beneath his heavy feet.

The door at the top of the landing slammed shut.

"Why don't you go fuck yourselves. Go on, get fucked," he roared.

At the foot of the stairs, he lunged towards an old dustbin and grabbed it before climbing back upward. Raising the battered metal container above his head, he sent it crashing against the entrance of his guardians' flat.

A scream was heard and the door swung open again. Someone came darting through the debris and ran down the stairs after him.

"You little shit!" The man was in his early sixties but moved swiftly in his pursuit of his former lodger. "If I ever see you here again, I'll call the police. I mean it, Ricky. All these years, we've been nothing but good to you. You've totally taken the piss out of us both."

His South London accent cracked and fired like a small machine gun.

Ricky Gomez had returned in an attempt to steal money from his guardians, a couple who had indeed previously given up their own lives to become his foster parents.

Although seventeen pounds and twenty-nine pence wasn't a lot of money, it could easily supply him with wine and sweets for the next few days.

During school, Ricky Gomez had shown far more potential within the Sunday football leagues than his team mate Andrew Baker. But his shambolic home life and penchant for cheap alcohol and drugs had dulled both his talent and enthusiasm for the sport. And while Andrew excelled on the pitch, Ricky deteriorated.

He quickly limped up the road and rounded the corner and was hastily joined by a scruffy young boy. "Rick, I see you got the money. Gimme it. I mean it. Give it here."

"Piss off, kid."

"What's the matter with you? You want to kill me? You know I ain't had nothing since two days. I need it, you greedy bastard, give it back."

Ricky Gomez turned and pushed the boy harshly, which sent him plummeting to the floor. He then kicked the boy heavily in his ribs.

"Fuck off. And tell your stupid mates to fuck off as well. You're all a bunch of wankers," Ricky spat.

The boy sat up and held his chest, looking back at Ricky, who walked away quickly. The look on the boy's face mirrored that which was firmly stamped upon Ricky's mind: *You'll regret that.*

LV Metro

London.

"Hello...? Yes, this is Detective Inspector Jack Sargent." He enforced the word *Detective* after hearing the person on the line omitting the title, wrongly referring to him as plain old Inspector.

"Okey-dokey. So... a body...? It that what you're saying?" He ran his hand through his hair and rubbed his eyes with the palm of his free hand. "Two? Three bodies?"

The line was bad. As he struggled to listen, he could hear faint voices in the background. American.

The man continued with a kind of easy drawl, "...a case of yours not so long back, it's matching an incident we got down here in Clark County..."

Jack looked at his pen whilst listening, evidentially nonplussed. "Yes...?" he answered lazily.

"Well, yeah, us folks here at the LVM, at this point, believe them to be related."

"Okey-dokey."

"What was that, Sargent?"

"Okay... erm... what else?"

"Yeah, we're the LVM..."

"Okay," Jack said, only half musing about who the folks at the LVM actually were. "Can you tell me more about the connections...?"

More pause on the line. "...Yeah..."

Jack Sergeant grew tired; he'd been awake for well over twenty-four hours. The pain in his back had subsided earlier that day but only now did it choose to return with an unforgiving vengeance. Aside from that, the conversation he was having, even without the annoying delay, was going nowhere.

"Would you like to tell me, then?" he asked, exhaling heavily.

"...tell you what, Sargent Jack?"

"My name is Jack Sargent," he said, almost automatically. "Detective Inspector Jack Sargent."

More indecipherable interference. "What?"

"You say that you have a case in Clark County that you think may be related to... what exactly...?" Jack said, still writing – writing nothing to do with the conversation he was having.

"...your asphyxiation case..." The man on the phone obviously struggled with the report from which he was evidently reading, as he seemingly consulted a colleague in the background for help. "...asphyxiation case. London, from five months ago," he said finally.

Jack's ears pricked up as he dropped his pen. "I'm sorry, what did you say your name was?"

"I told you already; the name's Sheriff Josh Morrison, I'm with the LVMPD... In Vegas. Basically, somethin's happened down here, a three way homicide, and we think it may be connected. It shares some of the same criteria..."

"Okay, what is that criteria, Sheriff?" The line became crackly as the voice spoke through the crumbling static.

"...the cigarette..." A crackle, then finally the line went dead.

***

The following morning, Jack hadn't slept. Ollie Travis drove them both to the office. His young partner was typically upbeat, a characteristic which seemed, curiously, all the more enhanced whenever Jack was particularly fatigued.

"Ollie, you remember the cigarette thing?" Jack asked, turning the volume down.

"The one we couldn't ID?"

"Yeah... Phone call last night, guy from Las Vegas"

"Vegas? Who was that?"

"Some guy called Morrison. We're going to check it out first thing. From what I am able to gather, I think what they are trying to say is that they have an open case over there where the details are similar... I think."

Ollie turned the volume up again. Bon Jovi was loud, however, both Jack and Ollie's thoughts turned to the *Bolter* homicide.

Not a year had passed by since the case. Richard Bolter, a forty-five year old electrician had been asphyxiated. He'd been found in a building in London's fashionable South Bank, choked to death due to, they firmly believed, forced inhalation of smoke. It was certain that someone had blown smoke into his lungs and trapped it inside by forcing his mouth and nose shut.

There was severe bruising to his face and neck due to his struggles against someone strong enough to hold his mouth shut for a long length of time. But the assailant had worn gloves and the only prints the forensics found were the victim's.

Besides the cigarette lead, there was nothing else to go on – just a body tied to a chair with smoke still rising from his throat. With bruises also applied on the remainder of the victim's body, he was brutally beaten and maimed in the extreme sense of the word.

After relating the morning's new developments to Ollie Travis and Superintendent Rob Wright, Jack presented to them his proposal, suggesting the way ahead for the next couple of foreseeable days.

"It's slim, and Ollie, you'd argue it's not much to go on, but the connection Sheriff Morrison referred to is the cigarette itself."

He silently awaited the inevitable exchange. Indeed, Wright and Travis cut their curious looks at one another, suggesting their confusion. Jack continued. "A very rare usage of this high class manufacturer suggests to us that it should be seemingly easy enough to identify who smoked it."

"Excuse me, but what the hell does that mean, Jack?" Rob Wright was ugly when he frowned.

Jack rubbed at the pain in his back. It was never enough

to totally delete the discomfort, but doing so put him more at ease. *It was better than not doing it*, he thought.

He went on. "Well, those privileged enough to be recipients of this exclusive tobacco obviously move in some ridiculously upscale places, Rob. Arabs, Wall Street guys in New York, people like that. An actual licence has to be obtained to receive this merchandise and smoke it."

"Are you serious? It's bloody' tobacco!"

Ollie cut in. "Jack, this Morrison guy thinks it's the same assailant?"

Jack nodded. "He told me he's ninety nine percent."

"What has an electrician from Brixton have to do with three Islamic Russians in Las Vegas?"

"I reckon the answer to that will tell us who killed them. Like I said, it's slim."

Ollie loathed office work. For the next twenty four hours, he was grudgingly screwed to his desk making enquiries, some of which he struggled to understand himself.

Jack looked on – Ollie was always good at looking like he knew what he was doing, but Jack believed in him. He was the only one who did.

Eventually, through differing time zones and long phone conversations to various mob criminal investigators and police chiefs across the Atlantic, they had gathered up something quite interesting. They finally received a list detailing unique members who were privy to the pre-eminent tobacco. It consisted of merely four names.

Carlos

It had been a long morning and nothing was going right. Dusty tradesmen stood around idly. Carpenters were waiting for plumbers to finish as decorators were waiting for carpenters to finish. Some men couldn't even begin their work, owing to late deliveries. The site was a shambles due to bad management and supervision.

Carlos Tutola's mobile rang, the builders' merchant informed him that the materials he'd ordered had arrived at their yard.

James Kelly came dashing through the entrance, his phone firmly clamped to his ear. "Oh crap, this ain't good. This definitely ain't good. Okay… I'll tell them…"

He looked around at all the workers and awkwardly attempted to round them up. "Okay guys, listen up, the client's here. The client's here *now,* guys."

The sight of James Kelly being in distress was nothing new, his manic behaviour was an occurrence to which most of them had been accustomed for some time.

"Get back to work all of you!" he shouted.

"Hey buddy, we *are* at work," a burly man in overalls called out, "and, anyhow, who gives a damn if the client's here?"

"I do," James Kelly screeched. "I'm supposed to be running this gig. If anything goes wrong, it's my ass on the line here, so do me a favour, please, at least make yourselves look busy."

"Are you kidding me? This is all your fault. You're responsible for all this mess anyhow. I'm supposed to be doing the lighting in the main corridors upstairs, and I've just been told to come back later 'cause there's six guys up there still boxing pipes that should have been finished yesterday. I'm stood around doing nothing. You're hiring and firing at will and, to top it all, you spring more work on us…"

"Okay, okay, I didn't know about the new extension till three hours ago. Three hours! They told me at the last damn minute," Kelly shouted.

"Well, like I said before, who gives a damn? Frankly, pal, I'm past caring."

"You guys don't understand. The client, she's a real pain in the ass. This is fucking real, you morons."

James Kelly's dialogue was peppered with fretful weeping, and some of the men shook their heads piteously.

"Believe me, I know; I spoke to the bitch. She's a real ball buster."

"Listen boss, I don't know what all the fuss is about, she's just some broad," said another.

"Jesus Christ, what do I gotta do to make you fucks understand?"

"Why don't you get out of here and let us get on with what we need to do? Because, like I said all along, no-one gives a fuck."

Everyone laughed.

Rose Benoit chose to speak only when the laughter had finally subsided. "So, no-one gives a fuck. Is that so?"

The woman had already entered the room, elegantly dressed and maintaining her official status.

The noise dimmed to absolute silence. Radios were switched off. Mobile ringtones ignored.

Carlos looked on, reluctant to leave and collect his materials until the showdown was over.

Rose threaded herself through the expanse of men and tutted. "Most disappointing." Her English accent cut through the air like a freshly sharpened knife. "You know, I have been in meetings with other contractors who would jump at the chance of such a handsomely-paid opportunity. *They* would give a fuck."

"Hey lady, it's no big deal," someone called out. "The work's gonna get done, you know. Especially if Kelly gets moved off outta here. The guy's a nightmare, always yelling and putting people on edge, man."

A low mumble of agreement could be heard.

Rose walked towards the man who had spoken. "The reason Mister Kelly would appear to be of a slightly stressful disposition is due to me, actually."

She took the man's hard hat from his head and placed it atop her own. Then, looking at her reflection in a gigantic mirrored wall, she adjusted it, stylishly tilting it to one side.

"Truth be told, I am on his back. Constantly. I grill him relentlessly, demanding regular updates as to the progress of my property. Indeed, quite frankly, I could honestly say that I am making his little life unbearable. But this is only due to his being grossly unprofessional, for if Mister Kelly applied himself with more astuteness, more competence, we wouldn't be in this mess."

She turned, glancing back at the man in question. Kelly looked forlorn, twiddling his thumbs.

Rose went on. "Gentlemen, this job is to be completed. I hired you all on the proviso that its completion would be by the twenty second of this month, it is now four days past that date. I am not the kind of person whom accepts that kind of inadequacy. I am tired of paying money for labour that remains to be undertaken."

Rose Benoit walked around the dumbfounded men, holding the attention of all one hundred and thirty nine of them in the palm of her hand.

"There is to be two further weeks of labour. By the end of such time, I shall receive my completion."

A few disgruntled misgivings were sounded, although quietly.

"This is my house, gentlemen. If you have an issue and feel a lack of confidence in meeting my requirements, then hire up, acquire more manpower to aid in the overall assistance of this place. It doesn't take a fool to see that further recruitment is needed. I mean, take a look around and see the results as they speak for themselves."

A long silence followed Rose's speech, further enhancing her command of the large room.

"Hey pretty lady, are you from England or somewhere?" a young labourer called out, but by this time, Rose had said what she needed to say.

She walked towards the entrance, then looked back at the room full of men with their mouths ajar.

"You!" she barked at James Kelly. "Come!"

She walked from the room as the foreman ran towards her and followed her out.

All the men cheered, Carlos couldn't believe his eyes.

None of the gathered men ever saw James Kelly again.

Diamond Suite

Jack had been waiting all evening for the call. He was caught completely off guard when his mobile phone finally buzzed. Indeed, Sheriff Josh Morrison's amiable ramble was assurance enough to relax and curb all previous doubt.

"Well, Sargent, I've got a few things for ya here," he said. "It ain't pretty, but hopefully it might just wing us closer to what the hell's going on!"

"I appreciate this, Sheriff."

"Hey, don't mention it, Sargent." Jack chose not to amend Morrison's misunderstanding. "You and I have to talk. We got a connection, so from now on, we're a team. That's how I do things, Sargent, buddy."

"That's good to know, Sheriff."

"Those Russian fellas, they've been ID'd."

"Okey-dokey," he said.

"What was that, Sargent?"

"Oh, nothing. Yeah, carry on."

"I have their history, I'll send their names to you shortly."

"Okay."

"Right, there was a maid working her shift, possibly between the hours of 1pm and 4pm. She reported something to a manager at the hotel. They rejected the statement she made, but obviously, you know, when they found out what had happened to those guys later... what state they were in... they had to consider it."

"Right. This maid, what was in her report?"

"She was working in the apartment opposite and overheard the three of them talking. As far as I can tell, these guys were damn pigs, you know, greedy, excessively deviant. Rich kids. They dialled random hookers from the apartment, hoping at least one would show up. One did. Beat the crap out of her."

"The maid heard this?"

"Yep."

"The managers ignored her?"

"Unfortunately… damn it. Ya'see, Sargent, this hotel is one of the most exclusive damn places in Vegas, hell, even the world. You think the manager of that casino is gonna take the word of a migrant worker and disturb high-ranking guests?"

"Yes!"

"Wrong. They should've did, obviously, but, damn, life ain't like that. Wish it was."

Jack felt a little easier when he heard the frustration in Morrison's voice. He appreciated the familiarity. "So what happened?"

"Okay, so the maid heard them talking about it. Specific details. It was a thing for them. They did it all the time. Apparently they argued about who was gonna go first. As soon as the girl arrived, they would force her, make her beg, and leave her black and blue. It excited them, they thought nothing of leaving the girl for dead. Cheap girls were better because the likelihood of an investigation was almost zero… Their words, not mine, Sargent. Damn them. Anyhow, it was all the more important to these guys, however, that this poor girl had to be either using or fully dependent on hard drugs. They lusted at the control of actually not paying the woman in the end, after putting her through all that stuff for nothing… if she survived. Well, they did all the above, and then some!"

Jack was silent. His mind reeling and trying its best to properly assess the information.

"You mentioned about the apartment opposite?"

"Yes. The main penthouse apartment. What the casino calls the Diamond Suite. Usually reserved for filthy rich heads of state."

"Any info?"

"It was an arrival. A couple of women stayed for two nights. The evening maid said there was music coming from inside at the same time of the later homicide. But the room was empty, a manager went up there making courtesy calls only to find the stereo blasting and the remains of a party. Obviously these two chicks went down on the strip."

"Right," Jack sighed. "Oh, I think I've just received your ID reports. What did they do for a living? You said they were rich kids."

"All in the report, Jack. These fellas were traffickers, anyhow."

"Traffickers? Like, sex traffickers?"

"Yes indeed. Bad fucking guys. One of them, the one who's face and skull had been smashed, ran the whole operation. They dealt mostly with young imports from Zimbabwe, Mozambique, Zambia, their stock in trade. He would send them all over the world to be abused and to make money for him. The turnover this guy's traffic accumulated was megabucks. It could easily afford him trips to Monaco for the racing and trips to Vegas with his buddies to gamble and abuse whores in hotel rooms. His trips to Africa and Asia were mostly business."

"Okay, I get that, but why are they dead? Rival traffickers?"

"I'd say so, only, something don't add up to me. Someone definitely came afterwards, we know that. But there was no sign of forced entry. These three dudes were *big*, Sargent, big as barns, I tell ya'. To quell the three of them would definitely have needed even bigger guys, you know? No evidence of a large group of men was found in that apartment. No army. There would've been a struggle, but the apartment was immaculate. Whoever did this was big, Sargent. Big meaning important, but big in stature, too, I guess. Sargent Jack, buddy, we're looking for one big son of a bitch here."

Claw Hammer

"I just heard on the news feed that the Baltimore heist was intercepted," Ollie reported as he stepped into the car.

"Yeah? For the third time?" Jack asked as he pulled off.

"So they say, but who knows?"

"Did you know it's the single largest hold-up in history?" said Jack, "People downtown are saying that the money was astronomical. But that's not the half of it, the goods were weapons, nuclear, all that kind of stuff."

The magnitude hardly registered with Ollie Travis, who was looking out the window at two female cyclists.

"Okey-dokey. Well, anyhow, our friend Morrison in Vegas told me something last night. Said that the three guys in the Las Vegas hotel were part of the heist, but somewhere along the line they were prevented from undertaking their duties."

"Prevented? More like completely devastated."

Jack sniffed. "True, Ollie, true."

"Where are we going, boss?"

"We just got word about a scene, forensics are all over it already. One male victim. Details are strange, that's all I heard."

When they arrived the place was already swarming with people. Somewhat reluctantly, they both walked through the perimeter of the scene, immediately noting the gruesome results. This was now the eighth crime scene in four years where they had discovered particularity frightful details. They were beginning to refer to the sequence, linking the murders, giving them a title.

"I know, a little messed up, right?" DCI Burke appeared behind them. Seemingly proud he had been among the first on location. Jack and Ollie looked at each other.

"It took us a while just to take in what we were actually seeing. What kind of human being could even think of such a thing... With nails? Sick bastards."

"Yes, Burke, we can see for ourselves," said Ollie, aware that Burke was becoming trying for Jack. "Unless there's anything else you'd like to do here, you are welcome to leave any time you like."

"I know when to take a hint, Travis. We were just about to make a move anyway."

"Good," Jack muttered under his breath with a wry smile. Ollie Travis knew Jack wasn't capable of uttering anything remotely derogatory without excusing himself with an *only joking* note at the end.

Burke sauntered off, loudly gathering up his colleagues.

Ollie assessed the crime scene. "This is mad, boss."

As always, Jack ignored his partner's shock. "Do you notice how the nails have pulled parts of the skull away?" Jack glanced down. "The assailant left some of the nails still positioned in the victim's skull. Why did he do that?"

Ollie flipped open the spec details. "Victim's name is Roger Malone. He had been living in London for two years after moving from Manchester, where he's from originally. Bit of a wide boy."

"Ah, maybe treading on someone's toes?"

"Must've been some big toes, boss."

"True. Get on to the Manchester lead, find out if this Roger Malone still had people or family up there."

"Roger that, boss."

"Ollie, show some respect will you?" Jack looked sadly back at his colleague.

"Sorry, Jack."

"Okey-dokey, the hammer over there, it was used to bang the nails into his head, but not to fatally penetrate the brain."

"The guy was still alive?"

"I fear so, yes. In fact, I reckon the nails didn't kill him at all, they just added to the man's discomfort."

"Torture, then," Ollie said.

"Yep."

"He doesn't seem to be tied, or held in position."

"That's right, and no marks that would suggest he ever had been. No signs of struggle."

"Drugged?" offered Ollie.

"I reckon. There's no other way our perp could've done it otherwise."

"Well, what would've been the point of drugging him if the victim wasn't able to feel it?"

Jack nodded. "But saying that, maybe the assailant issued an anaesthetic to just his limbs so he was unable to move. Maybe he felt everything, unable to do anything about it."

"For crying out loud, it's another one of *those,* right?"

"Indeed, Ollie, this is another one by the *Animal.* We're dealing with an extremely angry guy here."

Kimmy

Puerto Banús, Costa Del Sol

The end of season had finally arrived, and with it the onset of summer. The rigorous training had ended, Andrew Baker looked forward to a well-earned break.

The VIP suite was huge. The windows, which curved their way towards the veranda, opened out onto the still night. The faint licking of the waters that encompassed the marina merged with the reverberant sound of bass from a distant nightclub. Kimmy, his latest fiancé, lay sprawled upon the bed, a light nasally snore eased from her tiny nose.

She awoke with a start as Andrew stumbled through the door. He clomped through the room, loudly announcing his arrival.

"Drinking already?" she said, squinting. "We haven't been here twenty four hours, and you're almost paralytic."

"I never realised it was any of your business."

He stopped at the bed and scratched at his backside, smelling his finger afterwards.

"You're disgusting," Kimmy said and rolled over, turning her face away.

Andrew undressed himself, throwing the remains of a newly purchased *Gucci* suit to the floor. She could smell his naked body as he pulled the sheet from the bed and threw it over to the other side of the room.

Kimmy screeched. "What's the matter with you?"

"Hey, you were meant to wear that sexy underwear I bought for you earlier. Why ain't you wearing it now?" His speech was slurred due to the Tequila he'd consumed earlier.

"Andrew, it's three o'clock in the morning. I'm in bed. I was asleep."

"What the hell's the point of buying you expensive shit

if you ain't going to wear it?"

"You're drunk. Go to sleep."

"Take those shit pyjamas off."

Kimmy huffed and sat bolt upright before quickly bouncing from the bed to retrieve the sheet.

"Where do you think you're going?" he stammered. "Why aren't you wearing the underwear I got you?" He darted over the bed and grabbed her before she could reach the sheet.

"I said... the underwear... Why aren't you wearing it?"

"Get off me!" Kimmy fell back on the bed. He landed on top of her, pinning her down, pulling her arms up. "Get off me, Andrew. Stop it."

"Listen, shut up. I just wanted to know why you weren't wearing that stuff I bought for you, that's all."

For a moment Kimmy didn't move, then Andrew released her, rolling away. He smiled and switched the bedside light on.

"Well, there was no need in waking me up though, was there? I was asleep. You could've asked me that in the morning."

"It *is* the morning," he said with a cheeky grin.

Kimmy finally retrieved the sheet and threw it over him. She slipped herself under it, joining him.

"Sorry, Kimmy. It was just a mad night earlier. I was fired up, out with the lads, you understand."

She glanced over at him. His cute face now absent of the menace she had seen earlier.

They pecked each other on the lips and Kimmy helped him as he pulled a vest on. They ordered grilled chicken and mayonnaise sandwiches from room service.

Kimmy told Andrew about all the places she wanted to go for the next few foreseeable days. Shopping at the boutiques that overlooked the yacht-strewn Alboran. Drinks inland with some of his team-mates' families. Later, surrounded by the sunset and palm trees, they would gorge on Argentinean grilled lamb at the restaurant they had spotted earlier when they had arrived.

They laid there together, silently looking at each other. Kimmy tenderly touched his face, her smile danced in the partially broken sunlight that shone into the room from behind the shades.

As he punched her in the face, her smile slowly transformed into an awkward grimace. Blood instantly oozed from the raw cut he'd just made. He banged his fist into her face again and she scrunched her eyes shut.

Her comprehension was slow but eventually she wailed, quietly at first. Andrew quickly shot up and straddled her. Kimmy, still in shock, failed to notice him above her as she placed her hand to her fractured jaw. He grabbed her small arms and easily tucked them under his knees at her sides. He punched her again, three times on her nose, twice on her left eye, and lowered himself screaming into her face.

***

Red, Andrew's manager, was called and the pair of them spent a mere twenty minutes within the breezy office at the local Marbella Policia before they were able to freely walk away.

The director general had smiled fondly as Andrew signed his autograph with a thick marker pen on a wide, laminated picture of himself from four seasons ago.

***

Andrew had demanded Kimmy return her silver engagement ring.

After three days of waiting, Kimmy had to borrow money from the English embassy in Andalusia to fly back to the United Kingdom. With her face still resembling an animal that had been run over by a speeding truck, she made several attempts to report the details of the attack and rape to the police. The process was slow and draining for Kimmy and her working-class family. With a rather hushed trial set for the following spring, she went against the wishes of her lawyer and tried to sell her story to the British tabloids. The published results, projecting her as a pariah and jobless gold-digger who falsely accused Andrew Baker – soccer genius and national treasure – of violently raping her, did nothing for her image and chances in court.

Michael In The Cupboard

Situated deep in the heart of the city's business area, Rose Benoit had personally selected Canada Square for its views of the Thames River.

It had barely taken her twenty minutes to find what she was looking for, down in the depths of the building. She walked past the postal managers and maintenance men who were suddenly quieted by the rare sight of their Chief Executive, the co-owner of the business. The overall chatter and conversations had been halted due to her presence.

She looked out of place, down there amongst the finger-smeared walls and scruffy posters of football team line-ups and page three models. A far cry from the onyx and marble of *Nubian Rose*'s upper echelons.

Rose was unimpressed as she mused about what they all got up to while unmanned by higher supervision. She momentarily considered sanctioning refurbishments and installing closed-circuit cameras.

She stood by the open door of the smallish office, her destination, casually tapping at the glass with her long fingernails.

"Hello...? Michael?"

"Yeah, who's asking?"

The sound of his own voice, and the manner in which he had answered, shocked his soul to the core as he turned and saw Rose Benoit. She held her position, eyeing him. She knew she was looking at the right man. A man who, it was related to her by one of her informants, was famous for taking advantage of female staff. Behind doors and in stationary cupboards. She'd been informed that numerous new arrivals were being duly questioned by the lecherous thirty five year old. He would size them up, making over-friendly contacts on shoulders with his wandering hands that outstayed their welcome. The occasional touch down the odd waist or leg. She'd heard details of how he made a name for himself for his groping hands.

"Are you Michael Beavis?"

"Yes, Madam. I'm sorry, err, I… yes I didn't know… it…"

She had walked through the door, shut it, quietly turning the key and locking it from the inside, by the time he'd finished his stuttering.

She pointed to a door on the left wall. "Get in there," she said calmly.

"Yes, err… okay, but this…"

"Through there, Michael."

"Okay… but…"

"Move," she whispered.

Obeying, he hastily shifted past the threshold. Once inside, they were in a small, dark corridor that contained two more doors on either side. Stationary cupboards. Perfect.

"Last one on the right, there's a good chap," She said, encouraging him with a small shove from behind.

"I… Err, this is the… cupboard…"

She interrupted. "Did I tell you to speak?"

" Sorry, you… no…"

"Okay, so why are you speaking?"

She pushed him inside and closed the door behind her. In the pitch blackness, she located the small switch to the dim light above them. He still had his back to her and, before he attempted to turn, she reached round with her left hand, tightly taking a hold of his crotch. She could feel his hardness already from underneath his trousers. Rose placed her right hand over his throat and pulled him back towards her from behind. His backside thudded against the front of her thighs and as she grabbed hold of his penis she bent him over slightly.

"So, Michael, I need adhesive, or something to that effect. Where might I find such an item?"

"I, don't… Err…"

"I asked you a question, kindly answer it."

Michael was now fully bent over. "This… is not…"

"This is not what? 'Tis but a simple question, Michael."

"I was going to… to say, it… This is err…"

Cutting in again. "Yes, Michael? Spit it out."

"Um. This is not part of… my job… err…"

"I see. Not part of your job? That's curious, Michael, because this isn't part of my job either, but guess what?"

"Err, yes…?"

"Unlike you, I am willing to make sacrifices, you understand? I'm willing to further myself from the confines of what is expected of me. I expect this too of others. People aboard my ship have to make sacrifices, Michael, and successful sacrifices are enthusiastically looked upon if they are of a certain benefit to me. Do you understand?"

"Err, but…"

"Do not make me repeat the question."

"Yes. I… yes, I do understand."

"I am now going to make a sacrifice of my own, you see, Michael. Do you understand?"

"What… I mean…"

"Do… you… understand?"

"Yes."

"Good boy."

The close proximity of the cupboard offered them little room for movement. She spun him around. He saw her in the dim light. Michael was captivated by her smouldering eyes, although they added to his insecurity. Her somewhat curvy physique contributed all the more towards his lack of confidence. He could smell the shea butter she had applied to her skin earlier in the day. Her smooth Berkshire dialect contrasted with his blubbering Middlesex.

"Get down on your knees." Enforcing this action, she prodded him downward.

Rose turned around slowly, her backside stared down at him.

"Do you see that, Michael?" He could indeed see that. He could see the wide expanse of bountiful ripeness enclosed tightly within her grey trousers.

"That's correct, you have the rare privilege of meeting my friends, my gluteal limbs, Michael. I would assume you'd know them better collectively as an ass," she hissed the latter part of the word, "and from this point on, this ass owns you, Michael. Do you understand?"

"Yes, Madam."

"Good boy. You will now be given an opportunity to show your obedience to that which owns you. Kiss the ass, Michael. Kiss your boss."

"Are you sure… this is…"

"I do believe my ears are playing tricks on me, Michael. When I told you to kiss my ass, I could have sworn I heard your voice. I hope it was my imagination."

Michael nervously moved towards her. "To the left, Michael, if you please. Kiss the left cheek first."

The air around them was silent, slightly cool, but he could feel his temperature rise towards the onset of perspiration and shameful fear. He planted a peck softly and was then ordered to kiss the right side. She grabbed the back of his head and pressed him into her. "Good. Good boy."

Rose held him in the same position and rubbed his face tightly against her buttocks. She could hear and feel him mumbling.

He was finally released and she turned herself around to face him once again.

"I asked you where the adhesive was, Michael," she said while gently touching his upturned face.

He found it difficult to speak as her palm rubbed against his mouth and nose. "On the, um, right, up there."

She looked up. "Ah, yes," she trilled, her fingers selecting a small container that she popped into her waistcoat pocket.

She stroked his hair tenderly. "Would you like to know one of my most loathsome pet hates, Michael?" Michael mumbled and nodded nervously. "I detest the idea of anyone or anything contributing to the discouragement of female progression within the workplace, especially within *my* workplace." Michael mumbled again. "Tell me, Michael, is this one of your issues, too? I most certainly hope it is. I make this a prerequisite. Anyone who comes to *Nubian Rose* is made thoroughly aware this is of major importance. It's kind of *day one* stuff, if you will."

"Yes I know, because… when I…"

"Your department has the highest rate of resignations, Michael. If you have an issue with younger, more vulnerable female staff, then I suggest you hire more mature and experienced females." Rose looked down at him. "Do you like my suggestions, Michael?"

He nodded.

"Now, Michael, be a darling and unzip your trousers," she said, while inspecting her long nails and the tops of her hands. As he opened his mouth, Rose continued, "You shall learn, boy, to do as I ask. When I give an order, you have no other choice but to fulfil it. Do you understand?"

Michael nodded and looked down and fumbled with the front of his trousers. After an awkward moment he finally managed to unfasten the zip.

"Good. Now pull your trousers down."

"But why?"

Rose frowned, the pain Michael felt was instant. The slap to his right cheek had the desired effect and, within a cloud of frustration, he hastily pulled at the button above the zip to enable him to remove the trousers.

Rose's frown softened. "Relax, Michael darling, you might cause yourself a mischief. But learn, boy. Learn by the mistakes you make."

He tugged at his waistband. Due to his impractical position, he grew more and more distressed at his inability to remove or even begin to lower his trousers.

Rose reached down and yanked open the catch above Michael's zip, before tearing at the offending garment – virtually ripping them from his groin. Michael fell back, owing to her forcefulness. Yet still she yanked on the trousers, Michael murmuring a few low-sounding misgivings. Her grip remained, pulling the trousers along with his boxer shorts off his legs. Doing this made his shoes slip from his feet and they plonked to the floor.

At last, Rose slowly rolled the trousers into a ball and threw them casually to the ground.

Amidst a click of her fingers Michael repositioned himself again before her. She pushed him back to inspect his manhood.

"Your penis, Michael. Most inadequate." She tutted and slowly shook her head. "For a gentleman who boasts such alpha credentials, you would have to forgive me if I assumed you were slightly larger in size, dear." Rose reached down and held it with her thumb and index finger. She pulled it upward and released it. Michael reacted as it twanged back.

"I have lady friends with bigger penises than you." Rose frowned, "In fact, looking at it, the thing is quite remarkable. It's actually provoking me to beg the question... how on earth have you been able to sustain a functioning sexual relationship with a real person."

Rose placed her hand over it and grabbed it tightly within her palm while looking him squarely in the eyes.

"I have punished men who were a lot larger than what I have here, Michael, darling."

Michael coughed and groaned as Rose squeezed. "You really are a small fish, aren't you, boy? A little tiddler. It is as if you are underdeveloped," she whispered, in a slightly childlike voice.

She moaned, smiling to herself, encouraging his penis greatly while kneading it.

"Anyway, enough. I grow tired of the insufficient contents of your trousers."

After a brief moment, wherein not a sound could be heard, he was pushed back on to the shelving unit directly behind, which sent the whole thing crashing down upon him. Printer materials and stationary were strewn everywhere at her feet, and Michael Beavis looking pitiful covered in the ruins.

"Mmm, you had better clean this mess up, Michael."

Though the man made several confused attempts to speak, yet again Rose interjected.

"Now, Michael, it's up to you, of course, but if I find that you have told anyone about what has happened here today, I shall come back here and tear your balls off. Do you understand?" She wondered if he actually believed her.

"Yes, yes, I do, perfectly."

"Just remember, Michael, my ass owns you. You belong to it. Do you understand?"

"Yes, I do."

"Good boy." She looked around and finally let him go. Gathering herself, she adjusted her blouse and smoothed her hair back in place.

"Of course, I could have you dismissed, fired for breach of responsibility. But you shall prove useful to me in the future. Among other requirements, I know exactly where to come if I need more adhesive."

She finally told him that after she left the cupboard he must allow five minutes to pass before he himself was to resurface.

He waited an hour.

Colloquy1

Julie: Baby, I just received your memo.

Rose: Apologies, honey.

Julie: You're so frickin' annoying, you know that?

Rose: …

Julie: So you're headed back here next week instead, is that right?

Rose: I'm afraid so. They're taking on more staff at *NB Lond* and I'm needed for their inductions.

Julie: Grown-ass folks over in London need mama's help, *again*?

Rose: Of course. These darlings need whipping into shape. You've been here, baby, you know the way in which one operates in London.

Julie: Yeah, dumb-ass place.

Rose: Quite.

Julie: Rose, I need to lose some weight.

Rose: I beg your pardon?

Julie: I'm getting big, babe. My sis said it's why I ain't had no man the last two months.

Rose: Little sister is incorrect, Julia. If you lose any more weight, I'm afraid you'll look like a stork.

Julie: My ass is getting bigger.

Rose: And? That's a good thing, baby. Seriously, you have the best ass in the world; do not waste all that talent.

Julie: There you go, talking that crap again.

Rose: Why is it crap?

Julie: Because everybody in the entire world knows *you* got the best ass in the world.

Rose: Not true.

Julie: Why? Who then?

Rose: …

Julie: And don't be talking about Sapphire.

Rose: Mmm, Indeed. She has a fine ass.

Julie: …

Rose: Yummy ass. Nice boobies too.

Julie: For crying out loud, Rose, just fuck the girl already, jeez.

Rose: Wait, hang on a second…

Julie: What?

Rose: You said a moment ago that you haven't had a guy in two months.

Julie: Yeah?

Rose: What about Rossi?

Julie: That kid from Cassa Mia?

Rose: …

Julie: He was like a child, honey. Like I said, he was far too young.

Rose: Explain, please.

Julie: You want the short version or the more silly-ass version?

Rose: Give me the definitive version.

Julie: …

Rose: …

Julie: Okay, before we ate we had to go to Foot Locker so he could check out some new kicks or god knows what. After, he took me to some Chuck E. Cheese joint. *I* paid. He needed a ride home so I took him back to Van Nest, which as you know is near my sister's place. He was a nice kid, I guess. I felt guilty when he invited me inside. I think he had mommy issues. I met her, the bitch was a hundred years old. She told me he can't sleep unless he gets his milk and cookies every night.

Rose: …

Julie: Yeah, I thought that would shut you the hell up.

Rose: He sounds like a dream.

Julie: Rose, don't make me slap you.

Rose: My ideal man.

Julie: Oh, enough already. Listen, did you book your flight?

Rose: Yes I did.

Julie: Let me cancel it.

Rose: Okay… why?

Julie: You remember Samuel Richardson?

Rose: Vaguely.

Julie: He's in London right now. I told him you were over there too. Says he'll fly you back to New York on his jet on the condition you'll allow him to pour you Champagne. His words.

Rose: Samuel Richardson, right?

Julie: Right.

Rose: He's one of Oleg's chaps?

Julie: That's right, he never made it to our little supper at *Private Eye's*, Oleg and his dudes have obviously been filling him in. I reckon he's a little jealous.

Rose: Okay, cancel the flight.

Julie: Done.

Rose: Merci, Madam.

Julie: This guy, Richardson, is an industrialist.

Rose: Yawn.

Julie: Rose!

Rose: Boring, darling. I am far more interested in our darling little Oleg. He's such a sweetheart. Extremely cultured. I actually believe I may have met him before.

Julie: Are you sure?

Rose: I think so. Although, I don't know for the life of me where.

Julie: You're usually good with faces, baby. Could you forget a face like *that*?

Rose: Perhaps you're right, although I am such a scatterbrain at times. Baby, did you cancel the flight already?

Julie: Yes, your highness.

Rose: Good show.

Julie: You sound nice, baby, you lay somebody?

Rose: Mmm, not as such…

Julie: Not as such?

Rose: Well, *I* was satisfied, put it that way. Yet, something tells my instincts that I might have enjoyed the experience far more than my *playmate*.

Julie: Quit playing, babe. How could anyone not be satisfied with the shit *you* got?

Rose: …

Julie: Answer me.

Rose: You know how heavy-handed I can be, darling.

Julie: Damn, Rose!

Rose: You know me, Julia. I am never satisfied unless I am putting the world to rights. I could not survive in a world where the intellectually deficient would go unpunished for their mistakes. The same could be said for the socially deficient.

Julie: Rose, baby, you scare the crap out of me sometimes.

Rose: If that were the case, why do you laugh?

Julie: A lot of the time, I don't know what the hell you're talking about. You're just weird, that's what I love about you.

Rose: I'm glad to hear that.

Julie: Don't forget, Samuel Richardson. Okay?

Rose: Got it, boss.

Julie: Goodnight, sweetie.

Rose: Is it? I hope so.

D Morgan

"Morgan, are you still there?"

"Yes, sorry. Tell me, what is it?"

"We've got her, Morgan."

"Benoit?"

"You sound dubious; am I to assume you disbelieve?"

"You can assume anything you like."

"What's the matter, Morgan?"

"I do believe you, it's just… I wasn't banking on this. Kinda thought you was gonna get someone else to do it."

"Well, please forgive us, but this is why you are here. Am I wrong, Morgan?"

"Listen, just ignore me, okay? Don't worry, before you start, I *am* up to the job."

"We know."

"Okay, what's the spec?"

"Everything will be placed within a file, you'll know when it gets to you."

"You think you could gimme the basics?"

"All in due time, Morgan."

"Okay, anything else?"

"Be in NYC on the sixteenth, night time. Civvies, *good* civvies."

"I hear. Anything else?"

"The file will be with you shortly. Morgan, keep low, and good luck."

David Morgan heard dial tone and instantly disassembled the phone, taking care to destroy the memory card and sim. He cursed.

He hadn't even completed his current assignment and now he was about to embark on not only a new one, but a highly anticipated, dangerous project that had been in the production stages for years. He cursed again, *anybody but me*, he thought.

Glass Bottled Mineral Water

Carlos was exhausted. Having virtually learned the majority of techniques relevant in ventilation maintenance, he was the only engineer on hand to mend the entire building's air-conditioning system, which had previously all but malfunctioned.

It was approaching midday and Carlos needed a break. He wiped his hands with a rag and walked towards the exit of the plant room.

The corridor was long and wide and resembled more of an expensive hotel than office space. He could hear the official but relaxed dialogue of the power-suited warriors amidst the doorways and entrances he passed. All the women seemed to be ridiculously attractive, the men, like they'd all stepped from the pages of GQ. He almost laughed at how different Wall Street was to the south Bronx. But with every step he took, he could feel himself becoming more and more anxious.

He took a deep breath and instantly took in an earful of her sweet voice…

"Well now, boy. What are we to do about this?"

A male answered. "It was a simple mistake."

Carlos inhaled deeply as he arrived at the main doors to her office, they were ajar, and in spite of everything else, he was glad he could feel the gush of cool air escaping out into the corridor; the successful results of his own handiwork.

"Do you think you could explain?" she asked.

"I'm sorry, Madam," the man said.

"Yes, I know… I know you're sorry. However, I asked you to explain."

"Nobody told me," he said, shakily. "I wasn't aware. She will be fired, I can assure you. I'm not going to let this one go. The service is unacceptable."

"Excuse me?" she asked.

"I, err, I shall fire her, for her bad service?"

"You think *she's* to blame? Are you being flippant, boy?"

"Oh no, of course not." The man backed off a little.

"And stand still while I address you. Move yourself back to where you were stood." He did. "If you are not being flippant, could you kindly explain why you think this is her fault? What possible reason do you have to actually support that?"

"Madam, I…"

Rose sighed. "Boy, I hardly know you. But you've been in my service for over a year. You know my requirements. You know the quality and the standard of which I expect. I demand the best and I receive it. I take it for granted. Like a well-oiled machine, it *must* function correctly. Whenever I do not receive the finest standard, things become awry, a lapse begins, a horrid, proverbial blot on the otherwise shiny landscape. Everything comes to a halt, and before we know it, the same thing happens again. By the time anyone has the time and inclination to do anything about it, we become complacent within the climate of the sub-standard. Mistakes are actually accepted. This is not how I wish to work, boy."

Outside the office, Carlos stood with his back against the wall, not even daring to breathe lest his presence be detected by the monster within.

"I'm sorry, Madam."

"Please do not say that again, boy." She grabbed at the bottle of water on her desk and inspected it. "Shall we go over it one more time?" she asked with the tiniest smile. The man nodded.

"Okay. The girl arrived in my office, with this." Rose held aloft the bottle. The man looked at it as if it were the very blot on the proverbial landscape she had said it was. "Now, I shall remind you… When Miss Benoit desires refreshment, she is to be forthwith presented with a tray, upon which she likes to see a litre bottle of still, a litre bottle of sparkling, both are to be confined within glass bottles. There should be at least two tall tumblers beside the bottles. A barrel of ice, and a small jar should also be in attendance, from which she might select a slice of lime, or lemon. If Miss Benoit has a guest, or in conversation with Miss Ross, or in a meeting with one or more clients, the request for water or refreshment should be doubled, or tripled, depending on the number of clientèle. The water should neither be freezing, nor should it be at or below room temperature. The bottles should never be plastic. The ice should come with a small pair of tongs. There is nothing difficult to understand. It is your responsibility to make your interns and service staff aware of your manager's requirements."

Her dialogue rolled out like sweet candy, but the way in which she spoke did little to put him at ease, its contents were like explosives banging against his nervous system. The man nodded.

Carlos frowned. Every time he witnessed her, albeit from afar, it seemed to be within a cloud of conflict or severity.

"You are to reinstate the young girl. And you are to inform her, and your staff, of what is required." She looked up at him. "Do I make myself clear, boy?"

"Yes, yes, Madam. Thank you."

"Good. Now you may go."

The man left hastily and Carlos sprung himself around a nearby alcove. Just in time, it seemed.

Separation

Ollie Travis stood on the corner in the relentless torrents, holding a cup of coffee in each hand. The rain was now penetrating through his jacket and onto his shoulders. Jack pulled up beside him and he quickly got into the car.

"Yeah, so anyway, thanks for being twenty-five minutes late."

"Talk to me, Ollie."

"Okay, Malone did have family in Manchester, a partner and three kids."

"Okey-dokey, any statements from them?"

"Nope."

"Why?"

"Because two years ago Roger Malone killed them all." Jack raised an eyebrow. "He was a loony tune, boss. His lady was having an affair. He knifed her and set fire to her house, where two kids were sleeping. He was tried, spent a year inside and got out early because of a medical appeal."

"Okey-dokey," said Jack easily, not at all hinting at the sorrow he felt for the two innocent children. "Malone being a criminal, it proves a pattern. The three Russians in Las Vegas, traffickers."

"Uh huh," Ollie agreed. "Malone and some of the others, they all seemed to be only just released from a long stretch or guilty of something prior to their own murders…" Ollie's voice trailed off.

"Okay, what else?"

"There was one more thing. I don't think you're going to believe this, boss."

Jack, struggling with his coffee, glanced over.

"The report came back from the coroner. There are no traces of anaesthetic in the victim, not even around the site, or anywhere. Not orally, or injections. You were right, boss, It's actually been confirmed that the victim endured the punishment clean."

"How did the assailant manage that?"

Ollie laughed nervously, "The killer was strong? I haven't the foggiest. The Russians were tied, so was Bolter. Malone wasn't. If this is an *Animal* murder then what's the link?"

"I told you before, it's just the…" Jack searched for the correct word, "energy. It's so detailed, but so meaningless all the same. We've seen some pretty messed up stuff in our lives, Ollie, but there's no need for the lengths this guy goes to. Seems unnecessary."

"I still don't believe Roger Malone and the Russians are connected."

"I do, I mean, true, they didn't know each other. But I'm ninety eight percent sure they were murdered by the same person."

***

The rain had stopped but the chill was unforgivable, and when the gusts of wind caught them as they walked towards the station, Jack and Ollie both gritted their teeth.

Inside the office wasn't much better in terms of warmth, so in an attempt for much needed comfort, conversation turned towards matters more familiar.

"It's his tenth birthday," Jack said. "I'm planning on taking him and his friends to that paintball place."

"Just make sure you don't get splattered," Ollie said while sipping on a large cup of coffee.

"Yeah, well, I thought I'd make a big deal. This place Daniel's living, they don't really have a lot of money to spend on the kids. They do get looked after well, the carers are okay, you know. It's just the funds are low."

"Are you any closer to finding out what's causing these tantrums he's turning out?"

"They say more tests, more interviews with him. That's another thing, Ollie, they say his medical bills alone are eating into the employees' salaries. In this day and age, it's terrible."

Ollie didn't know what else to say. He watched Jack lightly shake his head.

Jack Sargent's first encounter with Daniel Tyler had been accidental. The station had been staging fund raisers for as long as he could remember. There was always a barbecue or a disco, depending on the time of year.

Jack would never be present from such affairs, until four summers ago, when he was personally invited by Chief Superintendent Rob Wright.

On that day, Jack was the only police employee not discreetly stood with all the other awkward PCs and staff, drinking and wishing they were elsewhere. Everyone laughed at Jack's rubbish soccer skills, but the children fell in love with him. Not least of all Daniel, who appreciated the first ever male adult in his life to take an enthusiastic interest in him and his love of art.

***

Jack jerked himself forward in his seat. He groaned and reached around to massage the pain in his lower back.

"When are you going to get that medical, Jack?"

Jack shrugged. "It's not a problem."

"Your back's been crap since we started this *Animal* thing, boss. Sort yourself out."

"Are you still thinking about leaving me?" Jack asked. A question which was beneficial for two reasons.

"Yes. She says she'll consider giving it another go, only if I agree on moving to Cadiz."

"Cadiz? I thought she was going to Dublin."

"Change of plan. She said she wants to be near her mother. I've got a year to decide."

"I have to say, Ollie, I'm sorry for you. I always liked Beth; she's far too good for you."

"I know, and you always seem to be the first person to remind me."

"A year's plenty. She'll probably change her mind again in that time."

"I don't think so, boss. She's already applied for her visa and pre-booked a one way ticket."

"You'll regret it."

"Regret what? Regret leaving the UK, or regret leaving her?"

"Ollie, you decide."

Miles Away

Julie laughed to herself. Before she entered the restaurant, she could see him through the window waiting for her. The man looked lost, awkward, surrounded by people who knew instinctively he was out of place. He looked nothing like his photograph. The one he'd sent her wasn't even of himself when he was younger. It seemed to be of someone else entirely.

Her thoughts of cutting out and leaving left her mind as she began to feel actual sympathy towards him.

During her introduction, Miles did not rise from his seat and he shook her hand without showing the vaguest indication he was interested.

Julie asked for a white wine and cursed Rose Benoit for encouraging her to think outside the box. Her constant bombardment, telling her to consider dating men she normally wouldn't. Miles was one of these men.

He spent the next few minutes talking about himself.

"I work in a garage, and I like to spend my evenings listening to eighties rock music. I don't get out much on the weekend. I have a dog… Brutus, he's my best friend. To love me is to love Brutus. He's great though, I taught him how to jump up and flip himself over so he lands back on his feet like a cat. He can't do it so good, but he's learnin', you know, he's a real trier. If you take a look on *YouTube* you'll see all my videos of me training Brutus. Say, do you have an internet phone?"

Julie shook her head, "No."

"Ah, too bad. Because if you did, you'd be able to see Brutus do his flips. There is even one where I try doing a flip, but I fall on my ass. I tried to delete that one but it won't let me. I don't understand the settings. There are others I posted too, some of my mom."

"Does she do a flip, too?"

"No, she don't! I live with my mom, in her garage;

she's okay, bossy though. Always waking me and Brutus up when I'm late for work, busting my balls, busting Brutus's balls. Say, you ain't bossy are you?"

Julie nodded. "Yes."

They ate, he ordered grilled Chicken and halloumi burger with fries. Julie watched him. She felt bad about herself, resentful. She hated herself for wasting her time, for wasting Miles's time.

After a spell of time which went by during an itchy silence, Julie announced her intentions to depart. "Thanks for coming out here." she said, trying not to sound too engaging.

They stood, and after an awkward exchange wherein he offered her a badly planted kiss on her cheek, Julie fidgeted, searching for something to say that would cast closure on any potential future.

"I'm going to be very busy the next couple of weeks, but I was thinking maybe next month we hook up. What you think?" he asked, matter-of-factly.

"Um, well, I'm going to have to pass at that. I'll be busy for a while, too. Right up until next season, I mean, my schedule's pretty much got me working all the way up 'til thanksgiving." Her words reeled out easily; it was the first fully-fledged sentence she'd actually said to him.

"Well, ain't this a kick in the ass!" he said, seriously. "I sit here, thinking we're making progress, telling you my life story, you don't say shit. And then you got the nerve to blow me out."

She stared at him in disbelief.

Miles continued. "I don't usually come out here. I'm from Red Hook. Do you think I have time to do this every day, huh?"

"Well, okay, please forgive me if you thought this was going to be more than what it was."

"It's no wonder you're still on your own. I sure hope you don't do this to other fellas."

Julie threw her napkin on the table and grabbed her coat in less time it took for Miles to know what was happening.

***

Inside the Jeep, Rose was almost asleep. Her Kate Bush playlist had run its course long before she'd opened up her laptop to begin researching all the files relating to the new merger with *Nubian Rose* and Oleg Gribkov. There was a sizeable amount of data to revise, considering the length of time that had passed since the deal had been struck. Rose shook her head and rubbed her eyes while weighing up the immense magnitude of the situation. The partnership was already being talked about by Chinese heads of state and royalty in Monaco.

She checked her watch when she saw Julie appear in the rear-view, fifty yards away and walking towards the vehicle. She was early.

Rose signed out with a password and looked again in the mirror. This time, a man was standing next to Julie, he seemed to be close to her. On closer inspection, Rose saw him attempt to grab her arm.

***

"Listen, man. I'll slap you harder into tomorrow if you don't get outta my face! You understand me?" Julie said angrily.

She had lashed out, and the blow was instant, like a reflex; recoiled and ready for him as soon as he'd completed the shove he gave her.

As he nursed his face, Miles failed to notice Rose before she appeared next to him wearing a small black vest and baggy jog pants. She took Julie's hand and attempted to lead her away.

"Oh, so you're a dyke as well, huh?" he shouted after them. Rose persisted and dragged Julie towards the vehicle.

"Oh no you don't. You can't cut out after that. I got rights. I could call the cops here. It's assault I tell you!" His pitiful words matched the pitch of his voice.

"Go home, Miles," Julie called out, almost tripping over herself and her large heels.

He called out. "You fuckin' bitches, you're all the same!"

Julie dropped into the passenger seat.

"Here," offered Rose, handing her a box of tissues. Julie pulled a few off and began wiping away the make up around her eyes.

"What the hell, Rose? Is this all there is now? Little fucks like this guy?"

"Jules. I apologise. This is all my fault."

"Damn straight it's your fault. You told me he was a friend of yours."

"Ahem, correction, the gentleman in the photograph *used* to be an acquaintance of mine. But you are right, I failed to undertake the research." Rose leaned over. "Julie, I am sorry. Really I am."

"Uh-huh. Yeah, yeah, whatever."

Rose wiped at Julie's face with more tissue. "Julie, don't be like that."

Miles appeared at the window beside Rose. She flicked at the switch to lower it. "Yes? May I help?" she asked.

"That bitch in there… she's a damned bitch."

The gash Julie's palm had left under Miles' eye was pretty rough. It impressed Rose as she glanced at his face.

"Okay," she said. "anything else?"

"I shelled out over one hundred bucks tonight. At least give me your damn cell number."

Rose flicked the switch and raised the window again. Miles began shouting. His face creased, further enhancing his ugliness.

"That's it. If I ever see your face again, you bitch…"

Miles kicked the side fender of Rose's vehicle and began to walk away.

Almost instantly, Rose unhooked her seatbelt and placed it tidily to one side. Julie panicked and tried to place her arm around her shoulder, but it was too late.

"Rose! Let's just go back to yours, okay?"

Rose calmly stepped from the car.

"Rose, it ain't worth shit."

Miles hastened his retreat but Rose bypassed him, and at the same time firmly took a hold of the scruff of his neck. She walked him until they were level with the window of the restaurant.

"What the hell? Get the hell off me, bitch."

The first time, the window failed to break when she pushed him heavily against it. Instead, Miles bumped against the glass and the rebound quickly bounced him back down to the sidewalk. There was blood from his broken nose splattered on the glass. People inside had jumped from their seats.

Miles was easily subdued and was swiftly pulled up. Rose grabbed his shoulders and forcefully thrust him towards the window – this time sending him plummeting through it. The sound was colossal as shards of heavy glass fell inside the restaurant with him.

He lay unconscious, strewn awkwardly over a small table, scattered food and broken chairs.

Julie's mood had somewhat lifted by the time they arrived back at Rose's apartment. And three DVDs, barbecue chips with homemade watermelon daiquiris, spent in the company of her best friend was enough to take her mind off Miles. Rose also decided that Julie should take a break from dating.

Accident & Emergency

Somewhere Between Wembley And The North Circular Carriageway.

Ricky Gomez had been homeless for almost three years. Initially, time had been particularly difficult due to the transition from crashing on a friend's sofa to living round the back of an oily tyre garage just steps away from Staples Corner.

However, his pursuers still found him, in spite of his concealed hideaway.

Four in total, they all stood and looked down at him, their dirty faces furrowed in anticipation at what they were about to do. Tin foil and broken lighters surrounded his slouched form. One of his assailants kicked at his feet to rouse him.

"Ricky, get yourself woke. Sorry, man, the time is now."

Ricky coughed and looked up through squinted eyes. Their forms appeared before him like shadowy spectres.

"I told you. I said you'd get your money at the end of the month," he slurred.

"That was last month."

"Yeah, last month. I told you last month, and I meant the end of this month."

They began their work. His limbs broken for their missing one hundred UK pounds.

***

A week had passed, six and a half days of slipping between unconsciousness and crying for help. The cold October rain lashed at his skin. Heavy juggernauts loudly sped past, almost crushing him as he lay strewn on the edge of the bypass.

He was almost dead by the time a passing motorist broke down nearby.

It was Friday, close to midnight. The Barnet hospital bustled with speedy intensity. Medical staff barged his battered body through countless sets of double doors.

His skin was the colour of papier mache but at least the doctor pumped his system with enough adrenaline to resuscitate him.

Ricky's mind recoiled in mortal pain. He shrieked and moaned to Heaven from his mobile stretcher. Inanimate figures pecked unfathomable questions at him. He just wanted the pain to stop. His hankering for heroin was intense enough but the impact on his brain and body as he longed for more added to the agony of his broken ribs and legs and jaw and fractured skull.

After a heavy sleep, he awoke in a muzzy haze, which made him feel like the incident happened years before, although the pain was current, right there and then, fraying his senses.

"How long have I been laid here?" he asked.

The lingering nurse, checking her watch, called the doctor into the small room. Doctor Sidhu arrived.

"Three days," she said methodically. "Now, is your name Ricky Gomez?" she asked.

"Yeah, when can I get out of here?"

"Not for a while, we need time to put you back together."

She allowed the nurse to place a white plastic cup next to his bottom lip. Ricky shook his head, not wishing to drink.

"You need fluid, Ricky."

"No I don't."

"I need to ask you some questions," she said.

"No you don't."

"Yes, I do, and so does the police."

"Shit, I need to get out of here, where are my clothes?"

"I can see I'm going to have problems with you. You can't move, Ricky. The breakages you've acquired are limiting your movement one hundred percent. I'm afraid you'll be with us for a while." The doctor looked towards the door, as if what she was about to tell him was confidential. "In fact, at this stage, Ricky, there is a ninety-eight percent chance you'll not be able to walk again."

Ricky Gomez fell silent as her diagnosis lingered around the room. A slither of salt-water and blood ran down his cheek on to the pillow.

After much deliberation, the nurse finally got Ricky to moisten his throat and drink from the cup.

"I'll need more than water. I'm a user, did you know that?" he asked.

"Yes, we did, Ricky."

"Well, aren't you supposed to give me some, or something? Like methadone?" he asked.

"Of course not. The first thing we did was try and decrease your dependency by applying morphine. We've also found other things… How often do you take crack?"

Ricky squinted, teetering on the cusp of pain and guilt.

"All I'm trying to do is help you, Ricky."

Doctor Sidhu wasn't a pretty woman, Ricky thought, but she had an easy manner and spoke in a way in which he could understand. She seemed like a nice person.

"Crack for, I think, eleven weeks. I think. Before that, heroin for about sixteen months. But that's on and off." He sounded sincere.

"Okay, and you smoke it."

"Yeah. I injected a few times, not for long."

Just then, Doctor Sidhu noticed Ricky was growing pale at an alarming rate. He began to perspire instantly. She called the nurse once again, and three arrived in quick succession. His temperature was taken and read.

"What's happening?" he said, wearily.

"Ricky. You're having another attack." She sounded far away, although she raised her voice. "It's the shock. We're going to issue you with more pharmacological treatment… Ricky…? Can you hear me?"

Her voice trailed off. Ricky was then ushered back into

his mind. Visions of being stamped on by disgruntled parka-wearing scum fused with his mental recollections of all the terrible things he'd done years before. It always haunted him whenever he had the misfortune of falling asleep without the soft cushion of heroin to dampen his reality.

Dinner With Beth

Ollie opened the door. He knew his guest would be on time and fully appreciated his reliability, if only because the food was moments from being ready. Brown trousers and brown tweed jacket with a bow tie always made Jack look like a nineteen seventies school teacher. Ollie cut him a hopeless glance. It was the kind of thing that used to annoy him, now Ollie found it amusing. He imagined in a few years that he would actually find himself accepting Jack's reluctance to join anything current.

"Do you actually realise it's *now,* Jack? Like, not fifty years ago?"

"I don't know what you mean," Jack said, grinning slightly.

"Yeah, well, it's been a while since the Millennium."

"Ignore him, Jack." Beth gave Ollie a mini-shove as she passed him. "I think someone told him once that it was okay to be rude to guests," she said, while giving Jack a warm hug.

"He's not a guest. I see him every day. He's more like someone's least favourite uncle."

"Ollie, don't be so rude. Shut the door behind you," she said as she escorted Jack into the living room, first on the right.

***

Jack had only met Beth Travis once, but they spoke often on the phone, sometimes as much as twice a week. He had always thought, somewhat whimsically, that their first and only meeting had perhaps been a mistake on Ollie's part. He knew Ollie liked to keep his private life separate, but his distance keeping seemed a little drastic.

"Beer, Jack?" Beth asked.

"I should, shouldn't I?"

"Woooh, scary!" teased Ollie, making trancey movements with his hands. "Go on, Jack, go for it. Live life on the edge."

He received a soft flick of Beth's tea towel before she disappeared into the kitchen. Ollie plonked himself down on the settee beside Jack.

"Your trouble is that you've been single too long."

"Don't start."

"It's true, Jack. I mean, look at you. You're so uptight lately. I can definitely see a change in you."

"And you think I can't see a change in you, too?" Jack then hastily switched his voice down to a whisper: "Especially when I know you and Beth aren't getting on."

Ollie began to fiddle around with a remote control, finally he aimed it at the stereo system over by the wall.

Beth re-entered the room. "Not now, Ollie. Why must you always be playing that rubbish?" she handed Jack a bottle of *Sol*, before stealing Ollie's remote.

"I just wanted Jack to hear something decent, instead of all that classical music he's always subjecting me to."

"Excuse me?" Jack said with gusto. "I know more about all your head-banging music than you do mine."

"See? That's exactly what I'm talking about. Coldplay and U2 is not head-bangers music, Jack."

"Okey-dokey, well, it is to me."

"Me too, Jack," said Beth. "Only really boring people listen to that kind of music anyway. The beer okay, Jack?"

Jack viewed the bottle he was holding, and proceeded to analyse himself after a couple of sips. "Sorry to be a pain in the bum, Beth, could I have a shandy instead, add some lemonade?"

"Course you can, Jack," she took the bottle again.

Ollie glanced over at him dubiously, silently accusing Jack of being his usual self.

***

Beth's lasagne was delicious. It's bolognese sauce

peppered the front of Jack's napkin, which he'd tucked underneath his collar; he almost looked like a big baby. Ollie had again silently questioned Jack's table manners as he watched his boss mop up the remains with the excellent garlic ciabatta.

Jack's mixed salad was untouched as he finally threw off his napkin.

"That was absolutely lovely, Beth. Ollie's such a lucky man."

"Ah, don't mention it. I'm glad you enjoyed."

She began to clear the table as both men silently thought about loosening their belts, but didn't.

"Would you like tiramisu, Jack?" she asked.

"Oh, yes please. Only one sugar for me, please."

"Jack, you plonker. It's a dessert!" offered Ollie. "You're so English."

The jovial façade upon Jack's face disappeared, at last heralding time for *work talk*. Ollie saw it and was ready.

"You remember Josh Morrison?"

"Sure, Vegas guy."

"That's right. I have a confession to make to you, Ollie."

"You're not in love with him, are you, boss?"

"I've been in contact with him ever since the Homicide in Las Vegas. He tells me a lot of things – interesting things that are happening stateside." Ollie listened while Jack took the small pot of tiramisu from Beth. "It's actually more than his job's worth; the murder's far from his jurisdiction – homicides in other states. He's been informing me about all this stuff, Ollie. Last time we spoke, he told me about a guy who went missing. Latin American, nobody important, just a runner, courier, that kind of thing. They haven't managed to find him yet. Interesting stuff, though, because this guy was also connected with this heist in Baltimore."

"Okay? What's that got to do with us?"

"Think about it, Ollie. All these guys end up dead. Messed-up dead. Admittedly, many of them were monsters, rapists and such. Paedophiles. Not all of them. But they have one thing in common. One thing that connects them."

"Baltimore."

"That's correct. You know, there's intelligence in Europe and America that's not acknowledging this connection, Ollie. There's something else. There is a man. An off the radar man. Ex-army. Name's David Morgan. He's been going over these murders in more depth. He's part of an elite task force. Morrison was shaky on the details, but he said that this Morgan is in close proximity with the killer, and the killer doesn't even know."

"How the hell did you get this information, Jack? We work in London. Don't you think we're a little out of our depth?"

"Of course not. Listen, Ollie, don't you see we have a chance to actually do something special here?"

"No, mate. I don't. Have you spoken to Wright?"

"Oh, come off it, Ollie. Rob Wright's past it. You know that. Haven't you realised yet, he's not interested. He'd rather us go after kids who do over sweet shops."

"I don't think that's such a bad thing. Sometimes, Jack, it's better to cut out. This case is fucked. We are so deep in it. Not only is it disgusting, but we still have nothing. We are as close to finding this sick bastard as we were six years ago."

"Listen, Ollie. I'll level with you. I have a feeling. I feel something about this thing. I've decided to make it my life's work."

"Oh, god, Jack, that's a bit over dramatic…"

"Not really. Listen…"

Jack turned to face Ollie and readied himself for what looked like a pre-rehearsed speech, which made him look like he was about to propose.

"Okey-dokey, I'll say it. I want you to help me. You told me you haven't decided to leave yet. Please. One more time, Ollie?"

Beth Travis leaned against the doorway that lead into the kitchen. She looked at them both as they nodded to each other, their hands clamped together in mannish union.

Pitch Confusion

Due to a minor power surge, the temperature controls on the air conditioning units had failed yet again. It had taken Carlos all morning to identify which of the units were operational and which were in need of repair.

He was in the next room, adjacent to her office. All throughout the day, he had been able to hear large chunks of her conversations. Some had been mundane, finance and numbers, with no room for personal small-talk. Yet others had been colourful, such as her hour long phone smooch with a woman she'd referred to as *Madam*. It became evident to him she was homosexual. Or maybe not. The subject matter seemed strange and at times unnerving, yet it would have been a lie if he wasn't engrossed in her voice and the way she spoke to the woman about sexual exploits and empowerment in the same sentences. He was also privy to all manner of her undertakings, including her calendar for the rest of the week.

Of all the suited associates who'd ventured into Miss Benoit's office, it had been a woman named *Julia* who had been the most frequent. Possibly her Manager, or personal assistant, he could not tell. The lady was just as glamorous.

As he drained the water from the main unit into a mid-sized bucket, he listened intently. Their accents. He found it curious; Julie's Bronx drawl rebounded strangely well with that of Rose's, a voice he believed sounded a lot like Mary Poppins.

***

"Oh, but I couldn't possibly. You know I have to fly back to London tomorrow evening," Rose said.

"Just do this one thing for me, babe," Julie pleaded. "Oleg's got a big thing for you. It's like he's obsessed. And he talks like he's your people, you know? He knows all that bougie crap you know... opera and ballet and shit. The new block over at Madison is almost in the bag, Rose. They have shopfitters over there right now. All he wants is a tour."

"Okay, I shall stay until the weekend, then I must fly out."

Julie smiled. "Good girl. Say, have we come up with a venue for the party yet?"

"Non. I actually thought Europe, what would you say to that?"

"Only if it's Milan. Or Paris."

"Mmm, both good calls. Arrange trips, darling, also check out the west coast. I'll enquire with my London fellows."

Julie laughed and attempted to adopt her usually deficient British accent, "Oh, rather! Call the Queen Elizabeth too while you're at it."

Rose smiled. "Julie, you beast."

Julie checked her phone, her smile straightened. "So, Four Seasons, tomorrow?"

"Good heavens, Julie, you didn't say anything about the Four Seasons," she raised her voice and pursed her purple lips together.

"What's the problem? It ain't like you gotta buy a new suit."

"Oh, Julia, of course I do."

Julie's phone buzzed and lit up, showing a man's face on the screen as Mary J. Blige blared out from its tinny speaker.

"It's Raoul," Julie said sadly. She cancelled him and flung her phone back onto the desk.

"Ah," Rose said, slightly triumphantly. "So he's back. Raoul, the *funny* man!"

"Yeah."

"Oui, Raoul. How is my little friend, Raoul?"

"Well. He's still a comedian," she answered reluctantly, "and he's still scared shitless of you."

"Whatever for? I haven't even met him properly yet,

have I? I mean, you showcased him to me the other month at the movie theatre, but that was hardly ample time for which to make my estimation."

"It was for him."

"Really?"

"Sure, as always, you made that impression, you know, that stain of fear you leave on everyone you meet? He said he was weary, he said he never met anyone like you before. Said you were like a monster or something."

"Moi?" Rose placed her hand to her breast.

"Don't go playing the innocent card with me, as if butter wouldn't melt."

"Oui, it *would* melt. Melt all over my body."

"Can we be serious for one second, honey, you think?" Julie flexed her shoulders.

"Forgive me, darling. Okay. You met him earlier, right?"

"Baby, you'll never believe it."

"Talk to me."

"We've seen each other most nights these last two weeks. I know he looks like someone from nineteen seventy eight but he's real cool. We met near the Village, about 2am this morning. He'd just finished his gig.

"Right."

"There's a restaurant over at Bleecker Street, nice little place, a pal of his kept it open just for us. Rose, we were the only two there; it was so romantic. We ate some Cajun chicken and shrimp."

"Julie, tell me how you felt about *him*."

"So, I'm thinking, okay, he's made a real effort. I'm looking at the boy, and I'm feeling something, you know? He's real funny, kept on pulling out these one-liners and shit. I was laughing so hard I almost wet myself."

Rose cocked her neck, glancing at Julie incredulously. "Go on," she frowned.

"I was so drunk, I straight up shouted, laughed like a bitch."

"Okay, okay, so he's an amusing fellow. But how did

you feel?"

"I don't follow."

"Is laughter your only attraction towards this boy, Julie?"

She saw Rose was serious.

"Okay, here we go. You think that just 'cause I ain't attracted to him then the relationship won't work? Well relax, mama, it's already past second base."

"I beg your pardon?"

"I appreciate your protectiveness, baby, I really do, but he ain't no wife beater. He was a gentleman, and I wanted him. There really ain't no need for you to throw this one through the post-office window."

"Okay, so you two got down to it. How was he? And be honest with me."

Julie wiped at her eyes with the palms of her hands. "It's a grower, I think, Rose. Might take a little time to get him on point."

"So, he's rubbish," Rose announced.

Julie hesitated. "He is, babe, yes."

Rose smiled and removed her spectacles. "Well Julie, my darling, at least what he lacks in the bedroom he more than makes up for in his *huge* gag-reel."

They both laughed, after which Julie continued. "Oh, and yeah, Raoul, he's also got Tourettes."

Her use of the latter word was hushed slightly, almost tailing off into an indecipherable mumble, an attempt so that Rose might miss-hear."

"Julie, explain please."

"Oh for crying out loud. He's got damned Tourette syndrome, okay? Walking me back to my apartment. Scared the crap out of me when he went off."

"*Went off*?" Rose almost shouted.

"Like a firecracker. Straight up shouted, 'fuck, fuck, fucking balls'."

Rose's jaw dropped, thoroughly perplexed.

"'Fucking balls,' he shouted, 'shitty balls,' like, real quick. 'Fucking bitch, fucking bitch.' I couldn't believe what was happening, folks looking at us, and shit."

Rose laughed.

"It ain't funny dammit. Well, it is to him 'cause he uses it as part of his comedy act."

On hearing all from the next room, Carlos chuckled to himself. His head was buried under the AC unit while replacing the outlet pipe. Suddenly the sludge which had caused the blockage poured down into his mouth. He almost choked. He coughed and spluttered and quickly sat up to balance himself, but in doing so the side bracket knocked against the top of his head.

Julie could hear the shuffling from the next room, as tools clanged and a bang sounded. She moved over to the door and closed it.

"Julie, I love you so much," Rose said, still laughing.

"Well, it was mad heavy, girl. I tell you, I damn didn't know where to put myself. He told me he suffers from it the most when he's more relaxed."

"That's weird, I thought it would be the other way around," said Rose. Julie shrugged. "So, have you made any plans to meet up again? Perhaps go to the library?"

"It ain't funny."

"It could only happen to you," she said, still smiling. "When are you going to see him again?"

"On Friday, he wants to make me some food. He's a nice guy, really cool to be around. I like him a lot. But I think I need more time; who knows, something might come out of this."

"Jules, I hope so."

Just then, there was a knock at the door and a man entered. "Excuse me, Miss Ross. Miss Benoit. The guys from *J&C*'s are in the lobby."

Rose turned to Julie, "Darling, shall we go? I trust the issues next door have been resolved?"

"You're kidding? They still got some fool in there messing with that air-con unit. I don't know what he's doing, and I ain't too sure he does, either," said Julie.

"Well, never mind. We shall conduct our meeting in the boardroom."

Surrounded by Julie and several other hand-picked executives, Rose Benoit sat at the head of an enormous onyx table. The board room, one of her most treasured environments.

"So, I believe you wish to request for the representation of *Nubian Rose*, is that correct?" Rose asked.

"It is, Madam. We at *J&C*'s are extremely enthusiastic about the product we have commissioned and would deem it an honour to be even considered by *Nubian Rose* to represent it."

"And tell me, Mister Forde, before we both merge ourselves together, might we be reassured of your foreseeable forecast being a success, this being *J&C*'s maiden voyage, so to speak?"

Howard Forde looked toward his now useless support for help, one of them actually shrugged and looked down with an almost pained expression.

"Well," he began, unsteadily, "I think... in fact... I can assure you that our finance team boasts impeccable insight. As you put it, we are kind of the new guys on the block, but even in these early stages, our main objective is to deliver the very best in cutting-edge services. Today our credit department have sent you all the documentation."

He took a deep breath and shuddered in complete surprise at his own display of self-confidence. His eyes lit up on seeing Rose Benoit actually smiling at him from across the table.

***

Howard Forde was handsome, in a rugged way. He feverishly fumbled about, checking through his notes and specifications. Although obviously nervous, he had just the correct amount of conviction that kept him from being rebuked.

"Surely, Howard, is it not more of a usual procedure for a promotions company to approach the designer? Not for the designer to approach promotions?"

It was a valid query, but Rose knew the answer. This would happen often. Rose was aware she was in-demand.

"Yes, Madam. In conventional terms, obviously that is true. But we are vying for your support. *Nubian Rose* is so expertly established. Your promotional packages are obviously among the best in the world, and, if you'll forgive me for my familiarity," Howard nervously looked at his accompanying colleagues as he spoke outside the script of his pitch, "it represents you personally, Miss Benoit, and the way in which you conduct and control all your undertakings. I don't believe there is anyone out there who would look at you and your organisations and *not* wish to work with Miss Ross and yourself."

***

Rose surveyed the clumsy man in front of her. Howard's presentation wasn't very good. His stammer and reluctance spoke of his lack of professionalism. She also disliked the product, an android software system that had been produced especially for *Nubian Rose*. The test drive was boring and the application actually failed to function on the first attempt. The thing would have served absolutely no use to *Nubian Rose* and its eminently renowned team of designers. The potential was zero.

Rose smiled. "*Nubian Rose* would love to represent your item, Mister Forde. I speak on behalf of all of us on the board when I say we like what you have produced and we look forward to a long relationship with you."

Waiting

David Morgan had just completed six hundred crunches. The phone call was due, but its expected time had passed. He paced, between periods of frustration, plastic bottles of water and cigarettes. The following day, after laundry, falafels and more exercise within his small studio, the mobile sounded.

"Yeah."

"Morgan, I'm sure you'll be pleased to know, we received your report in good time. You've obviously been busy."

"A simple thank you would have been better. And nicer."

This was the fourth time he'd spoken to the agency, and in time he'd learned there was more than one person who'd make the call. This person, a man, was his least favourite.

"Indeed. We believe your payment would have already seen to that, or did you forget?"

"Okay, okay. I ain't received the file for the next operation yet, though."

"Relax. It shall arrive in good time. Meanwhile, do the research. We have also made preparations for your cover. We want you to be as comfortable as possible; you really have to be careful with this one."

"That's what you said last time."

"Morgan, you know as well as we do, this is no ordinary assignment."

"You got that right. So why the delay?"

"Many details need to be finalised, Morgan. Not long to wait now, just a few more days."

"You make it sound like I'm waiting for a wedding. Few more *days*? Is there any people working your end?"

"We understand your frustration, we know you are eager to apprehend the subject, Morgan."

David Morgan refrained from being honest and saying he wasn't eager at all.

***

"I'm not eager…" he said aloud to himself repeatedly later that night. "I'm scared shitless."

Bored also. There was only so much research and revision into which he could immerse himself before he realised he was going round in circles.

Trash Can Times

Lunch Period, Manhattan

"That'll be eleven fifty, pal." The burly guy behind the counter kept his grip on the small pot of raspberry white-chocolate ice cream, as if thoroughly protecting his investment, preventing yet another customer who might dash away without paying.

"Jeez, that's mad expensive. You ain't gonna pay for that, Carlos?" Tony said.

Carlos dug a little deeper in his back pocket to retrieve another five.

"I don't believe you," his friend went on. "You can't pay for that crap."

The man in the caravan flapped his filthy expectant hand, onto which Carlos paid.

"You fat bastard," Tony said as they stepped away from *Fred's Ice & Coffee.* They turned right, and crossed the main street, headed for Seventh avenue.

"You must be crazy, bro. Raspberry ice cream?"

"I like raspberry, Tone, what can I say?"

"Yeah, but *raspberry,* holmes? Jeez. I ain't never had me no raspberry ice cream before."

"Exactly, that's why you should try it, it's wonderful." Carlos laughed.

His friend's face contorted. "Damn, you speak like these dudes already. Just remember where you're from, Carli."

"Where *I'm* from? I'm from Jalisco, esé. You? You come straight outta La La land." Carlos scruffed his friend's hair roughly.

"You're crazy, man."

"Tone, I love it here; it's different, you know? I like being in a different place sometimes."

"Boy, this city is too big, man, makes me feel like a

freakin' ant. And it's far too cold."

"Maybe, but out here they got this thing they call an overcoat, you know?"

Just then Carlos glanced across the main pavement, he seemed distracted.

"What's the matter?" asked Tony.

"Guy over there. I recognise him from some place."

"The dude with the big hair in the deli window?"

"Yeah. I recognise him, but I can't place him."

"The kid looks like someone stuck in the late seventies. You sure he ain't one of your Rican buddies."

Carlos placed his thumb and index finger to the bridge of his nose.

His friend went on. "Anyway, so? Who gives a crap?"

"I seen him. I know I have." Carlos searched his mind. "Oh lord, let me think."

"Carli, so you're a detective now, huh, is that it?"

Carlos smacked his hands together triumphantly. "I got it. This guy…" he began pointing towards the man in question, almost attracting his attention. "He's a comedian guy. He's dating the lady I work for."

"Right."

"Well, I don't really work for her. She's one of them. I'm sure the dude's name is Raoul, or something like that."

"These broads you work with… *buena*? They hot?

"I don't work *with* them. I'm working at that building back down near Federal Hall. They own the place."

"Yeah, yeah, but are they hot?"

Carlos looked back at his friend, his expectant face waiting for an answer. "I don't know. I guess they're both pretty hot."

They stood on the edge of the pavement and looked both ways before dashing out on to the busy road, dodging the cabs and speeding people carriers.

Carlos could see it was definitely Raoul. They could also afford a clear view of the blonde he was kissing.

"Well, this bitch you work for can't be all that," Tony laughed. "because if she was, your guy there wouldn't be all up in that blonde bitch."

Carlos looked confused, and shook his head. "Foolish guy, just plain foolish."

Tony frowned. "Hey, hey, hey. Easy, brother. What are you talking about? We've all done it."

He took a hold of Carlos's shoulders and pushed him along.

"Yeah, well, not me."

"*No mames*! Are you kidding me? Carlos... the pretty boy? I seen how these womens look at you. How many times bitches be coming over to me and asking for your number?"

"It don't mean nothing, bro."

"You say you like it here, but you don't like these east coast bitches?"

Carlos shrugged. "Dunno. It ain't no big deal."

"Whatever, man," said Tony, trying to dip his thumb in Carlos' pot of ice cream – Carlos raised it high above his head and out of Tony's reach.

"New York folks are okay, I guess. But they're cold. They seem to have far too many things on their minds. Always in a hurry." Carlos sniffed, looking back towards Raoul. The blonde laughed as he kissed her neck.

"Dude, you've been here almost three years, are you telling me you ain't seen nothing? Not one broad you'd like to knock your balls against?"

"Yeah, maybe."

"Wow, we have a winner. Who's the luckiest lady in town? She got a big ass?"

Carlos was silent, walking on ahead while seemingly avoiding Tony's interrogation.

"Carlos, how come you never talk about what's on your mind? We're amigos, you know me. Why you never talk to me, man?"

He sighed. "She's the lady who owns the building I work at."

"*Neta*? Really? the bitch your Porto Rican buddy's been banging?"

"No, not her. It's her partner. I reckon they're sisters, or something. She's British."

"Hold up, British?"

"English, bro. And *fresa*, a real pain in the ass." Carlos looked down, deep in contemplation, deciding to continue. "But she's different; I never met anyone like her."

He now had Tony's attention.

"Christ, I ain't even met her, anyhow," Carlos shrugged. "And it ain't real, you know? Like, way out of my league."

Tony looked disappointed. "You're kidding me? What kinda bitch are we talking about here? Is she like the greatest woman in the world, or something?"

Carlos nodded. "Bro. I ain't witnessed anything like her. She's like some movie star."

"Kind of movie?"

"Dunno."

"Have you spoken to her?"

"No."

"What's her name?"

"I think it's Rose. Yeah, that's right… Rose Bernet."

Instantly Tony stopped, slapped his hand against Carlos' chest. "¡*No mames*! You're shittin' me, right?"

"¿*Mande*? What?"

"Oh my god, mother fucker! Are you for real?"

Just then, Tony dashed over to an overfilled trash can and snatched that mornings *Times* from the pile, quickly leafing through the pages until he came across the business section. "You mean, *this* bitch?"

He displayed the spread and stabbed at it with his finger so Carlos was able to see.

His heart began to beat heavily. Upon the page, a photo, almost filling the entire left side of the paper. Rose Benoit, enigmatic, smiling, her shiny yellow hair fell just below her shoulders. Flanked by Julie Ross and a small, old, pudgy man with a horrible smile. The man looked awkward, and ridiculously wealthy, especially due to his company in the picture.

"Carlos, *mi compa*," Tony said. "This is the bitch I was

talking about the other day. She owns this place, man!"

Carlos looked back at him. "This place? Bro, what the hell are you talking about, now?"

"Look around you, Carli. *This* place, man. Everywhere! She runs Wall Street and shit."

"Oh, good, so you're saying I should go for it, huh?"

The fret carved on Tony's brow remained.

"Man, no way! You should avoid her like the plague. She's a real man-eater. She's a dyke too, Carli. I really don't believe you, *esé*. The *one* girl you decide you wanna fuck in this whole shit-hole town turns out to be the most richest CEO in the world."

"I think that's... an exaggeration."

"I ain't lying, bro. Stay away. That lady is trouble. Her and that bitch friend of hers."

Meanwhile, Raoul paid his tab, and with his arm around the blonde, departed the small deli. Out on the street they silently walked past Carlos and Tony who, in an attempt to appear less suspicious, froze like statues on the spot.

When they were out of earshot, Tony continued. "Your buddy there, he's fucked. These bitches eat dudes like him for breakfast, man."

"You're jealous, I think."

Tony shook his head as they stopped underneath a giant sized M&M's sign. He grabbed Carlos's shoulders. "Holmes, listen. You're my only brother here. Drop this thing with this bitch. I'm telling you."

"I ain't marrying her, Tone. She don't even know I exist."

"I ain't fooling around, man. I heard some stuff about her. She really is bad, bad news."

"Wait a minute. What stuff? What did you hear about her?"

Carlos looked back at him soberingly; it was the first time Tony managed to properly gain his attention.

"Uh, a while back, my cousin Tony, he told me that he saw a bunch of them at night, in, like, a restaurant, round near Midtown,"

"What the hell was Tony doing over there in the night time?"

"I don't know, but anyway, he said this Rose bitch, she was a real nightmare. She was demanding shit all night. Either the food was too cold, or too hot. Waiter comes over, serving drinks and stuff, she spits the wine she was drinking in his face. Made a real bad scene, like, made everyone look bad, talking down to everyone. Like as if she was the fuckin' Queen of England or somewhere. She's a real hard-ass, Carlos."

"Okay, but… everyone knows she's like this, I think. It kinda like… goes with the territory, no?"

"Carlos, what the hell are you saying?" Tony's hands remained firmly clamped to his shoulders. His eyes were serious, sprinkled with worry.

He began to whisper. " Listen… I heard that people go missing. People work there at that place, they go off the radar. Tony, when he came here, he knew this dude, they was buddies, you know. This guy worked at that Rose Nubian joint you work at. The guy disappeared. Tony and his brother went to the joint, reported it. Those cops laughed them out the precinct. They tried the media. Again, no one took them serious. Carlos, I ain't lying."

"*Calmela*, Tony, relax. I ain't even spoken to her."

"I know what you're like. I'll admit she *is* hot," he nodded in slight agreement, but don't even think about it. Man, literally, don't even *think about it*. You have to get out of that place as soon as you can."

Carlos saw the desperation in Tony's eyes; he was stern, open-mouthed, and breathing heavier than before. He placed his hands on Tony's, reassuring him.

"I get you, okay. You have my word, Tone, I won't think about it."

Colloquy2

Julie: Oh, please tell me you ain't going back to London again.

Rose: Darling, I'm afraid so. Please don't tell me you forgot.

Julie: Pain in the ass. Third time this year, and it ain't even July already.

Rose: Please don't be mean to me. You know I have family there. I have certain responsibilities.

Julie: Babe, they ain't your real family, remember? Besides, Lord and Lady bougie-boo don't realise I need you here more than they do.

Rose: Oh Julie, you are such a beast. I thought you loved them.

Julie: Yeah, I do, but not at the moment. I'm sure if they knew their precious ethnic adoptee girl child left her best friend and partner to fend for herself as we dive head first into the largest, most lucrative deal we've ever had in our history, they'd most likely slap you the hell into last week.

Rose: …

Julie: Well?

Rose: Well, what?

Julie: Don't you think I'm right?

Rose: Oh heavens, Julia, please give me a break.

Julie: I'll give you a break, baby, a break on your arm.

Rose: Jules, behave.

Julie: I am behaving. *You* ain't. That's my problem.

Rose: Are you okay now? About Raoul, I mean.

Julie: Yeah, I mean, the same old story, right? Jeez, I really take the damn cake. I'm a moron.

Rose: Yes, well, you're *my* moron.

Julie: Oh wow, thanks.

Rose: Well, you said it. It's not that I wish to be so agreeable, but you have a point, you *are* a moron. You aren't listening to Rose, that's your problem.

Julie: …

Rose: I really wish you would.

Julie: Listen, do you really have to go?

Rose: Darling, you'd be coming with me if you weren't so busy. They did invite you, after all. However, I finally know how you truly feel about them, I shall tell them you declined with the utmost disdain.

Julie: What the hell are you talking about?

Rose: …

Julie: Uh, for crying out loud, when are you back, baby?

Rose: Mid-July.

Julie: Listen, missy, just fucking enjoy yourself.

Rose: Mwah!

Rossington Hall

Rose arrived just before three in the afternoon. Already, all members of staff were lined up outside the building's huge front façade. A smattering of familiar colleagues she had instantly recognised, mixed with many new faces.

The head housekeeper came rushing up to Rose as she stepped from her silver Audi sports car.

"Miss Rose! I can't believe it's actually you! Gosh, you look every inch the lady now. Where have you been all this time?"

She always was a fusspot, Rose thought. Yet the Housekeeper was mostly correct, as there was no excuse, Rose could have remained in contact with the woman more regularly. A heavy wave of guilt rippled inside as Rose thought of how kind and caring she had been all those years before, and how, during her time there, she had doted on her young charge. Rose held her tightly as they embraced. They spoke momentarily.

Rose Benoit, well travelled and fully acquainted with social etiquette and graces, had been in the company of Queens and Kings. She had been placed high upon pedestals by sultans and princes and had been worshipped by countless men who'd claimed she was a Goddess. But she had never felt more regal than on these rare occasions when she'd return to Rossington Hall. She walked past the house staff, and every one of them smiled, beaming genuinely at her.

Lord and Lady Rossington stood at the top of the steps, close to the entrance of their home, their kind faces glowing at the sight of her. Rose felt another stab when she approached and became aware of how aged they now appeared. They looked like a pair of presenters of a lovely gardening television programme.

But their voices were the same as always, charming and familiar. A feeling of home reassured Rose.

Embroiled within a happy fanfare, her event had now begun. Rose needed a drink.

The grounds to the south west of the building were exactly as she'd remembered. A tidy sprawling thirty acres, strategically designed, the panorama was breathtaking and had been as such for the last three hundred years.

Rose sat with Linda Rossington under the giant awnings of the elaborate west side of the house, overlooking the water gardens and hiding from the mid-July sunshine. Rose was already attracting the attention of almost all the mingling guests, especially after she'd changed into a rather fetching sky-blue dress, a flowing chiffon maxi with a slit up one side. Her straight bob was light brown and shimmered in the sunlight.

Linda took a firm hold of Rose's hand and sandwiched it between both of hers. "You're growing, my dear. You look more magnificent than I could've possibly imagined. We're so proud of you. We love you so much."

Rose felt the love, warmed by it. She sipped on her pink lemonade and turned to face her.

"We just wish to see more of you, dear. Especially your father; he misses you like you wouldn't believe. Sometimes, when we see you on the American news or something, he's so proud of you when they show your face."

"How has he been? I've heard he doesn't get out as much as he used to."

Linda's mouth pursed. "And I hear you've been speaking with that chatter-box of a housekeeper."

"She cares, Mother, that's all."

"It's true, though, he isn't as light on his feet these days. A month ago he was playing tennis with some friends and he had to call a halt to the game because he had a pain in his chest."

Rose sat up and frowned. "Now, Rose dear, relax, please know that he's fine. It was a minor thing that we sorted out. It wasn't any kind of heart attack."

"Are you positively sure?"

"I am. In fact, look over there." Linda pointed towards the lower green in the distance. A group of people had gathered, surrounding what looked like two people dancing. Thomas Rossington, once expertly well versed in the art of the tango, could sweep a girl off her feet at twenty paces. Rose smiled as she watched him engage their beloved housekeeper in a flourishing quick-step.

***

The sun poured down like honey, a truly glorious English Summer's day. Rose thought of Julie. She regretted not bringing her; they would have had fun and Julie might have even been successful romantically.

Still, she had engaged and conversed with many of her British *Nubian Rose* associates, as well as others whom she'd known from her time at the finishing school she had attended.

Rose remembered every one of them as if it were yesterday. One of them adored dogs, owning five wolfhounds, three Weinheimers and six Doberman Pinschers. Another had married a wealthy pastor. Rose posed alluringly as they all stood around, all guffawing at their memories of their deportment training under the tutelage of the hard task-mistress Miss Kingsley. Rose allowed them all to pine over her, inspecting her nails and admiring her hair and eye make-up.

Get Me Out Of Here, read her text to Julie Ross.

***

The man was largely framed, yet moderately young for someone so overweight. He was also beginning to bald.

Rose became watchful of him as the day furthered. A waitress approached and offered him a drink from a tray. He turned his back to her while casually conversing with another colleague, who in turn snatched one of the beverages. At last, the girl made her way to mingle with the other guests.

"Excuse me, where the hell do you think you are going?" he shouted. She smiled as she turned and walked back.

"I'm sorry, Mister Mitchell…"

"You will be!" he interrupted. "How dare you walk away from me, give me that drink here."

He snatched the glass and again turned his back. Everyone glanced over at the commotion. The other man made a remark and both men engaged in overstated laughter. The girl finally walked away.

"Giovanni Mitchell, a devilish man, dear. Please refrain from getting involved, Rose." Linda warned, as they both watched the uncomfortable scene. "I know how you feel. Nothing would be more appealing than confronting him, giving him a sound box to the ears. I too cannot abide him, but that poor girl, she works for him."

"Why is he here?" Rose asked.

"I actually don't know. He wasn't invited. But unfortunately he classes himself as a *friend* of the family." Linda emphasised her sentence ironically. Rose looked at her, confused.

"He's our accountant, dear. Unfortunately."

Rose placed two fingers to the bridge of her nose, "Oh my."

"He and Thomas have engaged in talks concerning sales of some of our lands down the hill."

Rose knew she was referring to the disused acres to the south of the estate.

"But I'm as disappointed to see him here as you are."

Rose tested. "I cannot remember him."

"You won't have, dear, he wasn't really on the scene while you were here, but for the past few years he's been sniffing around wanting land, waving money in our faces and basically being a pain in the bottom."

Rose adored Linda Rossington's choice of grammar. She had never failed in putting Rose at ease. Although, this was understandable owing to the fact that Thomas had, in a sense, married beneath him. Linda Rossington née Mills had caught his eye during the spring, some fifty years before. He was the handsome young eligible bachelor, rich, educated and single. She was the beautifully mysterious bohemian, born years before her time with alternative philosophies and flowers in her long flowing hair.

Rose curled the corner of her lip. "I do not wish to see him any longer. His presence is far from pleasing," she said.

"He'll soon be gone, Rose, worry not."

The housekeeper came huffing and puffing up the steps and plonked herself down in the chair next to Rose.

"I'm flabbergasted, I don't mind saying, ladies. Thomas can still dance like Fred Astaire, but I think my back's broken!"

"Really? Well, I think you're a genius, I really do," Linda Rossington said. "We really appreciate everything."

"She's right, today has been absolutely amazing. I thank you from the bottom of my heart," Rose said as she kissed her cheek and pressed her head to hers.

***

As dusk was nearing its end and the sky transformed into a celestial golden orange that rolled towards the heavens, Rose had maintained her surveillance of Giovanni Mitchell, monitoring his behaviour. Making a heavy mental note, she locked him away in her brain's attic.

The night ended with Lord and Lady Rossington in the kitchen with Rose. Just like the old times she had always remembered with such fondness. She loved them both. She wanted to see more of them but her busy schedule had always made it difficult. Rose chastised herself again.

"Father, do not allow yourself to be taken in by people like Giovanni Mitchell. I care not him being a good businessman, you are so much more than him."

"I take on board what you're saying, Rose. It's just that he's offered us many benefits in return for his affordable rates, a lot better than anyone else over here. And he's a good accountant."

Thomas Rossington looked at his wife. On her nod he continued an evidently premeditated announcement. "We are broke, Rose. Well, almost."

He lowered his head in shame. Linda rushed over to him and placed a hand over her husband's shoulder. Rose walked over too as he started to shed a tear.

"Hey, you." She knelt at his side and held his hand. "Please don't cry. You two should have told me of this sooner." Rose's heart twanged to see him so dejected. Still holding his hand, she stood up.

"I want to help. The pair of you must allow me to do so."

Professor Mittens

Over a year had passed since first being admitted to the specialist facility. An unhealthy amount of X-rays every day, spoon-feeding nurses and arduous recuperation practices – with the ominous threat of being permanently crippled.

Bizarrely, however, Ricky Gomez's health progressed. The process hadn't been miraculous, amidst the bouts of terrible withdrawal, both his legs suffered with asymmetric abnormalities after an extensive duration and, as a result, Ricky walked with an awkward limp from the left side, but he'd still proved Doctor Sidhu wrong for her early diagnosis.

Upon his release, he was at a loss. His problems, the lack of a place to live, and his habit with its perpetual need to be fed, resurfaced again like the inevitable storm clouds they were.

***

His partner was smaller, and easily slipped through the chute that led to the courtyard situated at the rear of the building.

Ricky waited all of ten minutes for his partner to return with a key to allow access into the building. Picking locks were like second nature, an ability he'd acquired while spending time in a home close to Holloway. The security latches were sophisticated and Ricky Gomez huffed and perspired in his attempts to disable the coils in the heavy-duty bolt mechanism.

His partner waited, patiently silent.

After almost two hours of fidgeting with his devices and tools, the door freed itself of its fixed placement. They breezed through into Sir Hyman Cruff's family home.

***

A year before, they might have trashed the place, trying on the QC's wife's clothes and grinding the bodies of his oriental fish into plush shag piles. But their determined expressions indicated the weight of their impending duty; they knew exactly what they were there for.

The building boasted two staircases, along with a third set situated back-of-house. The door was locked. Ricky's partner looked confused as he tried the door again.

"I thought you said your friend would see us inside, man," Ricky whispered.

His partner was silent. He scanned the room for another opening. Nothing, save for the door through which they had entered.

"I don't usually do these kinds of jobs," Ricky sniffed, nervously. "This is far too upmarket for me."

His partner reached inside Ricky's backpack and wrapped a large white cloth around his fist.

"Are you crazy?" Ricky asked, as his partner smashed the window in the centre of the door.

Ricky moved towards it, stepping over the glass and plunged his arm through the opening.

Unable to locate anything which might have resembled a catch on the other side, Ricky began to despair.

"You told me your friend worked security here, where the hell is he now?"

He took a step back and kicked at the door with the better of his two legs. After repeating four or five more attempts, making a raucous sound that echoed around the large room, his partner tried to stop him.

Ricky looked at the opening before snatching the rag from his partners hand, using it to shunt away any shards of glass from the edges of the opening. He placed his face to the gap and peered through, frantically gazing around. The opening was wide enough for his head to fit through. Ricky tried carefully to avoid the jagged edges as his partner attempted to dissuade him by grabbing his arm.

With his hooked wrist, he dislodged the night latch and the door moved, his hand and the side of his throat catching against the glass.

Ricky's blood was all over the door, the wounds stung slightly. After almost severing his ear, and with the mostly useless assistance of his partner, they managed to free his head from its trap.

They dashed up the staircase to the first floor.

"I thought you said your friend was security here. Why are we smashing windows and breaking down doors?"

Although his mute partner shrugged, Ricky was able to see the doubt and fear on his face.

They slowed when reaching the top floor and stalked towards the master bedroom. Once inside, it was too early to be buoyant or to marvel at the sight of their final destination, which, hidden behind an oversized painting of *Professor Mittens,* Sir Hyman Cruff's family spaniel, resplendently modelling his pointy hat and ruff, contained enough goods to afford their way out of the miserable lives they were embroiled in.

Suddenly, Ricky looked slowly up to the ceiling. His mind went blank. And all was darkness. A duration of time passed, as invariably it did at times, and the length of which he never knew. Then the same images returned. His real mother smiling at him when he was five years old. The disappointment of assorted teachers and guardians. Sarah Allen's tears of blood. The haze of illegal highs, both beautiful and horrific. And the big hooded jackets of his scally assailants whose intentions to kill him were unfortunately not realised.

And now, as he and his dumb partner stood with their hands up, surrounded by police who screamed orders at them to get on their knees, Ricky was calm. For that moment, he was unable to hear them, his ears ringing, in slow motion, his mind almost empty. His thoughts turned towards the foreseeable future; himself encased within the next bin they would undoubtedly see fit to throw him.

Multiple Tasks

Bank, London

The knock at the door was soft and lacked enthusiasm and power, telling Rose Benoit exactly who it was.

She had been inside her office all day. Owing to the amount of time she was overseas, staff meetings at London's wing of *Nubian Rose* had to be undertaken whenever she was in the UK. Her penchant for keeping abreast on all matters was a time consuming one.

"Enter."

Michael Beavis nervously stepped into the large granite expanse that was Rose's office.

"Close the door," she ordered calmly, unbuttoning the top of her blouse.

"I, err…"

"Thank you, Michael. Okay, just to let you know, I've had some rather bad news."

She surveyed him. He stood there dishevelled, his suit was creased, his tie was loose and at one point he actually put his left hand in his pocket – something Rose could not abide, especially in a meeting.

"Err, yes, Miss Benoit…?"

"My cleaning contractors telephoned me earlier, they told me they were unable to attend this evening. They apologised and promised that normal service would be resumed tomorrow. So now, as you are aware, I am in a slight pickle."

"Miss… erm, it's… the time is nearly 5pm."

"Michael, at present, I care little for the time and its restraints, all it does is fool you into believing that your home time is more important than my needs."

"Miss Benoit…"

"Michael, let me spell this out for you. My office, and the offices which surround, require your attention."

The man shook his head defiantly. "I have to go."

"Michael. This situation is not available for your discussion. I am aware you leave work at five o'clock, or sometimes earlier, depending on how many liberties you feel like taking, but we cannot do anything about that now. So, I want you to don an apron and get to work."

He stared at her with a slight aggressive bent, which amused her.

"Aprons are in the cupboard in the corridor outside the lobby. You may begin."

***

"Hi, babe."

"Oh my God. You're still at work." Julie recognised the number on her phone.

"Julie, it's always the same whenever I'm over here. It's like having a big drawer that was nice and tidy when I left, but when I return, the contents are all over the floor."

"It's because I'm not there to hold your hand."

Rose had missed her best friend, her accent sounded good on the phone and it made her long to be back in New York.

Rose laughed. "You reckon? Sure it's not the other way around?"

"I'm running things over here. A black woman in charge of all these motherfuckers, could you believe that?"

Rose smiled, "I could."

"Say, Oleg was asking about you again, honey."

"Say what?"

"Oleg."

"Julie, Oleg? Really? I'm very busy here. I have literally twenty eight appraisals to conduct tomorrow. I've had to speak to those blessed auditors all afternoon about the data *they* lost, and then tonight I have another date with this fool Richardson..."

"Yeah, but Oleg..."

"You sound like you're flapping, dear. Calm down.

Mister Gribkov… I suppose he's a nice fellow, you know; we share a lot of interests…"

"He said the same thing."

"Indeed… Interests such as Modest Mussorgsky and Pyotr Ilyich Tchaikovsky being but two of them."

"What?"

"He is also extremely well versed in the ballets of his native St Petersburg, however I would have assumed as such. Sergei Pavlovich Diaghilev is obviously his idol."

"What?"

"I'm sensing I've lost you."

"Damn straight."

"I told him I used to be a dancer. He adores dancers, you see, and not just ballet."

"You tell him I could dance, too?"

"Jules, dear, I don't think he's aware of *your* kind of dancing."

At that moment, Michael clambered through one of the doors that led to an adjacent room. Clumsily pulling the large industrial vacuum cleaner past the threshold into Rose's office while also juggling numerous cans and containers of cleaning materials.

"I've cleaned in there, I just need to sweep in here and clean the toilet and that's it. I'll be done," he announced boisterously.

"Julie, excuse me one moment. I'll call you back."

Rose slid her phone's screen to off, and gently placed it on her desk.

"Get over here," she said quietly. She looked down and inspected the nails on her left hand.

The realisation of his error was apparent as he stalled, wasting extra time.

Rose read him perfectly. "It would be wiser in the long run to do as I have asked, boy."

Her tone, although low, was threatening nonetheless. His lack of courage hurt his senses as he stumbled up to her desk.

"Michael, on a scale of one to ten, tell me how

discourteous you think you are?"

"Erm, I… I did…"

"Just answer the question."

"Okay, I'm sorry, Miss Benoit." At last, honesty came to the forefront. Rose appreciated it, however she still showed him no clemency.

"I know you're sorry. But do you always have to be sorry, Michael? I grow tired of people who come to me and tell me they are sorry. I hear it all the time. Do you think I like paying good money to people who are always sorry?"

He shrunk as she glared at him; his entire soul and body being fixed upright by those eyes.

She raised her voice slightly. "I make it a requirement to maintain a zero tolerance towards anything in this building that is below par, Michael. Anything rotten, I cut it off, discard it, before it grows, before it gets bigger and spreads itself around." She maintained a long pause, thus projecting his fear. He began to sweat.

"So the question is, what am I do to with you, Michael? Are you always going to be so sorry?"

Another pause offered him the green light to answer. "No, I'll try harder. I shall not be sorry. I just wanted to do a good job for you. Please, I do not want to lose my job here, please, I…"

"I do not wish to lose the quality upon which my design is based, Michael. I run a tight ship, as you may or may not be aware. I have no need for rubbish."

"I know, and I'll shape up," his voice quivered, bordering on tears. "I will prove to you that I…"

"Yes, yes, be silent." She waved her hand dismissively and placed a large ledger upon her desk. "What time is it, Michael?"

He looked at his watch, it read an earlier time than that displayed on the large black clock that hung from the wall.

"It's err… nearly quarter to nine, Miss Benoit."

"Okay then, you may complete the rest of your aforementioned duties."

"Oh, thank you, Miss Benoit. That's really kind of you…"

"Afterwards, you will repeat them a second time. I need thoroughness. Thoroughness is the key to my black heart, Michael. Then, you may leave." She looked up at him again. "What do you say, Michael?"

"Thank you, Miss Benoit," he said, deflated.

"You're welcome. You may continue."

Rose finally resumed her conversation with Julie. A while later, she selected a loud version of Schumann's *Liederkreis* in its entirety, one of her most favourite night-time Arias.

"I'll Do It By Myself"

Rollins HM Prison. Bridlington.

"I can't do it, man."

"You're kidding me, why the hell not?"

"Because, Ricky, I don't want it any more. I ain't doing it."

"You was okay before, you were on board, what's changed, man?"

"Because it's dangerous. This isn't the way, it's not going to help you. You'll fucking kill yourself, and I ain't gonna help you do it."

"Oh, right, I see, you pussy out on me right at the last minute." Ricky bore his teeth in anger. "We've been over this for three weeks. Spent hours speaking about it. Fuck. You ain't got nothing to lose; it's not as if you're going anywhere for ten years, so it's no skin off your nose. They'll give your cell a locking-down is the worst they'll do to you, *if* they see you do it, which they won't."

Adamantly, his cellmate shook his head.

Ricky jumped from his bunk and threw himself at the wall, before clawing at his hair with his clenched fists.

His cellmate moved aside in avoidance, allowing Ricky to undertake his by now customary convulsions of temper to proceed unhindered.

"You decide now's the time you wanna put your balls away. You evil, selfish bastard."

"Listen, I can't do it because they heard us, the screws out there. Are you flippin' stupid, or what? Did you honestly believe they didn't? These guards in here are animals, man. They'd chop me up if I did what you want me to do. There's hundreds of snitches in here that'll tell them about us."

Ricky wailed, still in the throes of frustration, gripped in withdrawal upon the floor.

"Well, why did you tell me you'd do it, then?"

"Because, you're a dirty junky bastard, I thought it would shut you up. How do you think I feel, having to share a space with a stinky little thief like you?"

Ricky had stopped moaning and sat up before slowly assuming a foetal-like position.

"Why do you think they've been aiding you? Helping you down the stairs and stuff? They've got eyes on you at all times, Ricky! Come on, man, have you not got a brain? Or have all those chemicals melted it away? They knew we was up to something."

***

The prison term was his second. At the start of his sentence he was so strung out, he didn't even know what facility he had been sent to. He was aware, however, that this particular prison was tough. The inmates were harder, which meant that the guards were roguish, sadistic in the way they would operate. The beatings he endured caused more weight loss.

His cell mate snored heavily and rubbed his huge genitals, oblivious to the ever-nocturnal Ricky Gomez stood in the middle of their cell.

"I'll do it by myself," he repeated, mantra-like, as if possessed by an invisible phantom.

***

His intended *accident* comprised of a horrific tumble down the iron stairs between the first and ground floor. The injuries he'd obtained, the fractured skull and six snapped ribs and broken thigh and ankle, were enough to spell his way out of the ugly hell hole for over a year.

S Freeman

Platinum Cars, one of the most reputable chauffeur services in London, was a firm with which Steven Freeman had been employed on a sub-contractual basis for roughly over a year. His good reputation and tidy appearance always provided him with work for the company's more higher-ranking clients.

An alert was received within the body of an email to make him aware of a new assignment. The day before, the customer was a no show. He'd had to wait close to ten hours before finally signing off duty.

The following morning he'd received the call. At last, the client was coming out. He stepped from the car, straightened his jacket and tie and walked around to the front of the Bentley Continental, opening the door for the new client.

"Good morning, Miss Benoit."

"Good morning," she said politely, surveying the new face.

Wrapped within a mini-skirt power-suit and heels, she was the picture of authority he'd been warned about. She popped herself inside and, as she seated herself, her ample thigh revealed itself to full effect. After closing the door, he walked back round the vehicle, perplexed by what he had just seen.

"Take me to our Indigo building on Chancery Lane first, I wish to make a stop before Victoria. Afterwards, you are to drive to Cannon Street. Thank you."

"Wow! Okay, no problem," he chirped.

The remark rankled. Rose glanced at him from the back seat. The blame she would lay with the agency, as opposed to the individual in the driver's seat.

Mtume's *Juicy* sounded from her handset. "Hi, babe, what have you got for me?" she asked Julie while looking out of her window at a cyclist.

"It's Forde. He ain't here… he's absent."

"What do you mean he's absent?"

Julie sounded agitated while relating details of Howard Forde's fourth day of non-attendance. She had asked his colleagues, but they seemed to know as much about his disappearances as she did.

"Worry not, Julie, dear, we'll bring him in. I dare say there'll be a perfectly reasonable explanation for this."

The vehicle turned the corner along Regent's Park.

"Are you coming back to New York tomorrow night, baby? Remember, we got that meeting with those bitches from finance."

"Ah, yes, I shall be slightly late for that…"

"Oh, for crying out loud, Rose, you always do this to me."

"Do forgive me, Julie…"

"What is it this time? Another one of those bougie operas open up on pudding hill lane?"

"Julia. Please do not be mean."

"When am I ever mean to you? I *should* be mean to you, damn."

"A gentleman from the Met wishes to speak with me about some murder or other."

Suddenly, the driver's phone sounded. "Shit," he muttered under his breath.

Julie continued, "Murder? Where the hell?"

"Not sure… over here in London."

"Was that what you were talking about the other day? Something that happened close to our joint near the water…"

"That's correct, over near Canary Wharf… some poor fellow."

Rose glanced back at her driver.

After a while of small talk, the conversation was concluded and Rose switched off her phone.

Her smile faded.

"Your name, please," she called. It took a few seconds to register.

"Who, me?" Steven asked.

She said nothing, her eyes were still clamped on his reflection in the rear view mirror.

"Err, Steven, ma'am. Steven Freeman."

"Steven. Are you aware that, while in my employ, you are not to use your personal phone under any circumstances?"

"I'm sorry, my phone rang, and…"

"Your phone is of no consequence here. It is to be switched off at all times. You are on my time. Have you chauffeured before?"

"Yes, Madam."

"Also, I really must stress, you are to speak only when I address you. Do you understand me?"

"Yes, Madam."

"Good."

Rose thought to herself. Two options presented themselves. Resume her day's appointments, or deal with this new development.

The following day she thought to herself more constructively. Nothing had been planned for the end of that particular night. She was to fly back to New York the morning after. She made the snap verdict and her mind was made up, sealing the fate of the first of Sarah Allen's killers.

***

That night, as Freeman pulled up, he saw Rose Benoit outside *La Cube, Clube,* already awaiting his arrival. It was dark but he could clearly make out her fresh new hairstyle. Stepping out from his seat, he strolled round to let her in.

Waiting patiently for further instruction, he remained seated, silent, and looking on.

Ever since Steven's reprimand, he'd been briefed by *Platinum Car's* human resources team and was now on his best behaviour. He had wanted to keep this particular position; it was the highest-paid job he ever had.

She spoke after the long silence. "Drive."

Steven started the engine.

"Head towards Sloane Square, if you please."

He silently obliged, cruising along at 40mph.

From her small vanity case, she pulled a tube of lip gloss and applied it to her lips daintily with her middle finger.

He quickly afforded himself a glance in the rear view.

"Keep your eyes on the road, Steven," she said softly, without even returning his glance.

The Implement

He had bragged and boasted to his colleagues at *Platinum Cars* of how he was in the fortunate position of seeing his sexy employer every day, how feisty and dogmatic yet receptive and generous his celebrity client had been.

But the following Thursday morning, inside the Bentley, he waited. His enthusiasm had disappeared over time due to the monotonous delay. Gone was the buzz he had felt at thoughts of his impending duties. The images in his head, of her attire and how revealing it could be, vanished.

Five hours of London radio and The Wailers' greatest hits was not his idea of a decent working day.

He fell asleep.

There in the back seat, he assumed the single rose had been left by the vehicle's previous clients. A remaining item that somebody else had failed to throw out with the trash.

He failed to appreciate its dark, almost blood-red petals.

He failed to see the irony.

***

Face down, tied to the trolley, Steven had been wheeled into one of the smaller areas. The disused warehouse was a cavernous shell of neglect, its roof full of missing panels telling of bygone times.

The sound of the heavy rain outside was constant. Loud gushing water fell heavily within a central well close to the interior, the result of long-damaged pipework.

Broken guttering, nineties graffiti, and brickwork lay strewn across empty thresholds. Smashed glass and grime; an unhygienic haven for crack heads and rats.

He had wept earlier. She had watched him as he wailed, salt water and saliva ran down his bruised face. The cold was numbing, and would encourage the chilling wind to claw its way into her victim.

Steven had aged pretty well, she mused. His image indicated the sound decisions he'd made in his life. Gone were the undernourished sinewy edges and dreads and gold teeth, replaced by a smoother more gentile appearance. And glasses.

***

Rose's leather bomber jacket was warm as she zipped it up tightly about her chin. She wore little else save for a pair of cork wedges that suited her exposed legs.

Steven had been sodomised for a lengthy time. He frowned and gritted his teeth as Rose moaned, her mouth opened wide, and her clown make-up unnerving. She used a barbed whip to hack into his back as she pounded him from behind. The large, cracked mirror positioned before him displayed the harrowing scene in all its grotesque glory.

He lost a hold of his consciousness, and while flaccid, Rose manoeuvred him easily.

He awoke, shocked and malnourished and panicked as a sense of doom hit him in his heart and mind.

Rose took hold of his head and cooed in his ear. "My dear, dear Steven. Welcome to your new home."

***

He awoke again.

Placed in the middle of a large, tiled area that once might have been communal showers. Steven was knelt and tied to a stake, his chest ached heavily and his heartbeat was rapid. He became aware of his different position, although unaware of the three hours that had passed.

She had removed her garish make-up and was as he'd remembered from before. Her face radiant and her eyes heartbreaking, she approached him.

Steven gritted his teeth and moved feverishly in

defiance and in attempts to avoid the poisonous contact he knew she possessed. He could smell cologne on her skin, adding to the scent of her leather jacket. A disgusting mixture of sensuality and authority.

Rose ignored his feverish forlorn glances. She adored the terror that gripped every inch of him. Effortlessly, she made a small but deep incision in his abdomen, puncturing one of his Hepatic veins with the aid of a spiked thimble-like device attached to the tip of her thumb. As his life's blood slowly trickled from his belly, she sat close by, outside the circumference of tiled thresholds that partitioned his blood. She seated herself close by. A large silver bowl of cherries had been placed beside her and she proceeded to pick at the ripe fruits with her finger tips.

Steven Freeman wept despairingly as Rose told him how sweet the cherries tasted.

He replied by muttering of the pain he was in.

She popped a cherry into her mouth slowly. After eating the luscious flesh of the fruit, she spat the pip out at Steven, hitting him in his face.

"Why? Why are you doing this? I drove your fucking car, that's all." His words only just audible as they cackled from his mouth.

"I bid you be silent now," she said.

"Please. Just let me go!" he cried out. The expression on Rose's face was void of emotion as she selected another oversized cherry.

"Please!" he called out louder.

"Dear, dear, Steven. It is bad enough having to look upon your ridiculous face without having to hear your horrid voice too. I feel that cutting off your head completely would be of great benefit to me."

For all the torture he had endured so far, Steven appeared suddenly defiant as he looked at her, frustration and hatred creasing his face. Rose was impressed at his newly acquired zeal.

She stood and leaned over as she took his head in her hands. She then placed her spiked thumb to his eye and pressed in slightly, applying dangerous pressure to his cornea. "Baby," she said, sensuously in his ear. "I want silence. Does Rose make herself clear?"

"Yes, yes, I'm sorry"

His crying had almost stopped as his brain responded instantly to her threat.

"Good boy."

She sat back in her chair and placed another cherry inside her mouth, spitting the pip out again at his face. More tears flooded his eyes.

The cherry pips, immersed in Steven Freeman's blood, lay scattered around him. While Rose had devoured the remainder of the cherries, he passed out. He awoke with a fever, and as his skin turned paler, he shivered.

Rose gushed at the sight of him, a feeling of inward pleasure danced within the pit of her stomach.

"Let me go, now. Just... let... me go."

"Um, I think not," she said.

"Please, I need to get out of here. You gotta let me go."

Rose burst into laughter. "Darling, you are tied to the centre of the floor that is being filled with your own blood. You'll be dead within forty-five minutes. Let you go? Of course not, foolish boy." Rose beamed, happily displaying rows of perfectly white teeth.

His head swam with an aching frustration as he saw her sweetly smiling at him. Hatred filled every fibre of his body with a dramatic intensity. Rose could feel the warmth of his frustration and repulsion for her emanating from him.

***

She had been incorrect in her estimation. Steven Freeman was still alive after a further ninety minutes. She had returned in order to prepare for his disposal and was dismayed at the sight of his groaning and movements.

Steven never had the chance to see the implement. Rose, now naked, stood behind him and held it. She moistened and kissed the tip, before stepping into its leather straps, fixing it to her groin, positioning it and brandishing it, wrapping her hands around it in a most male-like fashion.

She took him by the shoulders and instantly pushed him forward with such force his wrists and back were broken as they snapped away from the steak he was tied to. His nose was also smashed as it banged on to the edge of the cast-iron rim of a row of old washbasins.

He wailed as Rose tore what was left of his clothing. She screwed his torn rag of a shirt into a blood soaked ball and pushed it into his mouth and face.

"That thing with which you used to damage her, pales somewhat in comparison to my more superior implement, Steven, darling," Rose breathed, as she positioned it over his buttocks. "I can feel Sarah's smile already. 'Tis like sunshine."

Amidst the ever present sounds of wind and thrashing water, Rose heard Steven's insides rupture and tear as she rode him towards the hell that loomed above him, waiting.

Interval

Everywhere

Bob Lind. Elusive Butterfly.

The sun had only just begun to seep through into the early morning for a few seconds, but already its glow had transformed the sky into a radiant indigo that illuminated the infinite horizon. It signalled yet more durations of lovemaking, and she perched high on his lap with her legs entwined tightly around his waist. They held hands.

The blossoms of love they found in one another had only begun the previous fall. The deep feelings they both possessed grew in awesome abundance.

***

Times were different ten years prior to Rose Benoit's establishment with *Nubian Rose*. At that time she had been attending one of the more prestigious dance and theatre universities in Belgium and Bella Savoca had been the name she'd provided to the university as she enrolled. She had been highly recommended from her time served in the performing arts schools of Moscow and New York. By a certain time, her abilities were impeccable and she had chosen Brussels, in particular owing to its reputation.

Ever the perfectionist, Bella strived to be of the best ability possible. Amidst her rigorous training and her studies at the university, she also had a residency at a humble but trendy café situated on the outskirts of the city.

She had attracted his attention straight away during these performances and he would sit in the audience at every opportunity. The small five-man production she had co-written had gathered some favourable reviews, selling out on most nights, but only because of Bella's expert style and her fluent movements. The others who performed lacked her standard.

It was he, the handsome stranger in the crowd, who'd advised Bella to go solo one night after the later show of the evening.

His large eyes danced in the flickering half-light of the inn. His beard and rustic clothing made him look like a farmer from the nineteenth century.

"Let me tell you this: the way you dance and move your body is astonishing. I have never seen anything quite like it."

He was forty-one years her senior. She watched him as he spoke. His mouth was nice. She had always been a keen mouth enthusiast, always convinced words and voices could be magnanimously enhanced by the look of someone's mouth. She imagined kissing his lips. Maybe it was the lemon vodka going to her head.

"Where are you from anyway?" she asked. "And who made you such an expert on dancing?"

"Please forgive me if I gave you that impression, it was never my intention to appear so bold. And I am no expert, but a simple man of flesh and blood." He doffed his tweed cap, bowing humbly. Rose allowed him to take her hand, his palm felt like the bark of a tree as she shook it.

"I like passion – I like to see it. Some folks come, some folks go. Some folks got passion, some folks don't know. You are different. When you dance, you have so much passion that it spills out of you like the sea."

Bella was touched, but chose to remain somewhat aloof. "Well, you certainly have a way with words, there's no doubting that. Can *you* dance?"

He laughed out another lovely smile. "I have been known to step a little. I'm working on it."

She had to admit to herself as she sat opposite him, he was a gorgeous-looking man.

"You never told me where you were from."

"I am from everywhere." He got up and displayed a simple flourish of jazz. "I *am* everywhere."

"Well, *Everywhere*, if that is in fact your real name, you may at least buy me another one of these." She tilted her

141

empty glass before handing it to him.

She could tell by the way he moved as he walked towards the bar, it was evident the man was fluent in rhythm and movement, a true expert in the art of dance.

The inn was dimly lit and, by some time later, entirely empty. They talked through the night and ended up in each other's arms as they danced to the old gospel blues that was being constantly played via a badly hooked-up jukebox.

***

As time progressed, so too did their relationship. She moved into the humble studio he stayed at and soon enough they became a team. Bella unwittingly learned that *Everywhere* was a genius. The agility he unassumingly boasted was like that of a twenty year old Olympian.

He would tell her that he had taught himself. All the expertise he wished to convey to her was entirely his own work.

Bella was both fascinated and attracted by his vagabond rootlessness, his good natured personality.

("*I'm a drifter, baby, I scaled the rooftops of the world while no-one was looking.*")

Everywhere wasn't like most people his age she had encountered. He possessed a cool and fresh attitude. His enthusiasm was boundless. They became lovers.

Before long, every opportunity was spent dedicated to her, imparting all his wisdom on his *beautiful dancer*.

Part 2

Rigidly dedicated to her dance studies, *Everywhere* was proud of his receptive pupil. They had worked long and hard for the impending assignment. Each student was given a project. The hand-picked participants enthusiastically knuckled down. But what *Everywhere* and Bella so rigorously trained for was to be the first of its kind. She was to display a series of movements consisting of up to five techniques in one performance. She had lost three stone, an achievement she disliked, however it was vital for the success of her performance.

All the students were to fly to Paris. The presentation finals were to be held in the Montmartre district.

A few nights ahead of the flight, *Everywhere* and Bella were still preparing. At this juncture, *Everywhere* was now becoming truly astounded at Bella's abilities.

"Absolutely breathtaking, you are."

Submerged deeply within intensive concentration, she cracked a smile all the same.

"I do not understand how you haven't lost any more weight. Your body appears to retain your African physique quite curiously."

"Nor do I. Will there be a problem?" she asked.

"People will talk, some may even show their prejudiced views and say it isn't natural for a dancer to look like you. But a problem? Nah."

"I have a larger posterior which sticks out further than those of my female competitors. But I am more toned than I have ever been before. I even impress myself."

"Beautiful. You are my rule breaker; you are the ultimate exception to the rule."

"Surely, I am not that big," she declared, her hands ran over the surface of her stomach and posterior as she inspected herself in the mirror.

"Of course not, but you see, people dislike things that

threaten their status quos. Because you do not resemble a woman who is the same shape as a piece of rice, it may subject you to the odd query. But, please, my love, let us not get distracted in what has not, or may never even occur."

He nimbly swaggered around her, viewing her, checking to see if she was indeed using the muscles he advised for the respective moves.

"Perfect," he said, simply. Bella was still ignorant as to where his gorgeous accent was from. "Everything is perfect, beautiful. You have done everything I've asked of you. Truly amazing."

He shouted above the loud music that served to motivate her. She was silent as she remained on her toes, holding her painstaking position to a particularly unorthodox and complicated move.

"Not only are you breaking down barriers, but you do it with such stealth, such grace... beautiful." *Everywhere* applied more menthol balm to her calves and the back of her thighs to aid towards the blood flow in her lower body. She then undertook the next move, and held herself to it, still, statuesque.

Pure class, he thought, as he surveyed her. This was it, as far as he was concerned, she had completed her preparations. "Come, beautiful Bella, sit with me."

She jumped free of the confines of her exercises and bounded over to her lover.

"Do you have a hero, beautiful?"

"Yeah, sure."

"I am just curious to know, what sort of things served to inspire you."

"My mother," she said simply. "My real mother will always be my main inspiration. But all women, I suppose; women are strong, and strength always did turn me on."

"Are men not also strong?"

"Of course, but men have always sought to *gain* with their strength."

"Bella, I don't follow." *Everywhere* scratched his head.

"Please do not let my words offend you, but men will always seek a reward for their feats. A women merely seeks survival for the hard things she has to face. All she wishes to do is to get over, and get to where she is going. She sees hardship and aims to jump over it, simply to get to the other side. A man will want praise for doing this, or money, or gold, or a country. Men are collectors. Women are survivors."

Everywhere was silent until he at last cleared his throat. "I cannot argue with that, beautiful. Everything you have said is truth. A man knows nothing of carrying the world on his shoulders. In fact, we men only serve to weigh it down more heavily."

Bella was silent, She grabbed her bag and picked at its contents, before proceeding to pick at her hair with a large afro comb.

"Anybody else?" he asked.

"Josephine Baker."

"Josephine Baker?"

She nodded. "Indeed."

"Your hero?"

"Most definitely. I will always have such a huge crush on her, and who wouldn't? Beautiful. Talent. Oh my God. She was the *first*!"

Everywhere looked like he only half understood.

"And aside from anything else she did, she was big with the French Resistance during the war. Assisted against the Nazis."

"Wasn't she famous for all that comedy Charleston stuff?" *Everywhere* asked.

"No!" Bella frowned. "I'm not talking about all that silly stuff, rolling eyes and funny walks. She had to do that for white Americans who didn't wish to see her in more higher-ranking situ." She glanced at him, disappointed. "Is that all you think she did? You never heard of *La Danse Sauvage*? She had the whole of Europe knocked out! If I only achieve a tenth of what she had, wow." Bella shook her head. "She is *the* example, baby, she was the first."

"Okay, I see, she must have been extremely talented, but when you say the first… the first at what?"

"Well, she was black. Not many of us in those days crossed over. She made it big. High profile big. Exclusive parties, jewels, famous guys begged her for marriage. And she liked the ladies too, I mean, in those days… how hot is that? She shook her ass, big time! Naked at the feast, darling. She was magnificent."

He nodded.

Another period of quiet. Bella was aware she was capable of silencing the otherwise over-talkative *Everywhere*.

"I love you, Bella."

"My beautiful man. I love you too." It was the first time she'd said it to him, or to any man.

"Even while you are submerged deep in the technicalities of your modes and choreography, you still find time for things such as love?" the man asked.

"*Oui je fais, mon amour.* Am I to believe you are complaining?"

"You have changed my life, how would I complain?"

They kissed as she climbed on top of him.

Both agreed to engage in no sexual activity until after her presentation. The tension and yearning would lend itself perfectly to the authenticity of her performance.

Part 3

Backstage the atmosphere was electric. Dancers and students running in and out. Performers being assisted with make-up and elaborate costumes. Everyone's nerves were exposed and wired.

There was a lot riding on this night for many gifted young dancers. Not only a Masters diploma but the prestigious annual TEPITA award for most inspired performance. This was the highest accolade, the one towards which they all strived.

All eyes, as well as expectations, were on Bella Savoca. Her fellow students were only too aware she was gifted. And owing to her high pedigree and ranking, her fellows were expecting only the most lavish extravagance when it came to her turn to perform.

Away from the mind-boggling wash of frenzy, Bella and *Everywhere* were holed up in a small cupboard somewhere high up in the venue's upper floors.

"I know you must be as nervous as I, beautiful."

"Not at all," she said in monotone.

He frowned, "Not even a small piece of nervous? You must be a little apprehensive, Bella, otherwise… well, it just wouldn't be natural."

"What I am about to do *isn't* natural," Bella chuckled, somewhat acrimoniously. She glanced at *Everywhere*. He almost looked disappointed. She decided to appease him. "My love, I am excited, but nervous? *Certainement pas!*"

She took hold of his face tenderly. "Listen, do not worry. Nobody on earth could have done what you have done for me."

"After this night, you will go down in history for what you do here. You shall have people worshipping you, Bella." he whispered excitedly, as if relaying the most valuable information in the world. His smile was pure love, his perfect teeth invited her to kiss him, to love him.

"If you think me a genius, then it is entirely your own doing, *Everywhere*!"

He was uncharacteristically subdued. Bella assumed his mood was altered by the highly charged furore that encapsulated the evening. He reached inside his satchel and pulled out a small box before presenting it to her.

She lifted the lid to see a beautiful gold ring, sat on a bed of yellowing cotton wool. It was attached to a chain. Bella wanted an explanation.

"My grandmother's," he announced. The manner in which he took the item and proceeded to place it around her neck made her entire body tingle. "Her husband died for it, but his death saved her life. This chain was the price she paid; it was the only thing she had left. The woman travelled three continents before she was to find herself upon safe lands. I often believe this thing you wear now is magic, Bella." *Everywhere* lovingly positioned it so the ring lined centrally with her bosom. "I would never have believed, that at my age, I would still witness such beauty."

Bella wept. The tale of *Everywhere*'s grandmother melted her insides as much as his undying love for her.

***

Due to slightly unnecessary legal restrictions, tutors not affiliated with her university were prohibited a seat in the main auditorium. She sneaked through a side door and ventured down to the great hall, as *Everywhere* would wait in the wings.

"Bella, where on earth have you been?" a school official called, and rushed her towards the rear of the stage.

The tournament was just about to start. Like herself, the first dancer was solo. The girl, dressed as a geisha, was a friend and studying partner. Bella wished her luck.

All the remaining students resumed their limbering and flexing backstage. However, Bella was still. Her mind not on her impending duty, but on her lover. She truly believed the love they shared fuelled her expertise. Like a sunbeam on a huge, healthy red flower.

Part 4

Participant Number Twelve. Quiet Please.

All the props, the rear screens, all the effects machines, which had served to add drama to all the different performances thus far, were removed. There was no specialised lighting or embellishments. The entire stage was void of absolutely everything.

An elongated pause preceded Roberta Flack's *Angelitos Negros* as it instantly threatened the entire audience seated within the huge auditorium. The unnerving strings bounced around them like death. A lone figure drifted into their psyches like a mirage before their eyes. She wore no costume, no elaborate fineries nor fashionable dancewear. No make-up had been applied to her face or eyes. *Everywhere's* gift hung from her neck.

She drifted to the floor, motionless and dead-like for the agonising elongated intro. Half a minute had passed and people already shuffled uncomfortably in their seats. A moment further and she still maintained her lifeless position. Just to the left of the stage, one of the stewards, twitching in the darkness, poised and readied himself for any untoward controversy. He raised his talking device to his mouth and warned his colleagues to be vigilant.

Whispers were hidden by the loud soundtrack.

Roberta began to sing her pleading in Spanish and Bella sprang up like a slow tree growing, higher and higher. The agility of her contemporary styling already impressed. It was fluid and she mastered it perfectly as only a professional would. Her hair, tightly scraped back to her scalp, and her black Nike training leotard that she'd worn all day, accentuated her physique to maximum effect.

She then changed the movement dramatically and fused the two styles like no one would have believed, had they not witnessed it with their own eyes. The audience were unaware at first that the contemporary had an additional overtone, a sexual, but then again, classical presence was forcing its way into her vocabulary so naturally it almost escaped their attention. And then, ultimately, the audience applauded as realisation hit them dumbfounded.

That display of expertise and detail alone would have been enough to cinch the award. Only, Bella didn't stop there.

On her knees, up on her feet, on her knees, up on her feet, in time with the regimental drum shapes, the ease of the transitions were rhythmically timed to acute perfection.

Another influence penetrated into the mix as the now neoclassical style lent itself to yet more movements her spectators had not seen before, strangely, but easily welcome. The intrigue she wrenched from her audience was so vast people strained, others actually stood to witness the experience wholly before its end.

The subject matter of the words being sung begged the question – in the dusty vaults of time and shameful history, why are there no paintings of black angels? Why were only white models depicted in these many pieces of art? The spectators who could denote the lyrics, they too wondered what had become of all the black angels of history. The magnificence and sheer beauty of the lone woman on the stage made them weep. Tantalised and fully hooked on her every move, they were like helpless junkies.

Now that she had them in the palm of her hand, she began her highest, most taxing demonstration. The song was starting to enter its final crescendo. Her movements grew heavy and loud, faster and faster she swayed into a definite hypnotic trance. In this section, she incorporated a modern urban styling and combined it with something that resembled a tango. On her heels, then her toes, heels then toes, pushing her body back and forth, arching it painfully, turning and ducking. It didn't look possible, but at the same time it looked human and real.

Roberta's final verses were accompanied by something that happened. Something so inexplicable, so harrowing, that at least three of the spectators in the front stalls fainted.

Bella slowed, stretched out her arms full to their capacity, spreading her hands and fingertips, pulling as far from their sockets as she possibly could. She was again tree-like, poised, her eyes burned out towards the stage lights.

Rolling her body over itself, she then raised her left leg high and proceeded to quickly pirouette. This gave way to Bella dangerously spinning her body so fast that after a moment or so she looked like a huge umbrella. The speed was like that of a flick book. She then altered her weight on its imaginary axis, turning herself one hundred and sixty degrees. And repeating, like a constant life-sized fluttering orgasm.

The effects of the display were now truly *inhuman*.

The last bar of the song faded and Bella fell to the floor. Dead-like once more.

There she remained. Over a minute's worth of shuffling bastardised silence from the crowd followed. Just then, someone screamed out aloud from way beyond in the upper balcony, a cry of pain and love, a cry of witnessing a thing so unexpected. A cry to deflate the awful muted agony. That spectator's horrid amplified cry spread its message, an almost unanimous swoon fell through the first cracks of applause, the delay of which was so, so sorry, begging to be forgiven.

The figure remained strewn upon the floor, twisted, void of any movement. An ear-splitting roar from the crowd added to the, by now, deafening applause. People stood, some jumped from their seats into the aisles.

Everyone wept and mourned.

The curtain slowly began to close, the dead dancer remained.

For over ten minutes the roar of two thousand burned souls resonated, the loudest sound in Paris.

***

Wishing to avoid the praise and congratulations of her tutors and fellows, Bella managed to get away without too much trouble. The warm night still had a slight breeze as she departed the building by way of some steps from a basement exit. Her small leather jacket only covering her top half as her big oiled legs shone in the moonlight.

She waited all night. *Everywhere* hadn't even left a message on her mobile.

***

Bella was under obligation to fly back to Brussels with her company. The TEPITA award for most inspirational performance was in her luggage, and the worship she received for the dance that earned it was in unlimited abundance. She even received the world-renowned *Plus Estimé* prize from the board of directors of the tournament, handed to her personally by the eldest surviving member and winner of the membership.

All the distinctions did not matter to Bella, in her mind it was not only through herself that she was successful. The other half was still missing. Absent from this cacophony of kudos, *Everywhere* was as deserving of it as she.

By The Light Of The Silvery Moon

"Hello?" she asked.

A silence on the line, but Bella knew there was someone on the other end. It was two-fifteen in the morning. She'd barely been asleep since they arrived back at their quarters.

"Hello, Bella." His accent was Russian.

"Hello."

The caller wasn't sure how to deal with her aloof manner. More silence.

"Don't you want to know who I am, Bella?"

"You may tell me your name if you wish."

He laughed. "I had been warned of your tongue. So spirited."

"Just tell me where he is."

"Aha, so we move straight to the heart of the matter. Bella, you are nothing if not a fast mover. You still haven't asked me my name."

"I said you may tell me if you wish to do so, or did you forget?"

More silence, until: "He must've cried, Bella. If what I am led to believe actually took place."

Bella switched on now, her mind transformed, an impassive field of calm, disallowing a single milligram of emotion to be released.

"He's a known criminal, Bella, did you know that? Did he forget to mention that piece of information?" Silence. "Let me tell you so you understand, Bella. He had many enemies, he insulted a great magnitude of people. An entire nation to be exact, Bella. One cannot expect to avoid retribution for that level of criminality." The man waited, allowing Bella the opportunity to interject.

She waived her right to do so.

"So you see, Bella, an enemy of the state must be put down, wouldn't you agree?" More silence. "They said they were going to tear his legs off first. Being an old dancer myself, I could only imagine this would be quite upsetting for him."

Bella looked up to the moon from her window; silver, exquisite brightness, surrounded by endless black. She would cry later.

"Oh yes, Bella, I knew him. I knew him very well. We were once friends and deadly rivals back in the old gypsy years. We would dance and steal a million hearts from those Turkish whores." *Keep talking*, Bella thought. "Of course, he was obviously more gifted than I. I mean, he was a genius, was he not? It was said that when he was barely five years old, his grasp on the flamenco was unsurpassed for a child his age. What was even more extraordinary though, Bella, was that his disciplines were all self-taught. His family lived in the gutters close to the harbour. They had no money to send him to the academy, as mine had. While I had the best training possible within the pristine walls of my classrooms... he was knee-deep in shit while he danced the tenements, and he was *still* my superior. He was obviously more handsome than I, too. He was all things, he was everything, he was *everywhere*. He refused to compete when the world stage beckoned. This is where we parted, Bella, him and I. I became very successful, while he lived in poverty and joined those self-righteous rebel fools who sought to overthrow my fathers, *our* people. Just because some of us had a more comfortable life than he. His band of freedom-fighting idiots were slaughtered years ago. I should know, I helped seek them out. Your beloved, he disappeared. Elusive and cunning and very dangerous to my father's people and what they stood for. That was until two days ago." He chuckled.

Bella poured some sparkling water from a bottle she'd lifted from her minibar.

"And you, Bella. You! You were astonishing. Yes, I witnessed all. How could you *do* that? It was like watching something taking place at the apex of heaven and hell."

Bella appreciated his use of words. *Very inventive*, she mused to herself. "Thank you."

Silence, he was obviously taken aback by more of her detached manner. "Are you not in the least bit shocked, my Bella? While you were on that stage doing truly magnificent things, he was being stuffed unceremoniously into the back of an unmarked vehicle. I suppose I have ruined my chances of persuading you to dance with my company. It's far too late for that. Isn't that so, Bella?"

"Yes, it is."

"Shame. A huge shame. You are a genius after all, there is no doubt about that. But never mind, my sweet. I suppose it's a consolation for me, knowing that I was responsible for his destruction. I hope his torture was slow. I know some of those gentlemen personally. I have seen them in action. Their favourite thing they like to do, we call it the *arc suszter,* it's an old Hungarian term, where they smash his face with a large hammer." He became silent, aware of his own animated joy in imparting the details. "Are you shocked *now*, Bella, knowing that is what has happened to your beloved fool?"

"What is your name?" She was calm.

He laughed. "There really is nothing you can do about any of this, Bella…"

"What is your name?" Again, calm.

"I shall tell you my name, but unfortunately for you, your cause is futile. You may have heard of me, my name is Oleg, Bella, Oleg Gribkov. And now, as we both…"

Bella calmly replaced the handset. She then began packing a bag.

The Brandt Crisis Centre

Andrew Baker's defence against Kimmy McGuire was a resounding success. Never faltering in their pursuit of justice, his esteemed gang of barristers mercilessly drove her shameful false accusations back from whence they came.

The case had been important, if not only for the popularity-boosting fruits it delivered. His status as a victim magnified tenfold, wrenching utmost sympathy from the national public. His soccer training school had also started during his court case. Both girls and boys were welcome. '*Free of charge for under-twelves*!' read the slogan, furthering his reputation as a generous humanitarian.

The press seemed to stay one step ahead of him – snapping him jogging with kids in Greenwich Park and buying groceries for pensioners in one of the UK's largest supermarkets. The same store who had just recently hired him to be the charming celebrity in their television commercials.

It was inevitable that the press would attend the latest event in his calendar. Indeed, Andrew Baker's appearance at the Crisis Centre was anticipated by the local council, patrons, and even the mayor tweeted that he was looking forward to an outstanding opportunity. All concerned parties awaited him and his entourage with baited breath, but no one would have estimated the extent of hysteria that afternoon. The surrounding area was closed off, the traffic deadlocked.

It had been Red's design. A once and for all call to stamp out the last remaining strands of the infectious rumours that had hindered his client throughout his career.

The Brandt Crisis Centre boasted a defiantly positive image within London. Originally, it had been a simple facility for counselling and supporting abused women.

Over a period of time, expansion afforded them growth and their current larger premises.

Andrew arrived at the correct time. With Amber Diaz, his third wife, by his side, they looked the perfect couple. She smiled while he engaged in soulless conversations with approaching staff.

A few hand-picked fans loomed nearby and, in time, they were invited to speak with the handsome star and his beautifully small wife.

After a lengthy conference with the directors of the organisation, wherein they discussed finance options and ideas concerning better counselling techniques, Andrew, Amber and Red partook in a public talk with media and local government officials.

Red glanced at his watch, then at Andrew. During all the officialdom and media frenzy, his client had coped extraordinarily well. Thoroughly deserving of tomorrows inevitable golden press in the tabloids.

The main governor was unassuming, a most jovial fellow, although all afternoon Andrew and his entourage had thought him over-fawning and his speeches a little on the long side. "It's great to see you here, Andrew, to know that you took time from your busy schedule to visit us all today. Everyone here really appreciates it." The announcement prompted a somewhat lacklustre round of applause.

Andrew stood and composed himself for his reply. "I'm not really thinking about myself at this point," he sighed. "When I began the soccer school four months ago, I wasn't sure about it to start with. But as it got rolling, I found we were capable of encouraging these kids, giving them a chance. I got a buzz from it, got a buzz from seeing them play and helping them with their skills. I wanted to help even more." Andrew sounded sincere. He placed his arm around Amber's shoulder. "My wife was a victim. A long time ago she was attacked. I just wanted to apply the same thing to this place, victims of domestic violence, you know. Maybe make a difference to women who have found themselves in a similar situation."

Right on her cue, Amber Diaz began, woodenly. "Andy has been a rock to me. So supportive. Being a victim has not been easy for myself, or my family. When Andy came along, it was like a light being switched on. He never talks about himself; it's always what he is able to do for others."

"Fucking bullshit!"

A low but heavy sound, like a deadly gas escaping, could be heard after the outburst.

Someone else called out. "Excuse me, could we get security."

"Fuck the security, and fuck Andrew Baker."

Red looked around anxiously, angrily demanding something be done about the intrusion.

They all looked towards the rear of the hall. Two male nurses both moved towards the lone woman who stood by the door.

"If anyone touches me, I'll call the police!"

"Mae, you know that's not nice," said one of the female nurses to the woman. "You aren't supposed to be here until Wednesday."

Mae's face was scarred and rough and failed to even hint at its pretty past life. Her red frizzy hair stood on end rigidly and failed to move when she shook her head.

"You!" She pointed her bony finger directly at Andrew Baker. "I know what you did. You and your filthy horrible mates."

"My client doesn't have to sit here and listen to this," Red said to the head governor.

"No, it's all right." Andrew grabbed Red's clenched fist with his own in reassurance. He turned to his challenger.

"Just tell me, what is it that I am supposed to have done?" he asked.

"Andrew, enough, we don't have to sit here and take this nonsense," said Red. He shook his head and made to get up from his seat.

"He's a filthy fucking rapist is what he is…"

The gathered crowd released deep murmurs of shock

and disappointment.

"And when was this? When was I a rapist?" He began to sound arrogant.

"Twenty years ago. You raped her, you murdered her, you should rot in prison."

Her voice, although squeaky, was loutish and uncouth. Her face screwed up angrily, as if it were possessed by some hostile ghost.

"You let your friends attack her, then you finished her off, and attacked her with a baseball bat. Everybody here knows what you did, you filthy horrible bastard. They're too polite or too stupid to say anything."

"I could sue you for slander," said Red as he finally stood.

Mae cackled, like someone who'd spent a hundred years in a cave. "You sue me, mate, and you'll see how much I give a fuck about it. Who the hell do you think you're talking to? Do I look like the kind of person you could sue? You stupid prick."

Mae screamed as she was removed from the hall.

The atmosphere was strange afterwards, strained, contrasting drastically with the cheerful air of good humour earlier.

Red wrapped it up finally, awkwardly clapping his hands together as if denying the existence of the previous five minutes.

"Ladies, gentlemen, I think, err, this is what happens when women like that… are attacked. If that woman had not been attacked, she wouldn't have used that kind of language."

He'd hoped his speech was tangible, providing an epilogue-like closure. Even Andrew placed his head in his hands after Red's remark.

***

Amber Diaz smirked to herself in the people carrier as it ferried them back to West Kensington. She knew Andrew would now be angry. She knew he would make demands, later that night, and jump on her body as if it belonged to him. Before they were married, she would put up a fight, which was obviously pointless. But tonight would be different, tonight she would be silent; she was satisfied her disgusting husband was about to receive the press in the tabloids he deserved.

Love In An Elevator

Fall. Construction Site Unit Oversee.

It was a November night on Lexington Avenue. The cold rain poured down and the icy wind bit at the flags over Bloomingdales.

Rose was chauffeured up to the main entrance to her building and she stepped inside. It was mostly dark, save for minimal temporary lighting.

She began her inspection. Not only recording the progress of the work undertaken thus far, she also had to check the condition of the building. Then she would examine the temperature of the hot water in accordance to the boiler regulations, ensuring that new valves had been fitted to the main calorifier and its adjoining pipes. She produced her tablet and filled out her inspection graphs online, taking photographs when necessary. She smiled to herself, thinking about Julie's complaints at how they had to do such mundane tasks themselves. Rose had argued that they might actually learn something new.

The man on the ladder hardly took her by surprise. Admittedly, all she could view was his lower half, his head and shoulders concealed within a loft hatch.

She gave a little cough into her fist. After a slight loss of position on his ladder, he quickly climbed down and bent his head as it appeared from the recess.

"Hi," Carlos said.

He seemed apprehensive, although he smiled.

Right at that moment, she noticed that smile and kept it locked in her brain.

She had seen him in the past, when he'd been on hand to repair and undertake his maintenance duties within her premises, but had thought very little of it; she remembered seeing his face but had felt nothing.

"What are you doing?" she asked.

He began stammering in response only to be interrupted. "I hadn't expected anyone here. I was told this place would be shut up by now."

She looked around. Carlos noticed her effortless prowess, her elegant leather mac, revealing just enough of her legs. He made haste and stepped away from the ladder, only then did he realise the significance, the sight of this evidently formidable woman, actually addressing him personally.

"Err, yes. I'm here on my own, everyone's gone home."

Rose's mind raced when she heard that it was just the two of them. Her thoughts momentarily relishing images of what she'd like to do to this man knowing they were alone.

"I know it's late, but I had to finish a couple of things. I am sorry if I caught you by surprise," he explained nervously. Rose stared at him, expecting him to say something else.

"Oh, sorry, I'm... my name is Carlos."

He reached his hand over from a respectfully safe distance for her to shake.

Yes, indeed, she liked him, he was an extremely fine-looking man, she thought to herself. His bronze complexion illustrated that he reeked of California, or maybe even first generation Mexican. Obviously in New York for work, with a young wife, perhaps. She nonchalantly viewed his waiting hand, it was big and rough and was covered in a day's worth of oil and graft. Raising her eyebrows she looked back up at Carlos, who pulled it away after realising her refusal and wiped both of them on his overall bottoms.

"I'm sorry, I, um..."

She interrupted. "I am pleased to meet you, Carlos. My name is Rose Benoit, and I own this building."

Carlos looked downwards. "I'm sorry, Miss Benoit. I wasn't told you would be here tonight."

"Of course you weren't told, Carlos. Who on earth would tell you about the unexpected arrival of the Chief Executive?" She watched him, waiting for a reply.

"I don't, I…"

"My partner and I, we are personally seeing to the checks of these buildings ourselves. The simpletons we hired could not be trusted to tie their own shoelaces, let alone be deemed capable of drawing up progress reports. I suppose I'm to blame for actually recruiting such substandard fluff."

She noted his puzzled reaction and smiled.

"Carlos, I am aware all you wish to do is go home."

She began to stroll, her hands met and joined behind her back.

"But before you do, would you be so kind as to show me where the elevator control room is, for this section?" Carlos looked confused. "Apparently the computers are playing up, they keep on shorting out."

Carlos hadn't a clue what she was talking about now, watching her every move as she slinked around him. "The engineers, Carlos, I grow so tired of their constant lack of application. It baffles me how these chaps keep on getting it wrong. I might as well do the whole thing myself."

Rose had completed her grievance and was now awaiting Carlos for an answer.

"Well, Carlos? Are you able to show me or not?"

He asserted himself. "Err, yes, ma'am. I think it's directly above us. This space used to be two floors, and as you know, they knocked them away to allow for the high ceiling…"

Rose looked at the man nonplussed, as she had been the architect who had actually drawn up the designs. "So Carlos, the elevator?"

"Oh, it's over there, see?"

"Right, let us take the stairs. You shall lead the way."

Once inside the control room, it didn't take her long to diagnose the fault on the CPU, which was re-configured and re-booted.

While both of them were inside the large elevator on their way back to the ground floor, Rose easily detected his shyness.

"Thank you for the tour, Carlos. You have been the perfect host." Rose glanced at him.

"It was my pleasure, really... Miss Benoit," he said, looking at the floor.

"You may call me Rose."

"Okay Rose, thank you..."

"You may leave now. I suppose your wife or your girlfriend will be expecting you."

"I have no wife, ma'am."

"Oh come now, Carlos, do you expect me to believe that a fine creature like you is single? I do not think so."

"It's true; I live alone, over in Brooklyn."

"I see." The elevator touched the ground floor and the door opened smoothly but Rose remained inside. Carlos attempted his exit. "Where do you think you are going, Carlos?" She whispered as she peeped inside her sleek handbag.

"Err, I was going to leave now, because you said..."

"Stay right where you are, Carlos." She applied the honey balm to her full brown lips, puckering them. "Take your top off."

Carlos raised his eyebrows, "Excuse me?"

"I do not think I stuttered." Rose frowned slightly, gently placing her hand to her breast.

Carlos's look said it all to her. His big eyes, almost disbelieving, took in her image. After a moment in which he spent time getting lost in her unwavering conviction, thus realising this was no hoax, he started to remove his blue t-shirt.

"There. That wasn't too difficult was it, Carlos?"

"No, ma'am."

They could hear the wind whistling, it soared around the building outside. By now the elevator doors had closed again, Rose stepped closer to him. Carlos inched backwards slightly. She glanced down at him. He possessed the perfect physique, she thought, in a very neat shape, a nice colour, and hairless. Not too big, like those huge steroid kings who vied for her attention whenever

Julie and herself would grace them with their presence at the gymnasium near Chelsea Harbour.

Blatantly, she rolled the palm of her hand over the exposed flesh, stroking it tenderly. "How old are you, Carlos?"

"Um, thirty one, ma'am."

"A fine age," she said slowly. "You look younger."

He tried to avoid her strong gaze, yet found himself powerless to do so.

"Are you intimidated, Carlos?"

"Err, yes, ma'am, a little."

"Good." She slowly began to ease her fingertips upwards towards his face and before long she inserted her index finger through his lips and past his teeth.

"I think it's perfectly normal for a man to be intimidated once in a while. Suck my finger, Carlos." She came closer still, her powerful leather uniform occasionally brushing against his exposed torso. Rose surveyed his inept clumsiness, cruelly eyeing him. Carlos looked back, albeit intermittently, undertaking exactly what she had asked of him. She could see his silent questions and his boyish indignation trying their best to materialise, her female power fending them off with devastating ease.

Rose maintained her hold of his mouth for a very long moment. Inspecting him, her gaze was like a magnet, and in time his senses were drawn into it. He almost wept at how beautiful she was.

"Do you like that, Carlos?" she whispered.

"Yes," he murmured, nodding.

"Good. Good boy."

***

He watched her as she silently walked away. Shivering, he waited for what seemed like the entire night's passing.

He recalled his friend Tony, his words of warning battling miserably against Carlos' better judgement. Within seconds, Tony, and his advice, disappeared permanently.

Recollections

The meeting Jack had attended with the child adoption agency played out in his head like a horrible payment reminder. Pearl Brewster, the adoption agent, was an itchy little piranha-like woman who seemed to take great pleasure in being the bearer of cold, hard, bad news. It rankled him when he recalled their conversation. Wiping her foul vision from his memory proved difficult.

She had questioned Jack's intention of being a legal guardian to Daniel. Said it was curious that a *police detective* would want to sacrifice his well-established career. She was corrected for her mispronunciation of Jack's title a total of seven times. Jack even overheard Pearl Brewster telling Madge the whole affair was unethical.

The next meeting with Brewster would be the week Jack was to turn fifty. He knew time wasn't on his side, but as his thoughts turned towards Daniel's angel smile, he knew he had to be successful.

***

The following day came too soon, having had barely thirty minutes sleep. He'd arrived at the scene early with Ollie Travis, surprised they were the first.

They stood in front of the vehicle that contained the body. The man was naked and had been positioned in the rear seat of a battered Vauxhall.

While glancing at the damaged corpse, Jack recollected not only their surroundings, but also the victim.

"Steven Freeman," he announced.

"You know him?" Ollie asked.

"I remember him, yes. Old case, one of my first, actually."

They both approached and stood either side of the car,

looking in through the opened rear doors.

"A girl went missing, presumed murdered. This guy was a suspect." Ollie waited for more. "I've been here before. This is the school Sarah Allen attended."

"Who's Sarah Allen?"

"She was the girl who was murdered. There were two other suspects as well, as I recall, but they dropped them in the end. It was bullshit, I knew those three were up to something, horrible bloody kids."

Jack took a sudden intake of breath through gritted teeth, as the pain in his back began to bite from the base of his spine upwards. He wafted away Ollie's concern with a wave of his hand.

"You're so annoying, boss. It's getting worse. Get the bloody medical, will you?"

Jack surveyed the area and looked over to the school's main entrance. He seemed preoccupied, as if something was on his mind.

Ollie huffed and produced the specification report. "Are you ready?"

"Yes, right, okey-dokey."

"Whip marks."

"I think we can see that, Ollie."

"And his rectum has been ruptured."

"Okay."

"The whip marks predominantly feature on the back, but the assailant made sure he left lacerations everywhere."

"Ouch."

"If you see, even his face was hit."

It was a shocking scene, viewing Steven Freeman's remains. Pure horror on an otherwise mild Tuesday afternoon.

"Yep. This wasn't one of your average kinky sex type things; this whip was like something out of Roots, know what I mean?"

"Racially motivated, you reckon, Ollie?"

"Possibly," he shrugged. "Looks that way."

"Okey-dokey. Right, the rupture?" Jack asked.

"It's big, Jack," Ollie said, his eyes closely reading the crumpled report sheets.

"What is?"

"The thing that was used, to err…"

Jack caught on. "How big?"

"They don't know yet, doesn't say here, and the item wasn't on site. Pathology say they'll get the err, dimension, after their tests."

Jack shuddered. "They can do that?"

"Yeah. By probing, the err…"

"Okay, okay," Jack said shaking his head. "This isn't good, Ollie."

"Roger that, Jack, it's terrible," he declared, frowning. "Whoever did this had a serious thing about sadism. Possibly homosexual, definitely a freak. But it's almost certain, this is our man again," he blurted. "Feels like he's following us, while we follow him."

Looking upon Steven's mutilated body, Jack knew Ricky Gomez and Andrew Baker were in mortal danger.

"You wanna know what I think, Ollie?"

"Go on."

"Presuming Steven Freeman was innocent of the crime I mentioned earlier, right? Then what's he doing in a car next door to the school where that crime took place?"

"Revenge? Mistaken revenge?" Ollie asked, they both looked at each other.

"I remember something. Something is coming back to me." Jack looked over to the same lacklustre shell of a school he visited all those years ago and searched his brain.

Ollie knew Jack was onto something. "What's on your mind, Jack?"

After a few moments, Jack continued, "There was a girl. I'll always remember her. She was scared."

He stooped down, knelt close to the rear tyres of the vehicle.

"She said something to me."

He looked down at the ground and spoke quietly to

himself. "Why is this familiar? Why do I think I've missed something here?"

Ollie Travis was still silent and he began to feel invisible.

"I'm sure she implied in some way... or suggested... about something like this. See, Ollie, this girl was the victim's best friend. I think her name was Rachel or something. Anyway, Wright handled the case, made a total pig's ear of it. They held her for questioning for hours. At one point Wright thought she'd done it... She was in a hell of a state. Her mother died I think, shortly after. Poor girl. Pretty thing, she was. Kind of geeky – glasses, innocent type."

"You think this Steven had something to do with this victim's friend, boss, this Rachel?"

"Well, his DNA did come up when we investigated Sarah's murder. We found a small piece of her body in a carrier bag which also contained a tiny trace molecule of what turned out to be Freeman's hair. For a while, the odds were stacked against him. When the case went to court he was given a lawyer who got him off due to insufficient evidence, the hair molecule had been amongst other DNA belonging to other students. Freeman's lawyer argued that if his client was to remain being a chief suspect then as many as sixteen others should also have been tried. He also played the race card to the jury. Finally, he also stipulated in a roundabout way, that Sarah Allen, flighty and flirtatious as she was, had been around more boys than just Freeman that night. He basically branded her a slut... that she more or less had it coming to her. On hearing all this, Allen's friend, this Rachel, went crazy. Years later, Freeman did get sent down, somewhere up north. But that had nothing to do with this case."

"Yeah, in Bradford. Says here that he was released a couple of years ago."

"Hold on," said Jack, looking less tired. "That's it!"

"Sarg'?"

"I got it."

"You do?"

"Ollie, we have to go."

"We do?"

"Yep. We have to find a black woman, early thirties. Her name is Rebecca Sinclair."

Fresh Linen

Doctor Sidhu entered the room and viewed the sheets of paper upon the clipboard that hung from the end of Ricky Gomez's bed with a tatty piece of string. She inserted a thermometer into his left ear.

"I'm feeling a lot better," he mumbled from his bulbous, swollen lips.

"I know you're lying, Ricky," she said as she checked the evidence on the reading. Ricky looked up at her. Doctor Sidhu seemed more attractive than when he'd last seen her.

"Why do you have to lie to me? You want to leave so soon? Even you admitted the food in here is better than the stuff you get in prison."

Ricky gave his best attempt at a shrug.

"Well, the fact of the matter is that your central nervous system is still damaged. Whoever threw you down those stairs tried really hard to sever your spinal cord. I'm not even going to mention the breakages elsewhere. Plus, there were traces of diamorphine in your blood. More lies, Ricky. You told me you'd quit last time you were in here."

"I think that was a different Ricky."

"It's not funny," she said. It wasn't, but that didn't stop her from giving him a comfortable half-smile which lasted barely two seconds. *Rare*, he thought.

His ability to speak had improved. A gentle slur now replaced the indecipherable mumbo-jumbo from the previous three weeks. The fits had also lessened, although not entirely.

"You get some rest, Ricky."

She laid the palm of her hand on his forehead.

He lay within the fresh linen, and looked upward to the white ceiling. A warm glow hit him like soft wool as he ironically congratulated himself on a job well done. Tomorrow, he would allow the damage he'd inflicted on himself to begin it's reign of terror, to assault his senses, and to think of the inevitable day he would be sent back to the shit-soaked prison. But today, drenched in painkillers and ignorant numbness, and the care and consideration of good people who served to make him better, he slept soundly and danced in his dreams.

Frustration

The space around David Morgan was beginning to irritate. In the past, he had often operated from some unassuming hole or other, stylising his digs only with all the information he would need to make his assignments successful.

Rats, though, and the smell of faeces that constantly emanated from every surrounding wall, were mentally discouraging him from working in the manner to which he had grown accustomed.

His assignment details had at last arrived.

"Hello, Morgan."

"Can't you call me by my first name?"

He knew they couldn't. He didn't care. By asking the question he was just establishing the difference between basic human need and anonymous lonerism – his chosen method of work.

Morgan began. "Dmitri Uloosv, Isaac Riblikov and Cherz Pytivok. The three men in the Vegas apartment. Slavers. You know the extent of their injuries."

"They were part of the heist, you think, Morgan?"

"No, the Baltimore heist is fabrication and you know it is, you created it to smokescreen the media. Their injuries were horrific, by the way. Way out there."

The voice went silent. Subdued, Morgan thought, by the results of his harsh truth and the way in which he'd delivered.

"Are you still there?"

"So, Morgan, have you got anything else?

He huffed. "Banji Oyekan."

"Go on, Morgan." The voice sounded once again comfortable.

"Nigerian. Thirty-nine years old. Ran two laundromats and was a part-time witch doctor. This guy was a nut job. Performed female circumcisions, genital mutilations – all that fucking horrible crap."

"Okay, where is he now?"

"Venue Brownsville. Homicide, body in parts, including penis. Severe whip marks on his back. I mean *proper* whip marks, none of that sex game crap."

The voice was silent, so David Morgan had no choice but to continue his report.

"He was left for dead, although still alive, while rats finished him off. The time, from the very first infliction, to his time of death, I estimate as being close to ninety-five hours."

David Morgan glanced at himself in a small mirror that hung lopsidedly on the far wall. Though his face looked unhealthy, a week or so's worth of stubble, his exposed chest was strangely easy on the eye. Abdominal crunches and push-ups of differing radius's used up many hours of his spare time.

"Listen, I really don't feel like verbalising all this," he sighed. "Surely it would be better if I wrote it all up afterwards?"

"Negative, Morgan."

"Listen up," he sighed. "I'm used to fighting in the field. In the mountains, you know? This time last year I was heading operations in Baghdad! All I'm saying is that there are ways I do things, damn it."

"Morgan, we have already stipulated this. We do not appreciate going over your grievances. Once we have told you our requirements, you are meant to adhere. Look, we know this assignment is unorthodox, we know it is unusual, but we also know you are the best. The work you have done in the past is genius. Truly excellent. We simply couldn't do this without you, Morgan."

Account Book

For three long days, Rose had been holed up in Thomas Rossington's office. Sat cross-legged upon the floor, inspecting countless files and documents with her keen, deciphering eye.

Timing was crucial, and as she heard the housekeeper climb the stairs, she hastily read the final page of a book of records dating back almost four years before the woman arrived at the door to the office.

"Would you like a cup of tea, dear?"

"I most certainly would," Rose said. "All this checking is thirsty work."

"Oh, good heavens. You have been busy," said the housekeeper, taking in the sheer size of all the files and documents that were piled high around Rose like miniature skyscrapers.

"I have, indeed. And I'm still a long way to completion, I'll have you know."

"Can I help, Miss Rose?"

"I wish you could, I really do."

"Oh, the Lord and Lady, they really do appreciate all that you are doing for them, Miss."

Rose smiled, imagining the housekeeper eavesdropping while Thomas and Linda were expressing their gratitude.

"It's actually not much of a hardship. It's something that must be done, that's all."

Upon her perusal of the vast mountains of facts and figures, Rose found herself being reminded of her training in accountancy, the intense after-midnight sessions in which Julie Ross and herself would partake back in the days before they both became CEO's of their conglomerate.

The housekeeper carried a tray into the room and cleared a space before setting it down on Thomas Rossington's desk.

"Thank you. Are you not joining me?"

"I would love to, but I'll only be a nuisance, dear," said the housekeeper. "I'm an absolute nincompoop when it comes to maths and things like that."

Six custard creams were laid in a tidy pile beside Rose's tea. Rose nibbled a corner and left the remainder.

It hadn't taken her too long to uncover the cause of the financial problems the Rossingtons were encountering.

Giovanni Mitchell had been managing the affairs of the couple and their estate for almost ten years. Throughout the man's career he had been a most gifted and trusted accountant with a near-impeccable record. His uncle, a valued friend and wartime companion of Thomas Rossington, had preceded him, and had passed the lucrative position to his nephew before he himself passed away.

Rose had indeed noticed a decline in the way in which Mitchell worked the records. His first few years with the Rossingtons were perfectly logged, the quality and the way in which he'd maintained the files was clearly unsurpassed. As the years rolled by, however, it was painfully evident his services suffered. He began taking small amounts at first, and as time passed, more currency would disappear.

The most recent evidence of Mitchell's undertakings glared back at Rose insolently as it hid behind the lack of six figured numbers.

Upon learning these revelations, Rose sat silently glaring at the facts, wholly astonished at Mitchell's blatant disregard for the Rossingtons' affairs. His attempts to run them into the ground wasn't even clever or devious. Just embarrassingly crude.

***

Rose began her surveillance of Giovanni Mitchell. On numerous occasions, she attempted to make contact with him, with no luck. The excuses she received from his office were pathetically juvenile. Sickness, holiday, personal troubles. On one occasion he pretended to be away from his office when Rose knew it was actually him speaking.

Finally, she appointed a personal colleague of hers to resume all responsibilities at Rossington Hall.

Max

Meetings had been arranged for the remaining week of their stay. They had worked hard these last few days, they were tired, in need of a little light relief. It was quite late; the evening summer sun had by now dropped behind the buildings of the Navigli, the dark orange sky reflected beautifully upon the canal.

The bar was full and the music at such a level that enabled them to conclude their meeting.

Julie had practically created the theme of all the plans for a gala, an event in which they could showcase the *Nubian Rose*-Gribkov tie-in as well as their charitable undertakings. She had liaised with her New York management team every night with the aid of social link-ups via her laptop, while Rose would entertain herself elsewhere.

"We're dubbing it *The Event*. It's already being greatly anticipated by all the movers and shakers in London and Paris and Dubai. Rumours are already circulating, you know, about it being a charity thing." Julie, over excited, reeled off the information like a newscaster with a sugar-rush. "As you know, *Nubian Rose* ain't selected a suitable place to serve all our needs… yet. But we need to act fast if we're gonna see this thing come to fruition. The previous destinations were unacceptable regarding their respective size and capacities."

"How about here?" Rose said, simply.

They had spent the best part of that day traversing the length and breadth of the Quadrilatero della moda. Rose was confident somewhere within Lombardy's capital would provide the perfect opportunity.

"The Galleria Vittorio Emanuele II."

"Say what?" Julie's face stiffened.

Rose smiled. "It's obvious, darling, is it not?"

"Are you crazy? That mall joint?"

"Sì, certamente."

"Are you high? It's open to the public. You'd have to close off the whole damn area, how the hell are you gonna pull that off?"

"I have the mayor in my pocket, honey, did you forget? He owes me for what took place up in Como."

"Jesus Christ, Rose. It's a shopping mall!"

Rose nodded. "But a beautiful one."

Julie twisted her lips before sipping her *Aperol* spritzer.

They both thought about the vast preparations that had yet to be undertaken before a start date was made public. Oleg Gribkov, fresh from making his union concrete with *Nubian Rose*, made good his generous contributions and would undoubtedly be present, alongside other patrons and guests.

"Um, Rose."

"Yes, baby?"

"You remember that guy, oh damn, what's his name?"

Rose turned and looked at Julie, somewhat dubiously. She frowned. "Julie, what is it?"

"Oh, yeah, that's it, Howard Forde. You remember him?"

"The gentleman from *J&C*'s?"

"Yeah, right. Him…"

Rose's stern reaction forcefully prompted Julie to continue.

"You ever, like, notice how…"

"Julie, baby, if you want my opinion… then no! I do not think he's handsome."

"Damn it, Rose."

"You need a man that bad? *Him,* darling? He looks like one of *The Usual Suspect*s."

"One of the hot ones?"

"No, my love, one of the stupid ones. I don't even know why we gave him the position in the first place."

Julie had wondered the same thing. Countless times

she'd privately questioned the odd way in which Rose had granted *J&C*'s rather ineffective merchandise.

"Julie, was it not your idea – the work relations rule? Are you and I the only ones whom are exempt from it?"

"No. He just seems like a nice guy, jeez. That's all I was going to say."

"Julie, you know me. I'll go anywhere with you, If you told me there was a guy in Wyoming, or Seattle, we'd be catching a plane. But not this way, baby. Not now. Besides, he's horrid," Rose scrunched her nose up. "I think I might feel quite ill if I saw you with *him*, darling."

As much as Julie tried, she was unable to conceal the sulk upon her face. "I guess."

Aside from Julie's disappointment, Rose became aware of a sudden distraction apparent within her friend.

"What's the matter?" she asked quickly.

"Guy over there's been casing us the past ten minutes."

She indicated towards the man's direction with an almost invisible nod. Rose took a sip of her sparkling water and, after a moment, looked over, thoroughly unimpressed at the sight of the overweight balding man, glasses, mid-fifties.

Giovanni Mitchell was wearing the exact same suit he wore on the day of her party at Rossington Hall.

***

Julie caught a cab back to the hotel. Rose reminded her of the appointments they had made for the following day, finally telling her she would return in the morning, first light.

The woman Mitchell was bothering smiled in appreciation as Rose rescued her and steered him away with the aid of a tight arm lock, her hand clamped upon the back of his neck. "This way, if you please."

After being hurriedly rushed over towards the bar, Rose despatched him onto a stool and ordered a lemon tonic and a glass of beer.

"So, Giovanni, this is where you've been hiding whilst I've been in pursuit. Tell me, what am I to do with you?"

The man grinned, unpleasant and forced. "One or two things might suggest themselves."

Rose passed him a questionable glance, then placed her hand over his. It was pudgy and clammy as she picked it up and felt his childish fingers, which were smaller than hers.

"Okay, look, I'm sorry. I might have been avoiding you, Rose, but it's not what it seems."

He appeared familiar, reacting to her contact as if they had been old friends. His accent hinted at his affluence, although his voice was extremely high pitched for a man of his stature.

"I never really meant for all this to happen, you know. I've been under a lot of strain lately." Rose's fingertips slowly tickled and danced on the backs of his hands.

"All this business with the Rossingtons, I am currently in preparations to amend the shortfalls I made, please be assured of that."

Rose beamed, her smile dazzling him. "Well, darling, that is indeed a start."

Giovanni asked her if she wanted a fresh drink, and Rose opted for a orange vodka cocktail.

"To be honest with you, Rose, I thought you'd be a lot more ticked off than this," he said, watching her stir her glass with a plastic straw.

"What on earth would make you jump to that conclusion?"

"Well," he cleared his throat. "I had been told about how formidable you've become, especially when you've been rubbing shoulders with those New York types," he said, as she stirred his beer with a straw. "Do you come back to the UK often?"

"Not often. Maybe once a year. And only when I need to do so." She inserted his straw into her mouth and sucked the froth.

"I don't suppose you went over all the Rossington's

ledgers?"

"I want you to stop talking now," she said, her fingertips gently covering his ugly twisted lips. "I own some rooms, a modest apartment a stone's throw from the cathedral, you and I could be there in ten minutes."

Rose stared at him, her smouldering eyes adding a momentum to her hospitality. Giovanni took out his handkerchief and proceeded to dab it against his forehead, immediately drenching it with sweat. He stuttered in accordance to her suggestion.

"Of course, if you have plans for the evening, then we could always reconvene our engagement at a more opportune hour, at a more convenient place."

"*No!*" he shouted, then lowered his voice. "No, no it's quite alright."

"Gosh, you're sweet," Rose hissed, "and insatiable too, it seems."

She took his hand and they both stepped away from the bar.

During their cab ride, Giovanni shuffled nervously, drenching endless sheets of tissue with his perspiration. "Rose, are you quite sure about this?"

"Giovanni, ready yourself for a life changing experience."

***

The building was typical Milanese, a traditional old haunt and well kept. Pale terracotta masonry with light-brown shutters. The interior hall with its black timber and flooring was dimly lit but seemed stylishly sparse and at odds with its exterior. She allowed Giovanni into the main lobby and closed the door behind them both, locking it.

"I must say, when I ventured to that bar earlier, I would never have thought I'd spend the rest of the night with you, Rose. I consider myself an extremely fortunate fellow."

Rose hummed.

Holding his hand, she silently led him through a long

corridor, stopping outside a door towards the end of the passage. She unlocked it and they both stepped through into the room.

She switched on the main light.

"Ah, here we are," she said warmly.

"Yes indeed, Miss Rose."

The room was warm. A faint metallic odour merged with the smell of cardboard and wafted towards them upon the waves of muggy air.

"Would you like a drink, Giovanni?"

"Um, have you any wine?"

"Of course. I have some nice Chianti, although, I must say that I am most fortunate in being a recipient of a lovely case of Ferrari. Sparkling, dear, I know, but so, so crisp. And we are in Milan, after all."

"Indeed. A good choice."

"You pour." Rose pointed to the bar over in the far corner. "And yes, a fine choice, as it shall aid to cool us both. It was a gift from a Trentino farmer I knew from my time staying at Sirmione."

"Ah, you've been there already?"

"Si. Yesterday. My partner and I went to the Lake. Especially gorgeous this time of year, and such a sweet part of the world."

Giovanni located the chilled cases and pulled one out. "The lady you were with at the bar, was that your sister, Rose?"

"Julie? No, she's my partner. We both own *Nubian Rose*. I would have thought you knew that."

He gasped. "Oh, I had heard that you were one of a duo. Although I had no idea your partner was another foxy minx like you! But it's amazing, what you've done, with your *Nubian Rose* thing, I mean." Giovanni poured the wine into two glasses before handing Rose one of them. "So, what are you actually doing over here?"

"I have a lot on at the moment actually, Giovanni, dear. Among other things, there's this event we're planning that seems to have taken on a life of its own. But at the moment, I'm merely utilising my time to accommodate our engagement. Your engagement… with me. "

"Ah. Yes. Rose, I must say I am very excited." They both walked over to a large couch. He stood respectfully while Rose seated herself and crossed her legs. He joined her and sipped his glass. "Whenever I see you, say, in a magazine, I'll admit I become very aroused. Like now. This… engagement, as you put it, might just make me explode. I'm so happy." Giovanni placed his arm around Rose's back.

Rose gently took hold of his hand and caressed it. "Good," she said. "Me too, Giovanni, dear. I'm so glad you're here. It's so interesting to learn what other people might think of my latest project, especially as it's currently on the eve of its completion."

"Pardon me?"

"I've almost finished, Giovanni."

"I'm sorry, Rose, but you've lost me."

"I do apologise," Rose turned to face him. "Allow me to explain."

"Please do, Rose."

"If you'll notice, over towards the other side of the room, there is a man I have placed into a device."

Giovanni squinted and quickly glanced over, surprised. It was true, her upturned hand casually pointed to a youngish man, late twenties, Afro-Caribbean.

"It is an instrument I've decided to call 'the deportment enhancer'. 'Tis nothing too original, Giovanni. A combination of a couple of old torture devices, both traditional inventions, that I have merely joined together. I believe they complement one another in terms of encouraging good posture. Manners, rectifying behavioural problems, that kind of thing."

Giovanni was silent, his brain taking extra time to process. The man in the device was standing, but also appeared to be asleep or unconscious.

Suddenly Giovanni became anxious and motioned to back out.

"Err, okay, well, I think I'll be going now…"

Rose laid her hand on his shoulder and smoothly caressed the side of his neck.

"You are not going anywhere, darling."

"Um, no, it's time I was thinking about going."

"Now, let us both go over. Come, I'll show you."

She led him towards the man, who's left eye had opened slightly. Giovanni stalled. Rose gripped his hand firmly.

"Now, as you can see, he is returning from his nap. Poor thing, he passed out yesterday as I ripped out his tongue."

Giovanni reeled backwards and stumbled to his knees at hearing what she'd just said.

"I have to go. I am going…"

"Baby, before we continue, let me tell you this… You are not going anywhere until I tell you to. I hope, for your sake, you understand this."

"I can't. I have to leave, please…"

"Dear, I am most loathe to repeat myself. Please do not prompt me to do so."

Giovanni began to quiver.

Rose arrived at the man's side. His eyes opened, wearily.

"Giovanni, darling, meet Max," she said proudly.

He looked up in shock. Max wasn't tied, he stood unrestrained against a rack-like frame, the implements within which he had been placed looked horrific. The young man's face was slightly bony, rugged. Giovanni thought Max looked similar to some of the scruffy drug dealers who'd whistled to him whilst walking through the Parco Sempione.

His stomach heaved as he saw that Max was fully awake but at the same time wholly resigned, looking off into the distance.

Rose anticipated Giovanni's thoughts. "Correct, Giovanni, Max is my product. He is mine."

She rested her elbow casually upon Max's shoulder. "I

managed to break him, you see. He wasn't always this well behaved, believe me, Giovanni, but Max is a good boy now."

"But, Rose…"

"Giovanni, stand up, come." She smiled broadly.

Giovanni saw Max's eyes start to well a little as he reluctantly did her bidding.

"Come closer, Giovanni, let me explain Max's new way of life within the deportment enhancer to you." She stroked Max's face. "Now, atop his head he wears a bridle, basically it's just a variation of what is placed on a horse. Only, the one Max is so beautifully modelling for you, Giovanni, is a lot more uncomfortable due to it being made of iron. As you can see, there is a metal hook at the top of the bridle to which I have attached a chain. The chain is hung from the hook on the ceiling, this has Max loosely suspended, holding him in a permanently upright position. The spikes on the inside of his bridle which protrude into his ears also discourage his movement."

Through pure shock, Giovanni's breathing became laboured. The fear in his heart made him cry.

Rose went on. "Additional to that, if you see… the heretics fork."

She placed her left hand gently around Max's neck to demonstrate the implement, which was strapped very tightly in a vertical position to his throat.

Both Rose and Max shared the same ethnicity, but Max's yellowing sullen hue was jaded against Rose's beautifully vibrant copper. Giovanni, blotchy and awkward, became shameful of his whiteness, as guilt and self-loathing gripped him.

She continued. "This little babe is keeping Max's neck from dropping forward, you see? A measure with which I'm sure you'll agree should encourage marvellous discipline within my Max."

She raised Max's chin up with her little finger so Giovanni could see the device. The horrible thing wasn't very long, double ended with sharp spiked prongs at either end. One end would indeed fatally stab underneath Max's chin and up into the base of his jaw. The other end, if Max's concentration faltered, would stab at his throat. It was apparent that the process was already underway, as dried blood had crystallised down his front from the wounds it was leaving.

Giovanni flinched upon seeing that all of Max's fingers had been cut from his hands.

"Yes, unfortunately we had to snip away poor Max's digits, the naughty thing was quite simply uncontrollable by a certain point. I did not have much of a choice. It took us a good two or three hours to completely sever all ten, did it not, Maxy baby?"

"This is sick," said Giovanni in a slightly gravelly tone. "It isn't funny. It's horrible."

"At first Max struggled when I started with the pliers, understandably. But as time passed, he actually became quite used to what was taking place. I think he could understand my predicament and why I was actually doing it to him. In the end, in keeping with the whole flow of his punishment, I made him beg me to sever the last three, or was it four? I can't quite remember. And when I say beg, Giovanni, I mean I beat him until he screamed and shrieked like a small child. So, we got there in the end, didn't we, Max?"

Rose glanced at the man, his eyes met hers, responding.

"I suppose Max is my ideal man, as he is now, I do believe. Totally subservient, one hundred percent submissive to a fault. The poor boy would literally do anything I asked of him now. I shall demonstrate, Giovanni."

Rose turned again to Max. "Max, darling, show Giovanni what you would do for me. Lower your head and demonstrate to him the damage the heretics fork does to your neck. Now, if you please."

After a moment Max proceeded to drop his head. Slowly at first, but as the spikes within the bridle tore at his ears and the fork on his neck continued to puncture his throat, his determination prompted his efforts.

"Do you notice he does not grimace? His face void of any objection?"

Giovanni wet his pants. New blood poured down Max's front as he lowered his head, his empty eyes stared directly at Giovanni.

"This is based on acceptance, you see. He has been taught to undertake all tasks without the merest hint of irritation." Rose turned to face him. "Wouldn't you just love a thing like this in your life, Giovanni?"

Giovanni looked down at the urine on the floor in shame.

"A nice, young girl, small, pretty. One who wouldn't put up a fight if you wanted to fuck her, and she'd allow you to take it whether she liked it or not? Isn't that what every man desires, Giovanni? It used to be what Max wanted, but since I came along, I think I've managed to change his tiny mind."

She dabbed her middle finger at the dark blood that dripped from his neck and tasted it with the tip of her tongue.

"Good boy, Max, dedicated to a fault."

With both her hands, Rose positioned his head upward again, as if adjusting a model dummy.

She then poured herself more sparkling wine.

"Owing to my behest, and entirely for my own convenience, I had Max shipped over here so I could fit him around my work schedule. Incidentally, he had walked with a slump, his gait uncoordinated and clumsy, he leant forwards as he moved. I've always detested bad posture, Giovanni, it is so ugly and there is no excuse for it. I decided to use this as a theme within the plans I'd formulated for him."

Again, Giovanni's chin wobbled amidst his weeping. The oppression inside the room was pungent, seeping underneath Giovanni's skin.

"Max ultimately proved himself a tough one to break, and I have enjoyed every moment. He'd been abusive in the extreme sense of the word, trying in vain to overpower me. He had groaned and wailed and screamed in agonising frustration as I remained in constant control of him. After his third day, I had literally turned him into a wild animal, unrefined, and witless, but captive nonetheless. I'd enforced every single manner of rule upon him. Not a moment was wasted in beating him down. I basically threw all the rules I could possibly throw at Max, he was constantly chastised until he got it right. On his sixth day, I finally encouraged out his submissive side with the aid of his deportment enhancer, resulting in his current calm and obliging manner. It has taken seven days, Giovanni."

Rose smiled, as she picked at Max's knotted mess of hair.

"Max? Ma-ax?" she cooed, lovingly, in his ear.

He replied by blinking, glancing over to her side.

"Giovanni, would you like to try?" She turned toward the pathetic mess of a man on the floor. "Come." As Giovanni made an attempt to get up, his left leg went limp limiting the momentum to rise. He fell back on his side, like a beetle on its back. She stepped above and pulled him up.

All the while, Max looking up, silent, daring to pray for death. Far away.

Rose enthusiastically continued.

"This strip of metal that juts into Max's mouth goes all the way to the back of his throat. It comes graced with spikes, you see, Giovanni, and the more poor Max would attempt to speak, shout, scream, or even cough, the more his tongue would be torn to pieces. So, by the time I had finally broken him in, receiving all the servitude his mind, body and soul could offer me, I decided to be lenient. I released him from the bridle, and I then cut out his tongue. My darling Max was most appreciative when I forced him to eat it."

She went on, aiding Giovanni competently, but his legs were on the verge of once more giving way.

"So anyway, Giovanni, I then tested the results of his

deportment training. I asked him if he loved me. He was incapable of speaking coherently, of course, but I knew from the way he pleaded he was trying to tell me that he did. I rubbed my thighs and belly and ass all over his face to enable him to worship me correctly. He had passed my examination, Giovanni. I was most satisfied and I rewarded him with a sound beating. Indeed, I beat Max so hard that I'm sure he actually begged me to finish him off, to end him. But I refused him that privilege. I kept him afloat, just teetering between death and madness. Afterwards, he was then placed into his device once again."

Giovanni gagged. His mind coursing with hatred and frustration towards her enthusiasm and manner. His empty stomach heaved.

Leontyne Price continued Verdi's *"Pace, pace, mio Dio"* as Rose swayed over to the bar. She poured herself yet more Ferrari, and cradled the glass in the palm of her hand. She walked back to the two men.

Daring not to look in his direction, Giovanni knew Max was staring down at him. From the corner of his eye, he could just make out the blurry outline of his pleading face. He choked on the mucus caused by vomit and fear and his own cowardice. He couldn't look back at him. His selfish guilt twisted at his mind, turning it inside out.

Rose took a sip from her glass and purred in appreciation.

"So, Giovanni, you are at last up to speed. And now, I require you to assist me further."

Giovanni could take no more. Finding it impossible to look at her, unable to look up at all.

He braved himself with all his power to speak. "Please let me go. I'm sorry I dealt with the Rossingtons. I did not mean to steal from their accounts, please... Please!"

Rose looked nonplussed. She bent down and tilted his chin upward with her index finger to face her and smiled.

"Pleeease!" he screeched, "let him go, for crying out loud. This is terrible. It's just awful."

"You must hush, darling," Rose said slowly, fully undressing his soul.

A noise was heard from Max, a slight cough, his throat, maybe.

"Oh heavens, it sounds like our Max is getting up to his old tricks again." She turned to Max. "Come, assist me, Giovanni. Let us play with him."

Another tear rolled from the corner of Max's left eye. His emotionless face looked straight ahead at her neckline.

"The piece of music you are listening to, Giovanni, is a story about a woman who calls upon God to allow her to die so she may be released from the agony of living without her lover whom she believes has been taken from her." She glanced at Giovanni. "Is that not so undeniably tragic?" she asked, as she moved back to the bar and retrieved a small black device. "Such sadness. Such sorrow. Giovanni, slap Max in the face, if you please."

She returned back at Max's side and glanced at Giovanni expectantly.

"I... I can't."

"You can't? Why ever not?"

Giovanni's head began to nod, a repetitive but slight tick that suggested towards the onset of dementia.

"Because, I... I can't! Oh, God!"

Rose paused, and gave a minute cough into the edge of her hand. "I believe I have been a most gracious host, Giovanni. Accommodating and kindly. Whilst you have constantly moaned and groaned and complained like a spoilt child. I shall make this as straightforward as possible, dear. If you do not slap Max, I shall be forced to slap *you*. Would you like me to do that, darling?"

He looked downward. "No, I..."

"Good. Okay, Giovanni, proceed."

Max's expression remained, looking straight ahead. Giovanni noticed the eye contact when he was in direct proximity. He took a swing and landed a feeble hand upon Max's cheek.

"Well, darling. That was pretty worthless, wasn't it?"

she declared, "Not very good at all." She shook her head. "He is our slave, Giovanni. You are to issue him with a slap. Do the job correctly. Make it count."

Giovanni despaired as he looked deeper into Max's eyes; haunted, lost, deep wells of sorrow and pain. Giovanni failed to even attempt to understand what madness they had seen. He glanced at Max, apology and shame and sorrow embossed into his face. Max looked back, indifferent, unmoved. Giovanni then gritted his teeth and heaved his whole body to enable a better swing. He applied a harsher slap, but the impact did not affect Max.

"Better, dear. Although, still substandard." Rose sighed.

She took Giovanni by the shoulders and moved him aside, herself now face to face with Max.

"I suppose your errors are in fact my fault, darling. You see, Giovanni, I assume full responsibility. One becomes more experienced after one has been taught sufficiently. Obviously, I have not illustrated as well as I should have. For this, Giovanni, I apologise."

The slap *Rose* issued completely jolted Max's head to the side, a grunt could be heard a mere second after the heavy blow. His mouth opened and drooled a little. A graze surfaced almost instantly. Blood trickled down from the side of his eye.

"Giovanni," she asked calmly, "did Max flinch?"

"I don't know! Let him go. You have to stop this pure evil." Giovanni was now hysterical.

"I could have sworn he flinched." She tilted her head sceptically. "Did you flinch, Max, darling?"

"Please, let us go! Oh, fucking hell!"

Another heavy slap struck Max, this time on the opposite side of his face.

"So, anyway. Giovanni, that is how it is done. Would you like another opportunity to punish our slave?"

She looked down at Giovanni. On all fours, he heaved and choked.

Rose chuckled. "So be it, darling. Although, I fear I must warn you that failure to comply to my demands may hold the most undeniably cataclysmic results for you later on," she said.

She stroked the side of Max's bleeding cheek, rolling his blood within the tips of her fingers.

"Do you think Max longs for death, Giovanni?" she asked, looking at Max.

She bent and kissed both his eyes, softly closing them. Raising the electro shock device, she pressed it to his chest. As his body contorted under the shock of contact, she took another sip of her glass, purposefully ignorant of the terror she was inflicting.

Giovanni vomited before finally passing out.

She pouted, gazing into Max's eyes. Finally, his head slumped forward as his subconscious released him from Rose Benoit.

Max wasn't killed that day. He was kept alive, and at Rose's behest, was sent to an unknown location.

Nostalgia

Ollie was running late. Jack had waited roughly ten minutes before receiving a WhatsApp message informing him to wait a further twenty. He remained inside the car and straightened himself with difficulty. The pain licked at the base of his back like a fire and threatened to spread all the way up to his neck. Lately, being on foot was almost as painful as when seated, especially within the small driver's seat of the Honda.

"We got the Freeman data back from pathology," Ollie said, appearing at his side.

"Oh yeah, the err… the…"

"The phallus, yeah." Ollie helped. "The thing measured ten inches in length. Width three inches." he said, a little too enthused.

"For goodness sake!" Jack was disgusted as he put the measurements to the image in his mind. "What the hell is wrong with this man?"

They had spent the previous forty-eight hours separate. Jack had considered Ollie accompanying him at first, but thought it more beneficial to be by himself as he searched for leads relating to Rebecca Sinclair.

Jack Sargent personally knew Finsbury Park like the back of his hand, and Rebecca's great auntie's small house was only a couple of yards away from his own childhood street.

Ollie drove as they headed back toward the high road to Holloway which led to the station.

"So, Rebecca Sinclair?" Ollie asked. "Don't tell me. The girl changed her name and now lives in Manhattan?"

"Ollie, you'd be correct in assuming that I have not been in contact with Rebecca Sinclair."

"Okay, is that why you look so pleased?"

"Do I look pleased?"

"I know why you're pleased, boss. I'm not stupid."

"I am not pleased."

"Okay, well, you're *satisfied* that you have eliminated Sinclair from our business." He eyed him, dubiously. "You liked her, boss."

"I was fond of her, I guess, Ollie, yeah. I felt sorry for her. After I'd heard her mother died, I felt really bad. Never saw her again," he paused.

"So, today?"

Jack cleared his throat and began. "Okey-dokey, so, Rebecca Sinclair's mother's family are scattered. Her sister's nieces are based in Brixton area. Sinclair's father's family are up in Tottenham, they never met her but always wished to, unbeknownst to her at the time. The father, Emanuel Sinclair, or Manni, left Martha and his daughter when she was two or three."

"Did you manage to get a hold of him?"

"The man is sick. I saw him in a hospital in Enfield but couldn't get much."

"Life threatening?"

"Hip operation. But the guy suffers from schizophrenia."

"So, Rebecca? What happened to her after Sarah Allen?"

"That much I know already. She and her mother tried to testify against three suspects Rebecca claimed to be responsible for the murder. One of them turned out to be Andrew Baker."

"Baker, yeah."Ollie nodded. "He just got married to that singer from Canada."

Jack nodded too. "All three suspects were tried, they all got off. Freeman, like I said before, got sent down for something else more recently."

"Aside from Rebecca, was there no other witnesses? I mean, there must've been someone."

"It's funny you should say that, Ollie. There was another. A woman who was working at the school on the night of Allen's murder. Her name was Mae O'Connor. She had a florist's. They did the school prom, decorated the hall. When she saw the news the following day, she told us she'd seen three guys in the early hours with a heavy holdall type bag."

"Hold on, Jack. The murder took place in the early hours. What was Mavis O'Connor doing there at that time?"

"*Mae* O'Connor. She arrived early, before light the following morning, to remove some of their decorative things. This was the exact time Sinclair told us the attack took place. She gave a witness report, but it had been rejected when she couldn't identify any of the three youths."

"What happened to her?"

"I was told something, like she suffered from depression. They put her in some home, I think. Anyhow, after the attack, Martha, Sinclair's mother, died from an aneurysm and that's when things go dark."

Ollie scratched his head. "How dark, Jack?"

"Rebecca's family were all lovely people, very accommodating. They told me all they knew. But their stories conflicted."

"They're covering her?"

"It's more likely they literally don't know. Some of them believe Rebecca died. A cousin said that she moved to the states. Europe."

Ollie nodded, "Okay, *that* kinda dark."

"I thought about scanning for her, putting feelers out. In the meantime, we have to talk to Gomez."

"Ricky Gomez, one of the suspects."

"Nice homework, Ollie."

"Thanks, boss," he said sarcastically.

"No, it's good, I'm impressed. You've obviously done the research."

"Yeah, well, if anything, I'm enjoying the nostalgia. Some of those old photographs are intriguing."

They parked the Honda and Ollie switched the lights.

"Boss?"

"Yes, Ollie."

"That moustache you had twenty years ago is very, very upsetting."

Training Day

Julie had to lie to Rose about an unworkable situation regarding her proposal to Milan's city councillors and The Galleria Vittorio Emanuele II. Following their completion in Milan, Julie caught an early evening flight to New York, while Rose had escorted Giovanni Mitchell back to the UK. On her orders, they had posed as a couple while on the plane.

***

Giovanni was naked from the waist down. He stood in the middle of the small dingy room. Bruises collected around his face and a large gash under his right eye merged with its purple and black surroundings.

"Now, Giovanni, dear, it would appear that you are extremely overweight. A most rounded fellow, indeed. I should like to take the opportunity to train you, maybe encourage you to lose a couple of pounds."

The look on his face suggested he was unaware she was speaking to him. His mind lagged behind and was currently still tormented by his beating, which had taken place some three hours previously.

"We shall start with five push ups."

Rose strolled around him. Looking every inch like a contestant in a line up for the women's one hundred metres. Her tightly fitting black and gold bikini pants provocatively displayed her buttocks, which jiggled slightly. He stood motionless, watching her.

"Okay. So five push ups, when you are quite ready."

He wept. "I cannot do it."

"I want you to do five push ups, darling. Now, we can make this so easy, or we can make it extremely difficult. This is entirely your choice."

Giovanni attempted a last chance gust of acquiescence.

"This is all wrong. I am sorry, please…"

"You're still talking?" she sighed.

"No, I mean, I was just trying to tell you that I've changed my mind. I…"

"Okay, you've chosen to be difficult. So be it," she said.

Before he could say another word, she grabbed his throat with her right hand and his exposed crotch with her left. She pulled him up towards her. Although he was heavy enough, she applied the right amount of strength and accomplished the feat easily.

She then threw him to the ground violently. His obesity enhanced his collision with the floor.

He wept loudly now. Spittle drooling slowly from his grimacing mouth. He hammered his fist against the floor in bitter frustration.

"I will get my five push ups. I shall get them today. You have five seconds."

Giovanni rolled over in an attempt to get to his feet.

"Five." she said, as he struggled to prepare himself. "Four."

"Please, please, give me a chance," he begged.

"Three."

Rose knelt down almost on top of him and began touching his face.

"Okay, okay!" he shrieked.

"Aw. No need to shout, Giovanni, darling. In fact, if you raise your voice again, I'll sew your mouth closed; you'll spend the rest of your life communicating via sign language."

"Okay, I will do this, okay… Okay…" he hissed, whispering loudly with sheer desperation.

He managed to turn onto his front and then attempted to raise himself upward with his arms, using his knees instead of his feet, from which to pivot only half the amount of his weight. Incorrect.

"Straighten your legs, please. Keep your knees away from the floor," Rose advised, as she inspected her long nails.

He applied himself, and with painstaking effort, lifted off his first push using the tops of his feet. His belly hung down further than his small penis, and as he tried lowering himself, his left arm gave way and he slumped back to the floor.

Rose tutted. "Mmm, I'm afraid that doesn't count, darling."

"I'll try, sorry, wait…"

"Start again."

Rose was rigid, not allowing anything to get in the way of her receiving what she had asked of him.

After a period of time which he'd spent composing himself, he began the exercise. His first lift was satisfactory, given his shape and size. Lowering himself again, he groaned as he lay flat on the floor.

"Good. Very good indeed. Four to go," she said. The man grunted and wobbled slightly, this time as he raised himself up. "Maintain your composure. Control your breathing… deep breaths, darling." Number two was complete.

As he lay there, coughing, letting time pass, Rose began to get impatient.

"Giovanni, dear. Do you expect me to sit and wait while your lack of application renders you idle? A little selfish of you, don't you think? You have three push ups left."

He slowly pushed up on his arms. His knees made contact with the floor again, albeit slightly.

"Knees, darling. Raise your knees. If your knees touch the floor again, I shall cut them off."

He rocked and wobbled under the strain of his own weight as his uninspiring fourth push up was complete.

"You disappoint me. You have one more to go. Make it a good one," she trilled.

The back of his head ached and the pain travelled around the circumference of his entire bulbous neck. The final push was obviously the hardest.

Rose was not pleased with the attempt. "Rubbish," she

spat. "Give me another – correctly, this time." He pulled up, once again with the aid of his upper legs and knees.

Rose stamped down harshly onto the small of his back, pinning him to the floor.

"Did I not just tell you to straighten your legs? To avoid using your knees? Did you not hear me?"

"Yes, sorry, I will…"

The last push up took almost seven minutes.

"Okay, get up."

He did this with questionable haste. Rose noted his enthusiasm. "It appears you are more acquainted with some movements than you are with others that you are less inclined to excel in. At this early stage, at least."

On standing, he looked at her, a slight seethe of anger glimmered across his mouth.

"Darling," Rose smiled, "I find your irritation charming. I'm filled with a delightful warmth, knowing I've rendered you incapable of challenging me." Rose moved closer, her face inches from his. "Go on, say something. Talk to me. Tell me how you feel."

Giovanni gritted his teeth, void of the ability to speak. His mind flooded with both terror and frustration.

"That's it, dear, allow your hatred to vent. Vent your misgivings to Rose, darling. After you've finished you'll fall in love with me as I release you from the pain."

Giovanni looked downward. He wiped the blood and snot from his face with his sleeve.

"Now, on the count of three, I want you to give me five laps. Move towards the door over on the far wall. You may start from there."

He traipsed across the room, reluctant and miserable.

"Three, two, one." She took a sharp blow on a silver whistle that hung from her neck to prompt his start and he slowly began a walk.

"Put your back into it, darling. I wish to see you running laps, not walking them."

He quickened his pace and already began to breathe heavily. His feet padded and flopped upon the floor.

She purposely let her leg restrict his way as he ran by her. He stumbled and instantly dropped to the floor at her feet. As he lay, he looked up at her. "Please, I'll do anything, have mercy." His Oxbridge whine was pitifully endearing.

Rose grinned. "Get up. Continue to do what I have asked of you."

On lowering her leg, he got up and carried on with his task. The noise he made as he stomped slowly around the room towards the start of his second lap annoyed her slightly.

"Raise your knees, and lift your feet as you run. Maintain the cohesion of bending your legs correctly, and on every step. In due time, this will build your upper leg muscles."

As he mumbled, she interjected. "If you speak once more, I will smash your head against the wall. You are not here to speak, you are here to do as I ask."

He was into his second lap. His belly was now red raw as it wobbled. His penis twanged and flicked below.

"So, lap two. You feel hot, and I see you are perspiring. This is good, as your body's temperature is regulating and your eccrines are obviously functioning well. Rose is impressed."

His heavy breaths were now beginning to turn into loud shouts as he gasped for air. His pace slowed under the pain.

"Check your speed – it is flagging. You must not reduce your speed. I want you to maintain the steady flow. This will test your limits as well as encourage self discipline."

She was waiting until he was level with her before she grabbed him back by the collar of his open shirt. Stopping him forcefully, he fell to the floor once again, this time landing on his backside.

"You should be aware of the hurdles in the way, darling… both in life, as well as on the racetrack."

"I'm sorry!" he wailed.

"Get up," she whispered.

His body was strained even more so as he got onto his

knees to lift himself. Rose had to stop herself from kicking him; the temptation to do so was almost impossible to resist.

On his third lap, his movement became slower still and Rose appeared at his side, joining him. She walked casually beside the struggling man. His face was deathly pale and drained of all colour, apart from his crimson eyes, and lips which were turning blue.

"Two and a half laps to go, darling. I must admit that Rose is far from being impressed with your overall abilities. However, she may give you a high score, if only for your determination."

His left arm suddenly dropped as the arteries to his heart became blocked.

Giovanni slumped forward and fell. His face hit the floor first. The groaning had stopped, and his leg began to twitch. Rose slowly stepped over him before hooking her foot under his side flank to pivot his body so he faced upward.

She assessed the results of her work. Grotesque and bloated. The man's chest still heaved, his indecent slobbering mass twitched and fought miserably against the oncoming permanence.

She stayed until his final breath, after which she contacted his office, letting them know of his untimely death. Giovanni Mitchell was fifty four.

Incompatible

Speed Dating Evening At Jovi's. Close To Washington Square Park.

He sat opposite her and smiled. Julie had stared, not over-incredulously, but in disbelief. It was inconceivable to her that someone like this would still be alive and kicking in this day and age. With his silver hair and beard, the man was almost seventy years old. His bow tie peeped from the top of the most sensible lambswool sweater she had ever seen. His image hearkened back to people who were in her mother's old school photographs.

He had been extra polite, however; the perfect gentleman, taking care in displaying his mild-mannered good grace at all times. He listened intently at her financial jargon, none of which he would have understood. And when she'd requested *Cristal*, she found herself sipping it moments later. In spite of her attempts to throw him off, Julie saw he possessed a charm that no man her own age occupied.

Yet, enthusing about New York Irish playwrights and the joys of Greenwich Village's beatnik era was not Julie's idea of the ultimate night out. She became impatient. Eventually, even his good-natured politeness agitated her.

Julie regretted being so rash, though. She also regretted her hastiness and wishing her time away, as if these engagements were disposable. She'd forgotten about just being, about spending time with people. She could almost hear Rose, chastising her from the back of her mind. Obviously, there wouldn't be any physical connection with this man, but there was nothing wrong with getting to know him. To learn something about him, and about life. She had been so desperate. Her foolish senses urged her time with him forward, and on to her final date of the evening, believing it to be her last opportunity.

But that wasn't meant to be, either.

Thoroughly unhappy now, Julie ran her hands over her perplexed face. There he sat opposite her, across the table. The man whom she'd tried to avoid all night. He was possibly the most unattractive man she had ever seen. He was the mafia type, an old dog. Chubby, with fat fingers and greasy hair. He breathed heavily. His thick gold chains around his neck were tight and gave the impression they were choking him right before her eyes. The stench of cigars and cologne insulted her senses and stung her eyes.

"Matti Corulla," he announced, hastily offering his hand for her to shake as if they were about to engage in a formal business meeting. "I work for a reputable company. My work is very important to me and so are my family and colleagues."

"Okay. Well, good."

He spoke seriously, as if the details would be of major benefit for her future. He took a swig of his hip flask. "So what are you in here for? You looking for a partner, huh?"

He pointed at her whilst he asked the question.

"I guess."

"You guess? You're in the wrong place if you ain't, lady."

"Well, I guess I ain't sure."

"Listen, you need to be a lot more open with me if you wanna get near *this* sugar." He pulled out his wallet, stuffed with dollar bills as if displaying some kind of famous monument. "You like the smell, lady? You like the smell of these fat benjamins?"

"Oh wow." Julie half laughed.

"Hey, you're impressed. Thought so. I had a feeling I could turn you round. I seen you earlier, I said to myself... Matti, she's the hottest broad in this joint, play it cool, Matti, and don't go in guns blazin', but I shoulda not bothered. I knew I could get me a piece of you." He stopped talking only to catch his breath. He heaved while taking another swig from his hip flask.

"Yeah, so, I gotta say you look damn fine. I bet you like

getting tapped, huh? You broads always do. You actually remind me of a hooker I knew one time."

Matti hadn't noticed Julie's listless expression. She cradled her chin with the palms of her hands.

"I gotta get outta here," she muttered.

"The fuck you mean, outta here?"

"You really are charming. You know that?"

"Yeah, sure. I knew that. Why?"

"Oh boy! I was being…" she paused and attempted to search for a clever word that Rose might have said in this situation. She failed. "…fucking sarcastic!"

The man frowned. "You should show me some respect, lady. I don't think you know who you're talking to."

"Okay, well, I ain't interested."

"What the hell are you talking about? I'm a businessman. Matti works hard, lady." He beat at his chest announcing more levels of apparent masculinity.

"Do you mind not swearing?"

"Are you one of them dyke bitches?"

Julie jumped on the opportunity. "Yes. Hell yes."

"Thought so. As soon as I saw you I could tell." He swigged another mouthful. "Shame though, you were pretty hot." Matti dragged a hand over his sweating forehead. "But what the hell are we doing sat here? You're wasting my time. What the hell are you looking for anyway?"

"I don't know, but it ain't you," Julie retorted, calmly but firmly.

"Yeah? Well you're one of those broads who needs to be taught a lesson, and I think I'll have to be the one to do it."

That was it. Julie snapped. "Let me tell you this: no one will be teaching me any lessons unless I wanna learn somethin'."

Her outburst dulled his previous rancour. Matti lowered his voice. "You better keep your voice down."

She went on. "And the chances of you teaching me anything, seriously? Are you for real?"

"I'm warnin' you, lady," he half whispered. "A bitch

like you needs to know when to shut the hell up."

"Is that right? Well, tell me…" Julie shouted, "tell me to shut up, you fat fucking pig. I dare you!"

The manager approached their table and asked Julie to kindly lower her voice.

"Excuse me?" Julie stood. "I'm being threatened by this bastard motherfucker and you tell *me* to be quiet?" she turned back to Matti. "So go on, bitch, tell me to shut up, teach me a lesson."

Matti adjusted his collar and crooked his neck arrogantly.

"Is this true, sir? Did you just threaten this lady?"

"So? She's a crazy bitch. I don't even know what the hell she's doing here anyway. She's a damn dyke."

"Sir, you can't use language like that in here." The manager seemed intimidated and virtually hid himself from Matti using Julie as a shield.

Julie noticed the level of background noise had all but stopped. She glanced around frantically.

"What the hell's everybody looking at?" she screeched, "Ain't you all got drama of your own to gawk at? What's the matter? You all never seen a black woman have an outburst before?"

Matti Corulla hid his face within a firm clutch of his stubby hands.

"Miss, please could you kindly lower your voice?" the manager repeated.

Within her arising bitterness, which was just about to explode to its limit – Julie stopped, and caught sight of herself. Her eyes flooded. The back of her throat felt hot and dry, and as she swallowed she choked a little. The first tear rolled down.

She felt like a child. As if someone had broken into her bedroom and read her diary. All the men she had ever met in her life had been mistakes. Her relationships were plane-crashes, if she was honest, every single one of them. All of them had been consistent with one horrible truth – she was incompatible with absolutely everybody.

Deal

Jack Sargent pulled the handbrake upward for the third time in almost as many minutes. More red lights, with more traffic; the dual carriageway was close to being gridlocked and there were no hopeful signs of it loosening up.

He glanced over at Daniel apologetically.

"It's okay, Mister Jack, we have to be patient, that's all." Daniel said, hope shining in his eyes.

"We were in a lesson with a man the other day, he was dressed like a bat or a bird or something. He told us that if we worry then it is really bad for us. Bad for our health and things."

"Why was he dressed as a bird?"

"I don't know. Maybe he thought we'd pay more attention to him if he was dressed in a costume, I think."

"Good thinking." Jack nodded.

"It doesn't matter if we're late, Mister Jack, as long as we have fun today. That's all that matters." Jack looked at his young friend, empathy moving him to finally come to terms with the Saturday morning traffic.

***

They were late. Almost an hour had passed since the start of Andrew Baker's soccer training school, but as Daniel had assured earlier, worrying was pointless.

Jack checked his watch as he waited outside the changing rooms. Sure enough, Daniel galloped towards the pitch like a horse released from its starting gate.

"Who's the kid?" Andrew Baker asked his coach. "I said no latecomers."

"Must be the one from the list; he was the only one who didn't show up."

"The retard? I was hoping he'd keep away."

"Andy, there's no need for that. Besides, he's already

paid up till the end of the month now."

"Yeah, well, I ain't got time for this crap. My boys here have already had an hour, the retard will pull them back."

"He's from an orphanage. He's not retarded."

"I don't care. You have to tell him to leave."

"Andy, it's their first day. What's the matter with you? Everyone's in the same boat."

"Okay, fine. But if he starts spazzing out, you're sacked, okay?"

Andrew turned to his pupils and blew his whistle. They were told to lap the pitch, and after their fifth circuit, some began to complain, others flagged, ultimately stopping altogether.

Andrew Baker was ill-equipped to accommodate the grumblings of thirty or more seven to ten year olds.

His coach was on hand to tell them that their hero had left the field due to a hernia he'd obtained earlier in the season.

***

They had forgotten about the mad rush of traffic. The multitudes of angry parents honking and weaving their way in and out of the queues had all but dispersed. All were a distant memory as Jack drove casually back towards *New Horizons*.

"Oh, Mister Jack, it was awesome. It was the single most bestest thing you ever did for me."

Jack smiled. "That good, huh?"

"Oh yeah! Andy Baker is a megastar. I wish I could be like him when I get to be older."

"I suppose he's pretty cool, isn't he? And look what he gave me earlier." Jack reached down and produced a sealed envelope. He handed it to Daniel.

"What's that, Mister Jack?"

"Open it and see."

He didn't waste any time tearing the light blue paper to pieces. He held the contents in his hands: a card featuring a Panini style mugshot of Andrew Baker from at least three seasons before.

Earlier, the gift had been handed over reluctantly. Jack had tried hard to be discreet, telling Baker in no uncertain terms that he might be in danger.

Andrew was typically detached within his arrogance.

"What the hell do you know? I feel bad for Steve Freeman and his family, I really do. But this ain't nothing to do with me or Gomez. Steve Freeman was into some bad stuff with some bad people."

This roused Jack's attention. "And what kind of bad stuff are we talking about here, Andy?"

"My name is Andrew."

"I'm sorry. Andrew."

"I've heard stuff about Freeman and his friends when he was inside. He used to be crazy, that guy. I tried to distance myself from him in the end. I don't know what he got up to when he was released from prison."

"He was a driver. He kept his nose clean."

"Yeah? Listen, Sargent, I'm not stood here because I want a casual chat with you. I don't really have the time for this bullshit. Freeman got banged because of the company he kept. Simple. You really are wasting your time. There's nothing to worry about; nobody's in danger."

***

Though the marker-pen squiggle he'd left upon the card was indecipherable, by no means resembling Baker's signature at all, Daniel was oblivious. Just to merely hold the relic in his hand was enough.

"Today's been brilliant, Mister Jack."

"Good. I'm glad, Danny. Look, it's important to us both if we do something exciting every time we meet up, okay? So I want you to think of something super-cool for next time."

"Okay. When are you coming next, anyway?"

"Maybe a week. I'll try and come sooner if I can, and

I'll tell Madge as soon as I know. Deal?"

"Deal, Mister Jack!"

Jack turned and looked at him as he smiled. The smile that was fuel to every second of his waking existence.

Sanctuary

Days drifted by, urged forward by the New York wind. The autumn leaves and scattered trash blew outside through the alley in the same way as his days turned into weeks. David Morgan was tired. Whereas before he was utterly sick of the sight of the inside of his apartment, now he missed it's familiarity. He hadn't been there in almost a month, owing to the extensive workload that seemed like it was growing with every passing week. Even a couple of helpers had to be hired after a certain time, owing to the rate his duties and surveillance were increasing.

The grocery bags fell to the floor, heavy apples and carrots toppling out. He flopped himself down onto his bed.

The cacophonous ringtone of his new disposable phone pulled him uncomfortably away from a much needed sleep.

"Morgan?"

"Yeah."

The silence that ensued inevitably prompted him to spill the latest report:

"Maximilian Jenkins. Twenty eight years. A gangbanger from Bushwick. This kid's a nightmare. Three homicides, one of which was a minor ten years ago. Been dealing drugs since he was eleven years old. School life was non-existent. Been in and out of bins and correctionals his whole life. Last stint was sixteen months inside Fishkill. He was paroled early, three months ago, released on some shitty grounds of diminished responsibility I ain't even got to the bottom of yet. This guy, Max, was good at only one thing… attending his PO meeting. Never missed one his whole life, presumably so he could collect his welfare. Now this is the strange shit I was telling you about. He had a passport. Jenkins never so much as took a shit past Manhattan Bridge. I mean, for the past six years he couldn't anyhow, because he'd been fitted with a scram. The device was found broken and discarded close to JFK.

His passport was handed in at a Western Union in Paris, fucking Paris, man, can you believe that?"

"Morgan, it appears you are developing more of an enthusiasm for this job. I think it's growing on you."

"Not really. It's just that this is getting strange, don't you think?"

No answer.

"Well, anyway, get this, our suspect flew to Italy last week, took a stop at Roissy Airport. Two days before Jenkins's passport was located. Listen, the kid was a menace, one of those real problem fucks, you know? But he's missing. He had a girlfriend, although she didn't give a shit that he's AWOL, but his brother has expressed some concern."

"Morgan, Morgan, can I just interject?

"Huh?"

"How is this relevant?"

"Excuse me?"

"Why so much information? This fellow seems like a nobody."

"Of course he is, don't you see? The evidence suggests towards our subject, right? A kidnap. Why in God's name is she picking off guys like Jenkins?"

Silence.

"Christ, don't you fools get it? I'll stake my life on it: Jenkins is dead, tortured, mutilated somewhere in some god-awful place. I'm using this guy to illustrate the lengths the subject goes to. The subject is insane, clinically, morbidly. Most-fucking-definitely."

Morgan huffed in frustration and slumped to the floor. He scruffed his hand harshly through his hair.

"All I'm saying… We need to go now, you bastards. I can nail the damned bitch *now*!"

"Morgan, hold tight. We'll give you the word when we're ready."

Colloquy3

Rose: I heard about your meltdown.

Julie: Don't tell me – those damned hens from the office.

Rose: I'm afraid so. Are you okay, my darling?

Julie: I can't stand it, Rose. Every stupid guy I meet. They're all damn stupid.

Rose: Oh, Jules. Please don't cry, baby.

Julie: I finally saw the real truth. It's my fault. The problem dates back to when I was a kid, when I used to think I was worth some kind of shit.

Rose: Julia Ross! Take that back. I will not have this.

Julie: Honey, it's okay, I just see the wood for the damn trees, you know? If it happens, it happens. If it don't, then hey… I'm cool. No more am I gonna go all out for these stupid men bitches.

Rose: That's okay, but don't be angry out there. I know how crazy you are.

Julie: Me?

Rose: …

Julie: …

Rose: Julie, I think you should travel.

Julie: Where?

Rose: Might I suggest… anywhere other than New York.

Julie: Atlanta.

Rose: And Atlanta.

Julie: What's wrong with Atlanta?

Rose: Julie, that doesn't count. That's not travelling; you have family in Atlanta.

Julie: Well, where then? I ain't going to no Morocco or Asia, or any of them funky-ass places you been to. This girl don't live in no tent.

Rose: Well, you should try it.

Julie: Listen, buster, if this is just your way of telling me you disapprove of me digging Howard…

Rose: …

Julie: I told you I liked him. That's it – end of story.

Rose: …

Julie: Well? Talk to me, damn it.

Rose: Darling, you are free to do as you wish. I have not said anything on the matter.

Julie: …

Rose: So, please, let us move on. Do tell me, what's been taking place since I've been away?

Julie: Everything's in order, baby. I'm running things. We're already receiving bank from the Oleg union. *Times* says we're the most enterprising thing to happen to the city in thirty years.

Rose: Did I not tell you that six years ago, sweetie? Was I wrong? All that hard work, the endless nights we spent together, rehearsing numbers and going over the stocks. That apartment! My Lord!

Julie: Yeah, yeah.

Rose: …

Julie: You're back here now, right?

Rose: I got back last night.

Julie: Okay, come round.

Rose: I can't.

Julie: Why not?

Rose: Because I'm horny.

Julie: And?

Rose: Baby, the way I feel right now, if I was to turn up at yours, I'd want some Julie pie.

Julie: …

Rose: You want to give me some Julie pie? I mean, are you able to do that?

Julie: Um, yeah.

Rose: Oops, I almost forgot.

Julie: What's that?

Rose: Julie, I have something to tell you.

Julie: Go on.

Rose: I have a man.

Julie: …

Rose: Hello?

Julie: You're fucking with me?

Rose: Non, mon cher. His name is Carlos.

Julie: Carlos? Sounds like a porn star.

Rose: …

Julie: Or a janitor. Is he hot?

Rose: He is. I don't think you'd think so. But I like him.

Julie: Wait a minute, I am freakin' speechless. The last time I heard you sound like this was…

Rose: Sapphire?

Julie: That's right, Sapphire. Wait a minute. Carlos? Where have I heard that name before?

Rose: Err, yeah…

Julie: Rose? Talk to me, what the hell did you do?

Rose: He's part of the maintenance team, you know? On Broad Street, Wall Street?

Julie: You're fucking with me, right?

Rose: I most certainly am not. Julie, he's really sweet, but not drippy, you know?

Julie: Where the hell did you, um… how did you come to be in close… um…

Rose: We chanced upon each other. You know me, baby. I do not go around looking. The moment I first engaged with him, I had this feeling. I think we had one of those click moments. He's so unassuming, easy, you know? Just normal. Actually… he's an absolute darling.

Julie: He must be. I ain't never heard you talk like this about no guy before. What is he… superman? Like, the bionic guy or some shit? He must be some kinda great.

Rose: Maybe. I quite think he might be. If he tows the line, he'll be just fine.

The Art Of Deception

Monday morning, Ollie was driving. They were both silent due to another disagreement. This time about the jinxed case they were working on. The cigarette lead proved unfruitful. They finally received the official list of patrons who were privy to the high class cigarette and chased every one of the leads. The Arab and Chinese names who it was comprised of were just a bunch of overly wealthy consumers. Nothing more.

"We've tried looking through all the other avenues, airports, Arab contingents, custom made-to-order requests. All nothing. Led us nowhere, we've got nothing, apart from a migraine that's forming inside my blasted head."

Jack replied. "What about the patron's list? There's that additional space."

"It sounds like we're really scraping the barrel with that. Sounds like bullshit to me. It's empty because the space isn't attributed to anybody, that's why."

"Ollie, we've been told that, in the eventuality thereof, it's more than likely a collective patron, for example a company? Isn't that what we were told?"

"Yeah, I heard, but the source was real vague, Jack. What was it? Nubian Rose? Sounds like a perfume."

Ollie struggled. He widened his eyes to ward off sleep. Jack noticed he hadn't shaved.

"If you are sick, then don't come to work," Jack said as he sat in the passenger seat, sulking.

"You said that twice already." Ollie spat.

***

The car ambled past Moorgate. Both men were silent, tired and sullen.

The *NRL* building was plush and modern and looked like it had been recently refurbished. They sauntered into the grand lobby, an ornately crafted structure which resembled more of a hotel reception. The impressive fibre optic strands of light fell from high above, like a shimmering waterfall.

The receptionist was dressed to impress. She looked like she'd walked straight from the evening section of a Selfridge's catalogue.

"Hello. I'm Lucy. May I help you gentlemen?" she smiled.

"Hello there. My name is Detective Inspector Sargent and this is my partner Inspector Ollie Travis." Ollie was fast forming a low tolerance to the way Jack said this all the time. He knew he had to say it, but it was just so unfortunate.

"We'd like to know if it was possible to speak with Miss Rose Benoit?"

Lucy arched her eyebrows. She then offered a hopeless look, as if casting questionable doubt on his request.

"May I ask, have either of you an appointment with Miss Benoit?" Both men looked at one another.

"Yes, we do have an appointment," Jack lied. Ollie still couldn't believe how badly Jack applied himself in the art of deception. He almost smirked as he glanced upwards to the swirling glass stairway behind the reception desk.

"Detective Jack…" she said to herself, as she navigated her way to the appointments page on her desktop.

His attempt to correct her mispronunciation was cut short.

"I'm sorry, it appears your name is not on today's list of meetings. Are you sure your meeting with Miss Benoit was today?"

"Well, I thought it was. She rang me a few minutes ago, she said to just go straight up."

"Erm, Mister Sargent…"

"It's okay, Lucy, she'll vouch for me. Believe me, Rosey and me and Ollie go back a long way, we all went to the same school together."

Jack seemed to be malfunctioning as he attempted to throw an arm around Ollie's neck.

Ollie cut in, unable to concur with Jack's facade. "Err, I'm sorry, Lucy. I think there might have been a misunderstanding."

At that moment, the pain in Jack's back shot up his spine, he shuffled his weight from one leg to the other, to distribute the discomfort.

Ollie continued. "We assumed it had been arranged. We are sorry to waste your time."

"That's no problem, Inspector." Lucy smiled.

"Just out of interest, would it be possible to just see Miss Benoit now anyway? I mean is she in the building?" Jack asked.

"There's no way I can really tell you that information." Lucy was annoyingly professional.

They were back outside and Ollie was seething. "Go straight up to her office? Are you for real?" His face creased heavily in frustration.

"We were winning, Ollie. *You* screwed it up," he said, without conviction. "I was *this* close to clinching an interview."

"What is it with this case, Jack? It seems like you're coming apart. This ain't like you."

"We have work to do, don't you see? This Rose Benoit is the main key to get us through the door, Ollie." Jack sounded drowsy and started to slur his words.

"You've got yourself a problem, Jack. This has got to stop."

Ollie clambered into the passenger seat, "You drive."

"I'm not driving, you drive."

"Jack, I can't think straight. Drive the car."

"Ollie, I can't sit straight. *You* drive the car."

Howard Forde

At last, Julie thought to herself, almost breathlessly, as Howard Forde approached. Here was a man who liked her for who she was. Almost two months in, their relationship was going from strength to strength without the tiniest inkling towards anything going wrong. A record!

The night before, after leaving the bar at VU46, he told her that he loved her.

She was truly happy in Gristedes, as they purchased tomato pies and fruit. He looked nice, with his casual Armani sports coat and trendy quiff. She saw him differently than the time when they'd first met. Back then, he seemed scruffier, not as polished. It was only lately that Julie was able to see him within his true light. He had a generous and amiable personality. He was neither narcissistic, nor was he goofy or childish. Howard fitted perfectly.

They booked a table at Lowdes, close to Bryant park.

"What made you choose this place?"

"I thought you liked it here?" he asked, seating her.

"I do, but I know you don't often come up around here."

"What, Fifth Avenue?"

"Yeah, I guess. Midtown…"

"I told you it's far too busy round here. I always tried avoiding it as much as I could."

"I reckon that's what I like about you; you ain't like the guys you see in this place: Wall street, Yale flankers.

"Flankers?"

"Yeah, bankers flankers, you know?"

Howard laughed. *A nice laugh*, Julie thought, *like a steady rumbling at the back of his throat*. He always seemed to be amused by what he referred to as her *traits*.

"Didn't Miss Benoit attend Yale?"

"Nope. Though I did. Three years, business. Nah, she

went to Harvard."

"Wow."

"I know, right?" Julie sipped on a large flute of peach Bellini. "My sister," she raised her glass in a toast. Howard copied. "She's awesome," she said, almost silently. "Of course, don't get me wrong, I don't discriminate. I don't hate on these uppity white guys around here, of course I don't. But as you know, there is a certain... set. These guys take it seriously, I'm telling you. If it ain't Gucci loafers and a Hermes tie then you can forget about it. Hell, even *we* have protocol. But out of hours, it's just so dull. I've been in and around all this shit so long, I find all that stuff so lame."

"What do you mean?" he asked.

"Well, you know *Nubian Rose* is blue chipped, right? We have to uphold certain standards. Miss Benoit won't accept anything less than an Armani suit. I mean, if the mood takes her, she'll sometimes refuse a meeting if the guy's hair ain't right. It's that bad sometimes. She's pretty hard on that kinda stuff."

Howard looked confused. "Does Miss Benoit dislike you and I dating?"

Julie chewed on the question for a moment. "My partner ain't taken on the idea that you and I are dating, no. But that's only because we're covered by *NR*, you know. Rose, that is... Miss Benoit, she don't date people. It's not her bag. She sees people, sometimes. But it's not really dating. I ain't saying there's anything wrong with that, but you know, that's not really my bag either. I mean, I'm one of those people who likes to be in a relationship."

"So what makes me your bag? That is, if I am your bag," he asked.

Julie was momentarily silenced. She swallowed the remainder of her drink. "I guess it was because it was a gradual thing. You didn't force it and neither did I."

"No, I wouldn't dream of that. I think, especially these days, people want things done too quick. Everything has to be fast and *now*. They're crazy, know what I mean? Like, it's a race or something."

"Howard."

"Yeah?"

"Do you want me?"

"Of course I do."

"Have you always wanted me?"

Howard was about to answer but paused. He looked down and inhaled.

"I do remember the time when I first saw you. I must admit, you were the first face I remember at *Nubian Rose*. I did find you very attractive, but I guess at the time I just wanted to make a good impression."

"Howard."

"Yeah?"

She looked down. "Why is this so… good?"

It was a question she'd been desperately trying to refrain from asking, but she couldn't hold it back any longer.

Howard unfolded his napkin. "I just like you. I think you are amazing." He half smiled and looked her in the eye. Genuine.

After a long comfortable silence, their eyes intently taking in each other's, she shook her head. "Are you shitting me? No one says that shit."

"That's it," he pointed. "That's what I love about you, Julie. You ain't, or you don't appear to be, afraid. You remind me of someone who's really strong. I can see a fire in you."

He glared at her now, intensely, as if warming himself upon the fire he implied she had. Julie could feel it glowing within the pit of her stomach, so strong it almost made her feel nauseous.

Their food arrived, the waiter had to make two journeys to their table before noticing the generous tip and realising that they'd left the restaurant.

"Mister Jack, I don't like it when you're late. It makes me think you aren't going to come at all."

Jack had scolded himself after his dressing down from Madge, but that had questionable impact when compared with that of Daniel's forlorn eyes.

"Please forgive me, Danny. It won't happen again. And I know I've said that before, but I mean it this time. I promise."

The boy warmed, a smile returning to his gorgeous face. "Okay, Mister Jack, I believe you."

***

The football they played this time was hilarious. Daniel had fallen to the floor numerous times, immersed in fits of desperate laughter. Jack's skills were getting worse.

"What do you do, Mister Jack?" he asked, eating a dark red apple, white foam dribbling down his chin. "What do you do in the day when I'm at school?"

The bus was almost empty, off-peak time.

"You know what I do, Daniel. You know I'm a policeman."

"I thought you said you was a detective."

"Yeah, well, I am a detective, I…"

"Is it true that it's a detective's job to solve murders?"

"Who told you that, Danny?"

"Joey, in my class. He's my friend. He said he watched a film once and there was a detective who had to find a man who was guilty."

"Well, that's…"

"What does guilty mean, Mister Jack?"

The bus rolled away from Mayfair and Jack checked how many stops were left before they had to alight.

"When somebody has done a naughty thing, or something bad, well, that makes them guilty."

"It means when someone is bad?"

"That's right, Daniel."

"Are you guilty, Mister Jack? I'll bet you aren't."

"You'd make an excellent detective, Daniel. You've just said that I wasn't guilty, and that's correct."

They high-fived and Daniel pressed the buzzer to alert the driver to stop at Regent's Park Zoo.

"Mister Jack?"

"Yes, Daniel?"

"You were only half right... when you said that you wasn't guilty."

Jack glanced back at him. Daniel's eyes, as before, were momentarily saddened. The pain in Jack's back was nothing compared to the stabbing in his heart.

"Daniel, I shall not be late again, okay?"

Unfortunate

David Morgan's colleague had just left. Obviously, remaining anonymous was paramount if they were to see their work become a success. But Morgan longed for some familiarity. He wanted to engage with his colleague about matters unrelated to their investigations. About music, or the latest John Grisham novel. But as he looked at the large case file he had delivered, he knew living like a hermit was essential.

***

He dialled the number and waited almost thirty minutes, until…

"Yes, Morgan, tell me."

"The subject travels extensively. Mostly from JFK to Heathrow, but she flies everywhere, really. I've drawn up and provided you with a partial list of the subject's air activity. Most recently in Europe, she flew to Malpensa airport in Milan, although as far as my surveillance could tell, no homicide was undertaken. The last homicide that took place was a…" David Morgan paused to retrieve a file with the man's name he'd forgotten. "Giovanni Mitchell. A retired solicitor and chartered accountant. The victim's lungs had collapsed. His heart had literally been torn to pieces. Our subject has obviously qualified beyond suspect status. The subject is deemed a perpetrator and a highly dangerous assailant. I need a permit to place the subject in a box."

"Negative, Morgan."

"What the hell do you mean, negative? It's been over a year. All I'm doing is following her around like a damn fool while other people are being killed."

"Negative. The time would be incorrect for you to strike now, Morgan. We appreciate your frustration, we really do."

"There's people fucking dying here. You're telling me I can't save these people?"

"Morgan, we know it's unfortunate. We have others, just like you, working around the clock, to enable you to detain the subject."

***

David Morgan later regretted cursing and throwing his disposable phone against the wall in sheer frustration at his apparent lack of power.

Another phone was supplied.

"Is it safe, Morgan? Are we able to speak to you without the addition of added tantrums?"

"Yeah... apologies."

"Morgan, please help us. Help us to help you. Contrary to what you think, we are on the same side. We need you."

"Yeah, okay."

"Resume your cover. Carry on. We are very happy with what you have done so far. We are even more pleased about these latest strategies."

Redemption

The woman was youngish. Strawberry blonde hair tied in a boyish ponytail and her large eyes, nervous but somehow assured, remained gazing at him. She had been stood on her feet for almost an hour, and with every moment of her being there, Ricky Gomez grew more and more frustrated. Her job – to coax him to join, or merely consider setting foot inside *Everybody's Able*, a shelter for the homeless, a tidy contribution-based centre just outside of Bermondsey, South London.

She was younger than himself, mid-to-late twenties. She wore loose baggy clothing, and pretended to look as though she hadn't minded that Ricky hadn't offered her a seat. She slowly paced the length and breadth of his small prison cell.

"Okay, we'll try it this way, Rick…"

"My name is Ricky."

"Sorry, Ricky. I just wanted to know if you've considered what your next move is?"

Ricky laughed and shook his head. "Moves?" he asked, dejectedly. "I don't have moves. I never did."

"Well, maybe you might want to think about applying some? You know, like a plan? A step forward?"

"Do you know how many times I've had my head kicked in?"

He looked around at the murky surroundings that, even by normal standards, were pretty dire.

"I've been inside these places all my life. They say it starts from childhood. It doesn't matter if I'm in hospital, or inside here, or if I'm living inside a wheelie-bin. You do-gooders will always find me, tell me where I'm going wrong, tell me there's fresh water and a clean bed down at the centre. Well, you can kiss my arse. I ain't going anywhere."

She looked back at Ricky with a sorrowful look on her

face, disappointed, pleading.

He responded. "You can't help me – what did you say your name was again?"

"Sandy, my name is Sandy."

"Sandy. They've sent the best, what makes you any different? Fuck's sake, what is it about me? Why can't you bastards just leave me alone?"

After a long silence, wherein Ricky was waiting arrogantly, Sandy finally answered. "I've seen your file, Ricky. I like you. I was hoping you'd take a chance on me, too."

Sandy looked down at the floor, forlorn, as if what she'd said was now a waste of time, but went on regardless. "I didn't want you to end up like my dad, that's all. He was like you. I couldn't help him. I was too young. I know that's not your fault, and I know you're not buying it, but I wanted you to like me as well."

***

The heroin Ricky Gomez was able to acquire in prison was usually better than that which could be obtained while on the street. Lately, however, someone had been adding more rubble. According to the prison doctor, the effect the diluted junk had on Ricky Gomez was irreversibly catastrophic.

In his desperate pursuit of yet more diamorphine, the prison officials had no choice but to throw him in solitary.

It was after his third unsuccessful suicide attempt, knee-deep in the throes of withdrawal, and sweat and agony, that Ricky actually found himself questioning his willingness to consider what Sandy had said. As he was waiting for the pain to lose its grip, surrounded by the smeared faeces on the wall and the urine on the floor, he felt a strange sensation – redemption. It felt to him, as if from afar, that someone was purposefully stroking his head, somehow telling him it might just be okay. He finally relented unto himself. Ricky Gomez tried his hardest in his attempt to make this new feeling the main theme of his current retreat from drug use, once and for all.

Interval

Zack & Wayne

Oildale, CA
8-10 years ago

The sound pressure level of her rifle was almost 200 decibels. After firing three rounds of the weapon, she unhooked her ears and inserted a pair of plugs for extra protection.

Rose had previously received the majority of her firearm training at a range at Bakersfield. It had boasted more sophisticated amenities and her shooting neighbours had been friendly and encouraging. But following an incident which had prompted locals to urge the City mayor to lead an investigation, Rose had to relocate closer to her Kern County condominium.

When Zack and Wayne entered the gallery behind her, she immediately tensed as she reapplied her defenders.

"Reena!" they both called out loudly. It was the name by which they knew her.

"Reena, you stupid bitch, why do you have to be so damn serious?" Zack asked, popping open a can of *Miller*. "It's just target practice, you ain't no cop."

More men arrived, and after less than four minutes, Rose was virtually surrounded by fifteen of them; a collection of ex-servicemen and failed footballers.

"Is that Reena? Ask the bitch if she wants a beer."

"Nah, she's too serious. Bitch likes poetry and shit."

Rose had complained about the harassment. She had given detailed accounts about Zack Jackson and how he liked to begin firing his rounds whenever she was unprotected in an attempt to deafen her. Every single one of her grievances had been snubbed.

Just then, Rose felt a light hand casually slap her buttocks. The action caused uproarious laughter. She looked down at her three weapons that were laid upon the surface of her desk. Without glancing too far around her, she made attempts to assure herself that nobody was close by, although aware she wasn't alone, and she selected a glock pistol.

"Oh yeah, bitch. You bringing out the big guns, aintcha," Zack said, before slapping her backside again. "Listen, why bother? You and your lame-ass shot."

Rose unclipped the safety and fired all six rounds. Her aim was applied expertly. As with her rifle earlier, the shots were dispatched with precision to all the major locations of her target sheet.

"Wooh!" laughed Wayne, "Scary shit, boys. See? I told you she was a cop or a marine or some type of shit. I'll bet she's working for the damn government as a spy... Shit!"

"Nah, Reena's just one of those fucking students or some such. She ain't shit."

***

After firing her last round with a smaller calibre handgun, Rose began setting her weapons inside her case.

Loud rock music now played from a portable stereo and some of them were shouting and singing.

She slipped on her coat.

"Now, where the hell do you think you're going to, my pretty?" asked Zack.

"Let me pass."

The sound of the range rocketed with laughter and gunfire.

"Fellas, I believe the bitch wants to get on outta here."

"Aw, Zack," said Wayne, reapplying his sweat-stained baseball cap. "You ain't gon' let her pass now, are ya'?"

"Sure I ain't, what do I look like, a damn homo? Nah, I'm gonna get me some fun outta Reena this time."

"Just let me pass," said Rose, her eyes set fast on the exit behind Wayne who lumbered above her while moving closer.

"Okay, if I let you pass, what you gon' do for me and the boys here?"

Everyone whooped and sounded like a pack of hyenas.

"I have to go. Let me pass."

"Bitch, you ain't going nowhere. You's staying right where you are."

"But, Zack, she's the best shot in the county. She'll shoot you in the balls as soon as look at you."

"Hell, I know she's a hot shooter, and I wanna know why."

Zack held her arm, not too tightly, just enough to claim control.

"You think you's better than me, huh? You think just 'cause you's a good shot it makes you better than me and the fellas?"

Zack stood over a metre away from her but his breath was as foul regardless of his proximity. Rose breathed in through her mouth to avoid it's assault.

"I never said I was better than anybody."

"You ain't from round here, are you? Where you from? New York City, I'll guess. Just like you to be like them high and mighty motherfuckers up there in New York City."

Wayne laughed and approached them both. "Zack, Reena, loosen up, you two. Either get a room and fuck, or get the fuck out."

From her left, Zack grabbed her by the shoulder and emptied the remaining contents of his beer over her head.

Everyone laughed.

Rose spluttered, drenched in the stink of cheap ale. "All I want to do is pass."

"Oh, Christ, let the bitch pass, for crying out loud!" someone shouted.

"Well, yeah, just get on outta here. Just remember, you ain't shit."

Carrying her large case, Rose walked quickly towards the exit amidst the sound of triumphant laughter and gunfire.

Her poster, taken of Reena receiving an award for the most marksmanship qualification badges, was unceremoniously snatched from the notice-board and torn to pieces.

Success At Last

"Hello, my name is Detective Inspector Jack Sargent. Could I speak with Miss Rose Benoit, please?"

"This is she. How may I help?"

Jack almost fell backwards off his chair in shock.

"Err, hello, I was wondering if it was possible to arrange a meeting with you. I understand you are quite busy…"

"That would be no trouble to me whatsoever, darling," she cut in. "What sort of time would best suit you, Inspector Jack Sargent?"

Jack chose to abstain from correcting her for her misinterpretation, confused as to why.

"Err, could we say, tomorrow morning, nine?"

"We most certainly could, Inspector."

He had seen many photographs of Rose Benoit by now, glossy, well captured images from the media magazines of New York and Paris. But as he stared at his favourite, the origins of which he was unsure, he felt engaged: a mug-shot – a very striking image in black and white. Her almond eyes pierced through the centre of the portrait. Her hair was slicked back close to her scalp - severe yet elegant. She looked dangerous, in an urban R&B singer kind of way. The image conflicted with her accent.

Jack was mesmerised.

"I was under the impression you were American."

"Oops! I think you have blown my cover, Inspector. Will you hold this against me?"

"I, err, no I…"

As much as he tried, Jack was powerless against his own lack of articulation.

"I am teasing you, Inspector." Jack could hear her smile. "Yes, I am in fact British, born and raised."

"And you live and work in New York?"

"Again, guilty. You really are a most intuitive fellow."

He shuffled in his seat. The pain in his back had subsided. At last, a few moments of comfort.

"Don't you want to know what this is all about, Miss Benoit?"

"I have an inkling of an idea. However, I'm sure you'll make me aware of this tomorrow morning, Jack," she replied. He liked her familiarity, and he liked the way she said his name.

"Oh, okay…"

"Will that be all, Inspector?" she asked. Jack could hear a hint of seduction, a slight flirtatiousness in the tone of her voice as she said the word *Inspector.*

"Err, I noticed when I was put on hold the last few times I called you, there is the song from Carmen." Jack cringed. Within his attempt to prolong the conversation, he could feel himself blush most uncharacteristically.

"Ah, yes. *La Habanera*, a close personal favourite of mine, and Maria too, so, the stellar version, obviously."

"Yes, Maria Callas."

"Jack, you surprise me. You are obviously a cultured fellow. It appears we have much more to discuss tomorrow besides tiresome enquiries."

"Yes."

"So, Inspector Jack Sargent. Tomorrow."

"Yes, tomorrow… I will be seeing you tomorrow." He sniffed out a laugh at his own repeats.

"Good day to you, Inspector." Then dial tone.

Jack was in love for ten seconds, then suddenly got up from his desk and frowned as he saw Ollie from across the office.

"You poor fool," he said, shaking his head before burying it back inside the enormous file he was reading.

Golden State Highway

David Morgan glanced at the clock, the time was almost two in the morning.

"The subject has a record. One sole incident. An occurrence that took place eight years ago. Beat the crap out of some local senator's son in a gas station toilet just off Route 99, daytime, 1pm, approximately. Zackery J Jackson was severely assaulted and cut with glass. The subject supplied a false name to the sheriff's department. Reena Davies, I think. She was held there for the entire time it took Jackson to come out of his coma. Zack Jackson, huge guy from Bakersfield, regained consciousness after a month. He lost the use of his bodily functions. Permanently handicapped. They got him a carer. The Kern County police report read that Jackson refused to press charges. He died almost a year later."

From a bag, he poured the last of the broken *Doritos* down his throat. The dusty remains were bitter and unsatisfying due to both the fact that they were past their sell-by date and due to the lateness of the hour.

Tears Before Midnight

Madge stood in the lobby, her arms folded with a look of disappointment and sadness etched upon her face.

"He's been really patient, Jack," she said. "He's been so good, so accepting, and you've been really bad. You're late again."

Jack frowned. Although the woman was mild mannered, even in the times when she tried her best to assert herself, Jack was ashamed.

"I am sorry." He shook his head. "I really am sorry, Madge. Has he been trouble?"

"He hasn't thrown a tantrum if that's what you mean. But he's cried. He's struggled to keep it together, Jack, and you're really out of order."

"I know."

Madge looked tired and older than her years as she snubbed his reassuring hand. "So, what was it this time?" she asked. "Why so late?"

Jack was reluctant to answer, but for now at least, undisclosed information relating to the *Animal* case mattered less than complying to her question.

"I had a meeting with someone today, but they didn't show up."

"Okay, well, you should have rang us, Jack. It really is irresponsible of you."

"I know."

"So that's it? A meeting?" she said, becoming somewhat more agitated. "Someone didn't show for a meeting and that makes you late? It must have been someone pretty important."

"Madge, calm down, please. It's no one's fault but mine. Today has been horrible, a real awful day. Ollie and me are really up against it. We're getting nowhere, Madge. Everything we do seems like a waste of time."

Her face softened and became sympathetic. "Oh, Jack."

As soon as both their eyes caught each other's they welled in almost perfect syncopation.

Madge fought hard to fend off her desire to embrace him, an almost impossible achievement every time they met, which would break her heart that night, alone, before she retired to her single bed.

"It's not a waste of time, Jack. We have to do what we can." She smiled sadly.

"Thank you."

"Did you have your medical yet?"

"Oh, please don't start on me, Madge. Ollie and Rob are always telling me off about this blasted pain of mine, not you too."

"They'd be right, Jack. You look absolutely knackered. I can tell your back takes a lot out of you."

"Mister Jack?"

They both glanced towards the corridor. Daniel stood by the entrance near the passageway. He yawned and tucked his *Mutant Ninja Turtles* top into his bottoms.

"Daniel."

"Mister Jack, you said you wouldn't be late anymore." Jack openly wept as he knelt before the boy. "Is it because I'm sometimes naughty?"

Madge placed her hands over her mouth, herself now traumatised. Jack grabbed him up in his arms and held him tightly.

"Daniel. Don't ever think that, okay? You mustn't say such things. You have done nothing wrong. It's because *I* was naughty. It's my fault, I've been really bad. Madge has already told me off, okay?"

Jack and Daniel both regained their hold of each other, both hearing Madge sniff back her tears.

"Okay, Mister Jack."

"So, tell me again how old you'll be, Danny?"

"Mister Jack, I'll be ten, you know that already."

"Are you sure? I thought you were eight."

Daniel smiled. His *Stone Roses* haircut was shabby and needed combing and his huge eyes had now ceased crying.

They clutched each other firmly. A tight, silent bond which wiped away all past discord.

The Interview

Though Rose Benoit had ventured down to his crummy office on three occasions in the past eighteen months, her latest visit still took Michael Beavis wholly by surprise.

He had been ceaselessly searching for employment elsewhere ever since that fateful afternoon in the cupboard. In spite of his previous lecherous ways, he thought himself a good manager. He hoped he would be given the opportunity to be appreciated in another environment away from the harassment of Rose Benoit. Yet, given his satisfactory CV and credentials, he couldn't understand why the places he approached were evasive towards any potential future with him.

"Ah, good afternoon, Michael," she said, closing the door behind her.

He sat at his desk and fumbled. "Err, Miss Benoit, hello, what... are..."

"I sincerely hope you don't greet everybody in that manner, boy. You are supposed to speak up, announce the words, darling. Reply to your visitor... make your guest feel welcome and show enthusiasm towards their arrival..."

She proceeded to give him an example: "Good afternoon, Miss Benoit. I trust you are well?"

She prompted him to repeat.

"Good afternoon, Miss Benoit. I trust you are well?"

"That'll need some work, you shall practice in your spare time." Rose slowly walked over and stood behind him, but he remained seated. She placed her hands on his shoulders and began kneading firmly. "It appears you are tense, Michael, is anything the matter?"

"Yes, I'm fine, I... I am just preparing for an applicant," he said finally.

"I see. You are giving an interview?"

"Yes, Miss Benoit."

"Okay, well in that case, and seeing as I'm here, I shall conduct the interview for you. Just to lighten the burden from your shoulders. These tense, nerve-ridden shoulders." She continued to massage, applying him with her expert hands.

"Oh, that really isn't necessary, Miss Benoit."

"Nonsense. Get up," she ordered calmly. He obliged.

"Now, Michael, darling, why don't you be a good boy and show the lady in."

She lowered herself into his rather small chair. The sides of her thighs tightly confined and caught on the arm rests. She scanned the room, instantly getting a feel of the somewhat untidy office in which he worked.

"Are you still there? Call the applicant in here, boy, or I shall throw you out of the window."

Michael dashed to the door.

After a slight delay, Gracie Richards breezed into the office, followed by a frowning Michael.

Rose stood and shook the young woman's hand. "Good afternoon, Miss Richards. I am Miss Benoit, but you may call me Rose."

"Good afternoon, Rose." Gracie's ignorance of the Executive Manager and co-owner of *Nubian Rose* showed just how little homework and research the woman had done. Unless Gracie had something extra special to bring to the temporary secretarial table, the interview would otherwise be dead before it began. However, her big smile was very engaging, Rose had to admit.

"Take a seat, Miss Richards."

Both women sat and Michael loomed awkwardly. "This unfortunate fellow's name is Michael. You probably wouldn't believe it, Miss Richards, but he is actually the head of this department." Gracie looked up and smiled, faintly acknowledging his presence.

"Pleased to meet you, Gracie." He was loud within his attempt to appear friendly. He moved in towards her with his hand.

"Michael, you will address the applicant as Miss Richards," Rose said.

"It's okay, I don't mind. It's okay really."

Although the woman was being polite, she was unable to conceal her reluctance towards Michael as he shook her hand, which was being unceremoniously crushed in the process.

"Whereas, I myself, do mind, Miss Richards. Do you not agree that one should always address someone by their surname, that is, until invited to do otherwise?" Gracie was silent. "Would you like coffee, or perhaps tea, Miss Richards?"

"Oh, yes please. I'll have a coffee. And please, call me Gracie."

"Thank you, Gracie. Michael, two cappuccinos."

Without a word, Michael rushed from the room.

Rose smiled and viewed the pretty woman before her. Her blouse was far too small for her breasts. She looked like an actor in a soft porn movie, or at best, a model from a men's magazine. Rose was immediately drawn to her, already figuring how difficult it would be for Michael Beavis to behave himself while working with her.

Gracie Richards shuffled uncomfortably in her seat and looked away, only for Rose to maintain her gaze, thus making the woman more tense. Michael had left the door open and the office outside was dubiously quiet. Quiet enough for everyone on the floor to hear him in the adjacent kitchen uttering complaints to a sympathetic fellow employee about his employer and his hard-knock life. Rose and Gracie heard all, they both smirked at each other and the uncomfortable atmosphere within the office was averted somewhat.

Rose began perusing and acquainting herself with the applicant by way of her CV. The woman was competent enough, excellent communicational and organisational skills. Standard fare, and well suited to the position she was applying for.

"So, Gracie, what do you think you are able to bring to me? What can you offer our postal despatch department that others might not?"

"Well, I've just come here from a long period at the Post Office. I worked there for six years but I suppose I felt like I was part of the furniture. Not much elevation after a while. I couldn't really progress. I'm good with numbers. And I'm a good people person."

Michael strolled in holding a tray.

"Well, I dare say, Gracie, you do possess suitable criteria. If you don't mind me asking, how old are you? It does not specify here."

"I'm twenty four."

"Gosh, Michael, Miss Richards is twenty four." Rose beamed a huge smile, her eyes still on the applicant. "You sure you can manage that, Michael?"

Michael stammered, literally unable to answer the question.

"Pardon me, Rose, but is my age an issue?"

"Why, of course not, Gracie darling. Give Miss Richards her drink, Michael." He placed the tray on the desk. "Sugar, Gracie?" Rose asked.

"Um, yes, two please."

"Two sugars, Michael. She likes her coffee sweet." He fumbled and mistakenly dropped a lump beside her cup.

"Michael, really. So clumsy. I fear I must apologise, Gracie, Michael can be such an oaf at times. Isn't that correct, Michael?"

"Err, I…"

"Isn't that correct, Michael?"

"Yes."

"Here, allow me." She arose and bent over the desk. Gracie Richards was then presented with the ultimate view of Rose's cleavage which, due to their gravitational pull, almost spilled from the confinement of her black blouse. Michael was flustered and frowned at the scene.

Rose moved closer while she took the spoon and clinked it a few times inside Gracie's cup.

"There," she whispered, "I think that should meet with your satisfaction now, Gracie."

"Thank you." Gracie grew somewhat warmer at the attention she was receiving from Rose.

Rose watched her sip her first mouthful. "How is your coffee, Gracie?"

"It's nice, thank you." She nodded.

"I'm so glad. I simply couldn't bare it if it was unsatisfactory." Still whispering. Still gazing at the unassuming applicant. Her almond eyes holding Gracie's until she was unable to look away. It hadn't taken her long to fall beneath Rose's spell. Michael looked on, his jaw opening wide with a pitiful look on his face. Rose reached over and dabbed at a smudge of froth from the corner of Gracie's mouth with her index finger. Gracie closed her eyes, unsure of the deep feelings that were now swirling inside her head.

"My, my, what a pretty thing you are. Is she not pretty, Michael?"

"Err, yes. I…"

"Would you like to see more of her?"

"Yes."

Michael, and Gracie were both now fully hypnotised.

"Miss Richards, it appears the duty manager is quite taken with you. That's great news, don't you think?"

"It is." Gracie made no secret of her lack of regard for Michael, while thoroughly engrossed within Rose's gaze.

Rose moved in further and, in doing so, knocked over her own coffee. The spillage was nicely contained by the rim of the tray but Rose lowered her breasts into the warm liquid, dousing them.

"Oops," she said ironically. "Look at me, I'm so gauche." She stood, the coffee dripping down her stomach.

"Michael, don't just stand there, get a towel."

"Yes, yes, okay."

He handed it to her as if it was some important document. Rose held her arms up as if in surrender. She stuck her chest out. "Kindly pat dry my breasts, Michael.

Do it properly."

The man roughly rubbed the towel against her navel. Rose caught sight of Gracie's longing eyes. "My breasts, Michael. Dry my breasts. Can't you do anything right?" She quickly snatched the rag from his hands and slapped his face with it, before dabbing it against her ample shiny chest.

"I do apologise, Gracie."

"Please, it's fine," Gracie said, spellbound.

"Gracie. What must you think of me?"

"I think you are amazing," she said, almost silently.

"Why, you are such a sweetheart." Rose placed her hand on the side of Gracie's cheek. "You are not like Michael at all. I do not think he appreciates what I do around here."

A flicker of disgust upon Gracie's face. The thought was unacceptable. She shook her head disapprovingly at the accused.

"I like you, Gracie. I admire your intentions to elevate yourself. I do not think it necessary to delay the results of today's outcome. I speak on behalf of Michael and myself when I say you have been successful in acquiring your desired position."

Evidently excited, her huge smile shone from her face. Rose could tell Gracie was suppressing the urge to engage in a hug. She opened her arms and welcomed her. Rose ran her hand over Gracie's backside, squeezing it for Michael as he looked on despondently. The erection within his pants had evidently leaked, unfortunate that the man had opted to wear pale grey that morning.

"I have to be honest with you now, Gracie, you were selected for a reason." Rose released her. "There is a task I wish for you to undertake for me."

"Okay. I will try."

"It's pretty simple, really."

"That's okay." Gracie nodded.

"Well, it's more along the lines of a favour. I want you to keep watch over our Michael here. Every time he steps out of line. Every time he looks or leers at you, or makes you feel uncomfortable. Every time he engages with any other female members of staff in a negative manner, or in a behaviour that would be considered derogatory or offensive, you are to personally contact me, at once. Do you understand, Gracie?"

Filled with zeal on hearing her mission, Gracie nodded heavily.

"I couldn't bare it if I thought he were to take advantage of you, Gracie. So you just inform me, agreed?"

Gracie smiled again. "Yes, yes of course." A moment passed. Both women stared at each other while Michael lowered his head shamefully towards the floor.

Gracie moved closer and began to whisper. "Rose, I have a question."

"Talk to me, Gracie, you may ask me anything."

"What would you do?"

"What would I do?"

"To Michael? If I was to report something to you, if he did do something. What would you do to him?" she asked.

Rose sniggered. "Gracie, I do not think Michael wants to know that, do you?"

"Maybe, but I'd like to know, though."

"Well," Rose walked over to Michael and placed her hand on top of his head. "If I were to learn that Michael here had been a naughty boy, then you and I would be forced to strip him naked and send him out into the street." Rose smiled and Gracie's eyes lit up.

"Can you imagine that, Gracie, darling? Poor Michael would have no choice but to catch the bus home in nothing but his birthday suit."

Gracie smiled and was receptive, hanging on to every single word that passed through Rose's beautiful lips.

"Take this, for example." Rose grabbed at the remainder of Michael's erection. "This is exactly what I'm talking about, Gracie." Rose slapped it harshly and Michael jerked forward.

"Men are such incompetents," said Gracie, staring at

Michael pitifully, her eyes full of loathing.

"Most are, darling, but not all. Some do as they're told. I like those ones," Rose murmured. "Come Gracie, let us depart." Rose allowed her to exit the office first.

She looked back towards a dejected Michael. "Here, read Miss Richards' details. Make sure you familiarise yourself with her credentials. As from this point onward, Miss Richards is now your line manager."

She slapped the folder onto the desk and left the office.

***

One hour later, Michael was still seated at what was to become Gracie Richards' desk. He had just read the contents of what Rose had handed him before she'd left. Hidden at the rear of Gracie Richard's C.V was a note:

Michael darling...

I am delighted to tell you that I have selected you to attend a training course, enabling you to acquire a high level of ability in hospitality. The duration of the training is one month. By its completion you will receive a grade and paper for your time at the school.

Failure in receiving the grade will see you repeat the training until you achieve success.

Failure in complying to my offer will see you receiving a most unorthodox disciplinary.

I hope you are as excited as I am, Michael.
Good luck.

Yours, Miss Rose Benoit.

JK

"James Kelly." Morgan said.

Silence.

"James Kelly, New York Irish, construction site supervisor. His firm, PICR Engineering, was contracted with New York City council to undertake contracts on four buildings attributed to *Nubian Rose*. Three of these sites are in the Wall Street area. He worked a total of three months before being reported missing. The guy, by all accounts was good at his job, but he did show signs of becoming unhinged, especially in the later stages. Kelly was forty-two at the time he was reported missing. One son, nineteen, lives with Kelly's ex-wife. He's been missing for sixteen weeks."

Silence.

"Request permission to sit here and do absolutely nothing?"

Silence.

Jack's Dream

Rose Benoit had failed to accommodate yet another appointment. Jack, usually impervious, took her rejection like a hammer blow to his face.

Yet, regardless of the knock-back, he had not been sleeping well. Fatigue caused the nausea which finally prompted him to take time off work. For the first time ever in his career.

***

His back pain was agonising the previous night. He had spent restless hours tossing and turning and feverishly glancing at the artex above, unwillingly creating shapes from the horrible swirly ceiling.

Finally, he did manage to sleep. And he dreamt. Jack could not remember the last time he was aware he'd had a dream before. He'd never had vivid dreams as a child for that matter. The dream was still fresh in his head the moment he was released from it as he woke up in a boiling hot sweat. He opened the window and was instantly sick. All night his temperature fluctuated between freezing shivers and red hot fever.

Yet, the disturbing nature of the dream still followed him. It had involved Rose Benoit. He couldn't erase the images from his mind as he tried his hardest to eat some dry toast. An hour or so later and the night was disappearing as the sun began to rise, yet he was still unable to gather his flagging senses.

"*Even rich head and you.*" The words subliminally carved their way into the dream's nightmarish visions. They whispered constant. Rose had sent them to him and they floated around his brain, stubbornly refusing to be forgotten. Resembling dialogue in reverse, but what they symbolised or represented he could not tell.

Normally, Jack Sargent would remain professionally detached. Expertly steering his thoughts and dispelling anything that would otherwise demoralise him or his colleagues. His skill of remaining cool seemed to deteriorate as his dream only reinforced his uncertainty.

After a few hours, he had decided it was time to speak with Miss Rose Benoit in person. Face to face. This time he would not take no for an answer.

***

He found the journey towards Waterloo bridge somewhat surreal. As if it was not him driving the Honda, but something else. His vision was hazy.

Jack barged his way through the huge glass doors of the *Nubian Rose* building for a second time that week.

"Hello sir, my name is Donald, how may I help you?" said Lucy's replacement.

"My name is Detective Inspector Jack Sargent. I need to speak to Miss Rose Benoit."

"Ah, I am sorry, sir. Miss Benoit is away on business at the moment." Donald seemed sympathetic.

"Does she ever come here? Does she actually work in this building?"

"May I suggest that you make an appointment?" Donald said sincerely. Just then Jack's phone buzzed. It was Ollie. He was rejected straight away.

"Donald, I've already made three appointments, and I keep on getting stood up."

"I'm really sorry, sir. Perhaps…"

"Listen, do you know if Miss Benoit will be back later?"

"I don't, unfortunately. I'm so sorry, Inspector." Ollie rang again, only to be rejected a second time.

"Right, okay, I will make an appointment," Jack said.

The four valiums he'd taken for his back were doing nothing. The pain was now making it difficult to walk properly.

"Okay, why not?" Donald said. Jack didn't appreciate the young man's genuine manner.

"Right, you're in luck; I've got a gap on the twenty second of June. That's just over eight weeks' time. Would this be suitable, Detective?"

Jack Sargent was silent. He looked up at the idyllic staircase, grandly situated to the rear of the lobby. By now it almost seemed familiar to him.

"Sir? Are you okay?" Donald left his post and walked around the desk, joining him. He encouraged Jack away from the prying ears of his colleagues, and spoke low so only the two of them could hear. "I'm sorry, sir, but I couldn't help notice, you appear to be a little under the weather. Are you sure you wouldn't want me to do anything to help you? A drink maybe? Or a sit down? Is your back okay?" Donald placed his hand on Jack's shoulder.

"No, it's okay," Jack said, brushing it off.

"Okay sir, do you still wish to go ahead with the appointment?"

Jack slowly made for the exit, ignoring Donald's concern.

"Inspector…"

Jack was out the door.

His mobile rang again. "What?! What the fuck do you want?"

"Jack, where the hell have you been?"

"What is it, Ollie?" he said, almost screaming the question.

"You had better get back to the station."

"Why?"

"She's here, Jack. She's here."

La Grenouilles a la Provençal

As Jack charged his way into the main entrance, he noticed her straight away. The two officers laughed as she concluded her anecdote before kissing her teeth.

She didn't look real. A far cry from the troublesome menace of her mugshot. Her lustrous coiled hair bouncing upon her smooth shoulders like shiny black snakes, Rose Benoit's perfect face melted his insides. Her eyes, exotic, like those of some otherworldly beauty queen, hooked him and burned into his soul. She looked every inch resplendent in a cream mini-skirt suit with a matching fitted overcoat.

Jack felt in awe; the room seemed to stop in time. He blatantly gawked at her, his mouth embarrassingly ajar.

"So, this is the gentleman who obviously catches all the flies," she said, purely for the benefit of her two new friends, who laughed uproariously.

"Yes, that's quite enough," Jack said, glancing at the floor at Rose's feet. She unfolded her legs and raised herself to greet him.

"Good heavens, you look absolutely dreadful, Jack."

"I, err…" he stuttered.

Rose slinked up to him and extended her arm regally, offering him her hand. Jack froze.

"A gentleman is supposed to either take a lady's hand or issue it with a respectful kiss, Inspector."

She spoke with the same syrupy diction he'd remembered, and longed to hear again.

"I'm sorry, Madam."

He asserted himself and took hold of her fingers. He instantly identified a delicious scent of mango as he kissed the top of her hand. Rose glanced at him, her lips parted slightly, her tongue gently touching the corner of her mouth.

Behind them, the officers smiled at each other, laughing

at the Detective's fumbling.

"I'm pleased you came. My name is Detective Inspector Jack Sargent…"

"Jack darling, we need not go into the formalities. I am well aware of who you are. We have spoken before, remember?"

"Of course, Madam. I do remember," he said. Indeed, he remembered the two conversations he'd had with her like he remembered his own birth date; they were purely unforgettable. The photograph of her mugshot was still safely concealed within his wallet. As well as an A4 sized copy taped to the wall in the kitchen of his home.

"Rose. Please, call me Rose."

"Rose," he repeated.

"Listen, Jack. Might we conduct our meeting at a more exclusive surrounding?" she said, and looked around as if only slightly repelled.

"Okay…"

"I am aware this is the most optimal place you have to offer. It's very nice, however, it lacks a certain… *je ne sais quoi*. You understand, don't you, Jack, darling?

"Of course, Rose."

"I know a little place uptown more conducive, and more in-keeping with the standards you and I wish to maintain." Jack was aware Rose was speaking entirely for herself.

"Miss Benoit, I will escort you anywhere you wish," he said enthusiastically. The old Jack Sargent was back.

"Mmm, Inspector." She smiled. "So kind, so charming."

Rose linked his arm as they both turned and departed the station.

***

The interior of Rose's chauffeur-driven BMW had a *new car* smell. She was bombarded with a relentless string of phone calls. Jack noticed she spoke flirtatiously at all times, sometimes talking in German or French. And whenever using words which contained the letter L she would emphasise heavily with her tongue.

The lobby of the large Knightsbridge hotel was ultra-modern. The sitting room seemed exclusive as Jack clocked at least three celebrities in as many minutes. The level of service Rose easily amassed from everyone who'd approached was optimum.

They waited briefly for their table.

"You have a problem with your kidneys, Jack," Rose declared, simply.

Jack had been oblivious, rubbing at his lower back like it had been second nature. He stopped instantly. "Um, I do?"

"Of course. Are you a drinker?"

Jack thought, then shook his head. "Not really, not a heavy drinker."

Rose stepped closer to him and placed the palm of her hand upon the designated area. "You have high blood pressure, Jack," she said, massaging. "Does that hurt?"

"A little."

She was taller, he looked up at her as she placed her free hand on his shoulder. He felt a little uneasy at first as he allowed her to manipulate him. A feeling which soon passed.

"Are you a doctor, too?" he asked.

"I didn't train as a doctor, no." The pain gradually disappeared, allowing him to stand with a lot more ease. "However, I studied medical and neurobiology during a year off in Canada."

"Canada?"

"Province of Quebec, darling. A beautiful part of the world," she declared. "Jack, you should get this seen to. Your high blood pressure is the result of your kidneys inability to dispose of excess fluids."

Jack's forehead curved. "Are you sure? I thought it was just a bad back."

"I am quite positive. You need an operation.

Imminently. It's actually baffling how this information escaped your consultant while receiving your medical examinations, Jack."

***

The restaurant was huge, with décor which was stylishly current. Grey and white. The place was semi-full.

"Good evening, Madam Benoit," the manager said, greeting her. "May I take the opportunity to thank you for coming to see us again today. It is always an honour to receive you. I trust you have had a pleasant day so far?" He pulled her seat out, onto which Rose gracefully lowered herself.

"Mmm, oui. Merci, Giorgio."

"And Sir. Welcome." Giorgio was very pleasant, Jack thought, as he too seated himself. Each were handed a small menu and Giorgio left them a while. They both silently perused their cards.

Jack was astounded at the price tag of some of the featured main courses. He was way out of his depth and he would be the first to admit it.

Giorgio reappeared. "Would you like me to take your requirements, or would you prefer a few moments?"

"Are you ready to eat, Inspector?" Rose smiled at Jack.

"Yes, I think so," he lied.

"Very good. Giorgio darling, get me the *Grenouilles a la Provençal*, if you please."

"May I say, an exquisite choice, Madam. Might I suggest the basil brioche? It really would accompany your choice most expertly." With the use of his hands, Giorgio physically demonstrated the benefits of the bread, while smiling proudly.

"Oui, merci. That sounds divine. I trust your expertise and judgement, Giorgio."

"Very good, and would Madam like a visit from our sommelier?"

"Jack?" she asked.

"Yes?" he answered, obviously not hearing Giorgio's question.

Rose sighed and turned back to the manager. "Not at the moment, just some water."

"Thank you, Madam." Giorgio turned to Jack with the same respectfulness he'd shown to Rose.

"Did Sir manage to see anything on our menu that might appeal?" Jack definitely hadn't, although he was out to impress.

"I think, I will also have the *Grenouilles a la Provençal*, actually." Jack puffed up his chest to assert his swift decisiveness, regardless of his mispronunciation.

Rose smiled, aware he was applying a slight accent. She offered her assistance.

"Jack. Are you sure?"

"Oh yes. Very nice, the err…" he inspected the menu again, just to check "…*Grenouilles a la Provençal*. I actually like this, a lot."

After their food had been ordered, Jack thought to himself that he had only wanted a few moments of her time. This whole affair was overly extravagant for a few standard inquiries.

"So. Inspector," she beamed. "You look slightly bedraggled. Am I to assume you are a little under the weather, in addition to your back problems?"

Jack looked down at his scruffy shirt, his attempt to straighten his tie was beaten as Rose leaned over, expertly tightening the knot and lovingly brushing away any potential creases – he loved her lithe hands.

"I, ahem, thank you, Rose. I wasn't good earlier. I mean, I think I caught a bug or something. But I am feeling okay now," he answered honestly.

"That's splendid. I'm so glad." Rose smiled warmly. "So, Inspector, pray tell, I'm on tenterhooks, why are we here?" Jack fell in love again as she leant her elbows on the table and criss-crossed her fingers, while her eyes gave him their fullest undivided attention.

"Okay, well, the main reason behind my intention to

meet you was because I wished to talk about an incident that took place last June."

"Would this be the same incident that happened near Bank-side?"

"Yes. I understand it happened next to one of your establishments."

"It did, Jack. The last thing one needs while one is conducting a business is a murder next door. I mean, do you realise how unenterprising that is?"

"I could imagine it wasn't the best thing to hear about."

"No, Jack. It wasn't. But there you go, it's passed now. They often say that smoking is bad for one's health."

"Ah, so you were informed of the details?"

"Of course." Rose frowned, as if being privy to unreleased classified information was perfectly normal.

"Well, the majority of the reports were kept dark, especially as far as the media was concerned."

"They tell me that when you chaps found him, he was so badly beaten it took you two days to identify whom the body actually belonged to," she said easily, smiling slightly.

"Well, let's just say he suffered. There was obviously more than one assailant. All the victim's vital means of identification were damaged or blocked in some way."

"What a shame. Well, anyway, like I said, it was most inconvenient at the time, due to the event taking place at such a close proximity to where my operations are based. Although, Jack, I must confess, I always find the details of such matters fascinating."

The enthusiastic glow within Rose's eyes unsettled him.

"How long do you think it took for that poor man to die?"

"I… um, I'm not sure…"

"Oh, come now, Inspector. I am perfectly aware you know the answer to that."

Jack was shocked at her nonchalance towards what had happened, and her ill-concern for the victim.

"Well, we actually made an assumption based on the evidence we received. We thought maybe half an hour."

Rose looked blankly. When she was actually in the process of torturing Jason Bolter it had taken over three hours. She knew she was able to suffocate someone in less than a few minutes, but she dragged out the time, keeping him alive for as long as she could. It was one of her shorter sessions; one of her least imaginative. But she had enjoyed the basic beauty of the process. Before he died, Jason Bolter was made aware of the incident he'd caused which ultimately sealed his fate. She forced him to beg for his life for a sizeable amount of time, and she almost let him live. The asphyxiation came as an afterthought; once the idea came to her, she had to see it through to the bitter end.

"Tell me, Inspector, in all your career, what's the most gruesome murder you ever saw?"

At that moment, their food had arrived. Rose ignored Giorgio and two other waiters who dispatched their food, while her gaze was firmly locked onto Jack.

"Err, well. It, I suppose, let me think…" Jack stuttered. He then thanked Giorgio as the waiter positioned his plate before him.

Rose relented. "Perhaps later, Jack, hmm?"

He nodded in agreement then looked down at his plate for the first time. The frogs' legs, scattered, and so many of them, all engulfed within tomato and garlic sauce and dressed with fresh parsley. Jack didn't wish to eat now, although he kept up the pretence.

"Ah perfect. *Le Grenouilles* are simply divine. The chef always does a marvellous job. I'm so glad you selected likewise; this means we have something else in common aside from our mutual friend Maria!"

Although Jack struggled to keep up, he was still in awe of her, and proceeded to pick up a pair of limbs using his clumsy fingers. Rose, aware all along that he was bluffing his way through the whole thing, cut in again: "Jack, am I to believe you are unacquainted with this dish? You fooled me, didn't you? You naughty thing."

Rose smiled, but her eyes, warning and dangerous, were at odds with her beaming grin.

"I'm sorry, Miss Benoit. I suppose I only wanted to create a good impression."

"Gosh, you're sweet. However, Jack, firstly, I would appreciate it most highly if you would just be yourself. Lose the pretence. Nobody was ever meant to be anyone else but themselves, do you not agree?" Jack nodded. "Secondly. If you don't start calling me by my first name, I'm afraid I'll have no other choice but to spank you. Spank you hard. Am I making myself perfectly clear, Inspector?"

Jack was both aroused and scared at the same time. His heart swelled. "Yes, I'm sorry."

She smiled. "Relax, Jack darling, for I am merely teasing you."

Jack remained unsmiling as news travelled slow.

"Unless... you actually wish to be spanked?"

She leaned in and looked deeper, silently questioning him. Jack quickly turned crimson as he tried to avoid her cool eyes. The truth was, the thought of being spanked by Rose Benoit did appeal to him. More unexpected truths muscled their way into his head, whether he liked them there or not.

"Anyway, Jack, my sweet, I think we digress. Follow my lead. I do not think anyone will notice if you pay close attention." Rose daintily took hold of her cutlery with thumb and forefinger and gently sliced a piece of meat, fixed it with her fork and placed it on to her tongue. Seductively eyeing Jack she closed her lips and swallowed.

"Gorgeous!" she whispered breathlessly. "Try some, Jack. To try is to love."

She pierced another piece of meat with her fork and offered it to Jack, who took the bait. "Nice?"

He munched on the food and remembered what she told him about being honest.

"It's okay, it's not the usual type of thing I like to eat. But it tastes better than I thought."

Due to his assertiveness, things became easier. Maria Callas was the next topic of conversation, obviously.

"I remember just falling in love with her unconventionality. It is oft said by all those so-called experts that her voice wasn't universally perfect. Maybe Renata Tebaldi was the more talented soprano. She was obviously a spinto-lyrico and her delivery was dynamite, of course. But Maria... wow, the wide range she commanded. And she was so beautiful. I still have a total lady crush on her. To me, it's more about style, I suppose. The woman oozed the stuff... and tell me, Jack, what could be better in this world than a woman with style?"

Jack looked on, dumbfounded. He was out of his depth yet again. He himself had owned a couple of Maria Callas CDs. Rose however, seemed to be an expert on the entire genre.

All evening Jack still hadn't asked about the cigarette. Why was he allowing the sole purpose of their meeting to become secondary? He became confused.

"Jack, earlier I asked you a question. Your most terrible case? Tell me." She sipped her water.

"Well if you must know, it was something that happened maybe five, six years ago. But I'm not sure it's the sort of thing you'd want to talk about at a dinner table."

"Why on earth not?" she asked as she beckoned a waiter over. "Who said? I asked you the question, remember? 'Tis I who wishes to know, Jack." The waiter swiftly appeared at their table. "Darling, a bottle of Bordeaux, if you please."

"Of course, Miss Benoit." The waiter stepped away and Rose was silent, boring a hole into Jack as she waited for him to answer.

Placing his knife and fork on his plate, Jack shifted uncomfortably before he finally spilled.

"We found a guy. His legs had been smashed to pieces with a sledge hammer." Rose was transfixed. She sat back and prompted him to continue.

"Yes. So, it appeared he was still alive and was dragged and lifted onto a table where..." He paused, placing his hand over his mouth.

"Inspector. Is anything the matter?" Just then, the Sommelier came over with the bottle.

"Madam. Would you like me to pour?" Rose waved at him to do so and he issued fresh glasses. He poured a small amount for Rose.

"You may continue, Jack," she ordered, while inspecting the liquid in her glass.

"Sorry, yes, they er... Yes, on the table, where someone had cut his arms off and... I'm sorry I cannot say much more about this. Can we speak about something else?"

Rose looked regretful, casting her eyes sadly downwards as she lifted the glass to her lips. "Inspector, as you wish," she said sadly.

Her words made him feel like the loneliest man on earth. Jack couldn't stand it.

"They found him with his arms amputated and he was tied to the ceiling by his intestines. His body was hanging two feet above the surface of the table. The man was still alive when we found him. Please excuse me." Jack bolted up out of his seat, dropped his napkin on his uneaten frogs legs and walked to the men's restroom.

Rose smiled warmly. She remembered fondly the time when she had hung the man up by the lighting fixture. The victim, political backbencher Douglas Rossiter, was responsible for the deaths of six boys. The homeless victims were all aged between nine and eleven when he and three other politicians abused them in the late nineteen eighties. Rose had thought that the manner with which he was dealt was befitting.

Maybe five or ten minutes had passed before Jack returned. The table was empty.

He sat, feeling miserable. Forlornly, he took out his phone, two missed calls from Ollie.

Just then, Giorgio appeared. "Inspector Sargent? Miss Benoit has asked me to tell you that she just had to step out for a moment. She asked me to apologise, and says she will be returning presently."

"Thank you," Jack could breathe again. He resented the forceful manner she had demonstrated, and although he still hadn't asked her about the cigarette, he admitted to himself, he was fascinated by Rose Benoit. Why was she so enthusiastic about the details of degradation? It was difficult for him to tell if her interest in the macabre was darkly unhealthy or just esoteric whimsy. Yet she had intrigued him. It felt like she was weaving a web around his senses.

She re-entered the restaurant and slowly walked over to their table with all the poise of a catwalk model.

"Darling, important call. Did Giorgio apologise on my behalf?" Rose asked, as a passing waiter seated her.

"It's okay."

Jack thought of a question for her and was about to ask but Rose beat him to the finish line.

"Well Jack, that was a pretty gruesome tale. Tell me, did you ever catch the assailants?"

"We did. There were three guys. Gangster types, you know. They each got two life sentences."

Rose inwardly laughed to herself.

"Gosh, Jack, you're so brave. I must tell you that I always imagined myself in a police uniform. I would've liked to have been a detective." She sipped her chosen red and exhaled satisfyingly after swallowing. Jack could take no more and let himself loose again.

"I think you'd look amazing in a police uniform." He looked down as soon as he uttered the words.

"Jack, look at me," she coolly ordered. When he lifted up his head she continued. "That's so sweet of you." Her voice was just above a whisper. "Tell me, Jack darling, are you flirting with me?" Jack didn't know where to put himself, but she held him again with her unavoidable eyes, not letting him go for one second.

"Please forgive me, Miss Benoit…"

"Rose."

"Sorry, Rose, please forgive me…"

"I asked you a question, Jack. Answer it please." She

sipped again, her eyes closed in satisfaction while she savoured the taste.

"I, err, wasn't aware I was flirting. I was paying you a compliment. I am truly sorry if I have offended you."

"You really are very sweet. I like you, Jack." She tilted her head, surveying him. "Tell me, are you married?"

"No Madam, I am divorced."

"Aw, poor Jack. How long?"

"It's coming up to fourteen years now. I don't mind, we were too young. It's something I've become very used to, being on my own, I mean."

"Me too, actually. I prefer my own space. I firmly believe other people only serve to clutter your life, as well as your house."

"Yes, that's true."

"But what if the right person might come along? What are we to do then, Jack?"

"I don't think I'd like to be in a relationship now. People have changed since I was young. Attitudes have changed. Women seem different nowadays."

"Inspector, do not rule out the chance of love. What's wrong with women nowadays anyway?"

"I don't know. Women seem too much for me to handle. I remember dating a woman about three years ago. It didn't work out. She was too, err…"

"Dominant?" Rose offered.

"Yes, dominant. I personally preferred it when men were men and women were women." Jack looked around. He was becoming hungry now.

"I hear what you're saying, Jack. But I've always adored a woman with balls."

"Perhaps I'm too old."

"Nonsense, darling."

"Rose, may I ask you a question?"

"You may. Unless it's not the one about what I was doing the night Javed Iqbal died."

Jack laughed, only half understanding the joke.

"I just wanted to ask you… er…"

"About the cigarette filter."

"Yes. How did you know I was going to ask…"

"Jack, it's a perfectly good question. It's true, the ash that was found in and around the victim's body, belonged to the same cigarettes as the filter that was found outside the building. It's also true that the orders that are sometimes placed through our finance departments do include that particular brand of cigarette. I do not smoke very often but when I do, I personally smoke these cigarettes. I also use an exquisitely long cigarette holder, but that is just personal preference, Jack, darling."

"Okay…"

"However, as you'll appreciate, and as you'll already be aware, the dates attributed with the filter, and the ash and when the murder took place, are all conducive, and correspond with each other. The centre date was the twelfth of July that year. Yours truly was working in New York at that time, I'd been there for two months prior to the date and a further month afterwards."

Jack fell in love again. *She is so good*, he thought. All evening skirting around the issue. He wasn't coming for her with the accusation, only a random enquiry. Rose had told the tale so convincingly, she might as well have been on the stand in a magistrates court. She wasn't like anyone else he'd ever known in all his fifty one years. Rose Benoit was dripping with class as far as Jack Sargent was concerned. He sat there catching flies again.

"Jack, darling. You weren't hungry at all were you?" She looked disappointed.

"I'm really sorry, Rose. I did eat a few. And I ate all my brioche, look!" He held up the empty plate.

"You fancy a drink, Jack?"

"I don't really drink a lot. Well I used to, but… No, not at the moment."

"I was going to suggest drinking elsewhere, Jack."

At first, Jack was doubtful of doing anything other than going back to his apartment. But then, he saw her, that look, the eyes, her lips slightly opened.

"Okay, I would like a drink, maybe loosen up. I think I need it, Rose."

"Yes, Jack. I think you do."

Luvina

"You'll have to forgive me for the sharpness I subjected you to earlier, Jack."

"It wasn't a problem, really."

"Of course it was. You left the table amidst a whirlwind of distress. It was plain to see I'd upset you."

She saw he had no answer. "Truth be told, it's me, Jack. I always seem to push people. On the other hand, I do not consider this to be any kind of flaw in my character. I am just fully aware it makes certain people uncomfortable."

"Do you like to push people, Rose?" he asked.

"Of course. How is anyone able to prove themselves? How is a man able to show his strength? If that man is not tested, Jack?" Jack was silent, she went on. "Once I detect skill and ability and dedication in someone, only then will they receive my appreciation. It is unfortunate, and I will admit this to you, but if I detect weakness in someone, I tend to make things all the more difficult for them. I cannot help this, I'm afraid."

Her eyes owned him, holding him up. He was aware she was referring to him. He was powerless, unable to do anything about it.

Rose read him correctly. "On the other hand, Jack, I am aware that sometimes I can be a little unreasonable. I *do* make exceptions. Sometimes." She smiled at him, her eyes warming, finally.

Their next stop was Soho, and in a short while they were downstairs in a club that played the kind of music Jack didn't think Rose would have liked, knowing she was a classical connoisseur.

They had been seated for all of five minutes when *For The Love Of Money* by The O'Jays began. Rose jumped up. "Jack, get on your feet, you must dance to this with me."

"Oh, no, seriously, Rose, I can't dance…"

She took his hands, prompting him to stand. Rose proceeded to move. Jack was fixed with awe as he saw how fluent and graceful she moved, even at this early stage. He hated himself as he attempted to do likewise. It took a few moments before Rose noticed Jack's poor attempts. It was true what he'd said; he really was atrocious. Rose laughed and pushed him back to his seat. She smiled before really displaying her abilities. Jack was transfixed, enraptured by her movements as her shoulders fell in time with her hips and posterior.

After a couple more songs, both of which were similar, Rose came back over and joined him.

"You are a very good dancer."

"Why, thank you, Jack. I wish I could say the same about you."

"I'm sorry. I'm crap, I know. Two left feet."

"Two left feet? Two left everything, darling! I wasn't sure what you were trying to do; it was as if you were in the throes of some kind of mild attack."

Jack laughed. "You thought I was bad today, you should have seen me when I was twenty."

"I can only imagine what a scoundrel you were back then, Jack darling."

"Would you like a drink, Rose?"

"Mmm, get me a bottle of something. Make sure it's cold."

After a while they were once again deep in conversation. Rose wrapped her arm around his neck. People stared. They were both enjoying their bottled lemon vodkas.

"Well, I always could dance. I take after my mother. We'd always be dancing. A few years ago I starred in a couple of music videos, dancing, R&B stuff. Jamaican things. Hip-Hop, you know? It was easy. If you look at some of those videos made about seven, eight years ago, chances are you'd probably see me in the background shaking my tush."

Rose smiled rudely, as if recalling some salacious memory from her past.

In his attempts to steer their conversations from further risqué issues, Jack asked. "Do you see your mother often? I guess it's probably hard, seeing as you're so busy."

Rose looked at him and suddenly became aware of something. Something hidden away in the back of her mind. She tried to encourage it to come to the front. It was like something that was trapped in a door, unable to come closer and reveal itself in its entirety.

"My mother passed away a long time ago." It was her usual answer. The reply she'd always tell to people before she changed the subject.

"Please forgive me. I didn't know." Jack looked down to the floor.

"It's quite all right, darling." She eyed him, somewhat earnestly. He was oblivious of her inspection.

The women at the next table were lively. There were four in total and, after a short time, Rose and Jack could hear the majority of their conversations. Jack assumed they were off-duty hookers, while Rose knew them as professional dancers.

She quickly acted on impulse. "Hey Jack, what would you say to a lap dance?"

"Um, no." Jack laughed nervously. "Of course not."

"Oh, come on, it'll be fun."

"I've never had a lap dance before," he said seriously, shaking his head.

"Well. Guess what… I want a lap dance. And you're going to have one as well. You're so selfish, that's your trouble, Jack," she said, grinning as she stood.

"Please don't, Rose," he said desperately. "I wouldn't know what to do."

She bent herself and leaned over him. He could feel her lips touch his ear as she whispered. "Jack. My baby. You will know what to do. They say it's like riding a bicycle."

Rose walked over to the four women.

Jack glanced around nervously, then placed his head in

his hands. When next he looked up, he saw Rose dancing towards him, hand in hand with one of the women.

"Darling, meet Luvina. Luvina wishes to give us both something extra special."

Luvina was slightly shorter than Rose. She was Latino with dark hair and nice skin. Underneath her faux fur, she wore stockings and suspenders. Jack was forced to admit, in spite of his reluctance, that Rose had chosen the most attractive of the four women.

He was encouraged to take the woman's hand as they greeted each other. Rose resumed her spot and made herself comfortable beside Jack as they both looked up at Luvina.

The current song was faded down and *Candy* by Cameo began to play. As the bass kicked in, Luvina sprung into action and, like Rose earlier, started rolling her hips and belly in time to the music. She stepped up to Rose and straddled her knee, bending over her. Rose, looking up at the girl, eyeing her lustfully, placed her hands on her legs as she almost sat on her lap. Rose then produced a fifty note and placed it in the string of her thong at her hip. Jack looked on, he began to feel hot, his temperature rising rapidly. He covered his groin and his expanding growth. Rose was now holding Luvina's backside as her bronze gyrating navel was level with her face. She slowly pressed her lips against the area just above Luvina's crotch and licked at a barbed wire tattoo that surrounded Luvina's belly button. Jack's blood pressure threatened to erupt through the roof, his heart missing several beats.

After she'd finished with Rose, she moved on to Jack, stepping over him. He could feel Rose beside him, her gaze melting the side of his head. He looked up and saw Luvina lick her lips as she touched her breasts and stroked her stomach seductively. She proceeded to lower herself in between Jack's legs as she came close to his groin. She then raised herself up again, slowly bending over him. Just then, Rose moved in closer and placed her leg over Jack's, almost sitting on him. Physically and mentally he was pushed to his very limit. He felt his fluttering heart beat heavily against his ribs, threatening to break through. He became unable to conceal his full erection as the two women writhed on him.

"Put this somewhere." Rose whispered in his ear and placed another fifty in his sweaty palm. Luvina stepped in closer with her right hip almost touching his chest, encouraging him to make the payment. His hands trembled as he attempted to place the note into the other side of her thong clumsily. However, he fumbled and lost his hold of the money. The note was about to fall to the floor, Rose adjusted it so it was safely attached and held by the strap at Luvina's waist.

Jack knew everyone in the club was staring. He couldn't afford to be concerned. Rose gently spanked Luvina's backside fondly when it was time for her to go.

"Luvina! Mmm, mmm…" Her tone was orgasmic. "A beautiful girl, wouldn't you agree, Jack?"

"She was…" he said, reluctantly.

"But?"

"She wasn't half the woman you are." He looked down.

"There you go again. You are so sweet, Inspector. However, I think the man doth protest too much. I was able to see how much you liked Luvina by the size of *this* thing."

She placed her whole hand around his still erect penis, giving it a shake before releasing it again. Jack recoiled in embarrassment.

Cats & Dogs

The message Ollie Travis left in Jack's voice-mail bordered on frantic.

"Jack, I called at the office this evening, then tried you at yours. I've been ringing and ringing you all night. The lady at New Horizons... Madge? She's been trying to get hold of you too. She rang me. It's Daniel, Jack, something has happened. Where the hell are you? Listen, when you get this message, no matter what time... ring me straight away."

***

On to their next destination. The place was packed to the rafters. Jack glanced over the sea of bodies. Naked, leather-clad and encased in chains and unabashed dissipation. Men and women writhing, entwined with one another. One huge man was dressed as a scarlet octopus, surrounded by sacrilegious nuns and naked men entangling themselves within his rubber tentacles, sucking on them.

Jack fought against the urge to frown. The whole place seemed like a celebration of ugly indulgence. The people flaunted themselves, being rained upon by blatant carnal sin that dripped everywhere. He felt resentful. He began to perspire.

Rose clutched his hand, an action which, in spite of his surroundings, calmed his nerves.

The music was loud, pulsating through his ears and brain. She grabbed the side of his face and spoke loudly inside his ear, "You are nervous. Naturally. But fear not, Jack darling, no one here wishes to hurt you... Lest of course you ask them to do so."

He could still hear that honey in her voice, and it oozed into his brain.

"You'll be fine, my dear."

He wanted to believe her. He looked at her as they walked through the writhing pit of bodies. Her attitude and poise, even her walk, was perfection. The way she engaged with others, her smile. Those teeth!

Jack submitted. He was now literally just a huge walking erection for her.

"You love me, Jack," she said in his ear. Did he imagine that? He thought he'd heard wrong. He thought about begging her pardon. He could hardly believe she had said the words. If they *were* the words she'd said.

He nodded.

Jack was introduced as *a friend*, although, he felt like he was imposing, uninvited, as if his presence was offensive to them all as he walked through the main dance floor. Everyone seemed to know her. Women approached her, and Jack was shocked at how Rose fondled and kissed them playfully.

At last, stepping away from the frivolity, they entered through a set of double doors and once inside the cacophonous music was immediately muted as she closed them.

The room was large, and if Jack was honest, resembled that of a James Bond villain's study - Shiny black snakeskin, ceiling and floor.

"Welcome to my office, Jack."

"Your office?" he frowned. "You work here?"

"I own here, darling. Welcome to *Erotique*," she announced, "an establishment for the more discerning fetishist."

Jack nodded, and frowned, and looked at the floor.

"Right, Rothschild, Chateau Lafite," she announced.

Once Jack was seated, he began to inspect his surroundings. There was a one-sided mirror on the far wall that provided Rose with the ultimate view out on the dancefloor.

"You are now inside the ship's belly, darling. I must confess, Rose is the world's biggest ever voyeur."

"I wasn't aware you were, um… into this sort of thing."

"Why would you be, Jack? After all, we have only just met. Fear not, though, we shall go and play with them presently."

This is what scared Jack the most. The ever-looming notion to immerse himself back out to that debauched place was, in his mind, akin to the threat of death.

"I have many interests, Jack. I've always been an admirer of the subversive. Matters of the heart is another interest. Matters of love and hate. Life and death."

"Death?" he asked, his right eye ticking a little.

"Oui. Death." she said the word with passion, as if it represented a work of art. "Death is just as valid a subject as life, dear. We should all approach death in a way that should only contribute to our own success in life."

Jack's brain turned at the irregular words he was hearing. "Death, I think, isn't something to be trifled with, Rose. Death is the end of everything, I believe, and it's inevitable."

"How do you know this? To make such an assumption is tantamount to claiming one knows the secrets of the universe. Tell me, Jack, are you privy to something that the rest of us are not?"

"I'm not saying that, I did not mean that. I'm sorry, listen, I didn't come here to talk to you about death."

"That's a pity, Jack."

An intense urge rocketed through him. Anything to move the conversation elsewhere.

"Do you like pets, Rose?"

Rose's eyes widened. "Gosh, Jack, what an appropriate question," she said, smiling again. She stood and tilted her seat back. "How absolutely apt of you."

"What makes you say that, Rose?"

"Because, dear, I simply adore pets."

Jack hadn't noticed before. Only now was he aware that her seat was almost throne-like. Iron, and high-backed. It framed her expertly and made her look like an evil empress in some nineteen seventies Gothic horror. Its base was larger than average and had a black leather cushion that covered the seat. The armrests also had leather cushioning.

Rose moved her throne backward, then pinched a small key from a drawer in her desk.

"I have many pets, Jack," she said as she inserted the key into the side of the throne. It clicked and Rose then slowly lifted the top of the base upward with her little finger.

"You see, Jack, we, as humans, feel almost compelled to keep animals with us. I've studied such things."

Worried, Jack looked over, craning his neck to see if he could catch a glimpse without having to stand.

"It's an age-old process. Humans, by their nature, require their pets to serve them. To be, at all times subservient to their requirements. A well-trained pet is considered a shining example of the master's authority, their good behaviour a testament to their owner's expert training."

Completely off guard, Jack hadn't guessed, nor could comprehend the shameful coincidence of his modest query.

"That's correct, Jack dear. Come. Look upon my pet."

The entire contents of the seat was filled with a pile of fur. The object inside breathed. Jack couldn't make sense of what position it lay.

"Otis, dear. Out," she called softly. Instantly the furry contents sprang to life. Jack had to squint to make out the materialisation of a man, evidently dressed in what appeared to be an all-in-one dog costume.

"Jack, meet Otis. Come on out, Otis."

Otis struggled at first, evidently disoriented due to his incarceration, and with no assistance from Rose, he almost toppled out of the enclosure. However, he remained steady in his attempts to step down from the seat.

"Rose, how long has he been in there?" Jack asked, gravity in his voice.

"I wouldn't guess more than a day or two."

"And it's his choice to be closed in there, is it?"

Otis was now free of his former boxed prison and

began to act more enthusiastically, slowly displaying the characteristics of the animal he was dressed as. Jack heard the man panting from within his dog head mask. Now on all fours, Otis began to flit in and out Rose's legs.

"He's happy, Jack, don't you see? I think he's excited to see his master has a guest."

"Rose, I really don't think I should be here. I feel as though I'm intruding."

"Nonsense, darling. Look, he likes you."

Otis ambled up to where Jack was sat, and cautiously at first, began to sniff the floor close to his feet.

"Stroke him, Jack," she trilled.

"Rose, I…"

"Jack, my guest, stroke Otis."

Rose's voice was so commanding, yet so convincing. He'd attended seminars years before that illustrated the powers of speech and its virtues. Lessons of how to combat persuasion that might otherwise serve to surrender one's own power and control.

At the time, he'd passed with distinctions and flying colours. However, only now, as he stroked the top of Otis' head, did he realise that he had no problem with his own admission of defeat and failure.

"That's right, Jack, baby, stroke him. Stroke him for Rose."

Rose attached a chain to Otis' collar and proceeded to walk him around the office.

"Walkies!"

Jack, dismayed, looked down towards the floor.

***

It was purely by impulse, whilst spending almost thirty minutes queueing in the bar area, trying his best to ward off propositions from inquisitive kinky Minnie Mouses and Darth Vaders, he decided to veer off and take a permanent detour.

It hadn't been Rose Benoit that had encouraged his

decision to escape *Erotique*. She was everything to him: beautiful beyond doubt, enigmatic, a leader. It was himself he was running from. And while being engaged or probed by her, he felt inadequate, incapable of accepting his own ineptitude.

Jack hoped that, judging by her astute ability to read into him, she would be able to fathom it was indeed entirely down to his own insecurity that he'd felt the need to leave.

Even the restrooms were tidy and sparse. They seemed sublime, mellow even, with a zesty lemon freshness. Music could be heard only faintly now. Jack became increasingly frantic despite the relaxing climate inside the gentlemen's toilets. (Or *Tenors*. Ladies were *Sopranos*. There was also a *Slaves* facility.)

He searched desperately, glancing around for a simple exit, a window, a door, a gap.

Nothing.

He thought about dashing through the main exit, but the idea of subjecting himself yet again to the bizarre mass of rubber and chains was now inconceivable.

Were there really people like this? People who liked being abused? People who liked to abuse others? He thought to himself. The establishment, together with its inhabitants, seemed a million miles away from his sensible shoes and good intentions. Its opposition to anything nice and decent seemed obstinate.

Adjacent to a small unlocked store cupboard, Jack located a passage which lead to an office-like room. Through a small window he could see the night lights illuminating, beyond to freedom. He blew out in relief. He dashed desperately towards it, knocking over a tower of small but heavy boxes and flattened cardboard which was leant up against the wall. He tripped, and as he gathered himself, some of the boxes smashed to the floor, their glass contents making a colossal racket.

The music was loud, conveniently allowing Jack Sargent to continue unheard. Using a chair, he climbed up and was dismayed at the size of the gap. He opened the window as far as it could go and tried his best in placing both his arms and his head through. Seemingly unable to hoist himself through the window, Jack decided on a change of tactic. He kicked his leg up as far as it could reach to see if he could go feet first. Unsuccessful.

Once again he passed his upper half through. With sheer bloodymindedness, he managed to scrape his top half through at last.

He was stuck. His arms reached out towards the floor below while his legs thrashed around pathetically in the room behind him. His stomach hurt as he hung suspended in the window. He winced with pain and strained as hard as he could. He ignored the pain in his side and in his back. Now wasn't the time to feel sorry for himself, to feel regretful that he still hadn't received medical examinations that had been accumulating for years.

He groaned in agony before finally loosening himself free, taking the plunge whilst risking actual bodily harm, just to avoid going back into the building.

The fall was quick. He landed on his shoulder and elbow, which shielded his ribs and body mass. He yelled – the pain in his shoulder was tremendous. The effort it took just to turn himself on his back was beyond description.

Jack almost fainted, but finally, he'd released himself from the evil inside to the freedom of the rear courtyard.

"I must say, Jack darling, I am most displeased."

Jack scrunched up his face. The need to look up was pointless, but he did so in any case. Rose Benoit had changed. A black lacy fascinator perched at an angle on the side of her head and a tightly fitting rubber dress enticed Jack's heart to travel up to the back of his throat. Once again he felt nauseous.

Otis, her so-called *pet* stood at her side, struggling to raise the umbrella high enough, shielding her from the rain, which was now bucketing. With her fingertips, Rose still held the empty glass.

"How long does Rose have to wait, Jack?" she asked,

softly. "All this trouble just to avoid buying me a drink?"

"No. It wasn't like that."

With all his strength, he raised himself to his feet and brushed himself down while his untidy jacket was quickly drenched.

"I, I think I got lost…" It was the only thing his absent head offered. He recoiled at the comment.

"Save it, Jack," she said, striding towards him. "Come. We haven't finished with you yet."

She led him back inside.

***

Rose finally received the strawberry Martini she'd requested of Jack prior to his escape attempt.

He followed her as she walked nonchalantly through another set of double doors.

"I think you misunderstand, Jack," she said. "This is a new experience for you, I'll grant that; a cultural shock to your senses. But it is your silly inhibitions that permit you from embracing me, and what I stand for. Your shy barriers are limiting your sensibilities, darling."

"I'm sorry, Rose. It's just… I never considered any of this." He tried to be as assertive as he possibly could, to reason with her. "All of this isn't really me, you know what I mean?"

"Not really," she said simply. "I wish to take a hold of your reluctance. I want to rip it apart. There is always a little deviance in everyone, Jack. One simply needs to entice it from within."

Another comment that worried him, words that only dispirited him all the more. By this time they were in a large room, empty. Music played, but not too loud.

"You see, Jack, I find myself in the fortuitous position of living out my fantasies, converting them into real life. It is simply wonderful, and truly quite astounding, some of the strange and beautiful things that have taken place inside this room." Rose spoke in the same way a real estate agent would try to sell a property.

"You shall proceed in tearing down your walls, Jack darling. And I shall assist."

"Err, I really don't know what you have planned, Rose, but I think it's time I left."

"Nonsense."

"Rose, it really is getting late. I think I've been awake for two days."

He heard his own words echo around the room and inside his head. He made a poor attempt to check his watch. The time was approaching 2am.

Then blackness.

***

It must have been the music that roused him. He glanced around, for a few woolly moments he was unaware of his location. Until he saw Rose, smiling.

"Welcome back, darling."

He looked around. Otis was kneeling, chained to a short post. Whereas earlier, in Rose's office, the man seemed stupidly enthusiastic of his humiliation, playfully revelling in Rose's taunts and abuse, now Otis seemed withdrawn and sluggish, reluctant and waiting.

The door to the room opened once again. One by one they filed in: three, four… A total of ten women, all provocatively dressed in figure-hugging black rubber, their faces concealed beneath cat-woman-style masks. Rejects from the dance floor earlier.

They all began to rub against each other while dancing to the hypnotic music. Otis looked about anxiously. Jack took in the scene before him. He began to feel the ripeness of nausea in his stomach once again.

"I know you are rhythmically challenged, Jack darling. I chose something slower for you to move to. Dance, dear. Dance with my felines." Rose purred, joining the other women. She began to move her body provocatively.

One of them swayed towards him and took his hands.

He was led around, as if enticed to begin dancing.

"Rose," Jack called, wearily. "Please, I must leave now."

"You shall do no such thing, Jack darling. You'll stay and dance with my felines."

Jack shook his head, trying his best to fend off the bizarre assault. But it was her voice, calm and convincing. She sang the words to him, as if within a lullaby. Jack found himself yielding, having no choice but to do exactly what Rose Benoit had requested.

Again, he moved his body with no skill. His shoulder broken, the pain soared through him.

Rose smiled. Jack's dancing partner clasped his hands, and although she was gentle, every movement she administered was pure agony.

Rose hung nearby, entwined within the arms of her own cat-woman.

"Good boy," she trilled. "I think you are finally getting the hang of it."

The music got louder, and everyone moved a little more forcefully. Jack noticed Otis seemed more agitated. He motioned toward him. "Rose... I think your... your dog man... Otis, he..."

"If you kiss her claws, she might give you a surprise," she said, cutting him off, destroying Jack's good intentions.

"Rose, I think I've had enough."

"Kiss her claws, Jack darling."

"Rose, please."

"Jack. You are irritating me. Please do not irritate me, baby," she said, softly.

He looked into the face of the woman he was engaged with. In spite of her mask, it was evident the woman had beautiful eyes. They hypnotised him as she offered her hand. He briefly pecked at her fingers.

Rose tutted. "That won't do at all, Jack darling. You'd be extremely lucky to receive anything for that. Try it again, Jack, and when I say kiss them, really kiss them: suck them, stick your whole mouth around them. Make love to her claws, Jack darling."

Rose lifted her head to allow her cat-woman to nuzzle and kiss her neck.

Jack released a wail of anguish. He looked up at his partner once again, her beautiful eyes danced and laughed at his frustration.

Rose Benoit was at last satisfied. The kiss he issued was far more convincing. His feline placed her long claws around his crotch, she handled it expertly, making it grow.

"Jack, my sweet, you've arrived," Rose announced, her voice gleeful. "Welcome, darling."

Jack was pleased, encouraged by her words. More caution was thrown to the wind as he let his body wind down a few more notches.

He glanced over, watching as Rose rubbed her groin against her cat-woman's thighs. Her posterior slowly grinding.

Jack's erection was so big it began to chafe. His feline wasted no time in her attempt to stimulate him. His concern for Otis disappeared as his feline encouraged him to hold back, thus prolonging the pleasure she was creating.

One of the felines slowly walked towards Otis. She placed her hand on his head and began to stroke. Slowly, one by one, the others followed, and soon enough, they had him surrounded. Trapped and looking more anxious than ever, he attempted to pull away, his chain yanking on the post.

From behind, Rose gently took Jack's hand and cut him a reassuring glance. "This, unfortunately, is where we say goodbye, Jack, darling."

"What? Why?"

"Our time here has at last come to an end."

"But… why do *we* have to go? What are they going to do?"

She shook her head piteously. "Oh, my sweet, sweet Jack. There are times when it is better to hide oneself from the truth. Sometimes, ignorance truly is bliss." She stroked his cheek.

"But Rose, what will happen next?" Frustrated, he motioned towards the others – a couple of the women bent down towards Otis, one of them was holding his face. He tried in vain to pull away and another cat-woman stepped over him and straddled his back.

"I do not think you'll be at ease with what is about to happen to our four-legged friend, Jack."

Otis was unceremoniously positioned on all fours. One of the felines produced a baseball bat, while another wrapped her arms around him. His head was then clamped between another cat-woman's thighs.

"But... but..."

"Come Jack, we depart."

The door was firmly closed and locked behind them. Within a thick cloud of lust and self loathing, Jack sulked as he was led away. Already, thoughts and memories of the scene from which he had been so unceremoniously severed tugged at his brain.

Back inside her office, Rose poured him a glass of sparkling mineral water.

"I still don't understand why we had to leave, Rose. This is your place, surely you have the right to be anywhere you want."

"That's correct." Rose sighed.

"Well... I just..."

"Let me explain something to you. That little scenario belongs to me. It is *for* me. Not for your eyes, Jack." Jack's face displayed a cross between turmoil and bitterness.

"You like things like that?"

"I most certainly do, Jack darling. I get an immense sense of arousal whenever such things take place. I'll warrant that whatever is happening to Otis is glorious. A punishment a lowly animal like him so rightly deserves."

"Whether the man likes it or not?"

Certainly, thought Rose. "Of course not," said Rose. "I can assure you his torture is purely consensual."

"Torture?" Jack's voice leapt from his throat like a bullet.

"Yes, Jack. Raw, delicious torture."

"B… but, err…"

"I like torture, Jack." She eyed him, again he was elevated and dismayed in equal measures by the most enigmatic way her eyes came alive when she spoke of distasteful things. "I like to be cruel, Jack darling. I like to be cruel to people."

"But do you not think it's wrong?"

"Non," she said, her eyes closed.

"Miss Benoit, is there anything I need to know? About what goes on behind these doors?"

"That depends, darling. I dare say my telling you that I like to do naughty things to people shouldn't really disturb you that much."

"That man didn't really want to be there though, I could tell."

"Really? Did he tell you that, Jack darling?"

"No, but…"

"Jack, if I told you I wished to beat you, would you comply?"

He glanced at her, gravely regarding the question, confused.

"Yes, but I'm…"

"Darling. Would you comply?"

Rose moved towards him. His gaze hit the floor. She scooped up his glass and sipped at it before placing it to his mouth. Jack had no choice but to swallow the remaining contents. Finally she placed herself on his lap, cleavage staring him in the face.

"Would you let Rose fiddle around with you? Jack darling?" she whispered.

His eyes said it all. But out of pure adulation he reinforced the obvious. "Yes. Yes I would, Rose."

***

He found the sunrise depressing as he sat in the back seat of her BMW. It was actually a glorious dawn, fresh, and brightly emanating throughout the gaps in the façades of Marylebone, but it signalled only one thing. The end.

The pain returned. He scrunched his left eye closed, a stinging reaction to the agony as it shot up his spine. He thought it ironic, it beginning now.

"Make sure you get your back seen to, Jack."

"And my shoulder."

"Believe me, your kidney pain will only worsen if you neglect to address the problem. The pain in your shoulder is entirely your own fault. Trying to escape through small windows is both dangerous and ridiculous."

Jack Sargent nodded.

Sat beside him, she coolly applied moisturiser to her hands and neck. She was still as radiant as she had been at the station. He almost laughed at how long ago that seemed.

She studied him again in the same way she had done in the basement at the Soho bar. There was something recognisable about him. The feeling was slight, a slither. Distant familiarity, hidden deep down underneath a sheet at the back of her mind.

Meanwhile, inside Jack's mind, he was himself mulling over questions. Requests he'd failed to put to her and was, by now, reprimanding himself for not doing so.

Silence washed over them, until she said, "I know you possess that picture of me, Jack. I saw it in your wallet earlier. I'll wager you also have another. The kitchen. The bedroom, perhaps."

He was about to speak but she shushed him. They both knew his displays of dissent would not be viable.

"Do you look at it, Jack? At night time, before bed?"

Her reach was slow, deliberate. She clawed just above his forehead and proceeded to drag her talons through his hair, instantly transforming him from tired scruff bag to a somewhat more improved version.

"You might notice it is a booking photograph.

Complete with my very own number board. I wasn't always so well behaved, Jack."

"I had noticed. About the mugshot, I mean."

"Indeed. A long time ago, now. A couple of slightly undesirable chaps, one of whom had been a tad disrespectful. I simply couldn't take it lying down, could I, Jack?"

Jack shook his head.

"I had my posterior, as they say, hauled in before a small court somewhere in California. This was when I was a student. The charges were dropped when they realised I had acted in self defence."

The car pulled to a smooth halt and Jack looked regretful. "I'm sorry…"

"Why are you sorry?"

"That photograph, it's so fascinating."

Her eyes hypnotised him as he tried to look away but couldn't. "I find you fascinating as well, Rose."

Without dropping her gaze she slowly placed her finger to his lips to silence him from saying anything else that he might regret. She then drew in close to place a kiss on his cheek.

***

As Jack sat in his kitchen, failing in his best attempts to down toast and butter, his heart ached. His mind counted the strange collection of things he'd witnessed.

He glanced over to the photograph again; black and white, and over eight years old. The eyes! She hadn't aged, but that wasn't a surprise to him. Like she had said the night before: "*Black doesn't crack, darling.*"

Red Alert

"The subject has a past, quite chequered. Extremely chequered. The subject has been decorated in various fields. All papers and qualifications were attributed to her using false names. Attended the ******* school of arts in Berlin, studied towards a degree in classical compositions and concentration, whatever that means. Was part of a season of successful performing arts achievement in Paris nine years ago, the subject won the top award for most outstanding performance. While doing that, she attended ****** in Brussels, apparently it was their highest accolade, like ever, made quite a stir. Erm, went to a university in Accra, studied science and African politics.

"There was something else, too. There's a period of time, between maybe six to eight years ago, when the subject has left evidence in locations near Fairfax County. I would like some assistance with this, namely the connection with Langley, and I need to make a parallel whether she was detained in some way by the CIA. Please could you supply me with contact. There's been evidence that she has been trained in the art of combat. Physically, but also with armaments. Russia. Asia. If this is true, I, err... If this is the case, I strongly suggest we act now as the subject would be red alert. I have tried; I've done more than your requirements have instructed. And I'm afraid if I do not get a green light from you fucks soon, I'll be forced to go off radar and reprimand the subject myself. Over and out and fuck you."

Trouble at New Horizons

Jack was told to leave the premises. With tears in his eyes and void of all energy, he had no choice but to gather up the gift he'd brought for Daniel and depart *New Horizons*.

Not thirty minutes earlier, he had known instantly from Madge's reaction, as he came bounding up to the entrance, that she wasn't herself; her manner was austere and detached.

She spoke with haste as if she lacked all patience. "Jack, I don't think you should be here. Not today," she had said.

"He'll be okay, I just want to explain."

"No. You mustn't. Not a good idea, Jack."

She looked tired; her hair and clothes gave Jack the impression she'd either been in a fight or dragged through a hedge backwards. She scrunched her eyes tightly before opening them wide.

"Listen, Madge, I know what this is about. I know he hates me at the moment, but just give me a chance to make this right. Let me talk to him."

"Jack. I rang you last night, many times. Where in blazes were you?" Jack had never seen her so perplexed. "It was awful. The one day he really needed you, we all needed you. You could have sorted all this out last night. But not now – it's too late."

Madge wearily parked herself on a nearby chair by the wall.

"It was an extremely trying night. All manner of things happened. I don't think we can take much more."

Jack glanced down at her.

"He had an episode in the playroom. Smashed everything. Everything's broken, Jack. We placed him into a reflection period in his room and he smashed that up as well. He is… in big trouble." Madge paused for a moment to consider her next words measuredly. "And it's all because of you. You are a fool."

When he heard this, he looked downwards and, with his back to the wall, slid himself down it. He crouched and it was excruciating.

"Madge, I don't want to lose him," he said.

The woman shook her head despondently. "Too late, Jack. You already have."

After a few moments, they heard a commotion from the entrance. Daniel came rushing through in to the reception, a member of staff followed and called after him.

"You lied to me! You lied to me, Jack."

Jack stood. "Daniel, it's okay. We'll be okay, I promise."

"No it won't!" His screams were piercing and it was as if he was possessed by something Jack had never before seen in the child. "You're a liar. You promised me, Jack. Where were you? What was more important than us being together? You promised!"

Madge placed herself between the oncoming Daniel and Jack, as if doing so would protect Jack from some unforeseen violent onslaught.

"Jack, I told you," she called, over the commotion. "You should have rang ahead. You started all this. It was his bloody birthday, Jack." She too was crying now.

Daniel roared, Jack and Madge had to raise their voices above his squeaking cacophony.

"What do you mean, *all this*? What's wrong with him, Madge?"

"You promised me, Mister Jack. You promised... You promised!"

Jack attempted to shove Madge out of the way. But Daniel had stopped, the anger subsided. Madge's colleague had duly released her hold of the child, and he stood there. His face seemed torn, tear-stained, and raw with bitter heartache. He fell to his knees before softly laying himself upon the floor like an insect readying itself for death.

He wept. A constant quivering noise that ripped Jack's insides apart.

Interval

Garjana

Northern Xizang

Rebecca Sinclair made unearthly sounds. Moaning, screaming, terrible madness. After almost two hundred hours of defiant self belief, she finally refused the demons any more passage to her mind. Her tears had stopped falling only because, she assumed, she'd cried them all.

Hung suspended, seven feet from the surface of the ground, she was in darkness. The cold had been unbearable. That's when the tears had started. Her discomfort and its constant nagging on her mind was all she'd felt for the past forty days.

Every third day, Dip had ordered two younger monks to lower her down so that she might eat and drink. She devoured the tempting berries and paratha bread, but only on every other visit.

Dip advised her via the power of thought:

"This exercise is designed to teach us the importance of abstinence. It is meant to encourage you to put your mind back where it belongs, so that you might find detachment from what is happening to your physical body. When in these conditions, it is usual that the two paths present themselves. One is torment and hatred. The other is acceptance and peace."

Rebecca hung, silent, her senses only just receiving his silent words.

"This method you are currently carrying out is the first of ten ways. Obviously there are more trying, severe methods."

"Show me the next way," Rebecca said aloud.

***

Dip had no reservations about Rebecca and her abilities. In

all his years at the Garjana monastery the old man had never encountered a student with such discipline.

Dip, the most highly esteemed master-teacher and Sensei, was obviously forbidden to feel the remotest amount of pride, usually detached and emotionally centred only on his tasks of relating his vast knowledge. And yet, he found himself questioning his own inner senses as he felt a strange tingle of pleasure whenever he saw the fruits of what he had imparted on to Rebecca – or Aba, the strong-limbed West African migrant.

On the day of the grand tournament, Dip would later pray to Buddha, asking for forgiveness for the smidgen of pride he would inevitably feel on this day.

There were twenty in total. Twenty students remained from literally thousands who had fallen to failure and weakness. Some were said to have died in their attempts to gain spiritual enlightenment and expertly honed combative skills, but this was purely rumour.

They all lined up in four perfect rows of five, rigid, poised, and empty of all emotion.

Due to her height, Aba stood within the last row, flanked at both sides by four of her companions.

Dip appeared, and proceeded to walk to the centre of the hall to address them.

He called her name and Aba quickly jumped to her right, before offering the traditional sign of recognition. She then bounded up through the rows of her fellow students, all male, before appearing opposite him, bowing.

Dip bowed and walked away. He seated himself beside three younger monks. Aba stood alone, her hands at her side.

Another door opened at the rear of the hall, and Sul entered the room.

***

From his seat, Dip watched Aba, and recounted his many experiences with her. Her journey had been arduous.

Memories of the past two years flooded Dip's mind. He remembered when Aba had first arrived at the monastery. Smiling, slightly clumsy, her western clothes revealing more flesh than he cared to witness. The injuries she had incurred. The snapped collarbone when being forced to endure pain whilst being beaten with dull sticks. Her broken ribs whilst being flung against the ancient trees in the orchard. Her tears as she pleaded with him, begging him to stop the lengthy punishments of silence. Rebuking her attempts to befriend him.

The worth of all her hardships had paid him the greatest gift. The gift of receiving the most receptive student he'd ever taught.

They would often see Sul, sweeping the steps to their quarters and training halls. Gently tending to the gardens and lovingly caring for the beautiful butterflies. Quiet and mysterious, his hooded garments gave no hint of his age or the sinewy brick wall beneath.

Only Aba was aware Sul was the final test. The famous unconquered. The ultimate champion. Through him would be the only way of qualifying into the higher realm. She knew he was relentless, showing no kindness or quarter to lesser students. He would never tire of beating Dip's potential protégés into submission.

Few of the watching spectators knew of her abilities. They looked on, and although their vacant expressions gave the impression of the noble and restrained fighting machines they appeared to be, their innermost thoughts were awash with awe and fear. Terror engulfed the hardy strength they'd previously possessed as they saw the tall African woman skilfully obliterate what was to become their new tutor. Just when Sul was about to complete a shifty manoeuvre to quell her advances, Aba would counter with a speed and precision they could barely see with their own eyes. Sul began to grunt with exasperation the more his operations were blocked. His dignity hitting rock bottom as he shamed himself, shouting and insulting his opponent. She was devastating as she punished him, again and again.

In spite of the damaging attack, Aba made sure his injuries were distributed evenly, so as not to permanently disable him; the sign of a merciful and righteous warrior.

Aba stood above Sul, as he lay upon the floor, her stick remained poised at his heaving throat. His face dripped with sweat and blood, his bruises already forming. Fire roared from his eyes, as temper and indignation bled from every pore in his muscular body. She stared down at him, her eyes calm in her expertly applied position. Her heart, caged within her ribs and lungs, beat soundly, belying the rigorous movements she had applied to beat the champion warrior.

Just a flicker of a smile. It danced on the corner of Dip's thin lips as Sul submitted. He rose to his feet and bowed towards the only one who had ever bested him within the tournaments at Garjana.

***

The night fell upon the mountainside. Its dark blue cloak hung down, allowing the stars to shine upon the monastery. Aba dropped her backpack outside the door of Dip's modest dwelling, a simple hut constructed from rhododendron bark and wicker.

Kneeling on his mat, he was immersed in prayer. Aba dwarfed him as she entered, filling the entire space above. She lowered herself and knelt opposite him.

After a lengthy silence, Dip opened his eyes.

"I want you to stay," he said.

"This I cannot do."

"Very well. When you first arrived here, I was concerned you wished to learn only the combat methods and not much else. I am now confident, as you have scaled the mental lessons I've taught, that your search for discipline and understanding was truth and just… which is so, so admirable." He smiled. "You still intend on the ascent to the Gold Mountains, in the north?" he asked.

She nodded.

"The journey is treacherous. But I'm confident your strength will see the voyage a success. I have sent word of your arrival to a charge who resides in the north west. He shall see your passage safely and resume the next stage in your studies." He smiled again. "Further durations of harsh training await you."

"Father, I have a question."

"Ask."

"When I go back into the world, will I still retain all I have learned here? Or will it disappear?"

"If you maintain the goodness it affords, if your self-guidance stays true, then your skills shall always be a part of you."

Just then, a mood seemed to cover his face. He sat for a while as if thoroughly contemplating her question. He spoke to her, as he would in these moments, via the power of thought. "*I have talked with Khorvadjig, the twenty-fifth Buddha of Theravada.*" Aba nodded. She was aware of the deity, having studied the Pali Canon scriptures. "*I can only send you good things. Now you are leaving, it is not within my right to tell you that you are wrong, only advise you to be true.*"

She waited patiently, another long period of quiet followed, owing to his intermittent meditation.

"*Your competence is boundless, there is no denying. However, you are not as you seem. There is a veil over your spirit. I cannot see through it. Your truths are shrouded with thick curtains. Until this day, I have never known fear. Tonight, indeed, you bring confusion. I have asked Buddha for guidance. Nothing more I can say, other than travel safely.*"

Aba replied, thanking him.

Just as she was about to depart, a tear ran from Dip's eye. He lowered his head and this time spoke with his mouth: "Thunder walks with you. It is not hatred. But it is a passion, an energy. It is in your belly and in your heart. It is immense."

Everybody's Able

Upon entering through the small door, Ricky Gomez was immediately welcomed by Silly Sandy. In spite of previously meeting her in the prison, he remembered little. He had been forewarned of her effervescent colourful disposition, but her nickname, actually written in big letters on her t-shirt, confirmed he was in the right place.

He'd been released that morning, and now, armed with nothing more than an old Puma holdall, he'd finally arrived at *Everybody's Able*.

"The first thing we want to do is give you a role, Ricky." Silly Sandy's voice would have been annoying the week before, but as he sat in her small office, surrounded by books on psychology and substances and Mister Men, he warmed towards her in the same way as a vampire who wanted to give up drinking blood might. Silly Sandy, ginger hair, kooky eyes, and stripy trousers; he shook his head, as if disbelieving his genuine feelings towards her.

"When you're here, we give you a role. Responsibility. I want you to have some responsibility, Ricky."

"I thought this place was a shelter?"

"People are welcome to use it as a shelter. But this place is more like... um, an activity place. We provide facilities. Things that'll benefit the people we have here. Recreational activities. Before you start, I want you to know this isn't like playschool; we don't sit around singing Kum ba yah. But, if you wanted to do that... we could do it. If you wanted to."

In spite of her engaging positivity, Silly Sandy seemed nervous, she looked downward at times while talking to him. Something else Ricky found endearing.

"So, Ricky, a role. We do many, many things here. Rewarding things."

"Like what? I ain't doing no hard work," he said.

"Why not? Did you know that hard work is actually

pretty brill?"

"Ricky frowned. "Really? How?"

"How? I'll tell you, mister grumps. Hard work leads to experience. We make mistakes during hard work. We learn from mistakes, and they make us stronger. But the most beautiful thing about hard work is the ending."

"The ending?"

"Yep," she nodded.

"What are you talking about?"

Silly Sandy thought for a second. "Look out that window, behind you."

Reluctantly, Ricky stood and stepped over to the small window. He could see the rear of the centre, and, in doing so, a view of the glorious garden. Large leafy hedges meandered around patios underneath the overhanging willow trees. Flower-strewn borders adorned either side of the void. Lovely pathways wound themselves around unseen corners. Pergolas and statues provided intermittent attraction for all who were lucky enough to feast their eyes upon such beauty. Ricky tried his hardest to think if he'd ever seen anything like it.

"The ending, Ricky." Sandy sounded emotional. Ricky could tell she was proud. "This is the result of hard work, when everyone pulls together as a team. That used to be a scruffy piece of land. The office workers in the next building, they used to throw their rubbish down there. Working on the Garvey garden was hard, but like I said, there's every point; every piece of hard work has an outcome, Ricky. An ending."

"It's beautiful."

"It is, yeah." She waved off any further signs of pride and emotion and changed the subject. "So, Ricky. What do you want to do? We have some kids coming round tomorrow; they're great little dudes and dudettes. We play rounders with them sometimes. Or, you could help some of the other fellas expand on the garden. We've just got permission to work on the land at the other side of the building. Or you could just help with making the food?"

"How long can I stay?" he asked, slowly.

Again, Silly Sandy thought methodically about her answer. "Well, I would like to say you are able to stay here, you know, for keeps. But the local council tells me I have to say *until you're back on your feet.*" She put on a stuffy bureaucratic accent for the latter part of her sentence, which made Ricky laugh.

"People come and go. You don't have to stay here. You can walk out right now if you want. But it would be nice to have you here. To be honest, Ricky, I want you to stay with us. I can guarantee you will like it here. You have to believe me. It's true; this place is ace!"

Love In A Car

Rose was already looking forward to the following evening. She had not seen Carlos in almost two months. Whenever her thoughts had turned towards him, especially lately, she would gush and feel a glow in her stomach.

The remains of a previous conversation they'd had inspired her to treat him; she dressed in white. They had had a wonderful evening at *San Lorenzo*. Typically, the food was fabulous.

As they both left the restaurant and walked outside into the warm evening, the sky was dark and the stars sparkled like diamonds. He opened the car door and she slid in.

Rose kissed him while the car cruised at a low speed up the length of museum mile.

"Rose, I wanted to tell you that it's been a lovely night," Carlos said, fumbling awkwardly with his tie. He looked curiously out of place sat in the back of the limo. Rose unbuttoned the front of her small blouse as she watched his shocked expression. She eased it off and held it up draping it over his head before her index finger let the garment fall.

"Rose, the err… driver…"

"Take my bra off," she quietly ordered. "Reach around me and unhook the clasp."

Her face, expectant, serious, shone at him from her side of the back seat.

Cautiously, he moved in closer. The faintest sign of a smile tinkled upon her lips as he surrounded her with his arms before fumbling for the desired location. Rose neither leant forward to assist him in doing what she'd asked, nor adjusted her arms to enable him to easily reach. Instead, he struggled, his face so close to hers he could smell the cocoa butter. Her eyes bored into him like beautiful stars on the blackest night in New York.

She cut into his muttering, "With your left hand take the clasp, unhook the other side with your right. This is relatively straightforward, darling."

He slumped, lowered by his clumsy inexperience. Carlos was now face to face with the very thing he'd been ordered to remove. Rose could feel his large hands, awkwardly pulling.

Finally, the hooks detached and instantly the white silk *LaPerla* loosened.

Rose glanced at the back of the driver's head. "Now remove it. Slip it off, Carlos."

The inside of Carlos' head swirled. He could hear the smooth hum of the engine, and feel a semi-cool jet of air float around the vehicle between them. It fell easily into his hands. To avoid gasping, he applied a certain level of restraint when presented with the sight now before him. The expensive smell, the heart-shaped tattoo on her left breast and the barbed wire ring around her upper right arm; Carlos could never remember feeling so aroused.

"Kiss them, Carlos. Kiss my breasts."

Rose disapproved of the length Carlos had let his hair grow to. She ran her fingernails through it and pulled at it as she pressed his face against her left bosom. He licked at her nipple, it grew erect quickly. "Bite it. That's it, bite it, baby." she whispered.

Her hand then found the waistband of her trousers. She flicked the button apart at her navel and slowly pulled down the zip.

With ample space in the large foot-well to accommodate Carlos, he was prompted to his knees. Her big legs surrounded him, and Rose casually hummed as she guided his head towards her groin. His jaw was placed in position and when his tongue made contact Rose heaved a heavy sigh.

The feeling was explosive. She moaned above him as he helped her towards her climax.

She pulled him up and pushed him back down onto the

back seat. She straddled him, and he struggled to unzip himself from beneath her. She smiled at his desperate attempts to undress. She softly offered her assistance, and easily peeled back his trousers, feeling his protruding bulge, wanting to be touched, wanting to be free. His shirt was forcibly removed, buttons popping and darting in all directions as she ripped it from his body, almost breaking his arms.

She marvelled at his torso, bronze and in somewhat better condition than the previous time she had seen it. She placed her hands on its surface, as if declaring her ownership of it, claiming him, his belonging to her. Her long fingernails ran across his abdomen, lightly scratching. She smiled again as he flinched.

At last, he was placed inside her and she almost surprised herself when she let out a dull moan. His penis felt big, nicely fitting inside. Carlos looked up deep into her eyes. He used his finger to trace a line around her lips and kissed her, softly at first, but her heavy lashing tongue influenced him to engage more intensely.

"I want you, Rose," he whispered in her ear. She moaned and raised her upper body, dropping her breasts into his face again.

Her hands explored him, feeling, as they elegantly traversed the length and breadth of all she was able to reach. He groaned.

He grimaced at the pressure of her hips as they forced downward, slowly, harshly, and the intense sensation stung him to the point of pure ecstasy.

"Can you handle this, baby?" she cooed. He smiled at her, answering the question.

Rose gasped with sweet abandon as she pressed down harder still. Both rocked together backwards and forwards slowly and rhythmically for a lengthy duration of prolonged rapture.

Her body started to tremble and she moaned heavily. Together they both reached their climaxes, syncopated, in harmony. A rush of pleasure filled her head and stomach.

They were both breathless in the still cool air of the limo.

Rose was unaware that Carlos was falling in love with her.

The following morning, her driver was dismissed.

Orange Is The New Black

Jack Sargent sat alone. The room was small but curiously tall, an office for a cartoon villain.

The temperature was cold; Jack could see his breath but he was too nervous to allow the January weather into his bones.

The door opened and Madge stepped into the room followed by Pearl Brewster, the head representative at the governing disclosure and barring office, a woman who looked like an undesirable from *Orange Is The New Black*.

"Sorry to have kept you waiting, Mister Sargent," she said, while not meeting his gaze.

"Please, call me Jack."

Pearl Brewster seated herself.

Jack looked up at Madge. She stood at Pearl's side like an ailing, reluctant soldier. He knew from the forlorn look on her face, he was about to be presented with more bad news.

"I'll make this as easy as I can, Mister Sargent. After the checks were returned to us we found some major discrepancies that, in my experience, should limit your eligibility to adopt. I'm sorry to have to be the one telling you this."

Jack had no time to assess his options. His mind turned blank as he searched for something to come back at her with.

"Excuse me but… You are sorry to have to be the one telling me this?" he repeated.

"Well, yes."

"Really? Surely that's not correct. Don't you mean, you're sorry *I* have to find out like this? Or something like that?"

"That's what I said."

"No, you didn't. You actually said you were sorry that *you* had to tell me."

304

"Jack," offered Madge. He shook his head and raised his hands as if not wishing to dwell on the matter.

"Mister Sargent, whichever way my dialogue is interpreted, this still doesn't divert us from the facts. We take our job very seriously at the fostering council."

"Okay, so why has my application been declined?"

Pearl's pause was measured, almost predicting the repercussions of what she was about to say.

"This isn't easy for me, Mister Sargent. At the council we have access to all manner of applicants' details."

"Yes, I know. And you've checked me, you know how clean I am. In any case, you have all seen Daniel and I together. You are aware of the connection we have."

"Yes, but regardless of momentary connections you may or may not have with a child, this does not form the basis of a permanent stable home life."

Jack was incensed, he shuffled in his seat. "What does that mean? You know we're best mates. There was a time I was told by your colleague that I had strong potential. It was in the bag, like, last year. What the hell has changed?"

"Okay. On the twelfth of October, you spent a lengthy amount of time in an establishment called, um, *Erotique*, Mister Sargent." She mispronounced the word, Jack didn't bother to correct her. "Now, far be it for me to discriminate where an applicant chooses to spend his or her time, the fact you were at *Erotique* illustrates that you, at best, are a single man, a man with no wife or partner to contribute an even balance that might benefit the adoptee. At worst, it demonstrates your need to facilitate your obscure requirements."

"Mrs Brewster," Jack said.

"It's not up to me to discriminate. But visits to such dwellings do limit your chances, Mister Sargent."

"Can I remind you that I am a detective at the Met. My actions during the night of the twelfth of October were part of highly delicate operations concerning an ongoing case." Jack heard himself as he reeled off the excuse. He sounded formulaic and characterless.

"As I have said before, Mister Sargent, we do a lot of checks."

"What's that supposed to mean?"

"We know there have been many days, especially lately, that you have not attended work. The days after the night of the twelfth of October included. This process, at best, decreases your chances of retaining your full wage margin. This would contribute to a lower standard of living, if you were to become a foster parent."

"I don't believe this," said Jack, now looking at Madge, an unspoken plea inviting her into the conversation.

"We have to be seen to be doing our job correctly," Pearl said. "Our most prominent duty is to put the safety and well being of the child before anything else. Our job is to limit the risk of placing the child within a hostile environment." Jack agreed, but it was Pearl Brewster who now sounded formulaic, he thought to himself.

"With all due respect, Mrs Brewster," said Madge, rather timidly. "in spite of the evidence you have brought to light, it still doesn't change the fact that Jack is an upstanding member of the community. Daniel absolutely adores him and they get on like a house on fire."

"On the contrary, Miss Markham. All three of us know perfectly well that Mister Sargent has fallen out of favour with the adoptee. A development which was most certainly caused by his frequenting the aforementioned, ahem, alternative lifestyle club. But in any case, Mister Sargent would have still failed the check. I am sorry."

"Excuse me? Still failed? Why is that?" he said, his temper rising.

Pearl huffed impatiently and bumped her spectacles onto the surface of the table, almost breaking them.

"I'll be honest, Mister Sargent, you are an established Detective Inspector. You've spent almost your entire life dedicated to solving problems. You think, eat and sleep your work. Your work is your entire life, your world. Just tell me, when on earth do you think you'd be able to accommodate the time towards caring for a child?"

Pearl's face creased, an ugly arrogance that matched the conviction she believed she brandished.

Jack's thoughts turned to the very first time he and Daniel had gone out together. Daniel's face, whenever Jack arrived to see him would light up. It was an image that would always fill his heart with strength and warmth. Daniel was the only person in his life who truly loved him – the only person whom he loved.

Pearl Brewster had already gathered her files and was about to stand.

Quickly, Jack stood. "I might have failed your checks. I might have gone to *Erotique* on the night of the twelfth of October. I might have missed a few days off work and I might not have shaved in the last three days. But I can't just walk away from Daniel, not just like that."

Madge glowed defiantly. A silent union, filled with recognition and respect, passed through them both.

"Mister Sargent, you will have to walk away." Pearl said as she stood. "Failing to do so will cause you more trouble. I have seen this time and time again, I know how it ends, Mister Sargent."

L'événement

An Invitation

The Event: An Appetiser

Thirty minutes before, Tico Ramirez had been hurriedly dashing up towards the rooftop bar to deliver some fresh hors d'oeuvres. His suit, well made and fitted, had made him appear taller than he actually was.

Now, shortly after his beating, strewn upon the floor, weeping at the feet of Rose Benoit, he asked her why she was doing this to him.

"I simply like the way I feel when I'm fucking you, dear," she told him, while softly removing the droplets of his blood from her face and cleavage with a damp tissue.

His face was heavily bruised. Tico was told to undertake the remainder of his duties back of house, away from her guests and the camera crew who were already setting up their equipment down in the main hall.

Rose left him in the gentlemen's restroom so he could jump from the window while she departed.

Back Of House Rumblings

Michael Beavis wasn't alone. During his tenure at the hospitality training, he'd heard rumblings. Rumours that hinted at the tyranny of Rose Benoit. However, it wasn't until the week that preceded the *Nubian Rose: L'événement*, that all manner of shocking details about his employer were revealed to him by other, like-minded victims.

From the onset, arriving at his digs near Bleeker Street, to being ushered into the venue and instantly set to work with his new companions – the whole thing had been like a whirlwind. It's heavy force thrust him into a mechanical system of subjugation that was way above his control to change.

Yet, despite the laborious bondage into which he'd been placed, he still found time to acquaint himself with other poor souls who had equally been made to suffer in much the same way as he.

Danny Booker looked like a shadow of the man he formerly was. His seething cynicism hinted at an enthusiasm he once may have had. Caucasian, bullish, although round plumps on his torso now appeared where once was well carved muscle. He was American, but Michael was able to tell he wasn't from New York.

They both understood the importance of whispering at all times.

"So, Mikey," Danny began, "if we're gonna get this plan of ours into action we have to strike tonight. This whole event crap is a façade, and it'll show everyone in the world the truth."

They both sat at the foot of the basement steps, next to a goods-lift, somewhere within the bowels of the building. Michael watched Danny fidget and fiddle with his fingers.

Danny's face seemed haunted and Michael saw a tiny piece of himself while looking into his vacant eyes.

"If we can just get Tico on side, he'll be the catalyst. I think we'll be able to actually pull it off. I mean, we've been banging on about this thing for months. Tico gets pissed whenever we start talking this shit, but Mikey, we could actually expose her, who she really is. All these visiting fucking governmentals and celebrity fucks, do you think they know what she's like? They think she's this classy Wall Street pin-up supermodel bitch. None of them know she's actually a damned lunatic."

"Tonight?" asked Michael, solemnly.

"Told you before, it has to be. I haven't come this far for it not to be tonight, Mikey."

They both looked down, listening, aware their voices were becoming louder.

"Okay, okay. Do you remember everything we said last week, Danny, all the details?"

"Yeah, I got them memoed right up in here," he placed a large index finger to his brain, "but, like I said, we need one more guy."

"Tico, it is?"

"Yeah, Tico. We'll get him, get him on our side. Tellin' you, Mikey, it's gotta be Tico."

They both grabbed at each other's palm, a tight, sweaty demonstration of their unfortunate association, and how they could overcome it.

"Mikey, we've been here just over an hour and already two people are missing."

Valentino Dress

Discarding Milan, Paris and Dubai in favour of locations more regional, the Metropolitan Museum of Art finally provided the venue, the most directly obvious approach to showcase the exquisite tastes of Rose Benoit and Julie Ross as they celebrated *Nubian Rose*'s tenth year.

The expectant crowd, murmuring it's pre-elation, every one of them could smell the excitement in the air.

The lighting within the courtyard of the American Wing was dimmed, the interior's hum faded to a deftly silence.

The acoustic strumming and polyrhythmic beats of the intro to *La Vie En Rose* flew above the heads of fifteen hundred chosen guests, before Grace Jones proceeded to serenade them all with one of Rose's most beloved anthems. The western balcony was then lit up and Rose appeared within a vision of scarlet perfection, the Valentino dress she wore was both provocative and stylish. The uproarious applause resounded as all eyes were on Miss Rose Benoit. She waved, making her way down into the main expanse of the void below.

The volume was respectfully lowered, enabling Rose to verbalise. "Ladies and Gentlemen, thank you all so kindly for attending this most special event. It means so much to Julie and myself, and all our team who have put all their efforts into making *Nubian Rose* what it is today. Do enjoy yourselves this evening."

More applause erupted as the music was turned up once again.

Carlos stood surrounded by murmuring strangers. With empty glass in hand, he had just finished his raspberry and white chocolate smoothie.

Rose headed straight towards him, her almond eyes boring a hole into the centre of his heart.

"So, baby, at last, you see me in my natural habitat, what are your thoughts?" she asked, placing a chocolate-covered strawberry inside his mouth.

"I do not know what to say, you are like the Queen or something."

"Yes. A drag queen! These shoes are far too high. I adore heels, but *seven inches*? I really should know better."

Carlos gave an agreeable shrug, looking up at her.

"Darling, you are not drinking," she declared and a young waitress appeared, balancing a large tray. "Non-alcoholic?" Rose asked and the waitress handed Carlos a tall glass of fizz.

"Pink grapefruit and basil mimosa," declared the waitress.

"Mmm, good choice."

"I would prefer something with raspberry and white chocolate," said Carlos.

"No, you wouldn't. Come, there are a few people in this room I wish for you to meet."

She led him towards the woman who'd flanked Rose in the photograph that seemed to be adorned everywhere. He had even seen it displayed ten foot high in the main lobby of the building upon his arrival.

Julie was casually talking to three other women before Rose cut in and grabbed her and CeeCee Holmes together. "Guys, guys, may I introduce Carlos?"

Julie's exotic eyes widened, "Ah, here he is, the main man." Carlos kissed her cheek as she moved in towards him.

"You did good, Rose, baby." She dug her elbow into Rose's rib. "Shall I give him the official Julie intro?"

"Oui, you may," Rose said.

"Charmed to meet you, Carlos. I'm Julie, and this lady here is CeeCee. We're the ones who take up all her valuable time when she ain't with you."

Rose smiled sarcastically.

"It is lovely to meet you all," said Carlos, in his most formal accent.

"Likewise, Carlos. Just promise me you stand up to her when she starts playing up. Don't take no stuff from this girl, you understand me?" Julie advised.

Carlos instantly warmed to Julie's feisty attitude; it was like the New York version of Rose's British sense of humour.

"Jules, what choice does he have?" Rose asked, stroking the top of his head.

"What choice does *anyone* have with you, babe?" CeeCee Holmes asked.

***

A large crowd of people had converged within the outer rims of their quartet.

Rose, now privately engaged in a conversation with Julie, was being watched by all as she ignored the commotion and the discreet vies for attention from her guests.

"Jules, Oleg Gribkov? Has he arrived?"

"Hmm, yeah. I meant to tell you about that. His people called through, said he's delayed. Rose, relax, he'll be here."

"I hope so, I so wish to meet him again."

"Yeah, you see, there you go again. What's the deal with you guys anyway? Don't you dare tell me you've got a freaky type of thing for this old dude."

"Julie, dear, that's absurd. Why are you talking nonsense, tonight, of all nights?" Rose asked.

"Honey, it's as if you two have a shared past or something. Are you sure you ain't got the hots for mister Oleg McNo-leg?"

Rose laid her left hand softly to her breast. "Moi? Certainement pas!"

Back Of House Rumblings (part 2)

Michael Beavis had been awake for almost thirty hours. He barged through the kitchen doors holding more trays laden with used glasses.

"Mikey, go take a break, you look like shit," blurted the back-of-house manager.

He surfaced and found his way out on to the street. Dragging on a dreamy cigarette while seated on a grassy bank parallel to the building, he kept himself hidden from passersby.

"Hey English man, you got a cigarette?" Michael failed to notice Tico pull alongside him. He passed one over before the man took a light.

"You finished your shift, English man?"

"No, I got twenty minutes then I'm back in there."

"Yeah, bad luck. Me too."

Michael took a glance at his companion. The small man had a swollen eye and a large gash on his forehead.

"What the hell happened to you?"

"Ah, it ain't nothing, bro. I slipped and fell while cleaning the floor."

After a lengthy silence, spent eyeing Fifth Avenue's dregs, Michael glanced at Tico. The man was at least five years older than himself, Porto Rican – the silent type.

"What did you do?" Michael asked casually, belying the gravity of the question.

It took a while before Tico finally spoke. "I never did nothing, Mikey."

He ran the palm of his hand over his scruffy black hair. "I was minding my business. I didn't do nothing."

"You must have done something, I mean, she wouldn't just hit on someone who did nothing at all."

"Proves how much you know, English. All I did was ask for a job."

Silence. Michael exhaled, his eyes intense and wide,

contradicting his fatigue.

"You have to join us, Tico. Right now, the worldwide press is in there, in that building. The eyes of the world. We can expose her, all of us, get together and mess this up for her."

Tico whispered sharply. "Can't you hear yourself? It's talk like that can get you killed."

Michael shook his head dismissively. "Come on, man. It's worth a try, what have we got to lose?"

"Mikey, I don't want any trouble. All I want is for this night to be over so I can go home."

"Bullshit, you're just like the rest of us."

"Let me tell you something, the last time I heard someone saying all this crap, they was never seen again, you hearing me? Wanna know what they did to me? I'll tell you, man. She has this friend, big ass bitch, about ten feet tall, I'd say. They both took turns throwing me against the wall. Then, afterwards, this friend of hers, she beats the living crap out of me, every which way, fucked me, you understand? Like, for real. I mean, I was badly injured, you know? *Internally*, all that shit. Put me in Lennox Hill for over a year. Then they put me in a psychiatric ward for another three months because nobody believed me when I told them, they told me I was crazy for even *thinking* such things. When I got out, they caught up with me again, did the same thing. They're like freaks, perverted. She sits and watches, touching herself while this big ass friend of hers breaks my ribs, fractured my skull, fucks me in my tiny ass. You hearing me? When I healed after the second time, it was time for this Met Ball shit. Said I had to do it or it would happen again."

Up until this point, Tico had been mild, gentle.

Michael recoiled at Tico's irate vitriol as it spilled out into the cool night air. He wept angry tears that he rubbed into the lesions on his face.

"You don't know shit, English," he spat, before scampering off. Michael followed his silhouette as it magnified against the side wall, until he disappeared.

Meet The Parents

Linda and Thomas Rossington were slightly dazed from the relentless click and flash of the photographers, while graciously answering the inane questions of ridiculously young reporters and media people. Rose removed them from the jaws of the press.

"Rose, it has to be said, you're a natural. Your father and I, well, we're not so acquainted with the ways of being superstars." Linda said in a way that made Rose know she was indeed having fun.

"Look at your father, he looks like one of those walking dead type of things, you know the ones from the television, dear?"

Julie laughed as she approached them. "Hey! Mom and Pops." She hugged them both within the same embrace.

"Now, Julie. I hope you've been looking after her." More of a query from Linda.

"Mom? Are you kidding? Of course I am. I don't get much time to do anything else."

"Now, Julie, there's one thing that puzzles Thomas and I."

"Yeah? What's that?"

"*Nubian Rose* belongs to the pair of you."

"It sure does."

"So, why was it just Rose who did that wavy walk of fame thing? I mean, it was very nice, and it was all very Diana Ross-ish, but where were you, dear?"

"She don't let me do all that stuff. You know how big headed she is, hogging the limelight. I asked her if we could both do the walk and the speech thing, but she tells me to get back inside my box. It's awful, guys, the way she treats me."

They had both known Julie Ross long enough. Rose rolled her eyes and kissed her teeth.

"I'll let you into a little secret," she continued, and wedged her tall frame between them both. "There's something about Rosey that I think you gotta know."

Rose stood by, listening with only vague interest while pouting at Sapphire who was smiling at her from underneath a huge Egyptian statue.

"She's mean. Like, totally mean, to everyone, guys, not just me." Julie pretended to frown and look sad. "Sometimes she don't even pay me. I have to remind her to give me my paycheck. I'll soon be living on welfare. She's actually pretty damn bad at paying me anything, actually…"

Thomas turned to Rose. "Is this true, Rose?" he asked sternly.

"Okay, that's quite enough, Julia. Why don't you go and find your Howard guy?"

"Rose, simply awful… it really is."

"Apologies father, but I cannot warrant any of this conversation with any further input because it would insult my own sensibilities."

"Well, talking of sensible ties, *I'm here*!" CeeCee Holmes announced. "And Rose, you never told me your brother and sister had arrived."

"Oh Lord," said Rose and Julie simultaneously.

Rose eventually managed to break away. She grabbed Carlos and led him through the crowd. By this time Carlos had consumed three more pink grapefruit and basil mimosas. "Ease up on the pink fizz, darling." She smiled and kissed him. "I thought you said you didn't like them."

"They're growing on me, I must admit," he said, hiccupping.

"Baby, there are two people I want you to meet."

"You keep on saying that."

Fully aware Carlos was unfamiliar with such affairs, Rose saw that he managed everything with his usual unassuming manner. His diplomacy and easy-going nature impressed her. His comfortable smile loosely displayed his perfect teeth, as his mellow Mexican dialogue made her ravenous for him. She was immensely proud as everyone stared at the stranger by her side.

"Mother, Father, may I introduce Carlos."

Positioning herself between them both with her arms lovingly wrapped around their shoulders, she towered at least a foot and a half above them. He was taken aback at her introduction as he saw the elderly white couple, their warm smiles immediately welcoming him.

Rose could see his evident confusion. "Darling, Lord and Lady Rossington. You might say they are my adoptive guardians."

"You might indeed, and we wouldn't change a thing. We are so proud of her," Thomas Rossington said as both men shook hands.

"Well, hello Carlos, splendid. It's so nice to actually see you in the flesh," said the Lady. She offered her hand and Carlos gave it a peck.

"I feel very honoured to meet the pair of you both."

"Rose, he has a very kind face, do you not agree?"

Rose objectively inspected him, as if the question had debatable gravity. "I do, Mother, for he is kind. A true gentleman, something I am sure you shall soon learn as you become more acquainted."

"Okay, of course, of course. So tell me, Carlos, have you ever been to Britain?" Linda asked.

"Great Britain?"

"Well, yes."

"No, I have not. Not yet anyway. Is it true it rains all year round?"

Thomas laughed. "It pretty much does, Carlos. But Linda and I, we never minded the rain. Rain makes things grow, you see?"

"Thomas, please refrain from boring poor Carlos with your rain stories," said Linda.

"I am not boring him, I was simply going to tell him that without the rain we would not be able to be blessed with beautifully green lawns and such huge blossoming roses."

"Thomas, can't you forget about your blessed roses for one second?"

Carlos smiled, but only after he saw Rose laughing.

"Do you like football, Carlos?" Thomas asked.

"Yes, sir. Do you?"

"Well, I am a Newbury F.C. supporter, so I, err…"

"Oh, just ignore him, Carlos," Linda said, looking disapprovingly at her husband. "Rose tells us you play soccer."

"Yes, ma'am, I do. Well, I used to play it. But these days I'm usually too busy for that kind of things."

"That's such a pity," Thomas said.

"Tell us a little about where you come from, Carlos. That is, if you don't mind," Linda said.

Carlos thought for a moment. "Where I come from, my mother has a window house, um, like a glass house. She grows roses inside it all year. There are a few, um – how do you say? – parables, stories from the place I come from. Roses are sometimes celebrated because folks think they are miracles."

Linda and Thomas were now captivated, whilst Rose, her arm tightly knotted with his, smiled and glanced at him.

"Oh Rose, Carlos is adorable."

Rose cosied up against him even more, pinching his cheek.

"So you are in construction, do you have a specific trade, Carlos?" Thomas asked.

"You guys, is Carlos under interrogation here?"

"It's okay. I try to do as much as I can, you know… building, plastering and things. But I am an electrician, really, although I sometimes do a lot of plumbing, too."

"Although, not at the same time, guys, that would be fatal," Rose quipped. They all laughed.

Back Of House Rumblings (part 3)

The past three hours had been rigorous. Since his last break, Michael's duties grew all the more tiring, and the heat of the summer night only magnified the pressure.

Together with Danny Booker, he'd spent a considerable amount of time trying to convince Tico Ramirez of the benefits in joining them.

"It's vital, Tico," he said. "There really is no choice. Three more people have gone AWOL."

"So? Why is this my business? I told you two to quit with this bullshit."

"I'm going to say something, I will, man. Something to mess it all up. I'm going crazy with this shit," Danny was unravelling before their eyes.

"I think we all should. This has gone too far," Michael said, shaking his head. "We could do something about this. Right now."

"It's just a job, you stupid guy. What the hell is wrong with you two jerks?" Tico said. "It's gonna be over soon. Why can't you just get on with it and shut the hell up?"

"Come on, Tico, man. Out of all of us, you're the one who's been bit the worst. Can't you see?" Danny pleaded.

"Can't *you* see? I don't wanna end up dead. Just leave me the hell alone," he screeched.

The kitchen was yet again filled with trays waiting to be carried out into the hall. The kitchen staff busy to almost boiling point.

"You three," the head chef screamed. "Get those trays the hell out of my kitchen."

Almost running, they barged through into the gallery to serve the guests intricately-crafted appetizers, such as cream and asparagus filled tomatoes and smoked salmon and caviar tartlets.

The chef called again, "Get your asses in gear. We ain't even started evening service yet."

Later, Danny Booker and Tico were assigned to wash twelve large cases of dirty kitchen equipment.

At first, Danny had been discouraged in his attempts to persuade Tico to join Michael Beavis and himself, but in time he became relentless in his pursuit.

"You ain't gonna shut the hell up, are you? You're just gonna keep on going on and on. I can't stand it. It's worse than what she ever did to me, this constant fucking noise in my head!" Tico's eyes widened, warding off the immense wave of exhaustion.

The Plan

Michael Beavis slowly passed through a seemingly never-ending sea of people, and the smile he gave was customary, something he'd learned from the hospitality training he'd received. As Middle-Eastern sultans and feather-wearing R&B singers swiped drinks from his tray, he'd thank them in a way that made them believe he was enthusiastic and attentive.

While almost dead on his feet within the Sackler Wing, Rose placed her hands on his shoulders.

"Where's the smile, darling?" she whispered, while straightening his tie. "When I paid good money for you to receive the best training possible, I never expected your standard, and your posture, to slip."

She smiled down at him. Michael almost wept with an overwhelming desire as he saw how beautiful she looked.

"I truly loathe bad posture. It ranks the top-spot within my list of all time pet peeves."

"I am sorry, Miss Benoit." Michael puffed out his chest and straightened his back.

"Good boy. Carry on."

***

Another co-worker had gone missing, a burly Irish boxer they had referred to only as Jimmy hadn't been seen for over an hour.

"Has anybody eaten?" asked Danny.

Michael shook his head. "But I'm not hungry."

"I had some bread earlier," Tico said dismissively. "Can we get this over with? We only have five minutes break, remember?"

They were all crouched down at the bottom of the basement staircase. The place had proved to be the safest location for Michael, Danny and Tico to speak freely.

"You okay with this? I wouldn't blame you if you said you wanted out," Danny said.

"You say that shit to me now? You two have been riding me all night, and now you offer me the damned option to back out?"

Both men sadly shrugged.

"But I volunteered anyhow, didn't I?"

Tico then looked at them both, expectantly, prompting Michael to hastily relate the plan he'd conceived.

"In roughly twenty minutes, they're all going to be sitting in the other wing while they eat. Danny... you and me are gonna be serving till closing time, which is maybe going to be another three to five hours." Michael then handed Danny a crudely old-looking smartphone. "Take this. Keep it safe. At the correct time, take the photographs. And make sure you know where the video camera is on the device. We don't want to balls this up."

Michael looked over to Tico. "Okay, so you're gonna make the speech. You'll be finished in the kitchen after your next hour shift. Wait until a minute and a half, then make a dash to the centre of the entrance. Remove your shirt, show all that shit she did to you and say the words."

Danny Booker folded up the scrap of paper featuring his script neatly written in capitals, and passed it to Tico.

"Remember, little man, if you go down, we're going down with you. We got your back."

The Speech

The event was catered for by one of the world's leading chefs, who simply couldn't refuse the opportunity.

After service, Rose, who was seated at the head table with Julie Ross, stood, momentarily allowing herself to be miked.

"I half guessed they'd want me to say something, and I haven't really prepared anything, so do find it in your hearts to forgive me if I commit anything that would be deemed controversial. Those who know me sometimes warn me of my many faux pas. I am aware this sets people on edge, so for this I apologise in advance."

Rose's accent was delicious while amplified, and the seated guests were totally mesmerised by her perfect tones.

"Okay, well firstly, I wish to thank Miss Julie Ross."

An instant round of applause. She looked down at her partner who was sat by her side, grabbing her hand tightly.

"My closest confidant, and my best friend. This event is ultimately a joint venture. An enterprise over which this gorgeous girl and myself have been obsessing and slaving pretty much from the moment we both started. I remember when we first met. I was staying in Hell's Kitchen, she lived close by. The nights we would stay up. Three, sometimes four in the morning, oh heavens, just to get things right, you know, get everything we had watertight, so that by the time we did fly across town to Gramercy Park we were prepared. Julie and I have worked tirelessly to contribute to our *Children's Playground*, which provides fair opportunities to carers of the Trust's shelters. It strives towards better conditions for the impoverished women and girls, with whom we have worked very closely, and their carers, some of whom we are extremely honoured to have as our guests here this evening."

The inspiring words prompted a full standing ovation.

Rose resumed her speech. "You know, I actually can't

believe it, to think we are here tonight within its reality and realisation. Over a million people are now safe and warm." More applause.

"Thank you, you are very kind."

She remained on her feet, and someone passed her a large black feathered fan that she used to full indulgent effect.

"I would next like to thank my guardians. There are no two people more responsible in literally speeding me to where I am today than my beloved Linda and Thomas. I love you both, so dearly."

She raised her glass to the pair.

"I suppose I should also thank the booking agents for the availability of this beautiful place. The designers and interior lighting for their assistance, they have done a wondrous job. The sound people, who managed to get hold of all my obscure and hard-to-find musical selections... I myself offer you a personal thank you. To our magnificent team elsewhere, in London and Europe. And all those who were unable to join us tonight."

Another brief spell of applause finally died down, while a slight commotion could be heard over in the opposite end of the hall.

"This is all a sham, you people is being fooled... this is... bullshit!"

Everyone glanced over towards the main entrance, to where the heckler was cut short in mid-sentence. He was then forcibly removed by three black security officers who were almost three times the size of the small, slightly scruffy man.

The guests casually looked back at Rose.

"Oops," she said, raising her eyebrows. "I wonder what was his problem. Perhaps it was the Foie gras. Personally, I prefer rare but I understand that might not be to everyone's taste."

Every single guest laughed uproariously before giving their host another round of applause.

"Where was I? Oh yes." Julie poured Rose another

glass and placed it in her hand. "This all started as a small twinkling dream I used to have when I was a child. It was a dream that I held close. I never used to speak of it, but I always kept it alive by thinking that someday I would manage to turn it into reality. I don't mind saying that, through my stubbornness and the determination of everyone involved… look at us now! We did it!"

She held her glass aloft, to raise the toast. "To all strong-minded people who have aspirations, may you realise them – for if one is able to dream it, one is able to do it."

She took a sip as everyone cheered.

The Crowning Jewel

Rose had left Carlos in the capable hands of Julie and CeeCee Holmes as they both stole him away from the Rossingtons, before parading him around as if he were a new toy. Rose mingled herself within the crowd in the main gallery and addressed the representatives of the main charities and shelters, as well as some of her more discerning guests.

Although fleeting, Carlos had also met Sapphire.

It wasn't until it was time to be seated in the upper gallery for dinner that Rose saw him again. Grabbing him from the clutches of her entourage, she pulled him through a door, sending him flying into the room beyond it.

They were alone. "Are you enjoying yourself, baby?" she asked as she pushed him up against the door.

"Yes, you have many friends who…"

"Be quiet. Kiss me."

The charity auction was next on the list of the night's festivities. Their revered guests, who had already paid over six thousand dollars to attend, were then invited to bid towards a selection of grand prizes. A Bentley with the year's current registration had been donated by a prestigious London garage. Various properties and leased apartments in and around the French Riviera were also up for grabs. Finally, the grand prize had been announced. The item had been commissioned by *Tiffany & Co.* A Diamond Platinum fringed necklace, which was valued at that time at a whopping six and a half million dollars. The crowning jewel, literally.

Julie Ross was resplendently modelling the piece. As she mingled, patrons were able to view its beauty as it hung from her neck.

As the night wore on, guests only slightly dwindled as music and food and drink still flowed copiously throughout the entire venue.

Rose announced that they had finally totalled a staggering amount of proceeds, which almost topped the thirty million mark.

She managed to slide away to a small room, and silently had a moment to herself where she wept tears of disbelief.

She thought of Martha and Sarah. The simplicity of her life when she was a teenager. A strange feeling of emptiness filled her head. Silently focusing on the shiny marble floor, the reflection of light shone from a skylight above her. She was listless, as intermittent intrusions from assistants only slightly distracted her as they respectfully let her know certain guests were at last departing.

The evening, which stretched to the early hours of the following morning, had been a success. One event she would never forget. She courtly thanked all.

Rose took her man by the hand as she left the night behind.

She dealt with Carlos when they arrived back at the hotel, rewarding him for being the perfect gentleman, whilst blowing his mind with the pure ecstasy and sinful pleasures of her superiority and womanhood. Pleasures that would have made lesser men feel unsure of themselves.

***

As the dawn light transcended through the large window of The Waldorf's rear facing penthouse suite, Rose sipped on her iced coffee and stroked his head as it lay on her lap.

"So? Do you understand now, baby?" she asked.

"Yes, I think so," Carlos said. Rose wasn't convinced, judging by his listless expression.

"Do you want me to explain it again?"

"I'm sorry, Rosy. It's my problem; you know what I'm like, I have to have things explained to me more than one time."

Rose looked over at the purple and fluorescent skyline

that hovered above the jagged buildings of Midtown east, giving much thought towards how to make her repeat more accessible.

"Okay, baby. My real mother died when I was sixteen. Back then, a lot of bad things happened. I had nowhere to go. I travelled out of London, where I found work as a housekeeper at Rossington Hall."

"Rossington Hall. Right! The Tommy and Linda Rossingtons!"

"That's correct. Well, I worked hard. They grew fond of me. We would dance in the kitchen." Rose smiled at the memories that were passing through her mind. "I would make them listen to Whitney Houston, and they would cajole me with Glen Miller and Count Basie. They knew I had been underprivileged. They asked me if they might help me."

"Seems like... they were very good to you."

"I remember, it was a Sunday evening. I had just arrived back at the house. I'd been in attendance at one of Duchess Katherine Burton's bridge evenings, a place I would also receive elocution tutelage, although not by Duchess Katherine Burton herself." Rose smiled now at Carlos, who nodded, seemingly bluffing at following her narrative. "That evening, I joined them in the parlour, we would often gather there, especially on Sundays. We would play games like charades and Guess Who. After a while, Linda asked me a question. She said, *of all your dreams, what do you wish to do with your life?*"

Rose was transported back. She shook her head and, for a moment, she could actually experience the feelings of what her life was at that time.

"What did you say to her?" he asked.

She remembered what she'd said. These rose-tinted memories. The whole thing played out like a gospel. She would often find herself thinking about these events when she should have been deeply engaged in meetings with financiers and famous business clients.

"I told her I would like to see the best school in the

world." Rose saw his confusion. "Baby, I wasn't always this educated. I came from a very bad place, in a very bad time. I saw ignorance. And hatred. I was born from poverty, and I was born from a broken home. It made my heart ache. I thought that bettering myself would be suffice enough an answer."

Carlos tried holding back, but had to interject. "Sometimes, Rose, I don't understand some of the words you say."

"Okay, the only answer I was able to give her was that I would like the opportunity and the privilege to be properly educated."

"Yes, I understand that. But I don't know what you mean about hatred. What kind of hatred?"

Rose was silent. She breathed out and proceeded to relate what, years ago, she always believed would kill her if she ever actually verbalised it.

"My best friend, she was attacked."

Slowly, Carlos looked down and an ugly crease appeared above his brow.

"She died. I loved her with all my soul; she was like a part of me. Aside from my mother, she was my most treasured thing in life. We doted on each other."

Carlos's eyes watered, a tear threatened to fall, but Rose stopped its escape. He stared at her in disbelief. He was evidently shocked at her rare display of vulnerability. The thought of Rose being anything other than the superior, strong woman he always thought she was, was baffling.

"Her attackers. They were not as bad to me as they were to her."

Suddenly, Rose felt remiss. She reproached herself for being so open. She released herself of Carlos' arm and sat herself up, leaning against the headboard and closed her eyes.

Carlos's frown remained. Rose saw him, a darkness that she believed was caused by her account and its honesty. She remained silent.

He then moved, and sat cross-legged at the foot of the

enormous bed, straightening himself. He cleared his throat, coughing into his fist.

"Rose. Nothing I can say is gonna express the sadness I feel when you tell me this. I am sorry for you and your friend, I am sorry." He looked down at his hands and rubbed them together.

Rose eyed him directly. His concern touched her, more so than she assumed it would. He nodded quickly, head still downcast, as if fighting off tears. Rose reached over and placed her fingers on his face in an attempt to better see his eyes.

"I love you, Rose. My life, my Lord, I'll say a prayer for you."

Support At Last

David Morgan's self-control had collapsed yet again. Demoralised, and after too many rejections to mention, he believed his report was going nowhere, fruitless. Of his two phone contacts, it had been the least receptive of the pair that was the most frequent. He couldn't stand this person's stark indifference.

But he continued. "On August twenty ninth, this year, the subject hosted and conducted a charity event at the Met museum on Fifth Avenue."

David Morgan lit another cigarette. It was nearing 1pm.

"An incident occurred while the subject was making a speech after dinner. The subject was jeered by a Hispanic male, name of Ramirez, who was forthwith removed from the main dining hall at approximately twenty-one hundred hours."

He paced his apartment, after closing the door to his bathroom, blocking out the sound of constant dripping water.

"An in-depth search for Ramirez provided no results."

David remained stubbornly silent, waiting for his contact to make a comment. Finally. "Morgan, why is the man still missing?"

"Pardon me? Your question is a little curious, don't you think? *I* don't know why Ramirez is still missing, do you? During the hunt, we quizzed security at the venue. They told us Ramirez was passed to the 17th precinct, over on East fifty first. I struggled to conduct a meeting with the head DI. Nobody knew what I was talking about. The contact I made with various employees at the precinct, all listed in the previous memo, was extremely adverse, extremely hostile. And when I needed you, I received no support from you guys, either. The time I'd spent making this inquiry would have been better spent actually reprimanding the subject. But that still doesn't explain what the hell happened to Ramirez."

David Morgan paused, aware he was losing his restraint,

something about which he'd been warned, on countless occasions.

He cleared his throat and decided to try a different tack. "I don't want this assignment. I want out."

Immediately, the voice on the line turned on the charm. "Oh, Morgan, we've been through all this. All we want you to do is relate the reports to us, for *now*. As soon as we feel it's safe for you to turn the subject out, we shall tell you. Then you may go in and deal with the subject in any way you think is fitting."

"Yeah? And when the hell is that going to be? I was doing this shit when I was sixteen. I really don't feel I'm doing anything that's gonna contribute towards the subject's eradication. I just don't buy this shit."

After an awkward silence, the reluctant voice continued. "Listen, Morgan, we're obviously getting nowhere. Would it help if we put ADF on the line for you?"

This took Morgan by surprise. "When, now?"

"Presently. Yes."

He thought about it. "Yes. Yes, it would."

Within the seven hours that followed, David Morgan waited, passing the time via more abdominal crunches.

"Davey? Are you there?" said a voice, almost whispering. But the voice was warm, a much needed sound, it instantly melted David's icy acrimony.

"Where the hell have you been, Arlo? And why couldn't I just talk to you in the first damn place?"

"Calm down, Morgan. Remember what I told you: there aren't many folks who aren't listening."

Arlo Dante had been David Morgan's chief-in-command for his entire career. A hardened soldier in his youth, but he was neither a tyrannical bully back then, nor a stuffy bureaucrat now. He was a hero to every single soldier he'd ever trained. David Morgan had missed him.

"This mission... if you can call it a mission, sucks."

"Davey, I agree. From what I can gather, it's a total mess, and it ain't your fault."

"It's a stake out. I feel like a cartoon character."

"Listen, Davey, I looked at this gig, and I've been through the files. It's a weird one, I'll grant you, but it's also a worthwhile one. And do-able, you know? That's why they have you on it. I told them that you were the main man for getting things done."

"I can't do it, Arlo. I wanna come back."

"Davey…"

"I want out."

"Davey, listen to me." Arlo's voice grew level, curiously halting David's momentum.

"*I* want you to do this thing, Davey. I *know* you're the best. No one knows that more than me. You remember when we used to talk about that *one special*? That golden egg prize? Well this is it, you hear me? You thought all them tours over in Syria and Afghanistan were fulfilling? Well, they ain't nothing compared to this bitch. This is it, Davey. This is the one all the others in the future are gonna be measured against. The big one!"

"Okay, so what makes it so fucking special?"

"Your subject. Your subject, Davey. There's a lot riding on the whole thing. Listen, I can't say a lot, you understand. Your subject is insane, Davey, but it's a high-ranking case. We have to be careful."

"That's what they've been saying."

"Believe them, it's right. They know what they're talking about. Davey, how are you gonna finalise it?"

"You mean, I can eliminate?"

"Sure you can, who told you otherwise?"

"I didn't think…" David stuttered.

"Think about the elimination. Design the details from scratch, and leave room for any further add-ons these guys tell you."

David pulled on the exercise bar with his right hand and pulled himself up as much as his strength could allow.

"I'm going to rip her head off."

"See? That's the Davey I know. That's the animal I trained to perfection. Only an animal can kill another animal the right way."

No Exit

Jack Sargent sat listlessly at the traffic lights. This was North London on a Friday afternoon; the waiting was endless.

Thoughts passed through his mind with unsettling haste and urgency, conflicting with the stagnant congestion outside. He envisioned Daniel waving at him from his bedroom window at *New Horizons*, a look of sadness staining his beautiful face.

But Rose Benoit haunted him as she played out the key moments from his time with her. The sound of her voice, the way she had danced, the clothes she had worn.

Her dominant attitude, although it at first made him feel uncomfortable, now enthused him about the strong woman's morals of being in charge and being in control.

The images came swarming through his mind like ten thousand hornets, ready to sting at any moment.

He drove through the dusk of the evening, which mirrored the murkiness of his mind.

The photograph was still taped to the wall within his kitchen. He glanced at it as he traipsed through from the hall before plonking his meagre shopping onto the counter.

The hum of his mobile sounded. Ollie.

"Listen, boss. I think you need a holiday," he sighed. "And it's late, you should be in your bed."

Jack listened, the phone loosely attached to his ear, while still stood in the middle of his kitchen. He imagined Ollie, sat at the foot of his staircase, a heavy frown obscuring his eyelids after an intense discussion with Beth about the differences between divorce proceedings and the onset of a new life in Southern Spain.

"I'm sorry, Ollie."

"Jack, you don't have to apologise. What annoys me is that I've already told you what to do. It's really frustrating because we're not moving forward. The medical. You should have had it by now, Jack. You think I haven't noticed your back is getting worse? You need that operation."

Again, Jack glanced at the mugshot of Rose. He noticed her naked shoulders and surmised she had been wearing something low cut.

"I'm sorry about Daniel, I really am. But you should take time to sort it out. The more you're on the job, the more you're screwing up your chances with him. This *Animal* case is crap, Jack. It's embarrassing. I can't see a way through it. You should focus on what's important. What's the most important thing to you, Jack?"

Rose Benoit, Jack thought. From the depths of his mind, Daniel cried and waved, trying to avert his attention as Jack glared at Rose dressed in a shiny black Catwoman costume.

He hadn't forgot the words from his dream. Their bizarre sequence: "*Even rich head and you.*"

He recalled the sound of them like he remembered where he lived, unforgettable. He remained unsure of their significance. The words confused him as his brain tried to construct a meaning for them.

The cigarette investigation was over, there was no reason he would or should contact her again. All was lost as he fought against his feelings for the woman whom he'd only ever met once.

Yet, sat upon the chair in the centre of his kitchen, he dialled. No answer.

A large glass, misplaced upon the edge of an old straw coaster, covered in murky prints and grime, contained three quarters of Scotch and melted ice.

The first call, now over an hour ago, failed to wrench his gut as he assumed it would, perhaps only because of the other misfires in the past month since their meeting.

He tried again. No answer.

Three more times, just as fruitless.

There were twenty double rings before voicemail

offered it's rude, needless services.

Rose Benoit's personal phone. As he rang it for the ninth time, he imagined her handset in a drawer in an office somewhere in a building close to Southwark Bridge.

Or inside her handbag, which was being cradled by a friend as she stepped onto the dance floor somewhere in New York or Miami, surrounded by extroverted homosexuals and famous porn stars.

Or perhaps in her own private residence, placed on a bedside table awaiting her arrival after a long hot shower. Herself dripping, scantily half covered in the whitest towel he could imagine.

As he rang for the twelfth time, thoughts of his own obsessiveness, his own impulsiveness, still failed to discourage him.

On the following try, suddenly...

Tico Ramirez

"Jack…" Rose announced, immediately awakening his mind, immediately heralding a new era, an era of light and great things, disarming all prior despondency.

He fell in love with the way she emphasised the *K*, as she half whispered the name.

He paused, composing himself and trying not to display his lack of poise. "Hi, it is nice to… it's… Hi." Failing miserably.

Rose laughed. "Mmm, still possessing a case of the jitterbugs, I hear, Jack?"

"I'm sorry, Miss Benoit."

"Jack, please, if you apologise one more time, I will come round there and give you that sound spanking we spoke about when last we met. Do you understand me, Inspector?"

"Okay, got that." Jack still relished the thought. In the depths of his obsession for her, he'd actually dreamed what such an occurrence would be like. Imagining himself bent over her lap. Rose seated and casually slapping his exposed white bottom with her gloved hands.

"Jack, my sweet, I'm going out on a tiny limb here, but would I be correct in assuming you wish to speak to me?"

"I err… yes, I am sorry. I apologise, well, it's not really that important…"

"Is Jack okay?"

"Oh me? I'm doing okay, I guess. I've been busy these last few days," he lied, "trying my best to keep my nose to the grindstone."

"Be careful, Jack darling. Be sure not to press too hard; detectives rely on their sense of smell after all."

"Yeah," Jack snickered pathetically.

"Well, I suppose you and I are now friends, Jack. There's not much harm in speaking from time to time, is there?"

Jack's ears pricked up hopefully. *Friends.*

"Of course not. I'm glad you, err, I am happy you feel that way."

"Our evening," she chuckled. "Did I scare you, Jack?"

Yes you did, Jack thought.

"Of course you didn't." Jack said. "I have to admit that I wasn't ready for it. I think the words *culture shock* would be putting it mildly. But since I've had time to think about some of those things…"

"You're warming to them? You're curious, Jack, my sweet?"

"Rose," Jack thought to himself, the time was right for some big sincerity. "That night was very special to me. I cannot think of anyone I would have rather been with."

"I fear I might have corrupted you, you poor thing. Immersing you into acts so sordid. I'm so naughty."

"Rose. It was amazing." Jack caught his dark reflection in the edge of his microwave. He hated himself as he glanced at the pathetic silhouette of his face.

"Detective Inspector Jack Sargent." The first time she'd said his title correctly. "I can't believe how sweet you are. I could eat you!"

"If only," Jack thought and said simultaneously. A short breathy silence followed. "…I'm so sorry, Rose. I don't know what came over me. I never meant to say that out loud."

"I did warn you, Jack, that if you apologised to me again I would spank you… Do you remember?"

"Yes, but…"

"I am a woman of her word, Inspector."

"I, yes…"

"And if I wish to eat you, I will do just that. This is something for which *you* need not apologise."

"Miss…"

"You will only apologise to me if I ask you to do so, is that clear, Jack?"

"Y… yes, it's…"

"Good boy."

Jack remained motionless and poised within the centre of his kitchen. Breaking this position would ultimately sever his undivided attention.

"I think it would be nice to maybe hook up again. What do you say, Jack?"

"I think so, yes."

"And might I retain your number, I mean, for personal use?"

"Of course, that would be fine, and am I able to keep your number, too?" Jack enquired.

"You most certainly can. However, this is one of my business lines, of which I have many, so it may be a case of just waiting for me to get in touch. You understand, don't you, Jack?"

Jack would have understood anything if Rose said it was so. "Yes, of course. I could do that."

"Okay. Well, again, it was a pleasure to speak to you, Inspector. I look forward to our future engagements."

"Me too, I really will, and thank you for speaking to me, Rose."

"The pleasure was all mine, baby."

Dial tone.

***

Rose switched off her phone and placed it back onto the shelf.

"Do forgive me, important call," she said while still casually leaning against Tico Ramirez, her arm draped around his shoulder. He glanced over at his severed right arm and tongue and ear, the blood-soaked hacksaw and several of his teeth that dotted the room around them.

"Okay, my sweet, might we continue?"

He grimaced, nodding. Blood poured from his mouth, his pained expression creasing as he continued to nod in agreement.

Tidy Tuesdays

Ollie glanced at the bags around Jack's eyes. Dark and seemingly permanent, like water damage on the side of a brick wall or the rings of a chopped tree. He wasn't sure what had contributed to their momentum: Daniel. The *Animal* case. Rose Benoit.

Everybody's Able was awash with activity. It reminded Jack of an old maritime movie – all hands on deck, scrubbing the rigging. Indeed, everyone seemed to have their own jobs to do, their own duties, and appeared extremely happy about it.

"Oh, hi guys," said Silly Sandy as she bounded up to the pair of them. Jack and Ollie stood awkwardly while loud urban music blared from huge speakers above their heads.

"Never mind the sounds, fellas, we take it in turns and today was that scoundrel Lois's choice. I know... not like the music in your day, is it fellas?"

She ribbed Jack with a small elbow, albeit softly. Instantly engaging them both unintentionally with her amusing headgear, a garland of rotating plastic flower heads, smiling and turning, at least two of which were moving slower than the rest. Ollie smirked.

They looked around. Many people, young and older, were rushing in and out, emptying large bin bags of rubbish. A young woman was stood confidently upon the top shelf of a tall step ladder, rehanging the ceiling lampshades.

"Yep, as you can see, Tuesday is cleany-up day. Or, as I like to call it by its proper name... Tidy-Tuesday!"

"Makes me feel lazy. You do this every Tuesday?" asked Ollie.

"Nope, Tidy-Tuesdays happen but once a month," she beamed.

"Well, in that case, why don't you call it Tidy-once-a-month-on-every-third-Tuesday day?"

Jack nudged his partner. "Behave yourself," he said, and turned to Sandy. "Sandy? Is it?"

"That's right. Silly Sandy at your service." She offered her tiny hand, it felt warm and rough when placed in Jack's palm.

"Pleased to meet you, Sandy. This is inspector Ollie Travis and my name is Detective Inspector Jack Sargent."

"I know that, silly. You rang me yesterday," she tutted and rolled her eyes. "Your name should be silly, too, Jack. Hey let's all be sillies, huh?"

They were offered a drink before Silly Sandy sent someone to find Ricky Gomez.

"Let me just fill you guys in," Silly Sandy began, as they both seated themselves inside her small office. "Ricky's a total bloomin' angel. He's really turned a corner and he's so willing to help, now."

Jack and Ollie looked at each other. The comment was questionable to say the least. By this point, Ollie Travis had only been briefed of Ricky Gomez and his past by way of his case files. Thoughts of his criminal back catalogue ran through Jack's system like infected water. Of the three suspects in the Sarah Allen case, Ricky Gomez had always been the most subversive, the most long serving.

Silly Sandy reacted to their evident doubt. "Okay, okay, when he arrived he was a bit of a nightmare. To begin with, we actually had a little trouble. But you'd be amazed, fellas, seriously."

"Yeah! Amazed at how handsome I still am."

Jack and Ollie reeled round, their eyes met the sturdy looking man stood by the door.

His face was less bony, but his big, deep-set eyes still hinted at the years of abuse. He wasn't overly handsome, however, he'd aged pretty well for someone who'd spent more of his life on class A drugs than off them.

"Ricky, you look good," Jack said. He got up from his seat and gave him a healthy handshake.

"Thanks, Jack. I wish I could say the same about you,"

Ricky smiled.

Jack stared at him in disbelief. With all the horror stories he'd heard within the past fifteen years, reports of countless break-ins, drug-busts, beatings and imprisonment, he struggled to grasp the image of this cheerful man stood before him.

"You remember me, Ricky?"

"How could I forget a face like that, Jack? Time's been hard, my friend, but there was always a place in my memory for you."

Jack did a partially sufficient job of concealing his astonishment.

"But your image and sense of style hasn't changed. You can set your watch to that hairstyle, Jack."

Jack smiled and Silly Sandy laughed.

She left, allowing the three of them to use her office.

"Ricky, I wanted to ask, did you hear about Steven Freeman?"

Ricky lowered his head. "That was awful."

"Do you remember when you first heard?"

"I received a mobile phone a few months ago and I got a text from a friend. I couldn't believe it."

"When was the last time you saw Steven Freeman, Ricky?"

He looked up at Ollie and, for the first time, his tone grew a touch edgy. "Excuse me, but am I on trial here?"

"Relax, Ricky. It's nothing like that, Ollie's merely trying to find out the last time you spoke to him, that's all."

"I haven't spoken to him since we were at school. I think he moved away. I didn't even know he'd been sent down until late last year."

"What about Andrew Baker?"

"Huh? What about him? He's famous, yeah. I reckon he lived near me when I was a kid. The youngsters here, I tell them that, it seems to impress them. I used to kick a ball too, you know. I was better than him, as I recall, but I can't remember a lot of stuff from those days. Stevie though, when I heard... I was sad, he died so... badly. I mean, who does that?"

Their instincts suggested Ricky was being honest. His rugged appearance suited him and Jack found himself being drawn to him. He'd been given the heads up that Ricky's mind had deteriorated, that his memory was, at best, genuinely selective, at worst like a colander. It was true, his speech was below par but Jack could see the effort Ricky was applying to accommodate their enquiries. His left eye appeared half closed, a permanent disability due to the numerous beatings he'd suffered.

Jack steered the conversation away. He pointed to the photograph of Silly Sandy. "Ricky, she's funny. I like her, she seems nice."

"She's great, Sandy. Everyone loves her."

"I can honestly see why, Ricky. I commend you for believing in her."

"Ha, she did the same thing with me. She's amazing – she's the thing that holds all this together."

"Where do you think you'd be if you never came through here, Ricky?"

"I don't know. But I know I wouldn't be able to talk to you. It doesn't bear thinking about, Jack. Helping out here is my whole life."

They both watched Ricky as he habitually scrubbed at the back of his head with the palm of his hand. Like an itch, Ricky did this almost twice a minute.

"What's next for you, Ricky?"

"At the moment I'm working for the council. Another three months and they tell me I can have my own place. I really want to work in a kitchen."

"And?" Silly Sandy appeared again, holding a tray with three hot drinks and a plate of custard creams. "Tell them about your good news, Ricky."

"And... my name's been put down for an educational course type thing."

"Oh, Jack, he's a silly billy, isn't he?" said Silly Sandy. "What Ricky's trying to say is, there's this huge learning centre opened up near Wandsworth. It's being funded by the government. It's basically trying to get people who are homeless, or people trying to find work, an education. They enrol, then they can attend and receive their O'levels, A'levels, or whatever they want."

Ricky smiled proudly at Jack and Ollie. "It's ace, guys."

A photograph was taken using Silly Sandy's phone. And, before Jack and Ollie had chance to leave, an A4 sized print of them all had already been hung behind Silly's chaotic desk.

Somewhere

Rose opened the door and was slightly taken aback to see him stood there. He looked handsome dressed in his jeans and white polo t-shirt. She was pleased he'd cut his hair.

"Are you okay?" Carlos asked, inquisitively peeping in, hoping that Rose wouldn't turn him away.

"I'm good," she nodded. "I'm good, babe."

She sounded tired. The vibrant accent that normally coloured her voice seemed subdued. She leaned forward to allow him to kiss her lips.

"I'm sorry, I wouldn't usually come unannounced. I respect that you have to work, and that you need time to yourself and…"

"Baby? Hush. Come." Rose eyed him and silently beckoned him in. He followed her into the apartment. A large quilt lay on the sofa. An open book laid face down upon the floor.

"Are you hungry?" he asked. "Because I'm hungry. I want to make you something. I want to know if you'd let me do that."

Rose looked at him; her eyes, free of all make-up, penetrated him.

"I was worried about you, that's all. And I wanted to cook."

He sounded desperate. He blew out with a sigh, as if flabbergasted by the words coming from his own mouth. She smiled. His sincerity was truthful.

"I could eat, yes, and I'm fine. I just needed some time out for myself. We've been extremely busy these last few weeks."

"Well, I'm here now, see? Carlos at your service." He saluted, standing to attention.

Rose laughed.

"Right, tell me where your kitchen is again," he asked as Rose kissed her teeth.

He ushered her back to the sofa, sat her down, covered her up with the quilt and handed her the book she was reading, a huge opus about the Renaissance.

"Carry on reading, I may be some time."

Carlos walked through into the kitchen and opened the fridge. He frowned at the sight, pathetically sparse. It's entire contents comprising of a large floret of broccoli, one carton of Milo and a bunch of red grapes.

He began opening cupboards and pulling on drawers, finding nothing more than a pot of dried basil and one jar of Jamaican seasoning.

He appeared at the threshold of the main living area with a slightly disappointed look on his face.

"Rose, you have the biggest kitchen I have ever seen in my entire life. Why don't you have anything in it?"

Rose laughed.

"Seriously, I've got more things inside my knife drawer that you have in your entire massive fridge-freezer."

"I guess I should have warned you before I let you believe I had a vast array of food inside my house. But the truth is I eat out more often than not."

"That's an understatement."

"Well, doesn't everyone? I thought it was a New York thing."

"A New York thing, not to have *any* food, *anywhere*?"

Rose smiled at Carlos's overreaction.

"I have champagne? In the room next to the kitchen?"

"Yeah, I saw that, the champagne room… one thousand bottles of champagne! Is that what you want for dinner?"

***

It had taken Carlos almost half an hour to walk down to the Fayre grocery store and return. In the same time, Rose had reread an in-depth biography of Battista Sforza, and then studied Piero Della Francesca's portrait, obsessively.

Carlos pressed a button on a slimline mp3 dock, which took pride of place atop one of the higher shelves and the music began.

He emptied the contents of three large shopping bags onto the surface of the kitchen's central island. A plan began to formulate in his mind.

He began cutting vegetables, frying them up in some garlic oil. He added spices to enhance the flavour, mixing the ingredients with a stock he'd made from scratch. Momentarily, he would stop to taste. Once satisfied, he would again proceed.

The aroma coming from the hall and into the living area beckoned Rose from her seat. She appeared beside him in the kitchen and Carlos placed a small spoonful of sauce into her mouth.

"That tastes divine." She licked her lips.

"Spicy bean quesadillas with guacamole," he proudly announced.

Her eyes widened. "I had that before, but never like *this.*"

She marvelled at the unique way he had presented his native food to her. "I'm really going to look forward to this."

"Hey, it's no big deal. And it'll be ready in less than two minutes, Madam. Let me make you one of my chilli Mojitos to go with your dinner, or would you like some of that champagne?"

"Actually, the Mojito sounds delicious," she enthused.

Carlos mixed crushed ice, lime, chilli, mint, soda water and rum in the blender and poured into a pair of tall glasses he plucked from a shelf. He then led Rose to the table and pulled out her chair, as the lit candles flickered, setting the scene.

"Now you are seated, here is your Mojito."

His hospitality was pure, and it established his character beautifully. Again, Rose's insides glowed at how virtuous he was, how untainted he appeared to be by New York.

"No need to ask you what your first job was, baby. I hope they paid you well."

She watched him more closely now, his expert timing and efficiency seemed effortless. The table looked lovely, lending itself to his Mexican hospitality. The food, however, tasted even better. Her empty plate spoke volumes.

"Well, baby," she smiled. "You obviously know your way around the kitchen. I never knew you were so well versed in the ways of culinary expertise." Carlos was bashful and played himself down. "C'mon. Spill it." Rose dug.

"It's nothing – everyone can cook like this where I'm from."

"Wrong answer."

"Okay, okay, my mother taught me from a young age, we were always in the kitchen together."

"I thought so." Rose sat back. "Your mother taught you well. Very well indeed. I fully appreciate it," she smiled.

"You are very welcome."

Carlos looked into Rose's eyes. They both sat and saw into each other. The silence, and the time that passed, was easy and welcome.

She knew Carlos was a good man.

He knew Rose was all he wanted in life. Devoid of awkwardness, they both welcomed the love within the quiet moment they were sharing.

After a while, Carlos spoke, pointing to her speakers. "What is this we are listening to?"

"You never watched *West Side Story*?" she asked.

"I heard of it, yeah. What's it about?"

"It's a show. It's about two rival gangs in New York. There is a Shakespearean, Romeo and Juliet type element to the story." Rose was aware she was losing him. "It's very good. One of my favourite shows. Amazing on Broadway, I have seen it like a trillion times."

"I like this song. I have heard it before; it is famous I think."

Rose laughed. "The whole gig is famous, silly. Bernstein, you know?"

"This song is very nice, it err…" Carlos paused.

"Go on baby, what is it?"

"It's the words."

Rose silently waited. She always liked it when he struggled to express himself. His attempts to impress her as his grammar suffered.

"The words are very pig-niont," he concluded.

"Poignant, Carlos."

"Ci, poignant. They will now forever remind me of the way I feel about you. Is this okay?"

Rose tried her hardest to resist commenting and she succeeded.

"It's because I want there to be a time where we can be together, and it will be a time and place that will be more easier, easier to see each other. It is because I feel like this that I feel that this is our song, Rose."

"My baby." She reached over, tenderly stroking the side of his face.

Somewhere, from the second act of the soundtrack, ended.

They both got up and cleared the table together.

"Let me run you a bath, then I'll clean up."

***

The roll top bath sat proud in the back centre of a generously sized en-suite. Candles had been lit and the spicy scent of bath oil wafted about the room. As Rose undressed and stepped into the warm water, she felt herself coming alive again.

She began to think how much Carlos meant to her. Was she falling for him? She knew of his love for her, although, did she love him? She smiled every time she saw him; she enjoyed his company, and she loved the way he complied when she was unreasonable.

And that smile…

She stepped out and dried herself, then slipped into some sweatpants and a t-shirt and twisted her hair into a high ponytail.

She walked back into the living room and grabbed him from behind. "Baby, I just want to thank you for taking the time out to see me, making me feel special, tonight."

He looked back at her seriously. Her voice seemed different. Purer, as if it were naked, stripped of the luxurious air of power she previously brandished.

"Rose, you do not have to thank me, ever. The pleasure will always be mine. I'm the one who should be thanking you."

His voice was almost a whisper. Rose glanced over at him in disbelief.

They shared drinks up on the roof terrace, and watched the city night with its illuminated skyline. The city sparkled from up there. Central Park lay below them like a huge black carpet while Manhattan was surrounded by the other four points of New York city. Rose had always thought the architect of the building was a genius, affording her a panorama of the entire city so expertly.

Time passed as they sat in yet more congenial silence.

A little while later, Carlos said goodbye. He stood up and kissed her.

"I will call you in a few days, honey," Rose said, smiling at him.

He was the tonic she had needed. The following day she had two connecting flights to catch and business to attend to...

Deepest Red

Silly Sandy leaped up the stairs for one final check of the store rooms, where heavy boxes and bin bags filled with spare clothing were kept. On account of *Everybody's Able* being an old school, age old exercise books and textbooks lay piled on the floor and were covered in dust.

She'd been running the place for almost three years, but she still had many things to do. A trip to the council dump had been arranged some time the following week to dispose of the majority of junk that had remained for what seemed like decades.

Sandy walked downstairs and began to close all the blinds to the large recreation hall. She then decided to check up on Ricky Gomez.

"Hi there, Gordon? It's Sandy again, how are you?"

"Oh yeah. Hello, Sandy, I was just thinking about you."

"Yep, ringing again! I hope you don't think I'm a big pain in the bum."

"Of course not."

Ever since Ricky Gomez began at the borough of Haringey refuse department, Sandy relied on occasional reports from Gordon Reeves, a kind man who only ever had good things to say.

"How's he doing?" Sandy asked.

"Ricky? Excellent. He's coming on leaps and bounds."

"Oh, that's fab."

"Yeah, Ricky's been here, what, almost three months, and already he's figured out a routine. He's in charge of like, three others; you know, got his own team. He's driving the promotional vans for the council. And, you know what, he never complains about anything."

Silly Sandy's eyes welled up, pride and good intentions made her pale face glow, and the back of her neck prickled.

"I've been working for the council for thirty two years.

Everybody moans about the work, you know, *everybody*. They come through here, refuse collectors, dustbin men, whatever... I mean, it's normal; they're always complaining about all the crap, the smell. You know, it's depressing, really, even I know that. But Ricky, God love him, he's such a good guy. He's always so pleased he's got the opportunity to be working – I reckon he thinks he's privileged. Some of the other men laugh at him, but he doesn't care."

"That's so like him. He's changed so much in the past year. He used to be a big grumps, but now he's just amazing."

"And I hear you and him are, you know, an item?"

Sandy blushed. "Yeah, he said he wants to take me to the Chinese restaurant tonight, round the corner from here. He even sent me some flowers earlier."

***

The time was approaching seven o'clock. They had arranged to meet outside the restaurant at twenty minutes past.

Silly Sandy carefully put her roses into a blue thermos flask and topped it up with some cold tap water before placing it on the small windowsill of her office. She turned and looked at them proudly. No one had ever bought her flowers before, and the thought of someone sending her deep red roses made her smile joyously.

She walked through *Everybody's Able* for a last minute check before switching off the lights and locking all the doors.

Josefstadt, The Eighth District Of Vienna

Many esteemed guests were due to arrive. A sizeable contingent of wealthy thrill seekers of the highest order, already in attendance and cavorting to the waltz music in the main gallery.

Fashionably late, Rose Benoit, together with a smattering of magnificent companions, stepped down from her carriage.

As they entered, the place instantly became awash with lust and over-exuberant passion. It spread throughout the hall like an instant wildfire.

A drink was placed within her gloved fingers as the majority had already flocked to admire her costume. Information about the garment had even preceded its arrival – an ensemble that was being described as rococo-esque fetish. The rubber design had been commissioned by one of Europe's most gifted designers, who had only recently received awards. A collar of pure crystal diamonds hung tightly around her neck, which contributed perfectly to the entire creation.

Rose Benoit's dark blonde afro was tied either side into equal bunches, making it look like a huge heart shape on top of her head.

Her status was blatantly obvious. She held the entire room.

She glanced about the huge grandiose chamber. Some of the masks were truly imaginative; the creativity of many costumes exceeded those from last year's masquerade. In spite of her casual smile, she was most disappointed her confidant Madame Evangeline DuTvott was unable to accompany her. However, she was satisfied her fellow patrons were mostly beautiful, eminent, and on heat.

"Madam Rose. How adorable," declared Baroness Lucia, flanked by two silent but enormous African males. "You truly are the ebony Marie Antoinette."

They kissed.

"Baroness, your compliments make me buzz with pride, although I should say Antonia was more of an ivory Rose Benoit," she said, her dangerous smile dancing upon her lips. People noticed it.

"Of course, of course. Madam, meet my kings for the evening." Rose allowed the over-muscular twins to kiss her fingers.

Lucia glanced and licked her lips at the sight of Rose's exposed shoulders and the shine of her well-oiled cleavage as it flung itself forward in attempts to escape her corset.

"I take it, Baroness, that the Baron is holed up in the pit, awaiting his cuckold?"

"Ah, my sweet Rose, you are correct," said the dusky young Italian. "However, I would gladly sacrifice my two friends here if you were to agree to cuckold him instead." Her fluttering eyes pleaded. "Any excuse to witness your magnificent physique again."

Rose took her hands gently, "My darling, Lucia, you flatter me so with such tempting summons, and I would adore to facilitate you. However, alas, I fear I must decline. I have, unfortunately, other menial matters that serve to press my time."

Lucia looked downhearted; she sulked and used her bottom lip to its full effect.

"I hope your friends pummel the poor Baron well, my darling," said Rose, finally.

Lucia clapped with glee, before fanning herself, tittering as her escorts kissed her neck.

The sound of Verdi and Puccini mixed well with the grinding trance music. Rose sat upon the huge thigh of the extremely rotund Marchioness Richelieu, the host for the evening, and one of her most dearest acquaintances. The slave for the night knelt at their feet, dressed in nothing but a loin cloth. The slave would inevitably be passed around by most of the higher ranking aristocratic guests, although only after the Marchioness and Rose had facilitated him.

The Marchioness Richelieu fluttered her beautiful eyes

from behind her butterfly mask, and tried again to tempt her guest of honour. "It's name is Quito," she inclined towards her slave. "So named after the place I found him. My dear Rose, he is yours, have a slice of him, darling, before he is no more."

"But Marchioness, I would rather have a slice of you, than your horrid slave." The two women lazily kissed, Rose sucking on the Marchioness's long tongue.

"Rose, Rose, my darling, ever the tease. If my lover, the esteemed Madam DuTvott were here, I could almost guarantee the pair of you would have Quito's guts for your garters," she smiled, cheekily. "But you are quite correct, Madam Rose, he *is* somewhat undesirable."

Though the Marchioness was Thai, Rose admired her French accent. Born into the best lineage of Parisian aristocracy.

"Well, then, would it please Rose if I abused the little fellow?"

Rose instantly glowed, already perspiring at the thought of such a thing.

She was joined by others as they watched their slave disappear underneath the Marchioness Richelieu. Later, during the session, Rose managed to slip away unnoticed as her host allocated others to wrap long chains around Quito's body.

***

Aside from a candle that had been lit some twenty yards away, the place was otherwise in darkness. Ricky Gomez had been awake for a few minutes but he knew he was restrained.

The period of screaming was over; his tears had tasted bitter as they rolled into his mouth while shouting his demands to be set free. Violence had flooded his mind as vitriol spewed from his ever decreasing throat. Indeed, the period of madness and screaming had passed.

He had been positioned on the surface of the floor,

seated with his hands tied behind his back. With thick chain, his neck was tightly fixed to an iron post behind him, so tightly in fact he could feel the pressure as the links pressed against his Adam's apple.

He could hear the dull thud of music somewhere far off in the distance, the beats slow and repetitive. The ignorance of his whereabouts wore on, and his mind, quelled by both fear and boredom, called out silently.

His throat, painful as he swallowed, was dry and hoarse, yearning for moisture in the same way he himself yearned to be made aware of the reason he was tied up in a darkened room.

Hour after monotonous hour passed by. The flame from the candle would occasionally dance and, in doing so, threw a little light upon the walls close by. Still, Ricky was unable to identify his surroundings.

As more time passed, concentrating on the candle was by now the only fuel he had to keep his mind motivated. He saw the glow that surrounded it. He despaired. But in his attempts to vanquish the distress, the misery, he imagined thoughts of love as he remained fixed upon the candle's light. His ears now turned deaf to the constant muffled sounds of slow dance music.

This comforted him, and his mind eased itself to a near tranquil state.

Sleep was almost within his reach – not unconsciousness borne from pain or boredom, but a restful warmth that placated his mind and body.

But everything instantly fell apart. His world came crashing down around him, destroying the peace he'd created… as a door opened.

The light shone in the room like some beacon of death, flooding everything in a hostile silvery white.

Ricky forced his eyes shut.

Instantly, the music became louder. After a few moments he began to open his eyes.

The realisation of *her* was the most difficult to accomplish. She entered slowly into the room and into his senses like a maelstrom.

The candle was still lit. He looked down, and saw that his chest was naked, but he wore a pair of worn pyjama-type trousers. Looking up, the woman now dominated his entire vision.

Feathers fluttered from her coiffure. With her right hand, she reached down and gently touched his face, feeling it, daintily caressing the side of his head and his eyes with the tips of her fingers. Her other hand held a cream diamond-encrusted Venetian mask up to her eyes with the aid of a slender stick.

Rose became immensely aroused by his confusion.

He didn't understand.

The slap to his face was swift and excessively heavy. It took command of his attention and made him fully aware of the situation right from the beginning. The impact adjusted the position of his head, the chain painfully biting against his neck. She dispatched more heavy blows to the side of his face in slow successions. As she wiped his blood from her gloved hands with a white cloth, the reason for the barrage of violence soon became apparent as she breathed: "I simply loathe beards."

Ricky Gomez, although no longer homeless, had kept his longish hair and unshaven image. A look that had by now become synonymous with his character.

"Horrid. Dirty things," she whispered again to herself.

"Please," he started, urging himself with an assertiveness that he believed would benefit him, "why are you doing this?"

"Mmm," she groaned, simply, blatantly unconcerned for his question.

No sooner as she reached down again and placed her hand near his face, he flinched, attempting to avoid her tinkling fingers as they touched his eyes and mouth. The passion surged through her as she teased herself while tormenting him.

***

Hidden within the bowels of the Marchioness Richelieu's enormous Viennese townhouse, Rose stood at the centre of the fashionable windowless eighteenth century museum-like interior. A libertine's wet dream.

She had gone to great lengths to ensure her time with Ricky Gomez was as outlandish and indulgent as she could possibly make it. Thus thoroughly contrasting with that of the poor man's lifestyle and the pathetically hard life he'd led.

He was shaved first. With a large cut throat razor, she expertly removed the article that, in one form or other, had been on his face for the past fifteen years.

"My name is Gomez, I am British," he said, carefully. "I was supposed to attend my class yesterday. I am studying Maths and English. They are the only classes I do on Thursdays, or… yesterday. I do not know what day it is today."

She was beautiful. Her face flawless, like someone from a commercial in a magazine. Her eyes, almond-like and deep brown mahogany. He wept, but complied when she placed her fingers beneath his chin to lift his face for inspection.

"Good. Good. Very nice," she announced, smiling slightly. Ricky looked up at her, still extremely confused, yet somewhat mesmerised by his captor's allure. Tiny thoughts of admiration swam into his head. Her half smile faded and she spoke again. "Now, it's time."

The sensual moment crashed away like some forgotten myth, broken by the sound of her noisy rubber garment. It dragged across the floor as she moved herself around him. She reached over him, her rubber breast line smelled fresh as it pressed against his face.

Once again, his eyes fixed upon the candle flickering by the door behind her.

No time was wasted as Rose attached a large phallus to the front of his face before she removed the flowing rubber skirts she had previously worn. Her appearance was immediately transformed as her big legs and high heels served to only enhance his inferiority.

"What the hell are you doing?" he called, his muffled protestation sounding angrier. "Get this thing off my face."

She welcomed his noise.

The opening baselines of *Love To Love You Baby* enlightened the room and slickly coiled around Ricky Gomez's brain.

She lit a cigarette and let the curved thick smoke linger from her lips before drawing it back and duly exhaling, blowing the smoke down into his face.

"Now, baby," she announced demurely. "It's time, make yourself ready."

Pulling up on the dildo, she arched her eyebrows and her eyes fluttered on hearing him choke.

She gently offered him the back of her hand. "Kiss." she said.

Ricky kissed, as best as he was able.

While cruelly slapping his face, she moistened herself before making him enter her. After a while, she firmly took a hold of the sides of his head and made the process of her stimulation faster and harder, and the experience more enjoyable.

Rose Benoit moaned loudly above the tool of a man beneath her.

Due to her height, elevated more so by her tall footwear, he was pulled up even more, his restrained throat dangerously being stretched to its limit. Pushing up and pulling down, her backside and belly alternately rolled slowly with every thrust of the penis. The final push made her ecstatic, she pulled him in and kept him there, locking him in place.

She excitedly climaxed all over his face. A rain of pleasure arose and fell as her body became an immense tingling playground.

She smiled. "Splendid." A thin layer of moisture hung to her face and upper torso.

She reached down and held his face again, never

allowing him one moment where he was free of her imposing contact, her control.

"Tell me you liked that," she whispered. "Talk to me."

She slapped his face again and he nodded, reluctantly mumbling acquiescence. She smeared her climatic fluid in his face and through his hair.

"Good boy, I am glad you are satisfied, for now comes *my* delectation."

She offered her hand once more. Only fear prompted Ricky to kiss it.

The candle by the door, its flame was blinding. Everything in the room faded. The walls, the ornate furniture, his smiling captor above him, disappearing from view. Everywhere turned dark, save for the flame, its glow luminously prominent in a void of greyness.

Ricky Gomez

Ricky Gomez was slapped awake.

"After my usage of you, I may now proceed to beat you. Oui, garçon, I shall beat you most severely."

She held aloft the paddle nonchalantly, as if ignorant of the implement and the threat it posed with its blunted metal studs. She beat his face furiously, delivering a slow and perfectly timed onslaught that prolonged his agony. Aside from his splintered jaw and broken cheekbone, Rose seemed to delight while delivering blows to his eyes, his left in particular, so much so that it had been left permanently damaged after roughly twenty minutes.

His tormentor stepped away, and with his right eye he saw the candle. It appeared that the passing of time had not made it any shorter, on the contrary, it seemed it remained the same size. The realisation of this confounded him, dismayed by the harsh truth that this previous symbol of hope had not made the same journey within the violent hours thus far. It aroused his temper to boiling point.

"Let me go, for fuck's sake. I can't take any more, you're going to kill me," he screamed in frustration. "You have to let me go."

She pulled his head up as far as it would go, taking care not to break his neck. She then held it in place and drooled a long string of spittle into his mouth. The root of Ricky's tongue gurgled in an attempt to reject her fluid. She then poured liquid anaesthetic down his throat, his cries rapidly turned from low husky breaths to nil.

"There. That's much better," she declared, smiling down at him, caressing the inside of his mouth with her two fingers, distributing the liquid.

Love To Love You Baby remained constant, the song's slow prowess mirrored her own sexual inclination.

Yet again she slapped his face and offered her hand for him to kiss.

Ricky tried to scream with all the energy that remained inside him, to express his hatred of her. All he could muster were a few lowly wheezes of air.

"You would, of course, be incorrect in assuming that I should offer you some sort of blessed release. Or that I should display leniency," she shook her head. "I fear I must be honest with you, slave, I am immensely delighted at this precise moment. And this whole affair that I have designed, in all its entirety, promises to be so much fun. So, given that is the case, and purely on account of your rather pitifully pleading face, why would I call a halt to these proceedings?"

A couple appeared at the door behind her. Both were dressed as extravagantly as Rose. The gentleman was a harlequin and Baroness Lucia, though still resplendent in her feathered golden mask, had changed into her underwear.

Ricky moved frantically, his body desperately bucked. His limbs ached in his attempts to grasp the onlookers' attention. Rose turned to face them.

Baroness Lucia looked inquisitive. Gomez, screaming, silently, trying to distract the couple, pushing himself, striving to smash through the madness that was taking place.

"Darling?" she drawled. "So this is the reason you were unable to grant my request."

"My sweet Baroness Lucia, I can but only offer you my most humble pardons."

"You most certainly shan't, Madam. What you are doing looks absolutely marvellous and really rather gorgeous."

With her long bejewelled fingernails, Rose stroked Baroness Lucia's heaving bosom. "Too kind."

"May I inspect your slave, darling Rose?"

"But of course."

Rose moved aside and the Baroness came into his view. She stared at him easily, as if face to face with an insignificant object. She tilted his head up with the aid of two fingertips.

"Beautiful work, Madam Rose, absolutely exquisite."

"Why, thank you, Baroness."

"The attention to detail, the violent application. It's awe inspiring. Total devastation. It is no wonder you are among the greatest of sadists. A devilish rogue, my sweet Madam."

Rose Benoit shuddered. The compliment filled her with gleeful sunshine, quite literally her insides shone, thrilling her entire being.

"I have not gone too far?"

"On the contrary, I think your work is far from being completed."

Ricky despaired. His efforts to appeal to the two visitors were useless as he glanced at the three of them, kissing and smiling and totally uninterested in him.

Vampire

Quito was almost unconscious, embroiled within the embrace of the vampires who had arrived after midnight.

Although, in truth, Marchioness Richelieu's slave was a consenting and trusted employee of her estate, who regularly saw to housekeeping duties within her mansion, he might not have assumed he'd fall victim to twelve actual practising sanguine vampirists.

During a well-deserved respite, sipping on a glass of deep claret Bordeaux, Rose Benoit sat with them and keenly watched how they tenderly cared for their feast, reassuring Quito with safety but also sending him spinning into a state of terrible lust and fear. Rose envied their skill and etiquette.

A tightly clad Victorian Gothic, her face as white as snow, almost hidden by a large mask made from jewels and black feathers, bit passionately at his throat. He struggled against her advances lazily before she released him from her grasp.

Rose sauntered towards the woman, stepping over Quito. A hot sensation flashed over her upper body as she seated herself on the Gothic's lap and daintily touched at the small trickle of blood that slowly rolled down from the corner of her lips.

The vampire's dark eyes were hooded and captivated Rose as she stared into them. There was a hushed silence behind them as everyone roused themselves, leering, awestruck at the scene.

A fellow vampire approached them, no doubt hankering for a taste. Rose rejected him and licked the remains of Quito's blood from her fingertip.

"Rose, my sweet, there you are," declared Marchioness Richelieu, entering the chamber within a bustle of casual concern. "Baroness Lucia and I have been searching for you."

"Do forgive me, Marchioness," offered Rose.

"Yes, Marchioness, please forgive my darling Madam Rose. We all know how she likes to disappear. She is nothing if not her studiously independent self," said Baroness Lucia, still aided by her two gallantly-dressed African twins.

The now almost comatose Quito was gathered up by his large owner, she checked his teeth and pulled at his eyelids to check the whites of his sclera.

Baroness Lucia cuddled up close to Rose, draping her arm around her neck. She wafted her with a large fan made from lace and light blue feathers.

"Now, Rose," she pressed her cheek to Rose's and spoke in a hushed voice. "There is a fine array of treats that Marchioness Richelieu has supplied for our delectation. Would you perchance, care to accompany us both to the dining room? It'll be fun... we could tease each other."

Rose Benoit could smell the desperation.

"Very well, Baroness, if it pleases you," she said finally. "If the hors d'oeuvres are exceptionally tasty, I might even feel the need to be cruel to Marchioness Richelieu's slave."

"Oh good heavens," said their host, her hands pressed together with glee. "Please do."

"I now have a taste for his blood. The unfortunate fellow is growing on me. I think I might punish him after all, although I am not promising anything. I have, as you are aware, more trifling matters to attend to."

"Indeed she does. A most sumptuous display of boundless creativity, my darling Rose," said the Baroness, almost breathless. "Your peasant slave, what a work of art."

"Yes, I had heard you have your own submissive," said the Marchioness. "Please, Madam Rose, you know what we do is all within the name of enjoyment and pleasure, try not to kill the poor soul."

Rose smiled and broke everyone's hearts.

***

A waltz began in the main hall. Court dresses, tailored from the finest satins, flowed and pirouetted amidst the sound and vibrancy of the music. Garters were slipped from thighs and handed to top-hatted gentlemen as gifts.

Scarlet highwaymen, ornate dandy pirates, felines in polka dots and even Queen Elizabeth the first, all lusted after Rose Benoit as she held onto Sapphire, leading her in a passionate Pasodoble. The Baroness Lucia was seated, a single tear trickling down her cheek as she forlornly awaited her turn.

An Empty Canvas

In due time, Ricky Gomez learned to tolerate the heavy slaps to his face. Retaliation and anger only assured more punishment from his tormentor.

The same paddle was now being used to violently smash against his torso and limbs. After almost one hour of relentlessness, his chest, backside and shoulders had turned blackish blue. Blood inevitably sprayed the floor beneath him.

By this point, the effects of the anaesthetic had worn off as his cough began to sound once again.

Rose decided to refrain from issuing further doses, however; his outbursts would now be welcome and add a drama towards the next instalment she had planned.

A large square canvas was positioned on a tall easel behind her. Rose stood before her victim.

"Why... don't you... rot in hell," he said. His voice was like broken concrete as he tried his hardest to string the words together.

Rose moaned and purred to the slow, pulsating beats of kinky house music.

She stepped closer. A sickness arose in his stomach as he learned of how prepossessing she was, this unbalance alongside her brutality was both uncomfortable and perplexing.

She was silent, her face serene as he wept wretchedly. She watched his tears mingle with the blood.

"Please! Just let me go."

Rose tilted her head, as if contemplating his request, but grabbed both sides of his head. Moving in closer as if to kiss him, she instead wrapped her lips around his nose and slowly sank her teeth fatally into the hardy cartilage.

Her performance was slow, deliberate, her top teeth crunching down on his nasal bone. His eyes watered and his attempts to move his head, to shake away her tight grasp were again unsuccessful.

Slowly she pulled away. Her eyes shut, her eyebrows arched.

The bloody remains of his nose were still clamped within her teeth. She retrieved it daintily with her thumb and middle finger and held it in front of his eyes for them both to inspect.

Rose allowed her victim a lengthy period in which he chose to vent his frustration.

She used this time to wash his blood from her face.

***

Ricky Gomez was hysterical. Using up vocal ability he believed he'd previously extinguished. He screamed at her, animal-like, almost dehumanised.

Mucus and bloody drool slowly ran from his contorted, toothless mouth.

"You've had your fun. Let me go," he cried. "For God's sake let me go." A lisp had formed in his voice.

Rose watched him watching her as she discarded what was left of his nose on the floor.

Blood poured from the gaping wound in the middle of Ricky Gomez' face.

"You are a fucking animal… what kind of woman are you?"

"Unfortunately for you, darling, I am the kind of woman who would fuck your brain if I wished to do so." she said with a slight smile which belied the gravity of her comment. "I'm actually really rather bad. An extremely bad sort of person, dear. So, yes, that being the case, you are correct, I *am* somewhat of an animal."

A long pause followed as her words danced upon the air. They stared at one another, Rose calmly glowed as Ricky's grimace was awash with blood.

She submerged the tip of a long paintbrush into a glass of clear water which was conveniently positioned to his right. She dabbed the bristles thoroughly into his wound.

More screaming. Rose purred.

The crimson swirls appeared upon the surface of the empty canvas, already giving the bare white square an audacious sense of movement, especially when taking into account the way in which she had applied the brush.

Cologne and Madrid, two of the more inspirational destinations that had provided her with the food of visionary arousal into which she had immersed herself artistically. Rose loved the Renaissance. The grandiose, biblical and often violent interpretations of works by masters such as Raphael and Michelangelo, enraptured her imagination. However, she learned that she personally possessed a niche for watercolours, simple, relaxing scenery and a far cry from whimsical depictions of heaven and earth and risqué fatted nudes.

"I don't want to die. Please, you're killing me," Ricky screamed.

Rose noted the sound of his voice, like being submerged in sludge. She smiled.

She paused and dropped the brush into the water. Thirsty work. She sipped at her beverage and smacked her lips in approval of the refreshing red.

"What the fuck are you doing? Why won't you answer me?" Ricky screamed when she resumed her handle on the brush.

Using the gaping wound in the centre of his face as the source fluid to enable her to indulge in her work, it became apparent to Ricky that not only was he unwittingly providing her with his own consumption, unable to stop her from using his blood, but also that an image was transpiring on the canvas.

Rose could hardly hear his shouts and ramblings over Guastavino's *La rosa y el sauce.*

She swayed, her free hand held aloft and upturned like a gentleman duellist. Closing her eyes momentarily, she moaned in ecstasy.

The image was taking more shape. His ailing brain and psyche became intensely wired, and a high-pitched white noise pinged through his head. But, through all the harrowing waves of agony he could make out, a figure, a portrait of a person, was starting to appear.

A silent gap between the music created opportunity to speak.

"That's correct, my dear," Rose interjected into his inner thoughts, reading them and thus exhibiting her complete control, even of his soul.

"It is indeed a face you see. Well done, Richard."

The music began again, cancelling his chance to respond.

Of course, Rose Benoit had no need to study the small polaroid of Sarah Allen. She had had enough practice during endless nights, sketching the outline of her face with a pencil.

On numerous occasions, late night exercises were undertaken where she would study the way Sarah's eyes were shaped. Indeed, the unassuming image had been etched inside Rose's brain automatically. Knowing every facet confined inside the four corners of the glossy photograph.

She was obsessed with the way Sarah looked into the camera. It was her favourite image of her best friend. Taken almost twenty years previously, they were both fourteen at the time. But somehow, as time marched on, Rose always thought the image had also grown. Sarah looked mature. Young, but knowing, somehow privy to a mysterious secret world that Rebecca Sinclair would not have known existed back then.

Alas, Rose could not remember Sarah looking so aware at the time.

Ricky Gomez was staring long and hard into the completed portrait of crimson. Confused. Oblivious. Tired. Sniffing and bubbling blood and snot from his terrible orifice.

However, it was when he saw Rose swirl slowly around the easel that heralded his realisation.

Sarah Allen. Andrew Baker's girlfriend. The only

person in his life he'd raped and murdered, was back in his life and stamping on his brain.

"My baby," Rose purred before dragging on her cigarette holder. "I believe you've decoded our little riddle. Congratulations, mon cheri."

Completion

Every time he gained consciousness he was mortified to find himself remaining in the same crisis as earlier.

Indeed, the thought of being incapable to stay alive was the only thing he could use to comfort himself, to succeed in his yearning for death. To be set free.

Unfortunately, however, this blessed gift would not yet befall him. From passing out, he had awoken for a third time.

It appeared she was busy, and in the middle of doing something to him. His damaged face was inches away from her cleavage. He moved his eyes upwards to look at her, she was deep in her work, not returning his glance. She seemed unaware he had returned from unconsciousness, perhaps she didn't care.

He lowered his gaze to the small black heart shaped tattoo above her left breast, he concentrated on it. He then moved his eyes to the left to see a restricted view behind her, the easel, and he remembered Sarah. Her vision stabbed at his fractured senses with memories of what he and his young friends had done to her. These feelings enhanced further when added to the pain of all the bodily inflictions Rose had so far imparted upon him, bringing his soul into a state of mental paralysis.

The flickering candle, dancing and insulting him, still appeared not to have melted via time, still maintaining its infuriating insistence on remaining unchanged.

Yes. He was now back in the room.

"Well, good morning, my darling," she said with a smile. "I trust you slept well."

The choking noise he omitted as he attempted to speak was rebuffed. "Aww, I do not think I granted you permission to speak, did I?" she asked, with a mock confusion, before dispatching yet another punishing slap to the side of his face, followed by the compulsory kiss to her hand.

"In a short while, the hate you feel for me will be replaced by love. You will love your master, Richard…"

He grimaced, a pained expression to quell the agony.

"I understand you believe you have had a hard time since we were at school together. I am fully aware, Richard, of all the trying times and terms of survival you have had to endure to keep your head above the ground. But, let me assure you, my sweet boy, all that has happened to you thus far, you shall deem quite delightful when compared to what I am about to do to you now."

His eyes pleaded, but still appeared hopeless. She surrounded his face with her gloved fingers. He watched the tall plume of feathers which crowned her head, waft gently.

"Your comfort and well being is of no importance to me. As a matter of fact, Richard darling, any feelings of safety you might have harboured, any slight slithers of hopefulness that you once may have had, have now flown far away from you. They do not exist here, my sweet."

***

The slaps were more harsh now, like severe electrical shocks that spread throughout his entire upper body. The kiss she required from him afterwards was law, a must, a prerequisite.

"I know you long for death," she whispered. "I deny you this most natural of privileges."

The music was loud and Ricky could hardly hear her as she spoke. But he knew her now. He could decipher what she was saying to him without actually hearing the sounds. Instinct and terror formed his undeniable understanding towards his tormentor.

"You shall love this, boy."

On saying that, a sudden pain exploded from his chest and up his neck to his brain.

The blade she used was so sharp it took half a minute to register.

For Rose, the first slice was a waiting game, a duration in which she grew impatient, then, as he identified with the pain, she savoured, becoming aroused at his torment. He looked skyward in anguish.

She bent forward and lovingly caressed his face with her cheek and lips, kissing his tears as they ran down his broken skin.

"I think you told me you would slice me like a pig. Do you remember, darling?" she whispered. "Is life not so, so strange? It has an anomalous manner of not turning out the way one plans."

Danse Macabre sounded louder, drowning his head, flooding it. She resumed her slow and intermittent slices, each time checking his reaction to every single stroke. At times she would smile sweetly as his face contorted, but other times she'd frown slightly if he reacted in a way she deemed unacceptable. Sometimes he'd pass out again, only to be awakened by more levels of pain.

The pain became like food to him. It fed him, and after a lengthy time, he expected it. It reminded him of the days when he used to inject the debased diamorphine. The times in between were the hardest; they presented him with the terrors of reality. Some days, when the euphoria was absent, he was so disgusted with the daylight, with himself, and the sky threatened to clamp itself to his brain, it squeezed him down and screwed him to the surface of the world like a dead shadow. This encouraged him to abuse himself more constantly, intravenously, until every moment of his life was shrouded with the pillows of delusion.

He coupled the philosophy. He knew she wanted him to love what she was doing. To love her as she was doing it.

This revelation led to his ultimate acceptance. "Hurt me." He squeezed the words out, choking. "I do not want to die now. I want this pain… Forever."

He finally succumbed to her, waiting for what she did next. His mind had turned insane, belonging to her will.

She was absolutely beautiful as she completed her work,

she kept him awake for the whole dreadful time.

She sawed upward with her blade, from the base of his stomach to just below his throat, cutting through his centre. Her hands immersed, inside him, searching. Rubber fingers squelching and squirming. Playfully touching and pinching at severed tissue and intestine.

Ricky Gomez fell in love as the last thing he saw was her heart shaped tattoo above her left breast.

The candle, still the same height, flickered slightly. Even his life's breath failed to extinguish it.

kleiner Nachwort
petit épilogue

My darling Marchioness,

I hope that you are well, and that you are at last wallowing in your usual level of optimum luxury.

Just a small note, telling you that I feel absolutely dreadful with regards to my behaviour during the course of your most splendid weekend supper.

My departure, void of my physicality and courteousness, was wholly regrettable.

I apologise most sincerely.

As always, however, I have left you a gift. A mere token of the esteemed adoration I hold for you. I trust by now you've located it. I am privy to your obsession with art, I do prey my creation pleases you.

I'll also be sending an additional little something your way, which should meet your arrival on the morrow. Hopefully it should aid you in rectifying the chaos I have left. It's name is Max and he'll be on hand to do as you wish. You may return him when he has facilitated all your delectable caprice.

Forever yours, RB

Commissioned

"Ah, it is a fine piece. Just look at how the artist has utilised the canvas and managed to merge the light with the mood of the subject, the mood being obviously dark. You see? And reticent. It suggests nothing to the casual passerby, but enraptures and haunts the keen enthusiast, or those with the audacity to step closer. *The most beautiful eyes*! They just dare to be careless. Of course, she is a femme fatale, yet she has seen unspeakable horrors. I would stake my life on the very fact that this painting was borne out of an environment that is the absolute antithesis of what one might consider conventional. A menace lies just beyond the surface, an animalisation within, to corrupt all, from the most innocent child to the most hardiest of killers, and everyone between, methinks. All are in danger. To conclude, the expertly-honed ability of the artist knows no limitation. I'll hazard a guess the piece is valued at well over the ten million mark."

"Tell me, Marchioness Richelieu, has it a title?"

"Indeed it has. It is simply entitled... SA."

Broken Metacarpal

It was official. Gutless as ever, Superintendent Rob Wright's memo to Jack's office meandered through the proverbial houses in imparting that he no longer wished to be part of the *Animal* investigations, warning Jack and Ollie from participating towards any further time served on the matter. He'd also stated that other, higher ranking agents were to take over.

To Jack, Wright's lack of interest in the case was always unfathomable.

Jack waited. Seated beside Ollie inside the Honda as he attempted to punch in the numbers on an outdated mobile phone.

"They're ignoring us, Ollie. I know what they're up to."

"Relax, boss, I'll get through."

Sure enough, after ringing consistently for over an hour, someone answered, although it wasn't Andrew Baker.

"Hello, you've reached Stuart Redding. I know why you're calling. My client is currently busy right now."

Ollie placed a palm over the transmitter "Who the hell is Stuart Redding?" he whispered.

"Andrew Baker's agent. Calls himself Red," Jack said.

"Sounds like a dick."

Jack sniffed out in lazy mock amusement, while glancing at a young mother pushing a pram past the entrance to Kilburn market.

"Actually, with all due respect, he's growing tired of Sargent and you guys bothering him. My client has many things to do with his life besides being harassed by you lot."

Ollie could hear Andrew Baker chuckling in the background, there was also a woman present.

"That's a bit unfair. I wouldn't say harassment, mister Redding. It's more just a case of communication. Inspector

Sargent just wants to talk to mister Baker because he knows he was an old friend of Ricky Gomez."

There was a silence, then a lot of shuffling in the background.

"I'm sorry, what did you say your name was again?"

"My name is Ollie Travis, DI Travis. I'm from the office of Detective Inspector Jack Sargent..."

"Listen, Travis, this is pure fabricated crap that the media has cooked up to scare my client. They think that just because two guys who used to go to school with him twenty five years ago get murdered that this has something to do with my client. Well, it doesn't, okay? You, the police, the newspapers, media, you've got it all wrong."

Red spoke angrily, however Ollie could hear the desperation in his voice.

"Red, calm down..."

"Don't you bloody well call me Red! Who told you to call me Red? You absolute idiot."

"Hey, relax."

"Ricky Gomez was a homeless junkie, he always was. He's just missing, that's all, you'll probably find him in one of those soup kitchen type places, you'll see. Why don't you just let this go? It all happened years ago."

"Pardon me, mister Redding..." Ollie spoke calmly.

"Yeah, well, pardon you. Just get off my phone line!"

"Ricky Gomez's nose was found in a jiffy bag in a parcel facility within the central train station in Vienna."

Ollie glanced back at Jack. Jack looked exhausted and bored, still looking out the window.

"I, err, this is just rumours, though, surely..." stuttered Red.

"Not rumours. True. We haven't released the reports yet," Ollie said, gravely earnest. "They'll be in the press tomorrow. See, the thing is, the only newsworthy thing about Gomez is his relationship with your client. Being a *homeless junkie*, he had nothing else going for him. But unlike yourself, Jack Sargent and I aren't really concerned about the news. We couldn't care less. We just want to look out for your client and we need to speak to him, as soon as possible."

Red was dumbfounded, so much so that Ollie could almost sense him waving frantically at Andrew Baker in attempts to silence the giggling.

Afterwards, both Ollie and Jack sat in silence. The darkly overcast sky overhead, with its manic movements, created awkward gaps for the sunlight to shine down brightly on the wet buildings of Edgware Road.

"Fuck!" shouted Ollie Travis. He punched at the steering wheel, his fist making an unpleasant thud as it banged down heavily. He repeated, continuing a roll of offence upon the vehicle's Honda badge.

His eyes watered. And only now did Jack glance back at his partner.

"Have you broken your hand?"

"Yeah."

"Two dead, Ollie. Freeman, and now Gomez. How could we be so witless? We are literally going nowhere. Wright's going to suspend us."

"Yeah."

"I need to go home," Jack said.

"I need to get my hand in plaster," Ollie said.

Dunn's River

Carlos received her email. His heart skipped a beat when he saw who had sent it. It was simple and to the point. He'd read it on his computer that morning before he drove to work in his van.

Mi hermoso amor.

I hope you are well and looking after yourself. As you know, it has been nearly four months since we last saw one another. I thank you for your patience; I know it is difficult for you.

Your birthday is fast approaching, and as a treat I have decided to take you on holiday to Jamaica. Just you and I.

I remembered that you told me you have always wanted to visit the island. Please make sure you are available. I shall contact you soon with the details.

I am looking forward to seeing your face.

De Se Flor

He reread the message when he returned home from work that night.

***

She was happy on the plane as she watched him. Everyone seemed to smile at him. Rose noticed when people spoke with Carlos that he possessed a most charming and unassuming character. He was warm, and he provided her with a feeling she'd not felt since the days of her mother.

They landed at Sir Donald Sangster and stayed a few nights in Montego Bay. They ate local food and Carlos noted the difference between the yuka and pimento chicken sold from a push cart at Mahoe Bay and those that he'd eaten in Harlem.

She showed him her dancing abilities when they went to a beachside party. Her dancehall moves were so good that the locals assumed she was first generation.

They both enjoyed driving the Audi they'd hired, with its lovely air-con. They took turns to drive the A1 road to Ocho Rios, her intended destination for him.

She told him stories of when she was a child visiting her relatives with her mother.

Carlos listened while slurping his way through a delicious-looking mango.

"Your mom, your real mom, she sounded like quite a lady," he said while wiping the excess juice from his mouth. "It would be nice if you spoke about her, Rose."

A long pause.

"Baby. My mother…" Rose began. She surveyed the landscape set out before them as she drove. The flatlands flanked both sides of the highway and the encompassing mountains threaded themselves over in the distance, emanating a pale turquoise haze just below the southern hemisphere.

"It's okay, Rose, you don't have to say."

"Her name was Martha. She was my best friend. When I was a child I suppose I was very bookish, you know, a bit of a geek: glasses, teeth in braces, all that kind of stuff. She was very glamorous; she always tried to encourage me to be more feminine. I suppose I never understood at the time. But I was a good child, she knew that, well behaved, you know, and I did all my homework. She did well with me, the best she could. She never had any other children as far as I believe."

"So it was just you and her."

"Oh yes, It was always just the two of us. I loved that: video, pizza, dancing. And we were always laughing, there was always laughter in the house. She always knew how to make people feel special, and always put me first, before anyone. She'd have men, although only when she needed to."

After a thoughtful silence, Rose plucked her purse from the glove compartment and handed it to Carlos.

"Open it and unzip it from the side."

Carlos pulled out a photograph and glanced at it.

Rose Benoit was unrecognisable, wearing a thick cream-coloured sweater with a bright green Christmas tree emblazoned on the front. Sure enough, the thick braces, locked within her exuberant smile, reflected with the flash of the camera.

"I was ten, Carlos."

Carlos smiled, studiously inspecting the information within his hand. Martha was the picture of elegance, the woman driving next to him resembled her more than she did her younger self. In spite of the Christmas tree in the background, Martha wore a stylish leather jacket over a tightly fitting black dress, her arm tightly holding her daughter. Young Rose's eyes danced, joyous pools of light, happy just to be in the same room and to be held by this guiding enigma of a woman.

The happiness was palpable, Carlos's eyes welled up. He wasn't at all surprised that Rose had a copy hidden within her purse.

"This is lovely, Rose. I like it."

She glanced at him momentarily. She always liked his sincere silences, thoughtful and measured amid the almost childlike manners he possessed.

"Look at my hair, truly ghastly," she smiled.

***

The following morning, they walked the small trek to Dunn's River to see the falls before first light and she kissed him while the entire pool was tourist free. They held each other's hands and looked into one another's eyes as the big sun rose from behind the surrounding trees.

They ate well on the evening of his birthday. She raised a toast to Carlos as she demanded the attention of the entire restaurant. Everyone cheered and one local woman even came over and kissed his cheek as she held Rose's hand and congratulated her on her fine-looking man.

Back at the hotel later that night, she looked out from the balcony at the dark water beneath. The warm breeze, coolest at night, lapped at her skin in the same way that the waves gently touched the sand on the bay.

She saw him in the wet room. His toned body, wet and glistening, as the lukewarm water cascaded down it. Rose impatiently pulled her orange mini dress up over her head and threw it to the floor before joining him. Her breathing changed and became shallower as she was filled with anticipation of what lay ahead. Carlos felt her presence, he turned and took in her wondrous nakedness. His kisses were soft as his lips moved slowly along her shoulder and neck. His hands cupped her breasts and his finger gently pinched her nipples, which were now getting erect.

Rose weaved her fingers through his short, wet hair, her lips touching his in a tantalising sensual kiss that registered a glorious sensation within her body.

"I love the way you make me feel." He took her hand and placed it against his erection giving his comment gravitas and proof. He whispered gently into her ear. "I want to be inside you."

She adored his accent. But Rose would never reply, adding to her mystique and his frustration.

His skin was smooth, like velvet. She touched his chest and, keeping her gaze, she squatted, warm water gushed heavily upon them both. She leaned forward, her wet hair slicked to the back of her neck. She gently kissed his nicely sized manhood and took hold of it. Rose licked the bottom side of the penis from base to tip before taking him in her mouth. Sucking him slowly and gently while his eyes were closed, exhilarated by her teasing, almost overwhelmed to the point of submission. A long groan by Carlos sent Rose into another dimension on knowing what she was doing to him. His whole body shuddered as she slid herself upward against him.

She felt the coolness of the tiles against her back. One

of his hands held around her hip, the other positioning himself, slowly easing himself into her. Rose groaned as she felt the sweet sensation of all of him inside her.

She moaned. They picked up the rhythm, herself controlling the gyrations and slowing him somewhat if he skipped the beat by moving too fast.

She watched him, their eyes locked. *He is mine*, she thought. She orgasmed, shuddering, her body on fire. Carlos closed his eyes, tipped his head back and climaxed quietly. All the while the beautiful water ran over both of their bodies.

They held the same position, tightly holding each other as they melted together as one.

"I love you, Rose."

She was silent.

"I love you and it's hurting me."

Relieved

With fatigue fully wrapped around their aching bodies, Jack and Ollie shoved themselves through into the main lobby of the station.

Rob Wright loomed close, they could see him from the corner of their eyes during their attempts to avoid him.

"You two! Where the hell have you been?"

His yelling banged against the acoustics of the soulless entrance to their division.

"Why does he always have to act like one of those grumpy bastard boss guys from those cop shows?" whispered Ollie.

"Keep your mouth shut, Travis," Wright said, as they approached. "If I want your opinion, I'll ask for it."

"Yes sir? What seems to be the matter?" asked Jack.

"Don't play smart with me, Jack. Get your asses through my door, now!"

***

Superintendent Rob Wright looked worried. He sat before them, a fat wolf-like version of his former self.

He dragged his stubby fingers through his greying curly hair and exhaled.

"This thing, it's been going on for quite a while now, don't you think?" he exclaimed.

"This thing? What are you talking about?" asked Ollie.

Awkward silences, they heard music somewhere in the distance as it chimed from a radio, as well as intermittent drilling, sub-contractual tradesmen fitting new lighting over in the interview rooms.

"Spit it out, Rob," said Jack.

"I have warned you both, told you to sack it. Last month, last week." Wright looked at them both squarely. "I've told you to drop it. You have to drop it." Ollie looked back at Jack, who looked at Rob, who looked at Ollie. "Listen, it's out of my hands."

"You are joking?" asked Ollie.

"I've been getting a lot of heat from the Commissioner's office, they're asking why my Inspectors aren't closing cases. Scotland Yard's involved. What you two are doing, or should I say, haven't done, is making us all look like a bunch of pricks."

Jack and Ollie, frowning incredulously, glanced at one another.

"With all due respect, Sir, Jack and I, we've lived and breathed this case for so long. We think we're close to wrapping it up."

"Yes, but you're not, though, are you, Travis? We all know that's a load of cobblers. As for referring to it as a *case*, it's more than a bloody case – it's a fucking saga. You've been on it for ten bastard years, and who knows how many years prior to that."

"People are dying…"

"Yeah, I know, and they'll continue to die if I let you two carry on."

Warning

"I have to go. I have to go now, damn it!"

"Morgan. You shall do no such thing."

"This has gone on for far too long; I have to."

"No you don't."

"You cannot stop me."

"Yes, we can, Morgan."

"Okay, you can try."

"Morgan, do not disobey the detail."

"I will. I'm going."

"We're warning you, please hold back."

"Fuck you!"

"…So be it."

You're Next

It was mid-week. Andrew Baker ran across the field effortlessly as twenty hand-selected under-thirteens tried their best to keep up with him. Camera crews and newspeople were as typical to these events as his tired looking fiancé.

The rotund shape loomed in the corner of his eye while in mid-sprint. It stood apart from the usual entourage and supporters. A lone smallish dump of a man flagged on the sidelines, awkward in his big coat in the morning sunshine, indicating to Andrew Baker that it could only have been Jack Sargent.

He stood, despondent, glancing about at the darting action on the pitch. The fluorescent glare of the sunlight caused Jack to squint, limiting his view of some key occurrences that were apparently detrimental to the outcome of the game they were playing. Jack cursed himself for his lack of knowledge.

Superintendent Rob Wright's decision to separate Jack's team, including any foreseeable engagements with Ollie Travis, was both frustrating and welcoming in equal measures. Being unceremoniously dragged from their *Animal* investigations was equally as infuriating.

However, failing to pay Baker another visit would be as if straying from the line of his conscience.

At the shortest notice, Red had arranged their meeting after Baker's visit to a paraplegic youth centre nearby.

Seated in a trendy Islington bar, with his bored fiancé and two of his best friends on the next table, Andrew smiled as he posed for more passers-by. They held up their phones as if he were an animal in a zoo.

"Don't you get tired of that, Andrew?" Jack asked.

"The pictures? Nah. Why would I?" he shrugged. "Thousands of people want to take my picture. Why would I mind? It's a compliment."

"It would drive me up the wall. Mind you, I would presume you're a lot more extroverted than me, Andrew."

"You're here because of Ricky," he declared, before taking a swig at his bottled apple juice.

Jack thought for a moment. "Not just because of Ricky Gomez. Steven Freeman, too." Jack sipped on his lemonade. "I think... I know this is all connected. Don't you think this is too close for comfort? Like a coincidence?"

"It's a shame. It's disgusting, Jack, what happened to them. But what do you think is really going to happen? To me? I am constantly surrounded by security, pretty much around the clock."

"What do you think Ricky Gomez was doing in Vienna?"

Andrew shrugged, as if the question lacked merit. "Dunno, maybe on holiday?"

"Oh, come off it. Gomez? In Vienna?"

"Dunno."

"Aren't you even the least bit scared, Andrew?"

"I'll be honest with you. It's entered my head. I would be lying if I said I haven't thought about it. But scared? Nah. I'm confident nothing's really gonna happen, Jack. The thought of something happening to me, like it would in a film or something, I can't see it, Jack. Those two were nobodies, Steve and Rick, no disrespect to them, or their families. But I was one of the highest grossing earners this country ever turned out. All those ads, my television appearances, that shit song I did that went to number one in the charts. It all made me megabucks. I'm a millionaire, me, this kid from Ponders End, who would have believed that?"

Jack glanced back at the celebrity. Even past his prime, mid to late thirties, Baker was still annoyingly handsome. He spoke more eloquently, which was obviously the fruits of elocution tutelage. Well groomed and tailored, with his tweed suit and cap, he still possessed the British dandy image he'd had when he was a player.

Jack shook his head. "Listen, Andy, this is so serious right now. The three of you being suspects back then... you're next. Don't you see?"

"Okay, Jack, if that's the case, where's the rest of you guys, then? Where is MI5? Why aren't I seeing any danger signs or urgency? Why is it just *you* telling me this crap?"

"I cannot explain that right now, Andy."

Andrew raised his voice a little higher. "Can't you? Is that because I'm being told by my manager to ignore you?"

"Wait a minute... what did you say?"

"You heard. Is this why you're always on your own, Jack? It's starting to look a little like a joke, you know."

"Your manager told you to avoid me?" Jack asked.

"He did, yeah. Look, right, I like you, actually. I think you're okay. I mean, I feel sorry for you. You seem a little pathetic. I know you haven't got protection from the Met any more. I know you're off the radar, Jack, but don't worry about it. I'm not."

"Andy, you have to listen to me. This is real. You don't understand."

"No, it's you who doesn't understand, Jack."

"Is everything okay, Andrew?" Red swooped by like an overprotective school teacher.

"Yes. Everything's cool," announced Andrew, raising his bottle as a salute. "Me and Jack's just having a chat, that's all, Red."

Jack looked at Andrew squarely in the eye and offered one more attempt. "Andrew, you're next, if you don't take my help. I am warning you."

"Hold on, Sargent. You can't talk to my client like that. Don't you know it's libel? You aren't even a police inspector any more. You've been struck off."

"Who told you that?"

"I think it's about time you did one, *Jack*." Red said, mockingly.

As if in a trance, Jack instantly upped and limped from the table. It was finished. The potential to change their minds had now disappeared. The pain in his back gripped him once again as he exited the bar.

On seeing Jack depart through the door, Red shouted: "Yeah, go on, Jack. And please, don't come back. I'll have to call the police if you do. The real police!"

Always Friends

They sat within the stuffy plastic windows of the waiting room. Madge placed the *Twix* that Jack purchased from the vending machine into her handbag.

Daniel looked sullen, as if he had lost weight. He sat apart from Jack and Madge, miserable and silent.

"Hey, Danny, how are we supposed to have a good time if you don't smile? Jack is very sad, you know. He said he's sorry."

The boy shrugged. He was now ten years old but looked at least three years older. He glanced over at the train, which was drawing to a halt on the platform.

"That's not it, Danny. I told you, our train arrives at three-sixteen."

"I'm bored." he said. He stood and walked out on to the platform.

Jack lowered his head. "I can't stand this."

"Just give him time."

"The whole day's been horrible. He hasn't enjoyed any of it. I really don't know what else to do, Madge."

She moved closer to him and took his hand, an action that was unexpected.

"Listen, Jack, there's something I need to tell you."

"There's no need. I know Daniel hates me. I mean, it's plain obvious. Any fool can see that. Let's face it – I've ruined everything."

"It's Brewster, Jack. She's getting involved."

He looked up and then turned to face her. "What do you mean?"

"It took me five weeks to persuade her to agree about today. She was really reluctant. That's why it took so long."

"What's her problem?"

"Um, this is what I wanted to talk to you about. She has an interest."

"What do you mean, an interest?"

"I was talking to Mrs Rogers, she's a friend of mine, and she's just taken a position at the adoption agency, inside the same department as Brewster."

"Madge, what are you saying?" Jack said, lifting his hand away from her grasp.

"Pearl Brewster is looking to adopt. A couple of people have said she's got her eyes on Daniel."

He was calm at first. A soft time passed by easily before his face turned to a greyish map of lines. She pressed herself closer into his side. Madge knew him. By now she was well exercised in catering towards many of his reactions. She was pleased that he was ignorant of her love for him. Pleased only because she knew it would never work, it would never flourish into some beautiful escape. Her matronly frumpy wholesomeness would be no match for the otherworldly charms of Rose Benoit.

She would cry those sad tears later that night, the salt water adding to the decline of her ageing skin.

"I'm only telling you… because…"

"Yes, I know," he said. "I appreciate all your support, Madge. I am aware I've given you trouble all these years. I am sorry."

They both looked out onto the platform, Daniel was stood opposite, staring at the train time display, evidently willing the time onward.

"I really thought it would have been a good idea to adopt. He was my best friend. We both wanted it to happen. Perhaps if I'd quit the force I wouldn't be in this mess."

"Jack, you did your best."

"Wasn't good enough though, was it?"

"Jack…"

"Madge, we've just spent forty-five minutes looking for him because he ran away. He ran away because he hates me. He would never have done that last year, four years ago. We were meant to have a nice time at the seaside."

Daniel entered the waiting room and silently placed himself on the bench closest to the door.

The time now read fifteen-eleven.

**

The train ride went by as silently as Jack would have predicted. He and Madge had tried to coax Daniel to speak, to open up and talk to Jack.

The grey sky epitomised the darkness they all felt as they walked up to *New Horizons,* and Jack cynically huffed at the irony.

**

They stood in the lobby. Daniel had been dispatched to his room almost half an hour ago.

"I thought she'd be too old to be considered. It's obvious she's connected, which is crap, but surely, her age should be taken into account. How old is she, anyway?" He asked.

"Brewster? About forty."

"Really? I thought she was about sixty. I'm not being disrespectful, just honest."

"You're right, she does look older than she is," Madge smiled cheekily.

"Right, well, that's it. I suppose that's all there is to it. She's younger than me. *One of those... key factors that helps in the adoption process!*" Jack said the latter cynically.

"Jack, please don't be like that."

"I'm sorry, I really am. Perhaps I'm being selfish," he sighed, and as he did, Madge did the same. "The next thing I have to do is let go. If I do, he can move on. I didn't want him to hate me, or hate anybody for that matter. Hopefully, in time, he'll let go of that hurt. I'd be happy with that, at least."

They embraced, with Jack welcoming her firm grip and feeling comfortable with her closeness.

"Goodbye, Madge. For as long as you are able, please look after him."

"Of course," she said, slightly muffled with her mouth pressed against his shoulder.

He walked down the steps onto the dark street.

"Mister Jack."

He thought he was mistaken, that the little voice was just another one of the silent audible mirages in his mind that had lately been happening more frequently.

Nonetheless, though, he reeled around to face the closed doors. Daniel Tyler stood before them. An outdoor fleece wrapped over his pyjamas.

Jack dashed towards the child.

"Mister Jack."

Jack saw the tears in his eyes. He grabbed his shoulders and knelt to match Daniel's height. They hugged, a muddy embrace that wiped away the past three months as if they were cobwebs.

"Daniel. I'm so sorry."

"Me too, Mister Jack. I never meant to be mean to you."

"Daniel, you were never mean. I understand. You were sad, that's all. That's all it was."

Jack took a tissue and wiped at Daniel's tears, his big eyes like pools of virtue.

"Mister Jack, I didn't run away." Jack glanced back, confused. "Today. I didn't run away from you and Miss Markham earlier."

"What do you mean?"

"I was lost. I didn't know where you went. I was walking with you both near the boats, where the hilly road was, remember? I looked around and you weren't there anymore."

Owing to Daniel's one word answers and dark mood earlier, it had been Jack who had first assumed he'd ran away. Their reaction towards his absence had been quick, and they had dashed frantically in all directions during their search, obviously straying from the boy even more.

"You walk too fast, Mister Jack."

Jack laughed, a mixture of relief and heartache. Daniel reached inside his pocket to present him with an A4-sized piece of paper. Jack unfolded it and stared at the image.

Typically, not the tiniest corner was wasted in displaying what Daniel had to say. Jack's bearlike paw, a high five, the two people in the picture smiling with love, and the banner above their heads declaring that they would always be friends.

Regroup

Oleg Gribkov's disappearance was astoundingly low-key, Jack thought, *especially for such a well-established business mogul.* Jack knew the man was on the admissions list to attend Rose Benoit's function in New York, he also knew Gribkov never made it to the event.

***

After Jack re-connected with Ollie, they both convened in a small cafe off Hammersmith high street.

"I think we should go further, Ollie."

"Yeah? Well I don't. You know what happens when people do that."

"Yes, I do. Well normally, but don't you see? This is different. I wanna see where it's gonna take us."

"Wright's took us off it, Jack. And you can hardly walk because of your stupid back. We need to drop it."

"I can't drop it. I'm thoroughly opposed to dropping it," Jack said, shaking his head with a conviction Ollie hadn't seen since their early days.

"You honestly believe you could do this, Jack?"

"I do, yeah, I'm serious. What else have I got, Ollie?" he said, palms up. "And anyway, aren't you just a little intrigued? This guy is a freak. There's something in the nature of these murders." Jack eyed his colleague, noting his reaction, believing he was winning him over, albeit in a small way.

"The perverse manner the killer always operates is unlike anything we've ever witnessed before. Come on, Ollie, we've seen some strange stuff in the past, all manner of stuff, but *The Animal,* he's different; his murder's have an edge. Ollie, I'm on to something, and I believe you and I are capable of getting to the truth. We've helped them this far with what *we've* uncovered. Us! Don't you think we owe it to ourselves to see the whole thing through? Don't you think we deserve the chance to nail this sick bastard?"

Ollie looked at the floor, wide eyed.

"Because I do."

"Okay, you've got me. You said you knew how we could do this thing without Rob?"

Jack shuffled closer towards Ollie, and Ollie felt inclined to do the same. Jack continued in a more hushed tone. "I've been in touch with Morgan again."

"Okay, so tell me about this Morgan."

"He's done a whole bunch of investigations, stuff he's keeping close to his chest. He said he'd rather speak to me in person. He's a loner. Operates alone, off the radar."

"I figured that."

Jack nodded. "Last week we spoke for the first time; he said there's been homicides in and around New York City. Same stuff, you know?"

"Connected?"

"Ollie, these cases are about as connected as Rob Wright is to bullshit."

"Okay, where are we starting?"

"First things first. You know this Gribkov guy? He's missing. You and I are going to find him."

***

They caught a budget flight to Beauvais, Paris. The tip-off was vague but not enough to ignore. The straw-clutching stakes were only just above average but Jack had a strange hunch. They both knew it was foolish to neglect any of Jack's hunches.

A tactical police team was on hand from the GIGN to accompany them if required, although when securing communication for this operation, Jack learned that they too showed only minimum concern.

Oleg Gribkov

The room was large and its lighting set at a pitch that could almost render the magnificent architecture redundant. Not that it would have been one of Oleg Gribkov's main concerns.

"I had such high hopes for you, my dear. You have disappointed me," he said, in a manner Rose would have always assumed he would.

The heat of the night was electric. The rain began to pat gently against the large shutters; a storm was evidently brewing.

The old man continued. "I can assure you, if you kill me now, things will ultimately become so unbearable for you. You will spend the rest of your days praying that you died early in your childhood," he said, as if grimly retelling a bedtime story.

After much of this boasting, which Rose was reluctant to halt, she began. "Your threats are tantalising. I am genuinely aroused. Believe me, behind the walls of my labia lie rivers of cum, just waiting to flood and pour over your broken body. However, my dear, I shall not kill you. On the contrary, my intention is to actually dispense you with the most sizeable volume of violence without actually killing you at all. As you urge your body to shut down, to escape the monstrous things I will do to you, it shall be you who will be responsible for the only kill here tonight." Oleg looked on, his confidence slipping ever downward, like grains of sand inside an egg timer.

Rose always savoured this moment. "Ready yourself for the fruits of what you yourself have created. I have almost completed my life's rite."

Ollie

The huge estate was in darkness, closed due to a sizeable renovation. The smell of newly applied paint within the empty voids and musty wet plaster lingered ubiquitously.

Carefully, they both trod, an undertaking that was difficult for Jack, the agonising flinches limiting his ability to walk normally as they both ventured further into the ornate construction.

It was purely by accident how they chanced upon his body. At first they had to squint, the little or no light limiting their sight. It took a few moments for their eyes to adjust. It was only then that their brains responded to what they were actually seeing.

Oleg Gribkov was still breathing, and rapidly. His obese chest heaved in and out in quick successions. He seemed oblivious to them entering. He was lying on a table to which he had been tied.

Ollie motioned to Jack, suggesting for him to call for assistance. Jack answered negative. He looked around the room. There was a small window to the left, and an interconnecting door, no other distinguishing features were evident. Oleg's blood had spilled copiously on to the floor beneath him. He began to murmur, which turned into a loud chant, repetitively omitting something in Russian. Jack's limited knowledge of the language identified his use of the words *bitch* and *murder*.

He walked over to Oleg. His eyes were blackened and had evidently been pressed in, their wells brimming with yellow and dark red goo. His cheeks beneath seemed to rattle and shift grotesquely as he shouted, illustrating that his skull beneath had been irreparably damaged. His teeth had also been smashed and, as Oleg continued to shout, spittles of blood and bone abseiled upward from his torn mouth. The afflictions made Jack's skin crawl. The most interesting feature, however, was the perfectly placed lipstick mark on Oleg's forehead amidst all the bruised flesh. His chanting grew louder and Jack was forced to shout over the noise.

"Ollie, this has only just taken place. This *Animal* guy is still in here, Ollie. We've fucking got him, there's no way he's going anywhere. Call them, get them now."

In spite of the caterwauling, Jack was aware of a silence behind him. He felt a draught and a slight aroma that he thought was familiar.

He drew his gun and poised himself. Cautiously he turned to see Ollie being held unceremoniously by the throat. The assailant was taller than his colleague. The ice pick was long, positioned just inside the entrance to Ollie Travis' ear canal.

Ollie looked dumbfounded at Jack, helpless as his assailant affectionately stroked his face.

"Step away from my colleague," Jack shouted. "Step away from my colleague and put the weapon on the floor. Slowly."

It was evident now that the *Animal* was female, dressed literally from head to toe in a tightly fitting rubber body suit. No amount of her flesh was exposed. The woman's face was covered by a mask, it's grinning façade was unnerving. Her feminine attributes unnecessarily prominent.

Jack quickly barked. "Step away from my colleague or I'll be forced to shoot you."

He wasn't sure if the language she spoke was Japanese, but her words were calm and flowed comfortably.

With his one hand, he kept his gun pointed at her face. He steadily reached inside his rear pocket and switched on his memo recording device.

Affectionately, she nuzzled the side of Ollie's face with the ugly long nose that protruded from her mask.

"Jack," Ollie said desperately, seeking reassurance from his friend. "I'm scared."

His captor reached inside his mouth and delicately searched around with her sharp fingertips.

"Get the fuck away from him!"

More oriental dialogue replied to his orders, confident, almost seductive. Ollie gritted his teeth and drew a sharp intake of breath as she inched the tip of her weapon towards the direction of his brain.

"This is your last chance. Drop the fucking weapon and step away from my colleague."

A short moment passed and Rose heard Jack's finger depress the catch. The shot missed her as she manoeuvred herself, twisting expertly to avoid its range, while plunging the pick fully into Ollie Travis' head. Instinctively, she reached over and removed the shooter from Jack's grasp before he was able to fire another shot.

Ollie slumped to the floor.

As the gun now pointed at Jack, everything seemed to go into slow motion. His eyes flooded on seeing his lifeless friend fall at the woman's feet.

She began to walk towards him, prompting him to back up. The *Animal* omitted more indecipherable language. When Jack's back bashed into the wall behind him, she expertly adjusted the weapon in her hand and brought its butt down forcefully on his temple.

***

In between shifting consciousness, Jack was met with blurred images of the *Animal* stood over Oleg's body. He could at times hear the Russian screaming, although his loud outbursts weren't enough to wash away Jack's drifting back into unconsciousness.

"*Even rich head and you,* Jack. *Even rich head and you.*"

Recuperation

The nurse was nice. She had an assuring air about her that Jack was instantly comforted by. However, this was the only solace that he could afford, as doubts inside his mind served to torment him. His failure to bring his lengthy investigations to closure, thus deeming himself unable to seize the disgusting *Animal*, greatly contributed to his growing depression.

He'd been in the hospital for almost a week. The frustration he felt as he urged the days away was becoming a way of life.

Ollie's death. The thought served Jack like an icy finger down his throat. Cold, and blocking the passage for much needed air. He simply couldn't comprehend that his friend was gone.

Wright hadn't offered much by way of support. He'd been typically distant. "I told you two to give it up, you couldn't even do that right," he had said. "Sorry, but I can't help you."

Other acquaintances had been the same – detached, insincere. It seemed to Jack that no one cared about the *Animal* case and about Ollie Travis's death.

The nights tormented his senses.

***

The uncertain nature of the lead had proved to him that someone knew a lot about the cases he was working on. It was obvious months ago that someone was one step ahead of him. Perhaps the *Animal* was being protected. The mere thought of this made Jack's blood boil.

Anything to smash the case. Anything he could do to bring it to completion became all consuming. Jack was now convinced that solving the case was his true calling in life. This investigation was vital to his health and peace of mind.

Before he was released from the ward, he sent the memo recorder to a trusted friend who worked within his department. The acquaintance was the only person whom Jack had any confidence to decode the translations on the device. The sound quality wasn't the best but that was to be expected, seeing as the thing was concealed inside his pocket, and drowned out by the omnipresent wailing of the tortured Oleg Gribkov.

He also had to admit that his obsession for Rose Benoit did little for his sanity. The time he'd been given to recuperate was, to him, unnecessarily long. He resented every second of the endless days. In that time he would be consumed with thoughts of her.

He had called the number often. Sometimes it would ring. Sometimes it would go straight to voicemail. Never would it be a success.

Until one day, at precisely twelve o'clock in the afternoon. She had returned his call. His heart started beating again.

"Inspector."

"Rose?"

"It would appear you've been trying to contact me."

"I'm sorry, Rose. I don't know who else to call. There really is no one else I can talk to."

He sounded frantic. Rose reined him in.

"Jack, Jack, Jack. What are we going to do with you?" As usual, her enigmatic poise silenced him. "You've become a mess, Jack. What do you suppose I do about it?"

Please do something about it, Jack thought. "Do you really think I'm a mess?"

"Of course I do. And why wouldn't you be? Your partner dies in the line of his duty. No one seems to be interested. I can only imagine how upsetting all of this is for you."

"Wait, how do you know all of this, Rose?"

"I do read the news often, Jack, even when on American soil."

"That was on the news? The fact that nobody's

interested?"

"Jack, my darling, I read news from some rather eclectic sources. Besides, Rose is an expert on reading between the lines."

Jack mumbled, agreeing. "He was two days away from leaving. He was going to live in Spain with his wife. He was a good detective, and he was a good person. He didn't deserve what happened."

"Jack, I'm sorry for you. I truly am." Jack was again silenced. "This happens, my dear, unfortunately. But think of it like this, although people are taken from us, they are taken for the greater good. Your friend tried to save that poor man; you must have been so scared. Who knows? He might have died so your life could be spared."

Her buttery voice kept Jack clinging to her every syllable. "I never knew him, Jack, but I am glad you are still here. Sometimes one has to appreciate the sacrifices life deals us. Do you understand, baby?"

"Yes," he said. Although he didn't fully agree with her upside down philosophy. Her words tore him in half.

"Jack. I shall call you again tomorrow, see how you are getting on. The advice I'd give you right now would be to make plans... away from your police work! Give yourself a goal, or something to look forward to. Do you understand me?"

"Yes. Yes, and thank you."

"Sweet dreams, my Jack."

Indeed, the comfort Jack was privileged to be afforded whilst inside Rose's dungeon could not be confused with its torment. The blissful state he was in after the phone call – he could see no line that would divide his contentment from his misery. It was as if both were present at the same time.

Leopard Print Louboutins

David Morgan had been discreet. Keeping himself a fair safe distance from Rose Benoit. His small but dedicated team had grown to three colleagues. They were competent enough and he trusted them to keep up the façade.

Posing as Howard Forde hadn't been easy. He had grown frustrated with his superiors and the bizarre way they expected him to operate. But making these sacrifices had contributed to his subject's eradication.

Julie Ross had prompted him to update his image. He struggled with the concept of fine dining but, on the face of it, he managed to convince his new acquaintances of an apparent acuteness when speaking in depth with Wall Street friends of Julie's.

Julie had been nice enough. The woman was beautiful, and not his usual type at all. Although, given that he took his position at the Bureau extremely seriously, he barely had time to learn what his type actually was in the first place. He'd been living the single life for as long as he could remember. Julie Ross and Howard Forde had made love on three occasions.

So as not to cause Julie to assume something was amiss, he kept his queries about Rose Benoit minimal, but choosing wisely to ask of her vital questions.

By a certain time, he'd amassed a growing amount of damning evidence that would either see Rose Benoit imprisoned indefinitely; holed up in a closed-security asylum, or being escorted to a safehouse for eradication. Either one suited him.

Contrary to his prior feelings on the matter, opting to murder her personally would only debase him. Doing so would have made him as bad as Rose Benoit.

David Morgan had now completed his thorough investigations. His work was sent to his superiors.

Discreet as ever, and with total belief in his conviction,

he had decided Julie Ross would be the first to hear of Rose's exploits.

***

CeeCee Holmes looked good as she sat opposite. Julie was especially envious of the shoes. The leopard print *Louboutins* were beginning to become a major issue, as she spent the first half hour of their evening imaging them on her own feet instead.

Julie glanced down again for the twentieth time, incapable of subduing her feelings any longer. "CeeCee, I'm sorry but those shoes are so damn sexy."

Just then, she glanced at her phone, an alert sounded.

"Excuse me, baby," she said and opened the email:

Julie.

I guess this is as good a time as any to impart to you the nature of my business at Nubian Rose.

But first I just want to tell you that it wasn't my intention to hurt you in any way.

My name is not Howard Forde. I do not work for J&C's *and I have not created the products I previously showed your management team at the time of the pitch last summer.*

My real name is David Morgan, I work for a special unit division, a federal division here in America the full details of which I cannot disclose in the body of this email.

The following may serve to distress you, I warn you with the utmost caution of what I reveal below. Again, I say it is not my intention to upset you, but you must know the truth.

Rose Benoit. Your partner, your colleague, your best friend – is a sadistic, perverted and highly dangerous serial killer. She's been involved in countless murders for almost twenty years. She is deemed extremely dangerous by my colleagues. When I issue her arrest, she will automatically be certified insane. She will be incarcerated until the day she will be ultimately destroyed.

Julie, I myself have led the investigation and surveillance of Rose Benoit prior to, and for the entire duration of, our relationship. I regret your involvement in this but you were a vital ingredient in my work. If anything, you have contributed greatly to the whole program.

My best advice to you would be to sever all contact with Rose Benoit.

I did like you. I am sorry.

D.I. David Morgan F.U.I.

"I'm glad you like them, but keep your eyes off, missy, ya' hear? Same goes to her highness Miss Rose of Benoit." CeeCee Holmes finished her lemon vodka. "Would you like another drink? The night is young after all. You ain't gotta go home yet, surely?"

Julie Ross switched her phone off and got up from her seat.

"Julie? You okay? You look like you've seen a ghost."

She walked towards the exit.

"Julie?" CeeCee Holmes called.

The cold air out on the street had the opposite effect. Julie assumed it might have helped in some way to clear her head, but it only served to make her all the more unbalanced.

She dialled Rose's number three times with no luck.

What did the email mean? Was it a joke? Julie browsed for it again and reread it.

The fourth attempt was a success at last.

"Julie, honey, you'll have to make it quick, I'm really sorry but I'm already late for my flight," Rose said, as she hurriedly crossed the road from the airport car park. The silence on the other end of the line was inconvenient and made Rose's forehead furrow. "Jules?"

"He knows."

Owing to the uncharacteristic direction of the call, Rose knew exactly what Julie was referring to, but played ignorant for more details.

"Excuse me? Who knows? And knows what?"

"David Morgan knows."

Julie hung up and Rose was almost mowed down by a fast moving Toyota as she stood in the middle of the crossing that led to the airport entrance.

"Fuck," she exclaimed.

Awkward Silences

"You fucking bitch."

Although Julie spoke calmly, Rose was nevertheless unnerved.

The past three days had been strange, owing to the unfamiliar pattern of Julie's absence. Rose had been ringing constantly.

"Baby…"

"*Don't* fucking baby me," Julie said slowly, her Bronx dominating her otherwise Ivy league dialect.

"I'm sorry, Julie."

"Fuck off."

"Listen, is it me who's to blame for him telling us he was someone else?"

"You fucking knew!" A silence followed, which irritated them both, although Rose deemed herself undeserving to speak. "You didn't tell me. You sat there and let me fall for a dude who was a cop, or whatever the hell he was. You did absolutely nothing."

"I did warn you to avoid being in work-based relationships, Julie."

"Oh fuck you, Rose. Surely something inside must've told you that I was getting serious, getting closer to him. Couldn't you tell it was a big deal? I was falling for him; I told you I loved him. You could have stopped it." Silence. "You knew from the start, fuck's sake. That damned shitty product he wanted us to sell! I knew it was bullcrap. I should have said something. I supported you, like a stupid goddamned… I'm a dumb bitch, right? You actually made me look *more* stupid."

"Julie," Rose pleaded. A tear running down the side of her face.

"Go fuck yourself…"

The awkward swirly silences were equally as heart-wrenching as Julie's outbursts.

"Julie, I'm sorry. I didn't use you. I didn't figure you in any of this. I am ashamed. It's a shame and I'm sorry, but I couldn't sacrifice my intentions."

"Oh, so you sacrificed *me* instead, right?"

"No, I didn't mean it like that."

"Yeah, your fucking intentions… Your precious intentions? Killing guys, raping them and all that shit, yeah? Fucking them up?"

"Julie. You know what I am. You knew right from the start. I have told you everything. You knew this."

"Did you do Oleg?"

"Yes."

"Oh hell, Rose!"

"There is a story to that, baby, we have a past."

"Oh right, I get ya'. So you knew him too, right? Something else stupid Julie F Ross never knew."

"Julie, please don't say that…"

"Fuck you…"

The silence that followed seemed to last forever. In that time, both women's thoughts turned to the future. Its doubtfulness. Its unsecured, wobbly outcome was disquieting, alien. Rose knew Julie would keep her secret, but she also knew their relationship was crumbling right there and then on the phone. That was the saddest thing to contemplate; a life without her best friend. Without Julie Ross, there simply would be no *Nubian Rose*.

Julie read Rose's mind. "Yeah, I think it's safe to say *NB* has reached its peak. Would you sacrifice everything we created?"

"Of course not."

"Oh, okay, cool. You'll stop with the killing already?" Rose was silent. "Listen Rose, enjoy your damn life."

"Julie."

"Fuck. You," Julie said, before switching her phone off.

***

It was 3am the following morning. Rose answered the phone.

413

"Are you going to kill him?" Julie asked.

"Yes. Yes, I am."

The minute's silence which followed was weird. Then Julie hung up.

Husac

Jack had attended Ollie Travis's funeral. He felt cynical as he looked around at the mourners. Aside from Beth, Jack knew very little about his partner's family. But he was confident that he knew Ollie more intimately than the majority of those gathered up in the small function room that Tuesday afternoon.

He'd also been in touch with Rose Benoit. But, as her absence grew more definite with every day, he indeed despaired at the thought of not seeing her again. At times he saw a bright future, especially if their conversation was positive and upbeat. But the other end of the spectrum was dark.

Jack couldn't help but feel useless, sat in Wright's office, with the same anti gun-crime and police dog posters that had adorned the noticeboard for over twenty years, still there, faded by time and the sun.

He resented his current job, a new assignment that he had obviously been allocated purely to deter him from having anything to do with his previous investigations.

"It's not a big deal, Jack," Wright said, after he was passed the closure report on the expired *Animal* case, which was obviously now whitewashed. "It was out of my hands, what could I do?"

"That morning... you said to us to go down to the school and see Freeman's body. The pathologist report a month later with that damned phallus; we were *this* close." Jack indicated a small gap with his thumb and index finger. "You seemed adamant at the time to clinch it, just as much as we were. What the hell happened, Rob?"

"You're getting paranoid, Jack. It's not that complicated. They took over, that's all."

"*They*? You keep saying that. Who are *they*?"

After veiled twists and turns, Rob Wright answered. "They were just a bunch of assholes, you know?

Something to do with special Intel. It was out of my hands, Jack."

Jack viewed his boss, and saw his lack of concern.

"Why are you so relaxed? Any other circumstance you'd be shouting the odds. You've had heart attacks over much less than this."

Later, Rob passed through Jack's office. "Fancy a drink?"

Jack looked up. He'd spent the past hour tidying his desk. "Are you kidding? The last time you and me went out together was over ten years ago."

"Jack, I'm just worried about you. Just leave, get out of here."

"Oh, go to hell, Rob."

"You were wrong anyway, about Andrew Baker."

"What are you talking about?"

"He's just signed a contract with *The Sports Channel*, the guy's gonna be the new face of *Soccer Night*. The highest earning pundit and ex-footballer in history."

"So?"

Rob flapped his hands to illustrate the obvious. "So, he's still alive. He didn't get murdered by God knows what. You were wrong, Jack."

***

Time passed. Approximately one month after his recuperation, Jack finally received feedback from his colleague's department to whom he'd entrusted his dictaphone.

A meeting had been arranged, somewhere crowded and mutual. Saturday afternoon, the pub on the corner, across the road from Victoria coach station, provided the perfect venue.

Jack had been waiting for some twenty minutes before the youngish man arrived.

"Sargent?"

"Yes."

"Can I sit down?"

"Yeah, of course." Jack glanced more thoroughly at the man. He looked stressed and hurriedly windswept. Middle Eastern, long hair and beard.

"Who are you?"

The man shook his head. "Just call me Husac, my name is Husac, okay? I can't say my name to you. I have to get out of here in less than five minutes," he said with urgency.

Jack sat up. "Why? What the hell is going on?"

"Keep it down. Listen, your voice machine is here."

Husac palmed Jack a small piece of paper, which he in turn slipped into his jeans pocket.

"Why haven't you got it here? Did you find out what was on it?"

"Shut up and listen to me." Husac's eyes were welling up. "You've uncovered something sick, Sargent. It's a sickness. You will not survive it if you have designs to ride it. Leave it alone. Go home and do something else. Please, please believe me."

Husac looked around, then he stood, but Jack grabbed his clenched fist. "Just tell me what was said on the device, man." He looked up at him. "Please."

"You are dealing with something that is totally incomprehensible, like you wouldn't imagine. This isn't just your average freaky shit, Jack. And get your hand off me." he said, pulling it away.

"Please, just tell me what it said."

The look on Husac's face broke Jack's heart. All of a sudden he seemed older, the weight of the world hidden in his big brown eyes. The man readied himself and proceeded his announcement, as subdued as he possibly could: "'*Death for a million years in one night. I shall eat you. In one beautiful night. Go home, Jack.*' That is what that *animal* said. She even knows your name. Get out, Jack, while you still have your heart inside you."

Husac zoomed from the bustling pub as ten giggling women, sporting L plates and butterfly wings, passed him on his way out.

Jack urged himself onwards. Although he was still undeterred by Husac's warning, he still operated with a heart-skipping fear.

He had waited a few days to venture out to the address that had been typed onto the small piece of paper.

The public locker depot proved to be the destination, a do-it-yourself facility that was deserted.

He despatched the number that Husac had provided on the piece of paper and walked through the security entrance. Once inside, he located the locker easily.

The door swung open after Jack punched in the last access code. Neatly placed inside, his memo device sat encased within a translucent polythene bag.

Jack nodded to himself and looked round before grabbing it. Once it had been stowed within his inside jacket pocket, he noticed the A4-sized folder, which remained on the bottom shelf inside the small locker.

Jack once again looked around. Gingerly he took hold of the flat file and lifted the wide flap.

The photographs were well-produced but, in spite of their high quality, Jack could literally feel the colour disappear from his face, after which a rising nausea grew in his empty stomach like boiling hot quicksand.

Husac was still wearing the same navy blue hooded top. Flanked by the very same creature who had ended Ollie Travis's life. A fetish-style gas mask hid her face with a dark red rubber catsuit.

The first photograph showed Husac on all fours, *The Animal* sat on his back. His head was being forced down by the long heel of her boot.

The second photograph featured a close-up of *The Animal's* hand fully inserted, wrist deep, inside Husac's mouth. His eyes looking skyward, pleading, praying to either his God or to the monstrous *Animal* above him.

The third image was another close up. Husac was by

now deceased, his jaw had been pulled from his head, what remained of his face, bruised and severed, was being pressed against *The Animal's* upper thigh.

Jack was infuriated. He noticed her elegance, her fingers. The refined way in which the assailant displayed herself and her attributes was so shockingly graceful that it made his heart's rhythm slow and then quicken.

Jack's thoughts suddenly solved Husac's curious naming. The damned soul had indeed been made into a *human sacrifice,* a most cruel and bizarre last insult.

He grabbed the device from his jacket, pressing it to play. The Paris night had been scrubbed, replaced with a single message, especially for him:

"S'il vous plaît aller à la maison , inspecteur."

More photographs followed. Husac's drained, fearful expression. Piles of bloody intestine. Her nonchalance, and the expensive fetish-wear. Relentless. Blood. A poor life crushed underneath her sadistic cruelty.

Jack emptied his stomach.

Andrew Baker

The tools, placed strategically in rows in accordance to size and girth, in a perfect systematic order, began from the left and grew all the larger and more devastating towards the right.

Her tools, her shiny instruments, had been used before. Their sharp angular edges, she touched at them gently.

They were lovingly maintained, well crafted and undoubtedly of the most supreme quality. They had been purchased while visiting Berlin-Charlottenburg.

She'd departed for a lengthy time. Andrew Baker was alone once again and he cursed himself for his decision to remain aloof. He took another look at the tools. In spite of the confusion that was now clouding his thoughts, he remained steadily rigid, strong and stubborn. He tried his best to oust any shreds of fear that had the audacity to creep into his brain. He had always prided himself on his strength and male assertiveness, it hadn't failed him yet.

He hadn't forgotten the rape and murder of Sarah Allen. After all the years that had passed, he was still adamant of his own sense of righteousness, the arrogance and lust he'd felt at the time, he still maintained.

As if being ushered in, two men suddenly rushed into the large dungeon and immediately took hold of a pole each, huge ostrich plumes at the ends. They stood either side of a throne-like seat, directly opposite to where Andrew Baker was positioned.

Music began to play, a slow, gravelly beat-ridden noise; industrial, loud.

If Andrew was honest, he would admit to being confused, slightly intrigued, but he wasn't scared.

He waited. The horrible music, its German female moaning vocals, showed no signs of abating. His eyes grew tired as he focussed on the two men in the distance. They looked oriental, and young, *almost too young*, he thought. Both dressed identically in faded blue boiler suits.

He suddenly realised, as he looked downward, that he was wearing similar clothing.

***

Andrew Baker had been in the company of his entourage on the previous evening. The Mayfair club was busy, it was Saturday night, with VIP guests from Hollywood. Photographers were everywhere. His friends had laughed as he openly insulted his pregnant girlfriend. She hadn't even wanted to be there, but he'd forced her to accompany him, evidently for this sole purpose. She was actually grateful to the two women who were lustily kissing each other nearby, ultimately averting the attention of her bullies. Indeed, the sight was a welcoming one for the boisterous tanked-up men.

Rose had enjoyed it too. Sapphire was almost as tall as herself and her lips tasted sweet as Rose slowly licked at them. Through provocatively revealing slit rubber costumes, both women lithely touched each other's exposed flesh and ran their hands through each other's hair, just as Andrew loomed nearer. In no time at all, he was reeled in, like a fish with its mouth caught upon a huge hook, or upon the thorns of the dark red roses that were handed to all patrons upon entry to the club that evening.

***

After what Andrew thought seemed like an hour, she entered. Although now entirely different in her appearance, he knew it was her. He'd been stupid, letting her get the better of him, entrapping him. He felt ignoble at his powerlessness. He liked sex games, scenarios in which he could take control. This, obviously, was not to his liking.

Apart from a pair of spike-heeled boots, she was entirely naked, her body displayed for him like a huge sweet piece of fruit. He imagined kissing her breasts and sinking his teeth into other bountiful parts of her anatomy.

So engrossed with her body was he that Andrew initially failed to understand the significance of the huge pair of horns, fixed to either side of her clean shaven scalp. Andrew looked on arrogantly, undeterred, in spite of her bizarre appearance.

She walked coolly past him and lightly stroked his throat. His mouth tightened, his face screwed. He chastised himself again on his own shortcomings, his being in this unexpected situation.

Rose's eyes sparkled. The sight of him, her main prize, his hatred, almost made her wet herself with lust. She teased herself as visions swam through her head of all manner of outcomes she could have planned for him. All thoughts made her stomach glow and she brought her hand to her breast to steady her rampantly beating heart.

The two Filipinos began to move their fans back and forth as Rose approached them.

"Surely, you ain't serious!" Andrew called.

Ignored.

She clicked her fingers and the servants placed their fans against the wall and proceeded to adorn her with a small shiny garment. She towered over them as one of them tied the straps behind her, the other adjusting it over her front as she held her arms out. Rubber, the butcher's apron barely seemed of any use as it covered only her groin and a small portion of her stomach, her breasts still openly displayed. The rubber creaked over her body.

The servants worked quickly and, once they had completed dressing her, they grabbed at their poles once again.

"You might have trained your pair of faggots, but it won't be so easy with me," Andrew said.

They both followed her as she slowly walked back down towards him. They seemed fretful, their boyish faces indicating fear. On closer inspection, it was evident that they both looked absolutely terrified, yet still swinging their fans. The face of the left servant was badly bruised. His eye was deeply cut and he had blood inside his mouth, immersing his broken teeth.

Rose began. "Let me see you, boy," she said. And placed both her hands on Andrew's face.

"I'm not afraid of you," he said. "Why don't you untie me, so I can show you what a real man can do."

Her fixed gaze remained, and indicated she wasn't moved by his words. She ran her hands over the front of his torso down to his groin.

Andrew continued. "You think you can take advantage of me? Demoralise me? Really? You stupid bitch."

Rose smiled. Pulling apart a couple of press studs on his boiler suit, she took hold of his penis and testicles. Soft and flaccid, she proceeded to kneed and pull softly.

She felt the blood pumping up his manhood. "There's no denying the indication of an erection, darling," she murmured, in French. "It's the same in any language."

Andrew stuttered, before Rose placed her lips to his, silencing him. She breathed into him, presenting him with the control he struggled to accept. Drawing away from his face now, she moved back towards her tools, although still holding on to his groin.

"You think this is a game. I like that," she said, looking down at the collection of implements.

"How could it *not* be a game? What do you think you're gonna do to me? Torture? Kill me? How do you think you'd get away with that?" he said, his top lip curled in anger.

"Indeed, darling, good question," she stroked over a couple of knives.

He continued. "In fact, this is absolute bullshit. I don't believe any of this." He shook his head, as if his own disbelief wasn't convincing him enough.

"I'm glad you've come to this conclusion," she said, "as your collision with reality will be all the more impactive."

"I don't understand what you're talking about."

"Well, in many ways, your arrogance merely stems from the hatred you have of your current situation. This is

423

obvious. But also, it's the mystery, the mystery that lies in wait. The unknowing, unforeseeable future. Naturally, you *are* unaware of what is about to take place, you've never been in such a precarious environment and you detest it. That is why you disbelieve, because your disbelief is a mechanism to vanquish the lack of confidence you have. It has been this way throughout your entire life, dear, and it is precisely what is happening right now."

Her use of language, and her well-curved accent annoyed him deeply.

"What? What the hell does that mean?"

"Well, darling. Let me show you." Rose clicked her fingers. Hastily, one of her servants ventured up to her side. She moved back slightly and grabbed the man by the collar around his neck. Firmly pressing his head to her stomach she gently stroked his cheek. Rose then proceeded to drag a serrated knife against his neck, just above his Adam's apple. The crimson liquid flowed out instantly, pouring down her apron and onto her upper thighs. As she continued to cut his throat, red spray gushed out and covered everything. Soaking into Andrew's boiler suit, his spotted face looked on in terror and disbelief.

Rose's arms and upper chest were immersed in the glowing cherry-red liquid. The man struggled, uselessly pinching and grabbing at the tightly fixed hold she had around the back of his neck and head.

The other servant still swung his fan frantically, droplets of blood tarnishing the bright virginal whiteness of the plume.

The servant, now still, although his grotesque wound still flapping, slumped to the floor. Rose ran her bloodied hands over her flesh and over her apron, which creaked as she touched it. She dragged and smeared his blood onto her breasts and her posterior.

Andrew Baker vomited.

He looked up at her, purple rings surrounding his reddened eyes.

"Now do you understand, Andrew?" she sighed, lazily,

her eyes brightly boring into his soul. "Now do you see that we are, in fact, *not* partaking in something so merely trivial as a game?"

***

She had left the room.

As the music pumped from every possible source around him, Andrew was fearful, he grew frantic and began to lose his breath. His thoughts turned to the many occasions where police liaisons and counsellors had advised him to succumb to protection. After the murders of Steven Freeman and Ricky Gomez, he had been warned of such an outcome. Thoughts of Jack Sargent crossed through his mind. He felt ashamed of himself and of his own disbelief. How he'd insulted Jack Sargent and his good intentions. The gravity hit him in the back with the power of a sledge hammer.

The Filipino's body was still in the same position upon the floor, his front totally immersed in dark blood, knelt awkwardly before him like an accursed worshipper of the damned.

Steven Richard Andrew

Jack's main intention, to waste all the gas in the cheap cigarette lighter, became more like a challenge as time rolled by. It wasn't the pain from the hot metal on his thumb that made him stop. It was the thought...

He'd pressed down the button, burning away all the gas for well over an hour until the thought came flooding into his mind – the thought served him like a rescue team – the thought made his brain slowly turn, setting it on course for a helpful view, away from the dark thoughts that enshrouded it moments before.

Jack was back at the Paris school. The place was still under refurbishment, still in darkness. If there was a pain in his back, he could not feel it. Perhaps it had disappeared. Ollie was still alive and stood by his side. He was smiling at him. Ollie opened his mouth. "She will eat the world, boss."

"Ollie?"

"*Even rich head and you.*" Ollie said.

"What did you just say?"

"*Even rich head and you.* Jack, you said it yourself, can't you remember, you idiot?"

"I do remember, but I never knew what the hell it meant."

"Did you forget their names, Jack?"

"Who's names?"

"She went to school with them. She's already killed them. Oh yeah, she's an animal, Jack; she's the worst in the world."

Most inconveniently, Ollie's voice drifted off and turned to silence.

***

The rain began to pour heavily against the tall windows,

just as it had done the night Ollie Travis was killed. Jack indeed saw himself lying against the far wall. While Ollie lay motionless, his grey features looked serene, unsmiling, but peaceful. Towards the centre of the room, the tall, imposing female figure climbed upon the jittering mutilation that was Oleg Gribkov. Her full, statuesque physique lowered upon the bloody carnage of her prisoner. In spite of the horrible mask she wore, Jack noticed she was naked. Her large buttocks and legs, which knelt and flanked either side of the man on the table, dark-skinned and admirable, Rose Benoit straddled Oleg Gribkov in much the same way Jack Sargent often fantasised she would do to him.

But Jack was powerless to act against her grotesque actions. He could only watch as she slowly tore pieces of flesh from his face and neck and softly smashed away what was left of his teeth and jawbone with a small hammer.

**

The limits of Jack's vision afforded a view of Ollie, who winked and said the words again: *Even Rich Head And You.*

It wasn't until now that Jack, back in his apartment, decoded Ollie's message: *Steven, Richard, Andrew.* Rose Benoit had fooled him – she was guilty of all the cases Ollie Travis and himself had tried to bring to closure. She had indeed murdered Steven Freeman, Ricky Gomez and Andrew Baker.

**

"Will I ever see you again, Ollie?"

"You might see me again, Jack. I hope so."

Jack then fell into a deep sleep. A slumber, fitful and much needed, that he welcomed with open arms and was, indeed, received by it in the same way.

The cigarette lighter was empty by the time he opened

his eyes. An easy calm seemed to pass through his head. Jack picked up the lighter and studied it. The conversation with Ollie seemed like a million years ago, but the experience was fresh, revitalising.

Jack's previous motivation for doing the job he did every day was fuelled by desperation and fear. Now, with a new determination, he was filled again with love and an unyielding devotion towards his life's work.

That morning lacked the shackles of the past seven years as certainty, at last, flourished throughout his mind. His back felt easy, free of all pain, like it did when he was in his twenties. Jack Sargent knew exactly what to do.

'oops

It was thanksgiving. At this time of the holidays, Rose liked nothing more than spending Christmas in New York. She adored Times Square when it snowed, and Central Park when its lakes were iced over.

Rose had showered and was now naked, save for a pair of black panties, as she programmed in some loud Mozart. Walking into her study, holding a bottle of Cabernet from Château Margaux, she viewed the missed calls on her smartphone.

There had been nineteen in total, the most recent of which had barely just happened, not three minutes prior. She cursed Jack Sargent and poured herself a liberal amount into the largest glass she could find.

More calls from the UK were similarly ignored. Carlos was due to arrive and Rose wanted to concentrate her attention on him. She'd had a plan, something she wanted to try out. A re-hash of the time she and Jack were at *Erotique* where he'd witnessed what her cat-women were about to do to Otis. Two full days were about to be used up in lavish style. Rose grinned to herself at the thought of Carlos dressed as a dog.

But the phone kept on ringing, barraging its inconvenience against the walls of her velvety lust. She finally relented.

"Talk to me. I so hope it's important, for your sake."

"Rose…? Rose, is that you, dear?"

Rose gasped before she fell off her tall stool and landed on her side upon the floor in shock. Five hundred dollars worth of alcohol smashed to pieces on the floor around her feet.

It was the Rossingtons' housekeeper.

"Rose? Are you okay?" she sounded distressed, upset.

She picked herself up and stepped on the glass, cutting her heel. "I'm so sorry about that. Yes, yes, I'm fine. Is, err, anything the matter?"

"Oh, Rose, it's awful." The woman began to weep, her speech dotted with intakes of breath. "I, I don't know how to say it, dear. Oh, I can't bear it…"

Rose knew. Her eyes widened, strangely warding off the impulse to do the same as the whimpering woman on the phone. As she stopped pacing, she looked down at the blood from her foot joining with the red wine.

"She's gone, Rosey. Linda's gone now."

***

The wounds the broken glass left on her feet were deeper than she realised. She was forced to treat the larger ones with minor stitches. Her eyes watered as she cleansed them and finally wrapped a bandage around her heel.

She poured a drink and thought about the Winter roses she'd sent to Linda Rossington not a month before. A regular tradition, as well as in the Spring.

Thomas Rossington.

She would have to leave straight away.

After packing a small holdall, containing only underwear and a glass bottle of water, she hurriedly checked her apartment before turning off the main lights.

But some paperwork had been faxed to her, literally within the past few minutes. "Oh, for fuck's sake," Rose exclaimed.

***

The facsimile prompted Rose to be clothed and outdoors.

A disposable handset was despatched to enable Rose to engage in a much unwanted and inconvenient correspondence.

On foot, she marched towards the direction of Columbus Avenue via West 70th Street, the drawstring of her black-hooded sweater tightly surrounding her cold face.

She was almost at Yorkville when the phone buzzed.

"Are you wireless?" the woman asked.

"Of course."

"Good. First of all, did you see to your appointment? The private one?"

"Yes. I took him to the Château Sauvageot. Andrew Baker ended up dying on the wheel. I cut off his penis and placed it into his mouth."

"Marvellous, darling, you evil minx."

"With respect, can we make this quick? I have things to do."

After Madam Evangeline DuTvott's provocative laughter drew to a halt, there began a silence, and Rose sensed a disagreeable nuance.

"Madam DuTvott, talk to me, please."

"It's bad, Rose, darling."

"What do you mean? Andrew Baker?"

"Gosh, no."

"Tell me," she demanded, somewhat angrily.

"We have received and reviewed your latest offering. Who was that?"

Madam Evangeline DuTvott's voice was serious. Her once trilling, high pitched Russian accent was replaced with a stoical darkness – not as lovely.

"What are you saying, Madam?"

"You have to answer the question, Rose darling."

"It's Gribkov, despatched to you not a week ago…" Rose unhooked a small piece of paper from the back pocket of her jeans and read from it: "…it's ZZ-5171."

"Rose, you're in trouble."

"Why? Talk to me, Madam."

"Your latest, ZZ-5171, still has wheels."

"He lives?"

"Quite correct, he still lives. As you might imagine, we are very unhappy."

"I'm sorry."

"Yes, well, I'm sure you know that sorry won't really

get you anywhere, Rose dear. We were expecting you to complete the job." She paused.

Rose heard Madam Evangeline DuTvott sigh. "The deceased you brought for us was not Oleg Gribkov."

The Governing Board Of Executive Directors And Judges Of Metropolitan Policing And Law

All males. All fifty or over. They all sat in a row, unsmiling like miserable pigeons who'd been snatched reluctantly from their comfortable environments and well-paid positions.

Jack sat opposite, happily setting out his files, organising them on the table before him.

Chief Superintendent Robert Wright loomed nearby, shuffling in his seat on the outskirts. Everyone in the room could hear the whistling of his bad sinuses.

Some of the pigeons glanced at their watches, their expressions turning differing shades of furious.

More tea was provided, and neglected, as they waited.

From his briefcase, Jack pinched at his best Parker pen, the last item to be placed upon the desk with the rest of his things. He was ready.

"Gentlemen, please forgive me for my lateness. I'm afraid I was waylaid… Traffic?"

The pigeons didn't move. They all looked towards him, unappeasable, expectant.

"I would like to thank you all for agreeing to see me at such short notice. I am privileged to…"

"Sargent? Is it?" one of them asked.

"Yes, Detective Inspector Jack Sargent."

The pigeon seated second from the end to Jack's left coughed, somewhat derisively.

"Err, yes, well might we begin, Sargent?"

Jack smiled, failing to bite on their dispirits.

"For the past thirteen years, I have been attempting to operate towards the closure of one of the worst ever crime sprees in the UK. I have had the pleasure to work with many expert officers, gifted minds who've assisted in our endeavours to bring our assailant to justice. Ollie Travis, for instance, was a man who was loyal and dedicated right to the end. He was also my friend. A good man who died needlessly in the line of duty."

Although his voice was measured and amiable, Jack lowered his head, a little gravitas which failed to gain any recognition from the pigeons.

"Anyway, due to our lack of success, we quite rightly received a lot of criticism. Our abilities, as well as our mental health, were questioned. Sometimes we despaired; the task force I set up was stretched..."

"It's Sargent, isn't it?" another pigeon called out.

"It is, yes."

"This all seems a little self indulgent, don't you think?" The pigeon looked around at his fellows, he received their approval straight away. "We were asked to attend this meeting because we were told the Superintendent had some heavy information for us."

Expertly, cheerfully, Jack resumed.

"...Granted, it's been a long time. It's taken this long to ascertain certain details, details brought to light purely due to long case studies and investigations."

"Sargent, please get to the point."

"Rose Benoit," Jack said, simply.

Suddenly, the name vroomed life into the hard atmosphere like a new engine. Their bored expressions being turned upside down now.

Jack placed four A4-sized prints on the table before them. All of Rose Benoit, one of which being his favourite mugshot.

"Gentlemen, I'm sure you're all aware of Rose Benoit. World famous CEO of *Nubian Rose* in London, New York, Paris and Dubai?"

At least two pigeons shuffled uncomfortably in their seats.

"Rose Benoit. Glamorous socialite, friends with Marc Jacobs and Beyonce. A formidable taskmaster who regularly receives high ranking positions in worldwide power lists?"

One of the pigeons towards the far right of the room pulled out a handkerchief from the breast pocket of his shirt and wiped his brow. His neighbour did the same.

"Rose Benoit... The devil who cuts open her victims stomachs and strangles them to death with their own intestines."

Jack spoke the words loud now. Anger peppering his voice. The remains of the last sentence still rang around the room and inside their ears.

At last, the eleven members of the The Governing Board Of Executive Directors And Judges Of Metropolitan Policing And Law were finally paying attention.

"Gentlemen, in order to move this terrible meeting forward, I feel it necessary to go back. I need to tell you a story."

The pigeons had no choice but to listen. Their responsibilities clamped them reluctantly to this devastating new duty.

"Twenty two years ago I was appointed by Chief Superintendent Robert Wright as a liaison officer to the families of Sarah Allen and Rebecca Sinclair. Sarah Allen was a fifteen year old girl who was raped and murdered. Not only that, after being beaten to death, her assailants ripped her to pieces in their attempts to dispose of her body. Initially, we made about ten arrests and from that, three youths became suspects. The ongoing case was really bad. The accusations were diabolical. What those three guys did, at that time, in those days, my God." Jack shook his head, as if lost in a hazy mist of shame and regret, remembering those days, twenty two years ago.

"I think, at the time, Superintendent Wright saw me as a nice kid, you know, compassionate and well equipped to manage such details. The victim's best friend, Rebecca Sinclair was at the scene of the crime and became a witness, so initially I visited her mother. She was told they had a strong case by her legal team who were just a bunch of students. I mean, it was pretty bad, sending a load of kids who'd barely passed their BVC's. It was a farce. The prosecution was almost non-existent. Sinclair's mother died, and Rebecca was no longer deemed as a stable witness because she was prone to outbursts. The day it went to court was the same day of Martha's funeral. Those three youths got off."

"Jack, why are you saying all this now?" said Robert Wright, shaking his head.

"You aren't listening, are you? I'm telling them I was liaison officer for the bereaved." Jack stepped closer towards Wright, who scratched the palm of his hand with his bushy beard.

"Rob, did you know that was the same year as my divorce? Do you know why my wife left me after three years?"

"You always told me she thought you were boring."

"I was married to my job. I wanted to go all the way. I gave her as much consideration as I would to a grain of sand. You kept on telling me not to bother with the liaison job. I mean, why? You gave it to me in the first place. You said I should carry on with the DI work. I believed you. I never bothered with Allen's family, Sinclair, or her mother. I neglected them all, totally."

"Jack, I speak for all of us here when I say why the hell is this relevant?"

"Relevant? Oh, you want to know what this all means, is that it, Rob? Well, this is the thing, maybe if I had bothered more about Rebecca Sinclair she would never have turned out to be such an animal like Rose Benoit... A person who is protected, no doubt, by some of the people sat here in this room today."

The silence that followed was as comfortable as some of the images of Rose's blood-soaked victims, captured within their glossy confinements.

"And, saying that, Superintendent Robert Wright, maybe if you'd have written Martha Benoit's actual fucking surname instead of referring to her as Sinclair, then I, we, could have got to Rose Benoit a lot fucking sooner!"

All eyes slowly turned towards Rob. He frowned and bit at the inside of his mouth, which made him look like he was chewing gum.

"I heard the tape. When you interviewed her with Rebecca. She reminded you three times." Jack shook his head. "You stupid bloody idiot!"

The pigeons were now dumbstruck. Robert Wright now looked like an angry jealous husband.

Jack coolly glanced down at the main central-most pigeon who'd just picked up a glossy print of a mohawk-wielding Rose attending the Cannes film festival.

He spoke. "Are you saying that you believe Rose Benoit is a serial killer, Sargent? This, as you've deemed... *Animal* killer?"

"I am, Sir." Jack nodded, a face so etched with sombre gravity Robert Wright failed to recognise him.

"And you can prove it?"

"Yes, I can. I have been in connection with an agent who was observing our suspect in the US extremely closely for almost a year and a half."

"Morgan?"

"Yes, how did you know?"

"Works for an elite unit, federal investigations. David Morgan is one of their best, just about the highest ranking."

Jack nodded. "His whereabouts are unknown right now, obviously owing to his security, but he circulated his findings."

Robert Wright grimaced, shook his head as if to quell the shock of Jack's assertiveness. "Jack, I told you to step down. What the hell do you think you're playing at?" he said.

"No, no, Wright," said the central pigeon, waving for silence. "I think Jack is on to something. Carry on, Jack."

"Thank you," he said. "I have been liaising with Morgan. He sent me a large case study. He was very close to the suspect, close enough to speak to her on a daily basis without being compromised."

"Good God, Sargent," exclaimed the central pigeon. "You have this evidence here?"

"It's right here. Everything from her days as a travelling student, to her most recent murders of the three suspects of the original Sarah Allen case." Jack displayed the files in question for all to see as if they were a deck of magician's cards.

"Jack…"

"Oh, do be quiet, Wright," said the central pigeon, an agitated look on his face.

Three pigeons stood and reached over to inspect the files. Their contents were emptied and scrupulously viewed. The silence in the room was oppressive as everyone could plainly see the harrowing photo images of tortured victims, carnage enshrouded by blood and chewed flesh.

Jack looked at the men opposite, their stoical professionalism and lack of shock.

Endless reams of David Morgan's crude notes, his handwriting sometimes measured and neat, other times indecipherable.

Some time passed, almost ninety minutes. Tea and coffee was finally a considered option.

Central pigeon began. "Well, this is truly amazing stuff, Sargent. Compelling. And exactly what we've been looking for."

Jack looked over towards Wright, who began to rub his eyes.

"Wright," called another pigeon, "did Sargent ever attempt to submit these details to you?"

"No, he's only just received it," he said. His head resting within the palm of his hand. "I didn't even know anything about it."

"Tell me, Sargent, was it difficult trying to persuade your Superintendent for extra time to bring your investigations to closure?" asked an American pigeon.

Jack looked over again at a more roused Wright. He paused for a second.

"I actually like Rob. If I didn't, I would have walked years ago. But sometimes his decisions didn't make sense to me. They only ever served to stifle Travis and myself."

All pigeons, even the ones who had stood, glanced over.

"Hang on a second, I was told to put a close on Sargent by people from *your* office. I don't know why I'm being held over the fire here."

"Surely, Superintendent, you would have realised the strain Sargent and his team were under? And in spite of your misgivings, you never recognised his passion for the case? I mean, good God, man, he was on it long enough. And who is it who allocates his assignments? James Bond?"

"Oh, don't be ridiculous," Wright shouted.

"Ridiculous? A bit hypocritical to say that, don't you think, Superintendent?"

Silence, as the majority of pigeons resumed their hold on Morgan's work. Endless nightmarish images. Jack refrained from looking, easily resisting the almost nonexistent urge to view again pictures of Ollie Travis's autopsy and his greying skin. Andrew Baker was unrecognisable, his torn, mutilated body tied to an enormous cylindrical wheel. His bloody penis stuffed inside his broken mouth. Within the photographs, the tools she'd used to scrape away pieces of his body were cleaned and placed back in their expensive display cases.

"Jack. We're all really sorry about what you've had to endure. We regret it's been difficult and the frustration it has caused. Your partner, Ollie, well, Jack, it must have been bloody awful."

The central pigeon looked down and shook his head. Jack no longer saw him as a pigeon, but more like the genuinely courteous man he obviously was.

"You are a damn fine man, Jack. It's an honour to be working with you. We're only sorry it took us this long to approach you and the work you've been doing."

The man was possibly ten years older than Jack, but his firm handshake was strong and seemed bursting with good intentions, suggesting towards assistance and friendship.

"Rose Benoit?" Jack asked.

The man laughed. "I think we'll say no more on that matter, only, I'm pretty certain the general public is now safe. There's some very large blockades miles from anywhere in the Mojave that have tiny cells and even tinier water supplies." The man touched his nose a couple of times.

"We'll be in touch, obviously. I would like to send a, ahem, for want of a better word, *liaison officer*, to see you straight away."

They both stood and another handshake was applied, all his colleagues filed by and murmured their words of admiration and respect.

Chief Superintendent Robert Wright exited the room silently and unnoticed.

A New Hope

Due to Rose's uncompromising and somewhat mysterious private life, Carlos hadn't foreseen anything untoward for the first three weeks of her absence. They lapsed by quite easily, especially within the knowledge of their by now customary rendezvous, arranged for the end of every month.

A further month, and Carlos naturally was in a quandary.

He ventured the rainy walk across the street past the YMCA. The long subway ride up to Manhattan. The strange faces of night time Grand Central Station. The imposing towers of the city loomed over him and the closer he got to her apartment, the heavier his heart became.

His key, still within his possession due to her request to stay over while she was away in London, still fitted.

He stepped inside. In the past, the apartment had had an ambience of cool, of her, with an aroma of zesty lime and citrus. The place had always been warm and inviting, breezy in the summer months. He'd taken everything for granted. Her voice, and the way she implicitly held him with her conversation, which was always cultured and exhilarating, echoed in his brain.

Always with the tantalising apprehension of seeing her gorgeous body, of being next to her. He could still smell her skin, the most potent and most wild scent, which he never could put his finger on.

The place was cold. Carlos trudged through its now soulless voids. Gone was the wonder of her. Gone was the air of potential, which had always, up until this point, promised to deliver. And gone was her. Gone was Rose Benoit.

***

The place was deserted. Carlos shook his head and raised himself from the settee, the huge picture of a beautifully young Maria Callas glared out at him. He wished he'd asked Rose who it was.

He wondered what had become of the many bottles that had adorned the walls of her champagne room.

He entered her bedroom and slowly looked around. The small cabinet beside the bed was empty. So too was the shelf that had contained books on nineteenth century jazz, and seventeenth century torture. Again, Carlos shook his head, there was a deep facet to Rose he always failed to understand. The strange and macabre went hand in hand with the gracious and jovial.

He felt a sudden pang of resentment towards her and became frustrated. Why hadn't she told him of her intentions to disappear? He upped and rifled through the nearest drawer, nothing. Opening the huge wardrobe, he walked inside, nothing. Gone were the over-abundant collection of shoes; the garments, once hung in succession of colour and style and cut, also gone. Like her.

The sound was faint. He almost didn't hear it. But the moment he did, he reacted like a hound with the smell of blood in its nostrils. He darted around, trying to follow its direction. The sound grew louder when he left the bedroom. With his heart pounding, he opened the small closet door in the huge corridor. The sound remained, he was getting closer.

Inside the kitchen Carlos noticed a charger that had been plugged into a socket high above the storage units. He walked across the wide expanse of the room toward the central island. The sound was getting louder as he walked past and opened one of the unit doors.

He cried out. His eyes spilled tears when he finally saw the small cell phone. He took hold of it, glancing at it as if the thing were a piece of her.

Switching the volume to maximum, the song ended and began again, set to a continuous loop.

Yet, it wasn't until he actually thought to himself that Carlos fully understood its pivotal message.

Track 01: (The Cast From) West Side Story – Somewhere

Stulti. Monitum.

Jack awoke, furiously tumbling away from much needed valuable sleep like an unwilling child at a wedding.

He breathed in and rubbed his eyes open. Suddenly cursing on seeing the tablets he should have taken hours ago, he sat up and rinsed them down with warm water from the glass beside his bed.

A typically restless night. He rolled around towards the other side of his bed to catch his cool spot.

He slept soundly for a time, possibly up to two hours.

The chair in the corner of the room was normally reserved for strewn laundry and clothing and loose change. He had never actually used it, but as he heard it creak, the sound instantly snatched him awake once again.

"Rose?" he said.

The morning, still unaccompanied by its dawn, made visibility almost impossible.

Unable to move his arms, he made attempts to sit up and became agitated upon realising he was fully restrained. He heaved his stomach upward.

"Rose, is that you?" He squinted, his heart beginning to thud heavily. "Listen, the fact you are inside my apartment is bad enough, but you are in serious trouble, Rose. We seriously need to talk."

A side lamp was switched on.

Madam Evangeline DuTvott slowly sipped at a tiny glass. Jack grimaced, sheer indignation at having a stranger, an unknown intruder in his bedroom.

"Oh, forgive me, sir. Were you expecting somebody else?"

"Who the hell are you? What the hell do you think you are doing?"

"Be calm, Jack, please."

He screeched, "I am perfectly calm." Feverishly, he craned his neck for a more suitable view. "Who do you think you are? How did you get in here?"

"Relax, and I shall tell you."

Her voice was serene, her accent unobtainable, possibly Russian, belying her light-skinned Caribbean appearance. She made light work of her beverage, emptying the last droplets from above into her mouth.

"I am relaxed, I keep telling you."

It was evident the woman was somewhat rotund, large bosomed and statuesque. She stood, displaying her true, astronomical height, Jack frowned at the sight of her and his estimation of well over six feet. He craned his neck to follow.

The woman was superbly, if not bizarrely dressed. She wore a black open trouser suit, her cleavage and navel almost spilling out opulently from the front. A red bow tie was strapped tightly around her throat. Her auburn hair was tied into a two high ponytails.

Jack fearfully began to inch away as she loomed closer.

He shook his head. "You and Rose…" he proclaimed. "Why does this not surprise me? You're all the same. Murderers, freaks. You get your kicks being ugly, making people feel bad, torturing them."

She smiled, and now stood above him at the side of his bed, like a plus-sized grim reaper.

"There are decent people in this world, you know? Normal people who love each other."

Her lack of interruption provoked Jack to continue. He began to raise his voice. "Killing me, what's it going to prove? What's to be gained by all these murders?"

Madam Evangeline DuTvott reached into her side pocket and pulled out a small pair of leather gloves. Her admirable lips, opened slightly and pouted. She carefully slipped the gloves on her fingers.

He glared back at her. The woman, although not as beautiful as Rose, was still attractive in a slightly more severe way. He imagined them together easily, cavorting, dressed within suits of latex while humiliating slave-like men chained to walls. Her appearance sickened him.

"So this is it?" he began. "You! You're here to kill me? I am a man who has spent his entire life trying to do the right thing. To fight for what is right, and good. I am going to be murdered by someone who gets a thrill from seeing people being tortured, is that it? Another victory for evil over good, for chaos over logic?" Jack's eyes watered. "How was I to know she would have turned out bad. To look at that sweet girl years ago, I had no way of knowing she'd end up rotten to the core."

The woman placed an index finger to her lips and shushed him softly.

Jack's contorted features twisted uncharacteristically with base hatred. He shook his head, as if attempting to wipe away the image above him.

Her smile faded. Madam Evangeline DuTvott raised her left leg and stepped over him, the modest double bed was dwarfed and creaked loudly as she climbed on top of Jack, straddling him.

"You get the hell off me, you, you…"

Her lower body easily encompassed him. He shouted from beneath, pathetically.

"I told you to relax, Jack," she said. "Allow me to introduce myself. My name is DuTvott, and I'm here to conduct a meeting with you."

Jack Sargent murmured something incomprehensible.

"As you might have guessed, I represent a dear, dear colleague of mine. She regrets not being here in person and asked to send her regards."

Her voice was delicate, high pitched.

"What the hell has this got to do with me, now? Do you think I really give a damn about Rose Benoit after all that's happened?"

A faint smile returned to her full brown lips. She hummed.

He tensed. The muscles in his chest were awash with agony while underneath his captor. He was now weeping, his eyes watered with the anticipation of the imminent death he could now see.

Indeed, Madam Evangeline DuTvott produced a sharpened stake together with a small hammer.

"I'm glad that horrible fucking woman never saw fit to come here; my life has been shit ever since she darkened it."

"Ah, my darling Rose, she has that ability, to darken the light, I'm afraid. It's the gift she has. Oh, but is she not truly delightful?"

"No, she's not. She's diabolical."

With her left hand she smoothed his shoulder, stroking it as if to tenderise his flesh.

"Diablo, indeed! Devilish. That lovely mouth of hers, yummy." She smiled, raised her shoulders and shuddered with delight.

"Oh, fuck you."

"Yes, sir, she rather did. And I her, too." This time she grinned.

Her huge thighs surrounded him, he traced an aromatic odour, a sweet-perfumed scent emanating from her crotch and surrounding over-bountiful flesh.

She placed the stake to Jack Sargent's shoulder and drummed down densely with the hammer.

He screamed out, the pain bit him hard, as the sound in his left ear split and turned mushy.

Madam Evangeline DuTvott removed the offending article. She licked at the blood before inserting the stake fully into her mouth.

His other shoulder was subject to a duplicate punch, in precisely the same position.

She moved in close to lick at the blood, which was now pouring from the darkly-bruised outlets. Jack's body buckled in paralysing terror.

She swallowed a generous amount, before his wounds were sufficiently staunched. This took almost an hour. The noises her mouth made as she slurped were sticky and grotesque. She surfaced, and the lower part of her face and chin were covered in blood, which ran down her neck.

"I asked you to relax, Jack. It was never my intention

447

for you to die. Merely to disable you, possibly permanently. Our mutual friend did request I go easy on you. For me, Jack, this might be somewhat difficult. But I believe I have kept to my end of the bargain."

Jack felt dizzy. He turned pale as he looked up at her, his blood on her dark tongue.

"One thing I want to know," he groaned. "Why did she have to kill Michael Beavis?"

She looked down at him, her expression simple, easy.

"There was no point." He panted heavily after a while, laboured within his attempts to speak. "He didn't have to die, there was no need to kill him. He was just a normal fucking guy."

Her expression remained. Silently looking on, dutifully as if he were a baby on the verge of sleep.

"And Max Jenkins, we know he's alive." he said, struggling to catch his breath.

Madam Evangeline DuTvott caressed his shoulders again.

"I want you do be quiet and listen."

"Oh, go to hell. There's nothing you have to say that would interest me."

Slowly, she inserted her thumbs inside Jack's wounds. His chest arched, as much as it could while caged within her inner thighs. He yelped out, screaming in pain. His white face transformed to deep scarlet. His eyes bulging out, gaping skyward.

Madam Evangeline DuTvott's attentive expression was serene as she twitched her thumbs, pushing through muscle tissue to locate his fractured clavicle bones.

He groaned, a low anguished tone broken only due to lack of breath.

"Do I have your attention now, Jack?"

She spoke quietly, although Jack nodded profusely.

"Good."

A gorgeous smile danced upon her lips, she pouted as her accent drooled out her dialogue.

"That's very good indeed. Our mutual friend didn't

want me to kill you because, and this is only my personal assumption, I rather think she liked you. Yes, I refer to a past tense because I fear you shall never see her again, although, dear, that is another story. I can't say I agree with her, about you, I mean. I must admit I find you rather inconsequential. Kind of like a little, ahem, nobody sort of fellow. Do forgive me, Jack, I tend to be a little self indulgent. Tonight is not about what I think, my opinion matters not. My appearance here is of a little more importance. I'm sure, by now, you have realised I am the nearest thing they could find to a liaison officer."

Jack stopped groaning, his eyes pinged up at her.

"You mean..."

"That's correct, Jack. We all know each other. Apparently many of my colleagues were most impressed with your speech the other day, said it was... inspired."

He poured out a heavy moan, no doubt encouraged by her revelation, but also due to the pain of Madam Evangeline DuTvott's talons manipulating his fractured limbs.

"Oh God, why are they doing this to me?" he moaned. "You bastards... why is everyone so fucked up?"

"I'm here to demonstrate to you that there is nothing Jack Sargent can do about any of this. You have received warnings, good advice telling you to cease your actions. Advice you refused to take due to your idiotic will. In any other field, Jack, your tenaciousness would be deemed commendable, heroic even. But not this field, Jack. Did you not think it a little odd that your reconnaissance with David Morgan resulted in nothing more than impasse? Jack?"

He suddenly thought. He'd spoken to David Morgan twice. Communication which had been upbeat and productive. A third exchange had been arranged but was swiftly cancelled without any explanation.

"Morgan's still out there," he suddenly said, under his breath. "He'll get hold of the both of you. You are not gonna get away scot-free this time. Your time is over."

Madam Evangeline DuTvott tutted. "My Rose told me you were presumptuous," she said. "I had no idea you'd also be naive and ignorant. David Morgan belonged to me, Jack. We let him believe he was on a *top secret mission*," she said sarcastically. "The foolish man made regular reports to me personally, telling me his limited, useless information. He wanted to act, to reprimand Rose as soon as possible. I told him to sit tight and he behaved most childishly because he wanted to operate."

Jack began to cry. "This is bullshit. I don't believe it."

"Believe it, Jack. I placed him inside a box, a shit-stained safehouse he believed was his appointed habitation. And all part of this mission towards which he believed he was contributing. I kept him there until it was time for him to go."

Madam Evangeline DuTvott looked down at Jack. Moments passed as she permitted time for her information to sink into his brain. Ultimately, Jack wept like a child.

"Now, let us analyse your options, shall we? Your future. Little Daniel has gone and it's all extremely sad and heart breaking. There is nothing we can do about this, unfortunately. And Mister Travis met with a sticky end. An occurrence that was essential." She let out a lazy chuckle. "Essential, if only because it benefited you personally, Jack," she smiled, her long tongue snaking around the corner of her lips. "You see, my dear Rose refused to leave you all by yourself. She knew you were close to that poor gentleman, and she knew he possessed a perfectly healthy pair of kidneys."

Jack's laboured breathing ceased, again he glared up at her.

"Correct, Jack. She wanted him to be part of you. Permanently. It took her many hours. Aren't you a lucky fellow? A brand new set of fully functioning organs that have aided towards rectifying your lumbar issues."

"For fuck's sake," he screamed, his mouth twisting in agony.

"For *your* sake, Jack," she smiled. "She did it for you.

You sound somewhat dismayed."

Angry sparks of spittle splattered from his gritted teeth. Pure rage gripped him, indignation and terror.

"Come now, Jack, did you fail to notice your limp had disappeared? That the pain had completely vanished? Were you not alerted by the medical staff who helped you cope with the trauma after the Paris ordeal?"

Jack Sargent wriggled his body from underneath, heaving with all his strength to dislodge himself. His attempts did nothing; his captor was unaffected.

"Your love for my darling Rose, as you've mentioned, has by now depleted. It's perhaps for the best. This is an extremely wise move, Jack; it shall make it easier to move on. Cast her from your heart, dear."

Even now, deep in the torment into which he was being immersed, and in spite of all the horrible truths she'd uttered, Jack's heart wrenched the most when being told of Rose Benoit.

"I shall now keep this brief, I dislike talking at the best of times – even now, I grow tired. I'm not usually the talking type."

Her smile remained. It was a cool, unkind upturn of the mouth. Jack had seen Rose do the same thing, on that fateful night, when he thought he heard her tell him that he was hers, that she owned him. He'd fallen for it. He had forgotten. He had seen countless people smile in much the same way: Murderers he had arrested when all their sordid secrets were at last known. Drug dealers on the realisation that the only way for them was down. A false smile, their eyes always gave it away. Their eyes void of joy and sincerity – a lie.

The terror gripped him, merging furiously with the pain in his chest.

"The future, Jack. Now, I advise you to take more of a basic approach. Buy that labrador you always wanted. Nest yourself in the Hertfordshire hills or the Yorkshire dales and close your doors. Who knows? You may even meet an equally inconsequential mate while shopping for your groceries. You could go to the library together, or make your own Christmas cards. But, do not, under any circumstances, come back here, Jack." She closed her eyes, and inhaled through her nose. "I do not want to see you again. You do not want to see me again. For, if we do... well, unthinkable things, unimaginable things will take place." She whispered the latter part. "This is neither a threat, a promise, nor a warning. It is just something I want you to know."

Jack wept again. Madam Evangeline DuTvott spoke the words effortlessly as if entirely ignorant of their impact.

"Now, before I depart, I want to leave you with something to remember me by. Just a small token, so to speak."

Jack Sargent recognised it straight away. The sight of the long thin ice pick which had been thrust into Ollie Travis' brain, emblazoned itself into Jack's psyche so heavily that he almost forgot about his own dilemma.

Madam Evangeline DuTvott began.

Jack breathed hastily, a process he believed would help him cope. His heart felt as if it were surrounded by rusty barbed wire.

She undertook her task expertly, deliberately slow. He was thankful his bedside clock had fallen to the floor due to the earlier fracas; he was glad he was unable to see the time tick away, to be forced to concentrate on its tortuous ebbing.

She continued scribing on his upper chest. He knew she was writing words, owing to the fastidious manner in which she took her time.

When finished, she wiped away the blood that collected under the lacerations with the back of her gloved hand before taking a greedy lick. The remaining blood was rubbed heavily into his face.

"It's Latin. It simply means, *warned*."

***

The giant stepped away from the bed. Her enormous posterior bouncing within its tight encasement of black linen as she moved towards the door. Madam Evangeline DuTvott used his cell phone to call for an ambulance as Jack slipped into more unconsciousness.

***

He called out to her. Hours after the ambulance had despatched him safely to the Charing Cross Hospital.

"*I shall find Max Jenkins.*" he murmured deliriously. "*I'll find the kid and set him free.*"

Coda

Pearl Brewster watched happily as Daniel played and ran around the lovely garden. Lenno, the golden retriever, still only a puppy, would grow with the child.

The previous three years had been hugely difficult for Pearl. Aside from all the long journeys back and forth from Helsinki to London, her father had beaten cancer twice.

But the trips to the UK were paramount, however, and spending time forming a relationship with Daniel had been some of the most joyous times in her life.

She had the financial means to cater for Daniel's needs. His medical supplies to balance his moods were now easily attainable and the attention his health required would be unlimited. The boy could easily spend the rest of his life wanting for nothing as his inheritance was already in place and secured.

The finest education lay in wait.

In spite of his past scares, her father was a sprightly soul, and now in residence, forming a near perfect connection with Daniel. He would laugh and kick the ball around the garden with his new grandson, or spend long days playing catch by the river close to their home, while Pearl would make deep-filled fruit tarts for them all to enjoy in the evening after supper.

They were complete at last, being able to care for her father in his twilight years, as well as living for the child she had always wanted.

At night times, though, she would listen to her father, from her room adjacent. Oleg Jusiv Gribkov would lay awake, restlessly, frustrated, gripped by raw fear.

He supposed this sleepless, soulless terror was due to his guilt. Hundreds had died at his hands in those old times, not least his comrade and friend from those early days.

His dreams were black. Dark shadows engulfed him as he made attempts to flee, his age considerably slowing him.

Night after night they would chase, small shadows, slow in their hunt for his soul.

And yet, lately, they grew evermore disturbing. A larger shadow, more menacing and imposing than the others, would not leave his side.

The shadow was the blackest, darker than the darkest sea, blacker than his former sins. It grew bigger and bigger, providing him with zero means of escape. He drowned in it for a thousand years every time he slept. The hellish torment it delivered punctured his entire being.

These visions made him appreciate his waking up. He adored the sound of the birds in the morning, his daughter making bread and coffee in the kitchen.

***

But if he awoke in the darkness, he would cry and scrunch his eyes tightly shut. Somehow, the large shadow had found its way into his real life, slipping from his dreams and into his bedroom. It stands by the door, glaring, smiling at him. Its teeth sharply pointed. It is surrounded by knives and death, and it slowly moves towards him.